# The Family He Craved

## CAROLINE ANDERSON
## LILIAN DARCY
## MINDY KLASKY

Published in Great Britain 2015
by Mills & Boon, an imprint of Harlequin (UK) Limited,
Eton House, 18-24 Paradise Road, Richmond, Surrey, TW9 1SR

THE FAMILY HE CRAVED © 2015 Harlequin Books S.A.

The Baby Swap Miracle, The Mummy Miracle and The Daddy Dance were first published in Great Britain by Harlequin (UK) Limited.

The Baby Swap Miracle © 2011 Caroline Anderson
The Mummy Miracle © 2011 Lilian Darcy
The Daddy Dance © 2012 Mindy L. Klasky

ISBN: 978-0-263-25223-1
eBook ISBN: 978-1-474-00402-2

05-0715

Harlequin (UK) Limited's policy is to use papers that are natural, renewable and recyclable products and made from wood grown in sustainable forests. The logging and manufacturing processes conform to the legal environmental regulations of the country of origin.

Printed and bound in Spain
by CPI, Barcelona

# THE BABY
# SWAP MIRACLE

BY
CAROLINE ANDERSON

**Caroline Anderson** has the mind of a butterfly. She's been a nurse, a secretary, a teacher, run her own soft-furnishing business, and now she's settled on writing. She says, "I was looking for that elusive something. I finally realised it was variety, and now I have it in abundance. Every book brings new horizons and new friends, and in between books I have learned to be a juggler. My teacher husband John and I have two beautiful and talented daughters, Sarah and Hannah, umpteen pets, and several acres of Suffolk that nature tries to reclaim every time we turn our backs!" Caroline also writes for the Mills & Boon® Medical Romance™ series.

# CHAPTER ONE

'Oh, stop dithering and get it over with!'

Putting the car back in gear, Emelia turned into the IVF clinic car park and cut the engine. In the silence that followed, she could hear her heart pounding.

'Stupid,' she muttered. 'It's just an admin hiccup.' Nothing to feel so ridiculously wound up about, but she was tempted to drive away again right now.

Except she couldn't, because she couldn't stand the suspense another minute. She just had to *know*.

She took the keys out of the ignition and reached for her handbag. The corner of the envelope stuck out, taunting her, and she stared at it for a second before getting out of the car. There was nothing to be gained by rereading the letter. She'd nearly worn the print off looking at it, but she wished she wasn't on her own—

'Emelia?'

'Sam?' Her heart stalled at the sound of his voice, and she spun round, not really believing it—but he *was* there, not a figment of her imagination but the real flesh and blood Sam Hunter, walking towards her with that long, lazy stride, in a suit she'd lay odds was handmade. She'd never seen him in a suit before. He'd usually worn jeans or casual trousers, but he looked good in it. More than good— he looked even more gorgeous than she'd remembered.

Broad shoulders, long lean legs, and those eyes—spectacular eyes the colour of slate, fringed with sinful black lashes. They had the ability to make her feel she was the sole object of his attention, the focus of his entire world, and as they locked with hers she felt a rush of emotion.

'Oh, I'm so pleased to see you!' she said fervently. 'What on earth are you doing here? Not that I'm complaining! How are you?'

He smiled, those eyes crinkling, the tiny dimple in his lean, masculine cheek turning her legs to mush. 'I'm fine, thanks. And you—you're looking…'

'Pregnant?' she said wryly, as his eyes tracked over the lush, feminine curves that had grown even curvier, and Sam gave a little grunt of laughter and drew Emelia into his arms for a quick hug. Very quick, because the firm, round swell of her baby pressing against him sent a shockwave of longing through his system that took him completely by surprise. He let her go hastily and stepped back.

'I was going to say amazing, but—yeah, that, too,' he said, struggling to remember how to speak. 'Congratulations.'

'Thank you,' she murmured, feeling a little guilty—which was silly, because it really wasn't her fault that his brother's wife still wasn't pregnant when she was. 'So—what *are* you doing here? I thought Emily and Andrew were taking some time out from all this?'

'Yeah, they are. "Regrouping" was the word Andrew used.'

She scanned his face, really puzzled now; his smile was gone, and she felt her own fade as she read the troubled expression in his eyes. 'So—why *are* you here, Sam?' she asked, and then apologised, because it was none of her business. Only, without Emily and Andrew, the presence of their sperm donor was—well, unnecessary, frankly.

'I've got an appointment to see the director,' he said.

Hence the suit. Her heart thudded and she felt another prickle of unease. 'Me, too. I was supposed to come this afternoon, but I couldn't wait that long. Sam, what on earth do you think is going on? I phoned, but they were really cagey. All they'd tell me was that it's an administrative anomaly and he'll explain. What's an administrative anomaly when it's at home?'

He frowned, his dark brows drawing together, his firm, sculpted mouth pressing into an uncompromising line. 'I have no idea,' he said after a moment, 'but I intend to find out. Whatever it is, I don't think it's trivial.'

'So—what, then? Any ideas?'

He gave a quiet grunt. 'Oh, plenty, but all without foundation. They've written to Emily and Andrew, as well, but of course they're away for a few more days so they haven't got it yet. And they wouldn't tell me anything, either, but as you say, they were cagey. The only thing I can imagine is there's been a mix-up.'

'A mix-up?'

She stared at him for a moment, then felt the blood drain from her face. 'This is really serious, isn't it?' she said unevenly. 'Like that thing in the news a while ago about switched embryos. That was horrendous.'

'Yes. I saw the media frenzy.'

'I thought it must be a one-off, because it's so tightly regulated, but—what if it's happened here, Sam?' she asked, her blood running cold. 'There were only the two of us there that day, me and Emily. What if they mixed our embryos up? What if this is their baby?' Her knees suddenly weak, she floundered to a halt as it sank in that the baby she'd thought of as hers and James' might not be hers to keep.

Tears scalding her eyes, she pressed her fingers to her lips, her other hand going instinctively to shield the baby.

No! She couldn't hand it over to them—but if it wasn't hers…

Sam studied her in concern, his eyes drawn to the slender hand splayed protectively over that gentle swell. Please, God, no, he thought. The other batch of embryos had all died before they could be implanted into Emily, but if Emelia was right, then they'd been hers, her last chance to have her late husband's child, and when this baby was born, she'd have to hand it over to Emily and Andrew, and she'd be left with nothing. All the plans, all the joyful anticipation would be crushed with a few words.

*It's not your baby.*

The memory scythed through Sam, and he slammed the door on it and watched as another tear spilled over her lashes and tracked down her face. Oh, Emelia…

He lifted his hands and smoothed the tears away with his thumbs, gutted for her. 'It may not be that,' he offered without conviction, his fingers gentle.

'It must be,' she said, her voice expressionless with shock. 'What else could it be?'

What else, indeed. He dropped his hands and stepped back. 'Come on, let's find out,' he said, impatient now to get this over with. 'It might be something else entirely— something to do with the fees, perhaps.'

'Then it would be the finance people dealing with it, not the director,' she pointed out logically. 'No, it's something else, Sam. Something much worse. I think it *must* be the embryos.'

Her smoky green eyes were still glazed with tears, her lashes clumped, but she sucked in a breath and her chin came up, and he laid a hand on her shoulder and tried to smile. 'Why don't we find out?' he said again, more gently, turning her towards the entrance, but she hesitated, and he could feel her trembling.

'Sam, I can't do this on my own.'

'Then I'll come with you. They can't stop me.'

He felt her hand grope for his, and he threaded his fingers through hers and gave a quick squeeze. 'Ready?'

She nodded, tightening her grip.

'OK. Let's get some answers.'

She felt shocked.

Shocked and curiously light-headed.

She shook her head to clear it as Sam ushered her out of the building into the spring sunshine. Odd, it had been cloudy before, and now it was glorious. How ironic, when her world had been turned upside down.

'So—what now?' she asked, looking up at him for guidance and grateful for the feel of his hand, warm and supportive in the small of her back.

'Well, I don't know about you but I could do with a nice, strong coffee.' He smiled, but the smile didn't reach his eyes. They were strangely expressionless, and she suddenly realised she didn't know him at all. Didn't know what he was thinking, how he was feeling—which under the circumstances wasn't surprising, because she wasn't sure what she was thinking, either.

She tried to smile back, but her lips felt stiff and uncooperative and her eyes were prickling. 'Me, too. I haven't had coffee for months but suddenly I feel the need.'

'One car or two?'

'Two. I'll go straight on from there.' And it would give her the next few minutes alone to draw breath.

'The usual place?'

She nodded, and got into her car, following him on autopilot, curiously detached. It all seemed unreal, as if it was happening to someone else—until she felt the baby move, and then reality hit home and her eyes filled. 'Oh,

James, I'm sorry,' she whispered brokenly. 'I tried so hard for you. I really tried.'

She felt something thin and fragile tear inside her, the last tenuous link to the man she'd loved with all her heart, and she closed her eyes briefly as she pulled up beside Sam, giving her grief a moment. It was a gentle grief, a quiet sorrow now, and it was her constant companion. She was used to it.

'OK?'

Was she? Probably not, but she smiled up at Sam and got out of the car and let him usher her in. They'd gone, as usual, to the riverfront café they'd all frequented in the past. Before, she'd always had fruit tea. This time, settling into a chair opposite Sam, she had a frothy mocha with a chocolate flake to dunk, and a sticky Danish pastry, also laced with chocolate.

Comfort food.

And, boy, did she need it. Those few minutes in the car had given her breathing space but they'd done nothing to change the truth. A truth neither of them had come up with. A truth that changed everything.

She looked up and met his impenetrable slate-blue gaze, and wondered if her child would inherit those exquisite and remarkable eyes...

It was a different sort of mix-up entirely, something that had never crossed Sam's mind.

Something that should never have happened, an accident which he'd always taken positive steps to avoid in his personal life for very good reasons, and which he'd trusted the clinic to be equally careful of, but it seemed they'd failed, because this woman sitting opposite him—this very lovely, warm and gentle woman—was pregnant with his child, and she wasn't going to be handing it over to Emily and

Andrew, as he'd feared, because it wasn't Emily's baby. It was Emelia's. And his.

*Our child.*

He looked away, his eyes carefully avoiding the smooth, pretty curve containing a bomb that was about to blow his life apart. His child was growing inside her body—a body he'd had to force himself to ignore on every one of the occasions they'd met in the past eighteen months. Very few occasions. Hardly any, really. Just enough for her to get right under his skin and haunt his dreams...

His eyes dropped to the gentle but unmistakeable swell of their baby, and something elemental kicked him in the gut, just as it had when he'd held her. Almost as if he'd known—

Damn. He couldn't do this. Not again. And it wasn't how it was meant to be. It was supposed to be quick and clean and straightforward. His brother couldn't have children. This had been something he could do, a way to give them a desperately wanted child which he could legitimately love at a distance and have no further responsibility towards except in the role of uncle.

Tidy. Clean. Simple.

Yeah, right.

And then this. Some *administrative anomaly* that had totally changed all the rules.

He yanked his eyes away from the evidence and put his own feelings aside for now. He'd deal with them later, alone. For now he had to think of her, the woman carrying not her husband's child, but the child of a comparative stranger. And that wasn't going to be any easier for her than it was for him, he realised. Probably a damn sight harder. They said it was better to have loved and lost than never to have loved at all, but to lose twice? Because she was losing James again, in a way, her dream replaced with a living nightmare, and that was just downright cruel.

He met her eyes, the muted green smudged slightly with tears of pain and bewilderment, and his heart ached for her. 'I'm so sorry, Emelia.'

'Don't be,' she said softly. 'It's not your fault.'

His voice was gruff. 'I know, but—thinking it had worked, thinking all this time you were having his baby, and then to be told it isn't—you must be just gutted.'

She felt the familiar grief amongst this new rash of emotions, but also guilt, because the man who was the father of her child was sitting opposite her and even now, with the shock of this revelation, she realised she was aware of him with every cell of her body, as she'd been aware of him every time they'd met.

She tried to speak logically, to find something sensible to say to this man when James seemed so long ago and all she could think about now was Sam's baby growing inside her womb—

*Stick to the facts!*

'Sam, really, it's OK,' she said eventually. 'I never really expected it to work. The sperm quality wasn't good, James and I knew that from the beginning. It was always going to be a long shot if we tried it, and I know it sounds stupid but I was astonished when I found I was pregnant because I never really expected it to happen, so in many ways maybe it's for the best.'

'The best?'

Not from where he was looking at it, but maybe she had a different perspective altogether. She shrugged, her slender shoulders lifting in a gesture almost of defeat, and he had a crazy urge to gather her up in his arms and tell her it was all right, she didn't have to be brave, it was OK to be angry and sad and confused. But then she spoke, and it seemed she wasn't being brave at all, she was being honest.

'It's been harder than I thought. My in-laws were starting to suffocate me. They were completely taking over, as if it was their baby,' she told him, realising in surprise that, despite the sadness she felt that she wasn't carrying his child, for the first time since James' death she felt free.

Free of the suffocating and controlling interference of Julia and Brian, free of the obligation to share her life with them for the sake of their grandchild. She hadn't realised how much she'd started to resent it, but now, it was as if someone had opened the windows on a hot summer's day and let in a blast of cool, refreshing air.

But the air had a chill in it, she realised as her emotions see-sawed and righted, and it dawned on her, that instead of her in-laws, she'd be linked to this man, this stranger—this charming, handsome, virile stranger with the unsmiling mouth and stormy eyes—for the next twenty years or more. The feeling of relief was short-lived, and was rapidly being replaced by some very confusing emotions.

'I'm sorry,' he said softly. 'It must have been very difficult for you from the beginning, this whole process. Emily said you were struggling with all the emotional stuff.'

'I was—and of course I'm sad, but maybe it's time to let go—and anyway, it's not just me, is it? What about Em and Andrew?' she said, not allowing herself to think about Sam yet, thinking instead of her friends, because it was easier. Safer. 'I'm gutted for them, because it could so easily have worked this time and the treatment's so physically and mentally gruelling. To think they'll have to go through it again…' She fell silent for a moment. Poor Em. Poor all of them.

'I'm not sure they'll want to try again,' Sam said after a thoughtful pause. And thinking about it, he wasn't sure he could help them. He'd found it harder with each cycle, been more reluctant the more time he'd had to think about it, and now—

'It's such a mix-up,' she said, sifting through the clinic director's words and trying to make some sense of them.

'Tell me about it,' he said tautly, prodding his black coffee with a teaspoon and scowling at it.

He looked frustrated and unhappy, and she could understand that. She'd forgotten much of the conversation, the clinic director's words wiped from her memory by the shock of his revelation, but she remembered the gist of it, and as she trawled through it again in her head she was just as bewildered as she'd been during their meeting.

'I still can't really see how it could have happened,' she said thoughtfully. 'They seemed absolutely certain about what went wrong—certain enough to check the DNA of the remaining frozen embryos—which means that everything was properly documented, so why wasn't it picked up at the time? It doesn't make sense.'

'Because the embryologist was so distracted she didn't even realise she'd made a mistake. She was clearly not fit to be at work and didn't pay sufficient attention to detail, hence the confusion between your names.'

'What—Eastwood and Hunter? I don't think so.'

'But Emelia and Emily? They're quite similar if you're not concentrating, and she'd missed off your surnames, and spelt your name with an "i" in the middle, which just made it worse. And it was only when the new embryologist sorted out the backlog of paperwork that the inconsistent reference numbers alerted her. Did you miss that bit?'

'I must have done,' she said slowly. 'I wasn't really listening, to be honest, after he'd told us what had happened, but if she left off our surnames it makes a mix-up more understandable, I suppose…'

'Absolutely, but it's no justification,' he said flatly, dropping the teaspoon back into his saucer and leaning back. 'It's just attention to detail. It's critical in a job like that. If you're incompetent, for whatever reason, then you shouldn't be working there. It's inexcusable. They've created a child that should never have existed, put both of us in an untenable situation, and no amount of compensation can atone for that.'

There was a hint of steel in his voice, and she realised he was more than frustrated and unhappy, he was angry. Furiously angry. Because he didn't want some random woman having his child? Reasonable, under the circumstances. She'd feel the same in his shoes. But the embryologist—

'Don't be too hard on her,' she murmured. 'She'd just learned her husband was dying. I know how that feels.'

Something flickered in his eyes, and he nodded briefly. 'Sorry. Of course you do. I didn't mean to sound harsh, and it was the clinic managers who were at fault. They should have given her compassionate leave or someone to work with to keep a quiet eye on what she was doing, not just left it to chance. But that doesn't alter what's happened to you and the situation you've been left in.'

And him, of course. She wasn't the only one who was affected, but she was the only one who couldn't walk away— the only one in what he'd called an untenable situation. And he looked as if he'd rather be anywhere else in the world but here, so she owed him that chance.

'Sam, this needn't make any difference to you,' she said carefully. 'I'm not asking you to sign up to any kind of responsibility for the baby—'

He gave a hollow grunt of laughter and drained his coffee.

'Emelia, I signed up to give my brother a child. A child

who'd be brought up by a loving, devoted couple. A child who'd have not only a mother, but a father. I didn't sign up to be a sperm donor, to hand over my genetic material to a stranger and take no further part in my child's life. That was never on the agenda and it's not something I'd ever do, but that's not the point now. The point is you're having my baby, and I won't walk away from that. From either of you.'

A muscle worked in his jaw and she swallowed. Was that what she wanted for her child? A dutiful, angry father stomping about in their lives? She wasn't sure. She didn't know him—and he was right, he didn't know her. Time to change that, maybe.

'I'm not that strange,' she said, trying for a smile, and he laughed again, but his voice was gentler this time.

'No. No, you're not that strange, but you are alone, and you didn't sign up for this either, Emelia. You were supposed to be having your late husband's baby, with the support of his parents. Now, there's no possibility of that ever happening, and you're pregnant with a stranger's child—a stranger who's very much alive and involved with this, and I can't imagine how you feel about it. About any of it. Or how your in-laws will feel, come to that.'

Good question. How did she feel? She didn't know yet. It was far too complicated and she needed time to sift though it and come to terms with it before she could share it with Sam. Her in-laws were another question altogether, and she had a fair idea how they would feel.

'It's going to be horrendous breaking it to them. They've grown so used to the idea that this was James' baby, and they keep feeling my bump, Julia especially. Really, you'd think it was hers the way she just assumes she can touch me.'

He felt a stab of regret, because he'd wanted to ask if

he could feel it, felt a crazy need to lay his hands on the beautiful, smooth curve that held his child, but of course he couldn't. It was far too intrusive and he had no right to touch her. No rights over her at all. Lord, what a crazy situation.

'So what do you do? When she does that?'

'I let her. What can I do? She smiles this proud, secret little smile, as if it's all her doing, and she's constantly buying things—the nursery's so full I can hardly get in there.'

'And they're all things for James' baby, not mine,' he murmured, realising that this mix-up was going to have a devastating effect on so many people.

She nodded.

'That's right. And they need to know.'

She swallowed. She couldn't put this off any longer, and she needed time alone to think. Sam sitting there simmering with anger and some other emotion she couldn't get a handle on wasn't helping at all. 'I ought to get back and tell them.'

'Do you want me to come?'

She stared at him, wishing he could, knowing he couldn't, and he realised that, obviously, because he went on hastily, 'No, of course you don't. Sorry. You have to tell them alone, I can see that, but we need to talk sometime, Emelia. This won't go away.'

She nodded. 'I know—but not yet. I need time for it to sink in, Sam. Give me a while. Let me tell them, try and explain, and let me think about my options, because this changes everything. My whole future.'

Sam searched her soft, wounded eyes. She was being so brave about it, but what if it wasn't what she wanted? What if, when she'd considered her options—?

'If you don't want to go through with this, if you want

to take the clinic up on their offer—it's your decision,' he said brusquely, a painful twisting in his gut as he said the words—words that could end his child's life. Words he'd had to say, even though they went deeply against his every instinct.

Her eyes widened, her hand flying down to cover the little bump that he so wanted to lay his hands against, and she stood up abruptly.

'No way. This is my baby, Sam,' she said flatly. 'I haven't asked you to get involved in its life, and I don't expect you to if you don't want to, but there's no way I'm taking them up on their *"offer"*, as you so delicately put it. I'll have it, and I'll love it, and nothing and nobody will get in the way of that. And if you don't like it, then sue me.'

And lifting her chin, she scooped up her keys, grabbed her bag off the other chair and walked swiftly out of the café, leaving him sitting there staring after her. The relief left him weak at the knees, and it took him a second, but then he snapped his mouth shut, got up and strode after her.

'Wait!' he said, yanking open her car door before she could drive off. 'Emelia, that's not what I was trying to say. I just thought—'

'Well, you thought wrong,' she retorted, and grabbed the door handle.

He held the door firmly and ignored her little growl of frustration. 'No. I thought—hoped—you'd react exactly as you did, but you needed to know that you have my support whatever course of action you decide to take. This thing is massive. It's going to change the whole course of your life, and that's not trivial. You have to be certain you can do this. That's all I was saying—that it's your call, and for what it's worth, I think you've made the right one, but it's down to you.'

He thrust a business card into her hand. 'Here. My contact details. Call me, Emelia. Please. Talk to me. If there's anything you need, anything I can do, just ask. If you really are going to keep the baby—'

'I am. I meant everything I said. But don't worry, Sam, I don't need anything from you. You're off the hook.'

Never. Not in his lifetime. He hung on to the door. 'Promise me you'll call me when you've spoken to them.'

'Why?'

He shrugged, reluctant to let her go like this when she was so upset. Concerned for her. Nothing more, he told himself. Just concerned for her and the child. His child. His heart twisted. 'Because you need a friend?' he suggested warily. 'Someone who understands?'

Her eyes searched his for the longest moment, and then without a word she slammed the door and drove away.

He watched her go, swore softly, then got into his car and followed her out of the car park. She'd turned left. He hesitated for a moment, then turned right and headed home, to start working out how to fill his brother in on this latest development in the tragic saga of their childless state.

Better that than trying to analyse his own reaction to the news that a woman he found altogether too disturbingly attractive was carrying his child—a child he'd never meant to have, created by accident—that would link him to Emelia forever…

'I've got something to tell you.'

'Well, before you do, come and see what Brian's doing in the nursery,' her mother-in-law said, her face beaming as she grabbed Emelia's hand and led her through the door.

Why not? she thought bleakly. Why not do it there, amongst all the things gathered together to welcome their new grandchild? The child they'd thought they might never have.

The child they never would have. Not now. Not ever.

She sucked in a breath and stood there in the expectant silence, aware of their eyes on her face, their suppressed excitement as they eagerly awaited her reaction. And then she looked at the room.

He'd painted a frieze, she realised. Trains and teddies and alphabet letters, all round the middle of the walls. A little bit crooked, a little bit smudged, but painted with love. Stupidly, it made her want to cry.

She swallowed hard and looked away. Oh, this was so hard—too hard. 'I had a letter—from the clinic director,' she said bluntly, before she chickened out. 'I had to go to there and talk to him. There's a problem.'

'A problem? What kind of problem? We paid their last bill, Brian, didn't we? We've paid everything—'

'It's not the money. It's about the baby, Julia.'

Her mother-in-law's face was suddenly slack with shock, and Emelia looked around and realised she couldn't do this here, in this room, with the lovingly painted little frieze still drying on the walls. 'I need a cup of tea,' she said, and headed for the big family kitchen, knowing they'd follow. She put the kettle on—such a cliché, having a cup of tea, but somehow a necessary part of the ritual of grief—and then sat down, pushing the cups towards them.

They sat facing her, at the table where James had sat as a boy, where they'd all sat together so many times, where they'd cried together on the day he'd died, and they waited, the tea forgotten, their faces taut with fear as she groped for the words. But there was no kind way to do this, nothing that was going to make it go away.

'There was a mix-up,' she said quietly, her heart pound-ing as she yanked the rug out from under them as gently as possible. 'In the lab at the clinic. They fertilised the eggs with the wrong sperm.'

Julia Eastwood's hand flew up over her mouth. 'So—that's another woman's baby?' she said after a shocked pause.

Oh, dear. 'No,' she said. 'It's my baby.' And then, because there was no other way to say it, she added gently, 'It's not James' baby, though. It's someone else's.'

'So—where's his baby?' she demanded, her voice rising hysterically. 'Has some other woman got his baby? She'll have to give it back—Brian, she'll have to, we can't have this—'

'Julia, there *is* no baby,' she said, trying to firm her voice. 'The embryos all died before they could be implanted.'

She let that sink in for a moment, watched Brian's eyes fill with tears before he closed them, watched Julia's face spasm as the realisation hit home. The wail of grief, when it came, was the same as when James had taken his last breath. It was as if she'd lost him all over again, and Emelia supposed that, in a way, she had.

She reached out and squeezed the woman's hand. 'Julia, I'm so sorry.'

She didn't react, except to turn into Brian's waiting arms and fall apart, and Emelia left them to their grief. There was nothing she could add that would make it any better and she just wanted to get out before she drowned in their emotion.

She was superfluous here, redundant, and it dawned on her that their only thought had been for the baby. Not once in that conversation had either of them expressed any concern about her, about how she might feel, about where she would go from here.

Not surprising, really, but it was a very good point. Where would she go? What *would* she do? She could hardly carry on living here, in the annexe they'd created when James was ill—the annexe where he'd lost his fight for life and which after his death, with the IVF conversation under their belts, they'd told her she should think of as her home.

But not when she was carrying another man's child.

So she packed some things. Not the baby's. As Sam had said, they belonged to a child who never was, and they would no doubt be dealt with in the fullness of time. She closed the door without looking at the little frieze in case it made her cry again, and put a few changes of clothes in a bag, enough for a week, perhaps, to give her time to think, although with very little to her name she wasn't quite sure where she'd go. She just knew she had to, that staying, even one more night, simply wasn't an option.

She put her case in the car, then went through all the contents of the annexe, piling the things that were hers alone into one end of the wardrobe so they could be packed and delivered to her wherever she ended up, but leaving James' things there, lifting them one at a time to her lips, saying goodbye for the final time.

His watch. His wedding ring. The fountain pen she'd given him for his birthday so he could write the diary of his last months.

She stroked her fingers gently over the cover of the diary. She didn't need to take it, she knew every word by heart. Julia needed it more than she did. She touched it one last time and walked away.

Leaving the bedroom, she went into the kitchen and turned out the fridge, staring helplessly at half a bottle of milk and an opened bag of salad.

There was no point in taking it, but it seemed silly to throw it out, so she put it back with the cheese and the tomatoes—and then got them all out again and made herself a sandwich. It was mid-afternoon and she'd eaten nothing since she'd left Sam, but she couldn't face it now. She drank the milk, because she hadn't touched her cup of tea, and then put the sandwich in the car with her case for later, had one last visual sweep of the annexe and then she went to say goodbye.

They were in the kitchen, where she'd left them, as if she'd only been gone five minutes instead of two or three hours. She could hear raised voices as she approached, snatches of distressed conversation that halted her in her tracks.

Julia said something she didn't quite catch, then Brian said, quite clearly, 'If I'd had the slightest idea of all the pain it would cause, I never would have allowed you to talk him into signing that consent.'

'I couldn't bear to lose him, Brian! You have to understand—'

'But you *had* lost him, Julia. You'd lost him already. He hardly knew what he was signing—'

'He did!'

'No! He was out of his head with the morphine, and telling him she was desperate to have his child—it was just a lie.'

'But you went along with it! You never said anything—'

'Because I wanted it, too, but it was wrong, Julia—so wrong. And now…'

Her thoughts in free-fall, Emelia stepped into the room and cleared her throat, and they stopped abruptly, swivelling to stare at her as she fought down the sudden surge of anger that would help no one. She wanted to tackle them, to ask them to explain, but she wasn't sure she could hold it together and she just wanted to get out.

Now.

'I'm leaving,' she said without emotion. 'I've put all my

things in the end of the wardrobe. I'll get them collected when I know where I'll be. I've left all James' things here for you. I know you'll want them. I haven't touched the nursery.'

'But—what about all the baby's things? What will we do with them?' Julia said, and then started to cry again.

Brian put his arms round her and gave Emelia a fleeting, slightly awkward smile over the top of Julia's head. 'Goodbye, Emelia. And good luck,' he said.

So much for 'think of it as your home', she thought bitterly as she dropped the keys for it on the table. That hadn't lasted long once she was no further use to them. She nodded and walked away before she lost it and asked what on earth he'd meant about Julia talking James into signing the consent—for posthumous use of his sperm, presumably, to make the baby they'd told her he'd apparently so desperately wanted her to have.

Really? So why hadn't he said anything? Why hadn't he ever, in all the conversations they'd had about the future, said that he wanted her to have his child after his death? Asked how she felt? Because he would have done. They'd talked about everything, but never that, and it was only now, with it all falling apart around her ears, that she saw the light.

And they'd told him—had the *nerve* to tell him!— that she was the one who so desperately wanted a baby? Nothing had been further from her mind at that point, but they'd got her, still reeling with grief on the day after the funeral, and talked her into it.

And she was furious. Deeply, utterly furious with them for lying to her, but even more so because it seemed they'd bullied James when he was so weak and vulnerable, in the last few days or hours of his life.

Bullied their own son so they could have his child and keep a little part of him alive.

She sucked in a sobbing breath. She'd been through hell for this, to have the child he'd apparently wanted so badly, and it had all been a lie. And the hell, for all of them, was still not over. It was just a different kind of hell.

She scrubbed the bitter, angry tears away and headed out of town, with no clear idea of where she was going and what she was going to do, just knowing she had barely a hundred pounds in her bank account, no job and nowhere to stay, and her prospects of getting some money fast to tide her over were frankly appalling.

Her only thought was to get away, as far and as fast as she could, but even in the midst of all the turmoil, she realised she couldn't just drive aimlessly forever.

'Oh, rats,' she said, her voice breaking, and pulling off the road into a layby, she leant back against the head restraint and closed her eyes. She wouldn't cry. She really, really wouldn't cry. Not again. Not any more. She'd cried oceans in the past three years since she'd known James was dying, and it was time to move on.

But where? It would be dusk soon, the night looming, and she had nowhere to stay. Could she sleep in the car? Hardly. It was only April, and she'd freeze. Her old friends in Bristol and Cheshire were too far away, and she'd lost touch with most of them anyway since James had been ill and they'd moved back to Essex. The only person who would understand was Emily, and she and Andrew were away and in any case the last people in the world she could really turn to. It just wouldn't be fair.

But Sam was there.

Sam, who'd as good as told her to get rid of the baby.

No. He hadn't, she thought, trying to be fair. She'd thought he meant that, but he hadn't, not that way. He'd come after her, offered his unconditional support, whatever her decision. Said he thought she'd made the right one.

*If there's anything you need, anything I can do, just ask… Promise me you'll call me… You need a friend—someone who understands.*

And he'd given her his card.

She looked down and there it was in the middle, a little white rectangle of card lying in the heap of sweet wrappers and loose change just in front of the gear lever where she'd dropped it. She pulled it out, keyed in the number and reluctantly pressed the call button.

# CHAPTER TWO

'HUNTER.'

He sounded distracted, terse. He was probably busy, and for a moment she almost hung up, her courage failing her. Then he spoke again, and his voice was softer.

'Emelia?'

*How had he known?*

'Hi, Sam.' She fizzled out, not sure what to say, where to start, but he seemed to understand.

'Problems?'

'Sort of. Look—I'm sorry, I expect you're busy. It's just—we need to talk, really, and I've gone and got myself into a rather silly situation.' She took a little breath, then another one, and he interrupted her efforts to get to the point.

'I'm not busy. Where are you?'

She looked around. She'd seen a sign ages ago that welcomed her to Suffolk—where Sam lived, according to Emily, in a ridiculous house in the middle of nowhere. Had she gone there subconsciously? Probably. She'd been driving in circles, lost in tiny lanes, not caring.

'I'm not sure. Somewhere in Suffolk—close to the A140, I think. Where are you? Give me your postcode, I'll put it in my satnav. What's the house called?'

'Flaxfield Place. The name's partly buried in ivy, but

it's the only drive on that road for a couple of miles, so you can't miss it. Look out for a set of big iron gates with a cattle grid, on the north side of the road. The gates are open, just come up the drive and you'll find me. You can't be far away. I'll be watching out for you.'

The thought was oddly comforting. She put the postcode into the satnav and pressed go.

This couldn't be it.

She swallowed hard and stared at the huge iron gates, hanging open, with a cattle grid between the gateposts. A long thin ribbon of tarmac stretched away into the dusk between an avenue of trees, and half hidden by ivy on an old brick wall, she could make out a name—something-field Place, the something obscured by the ivy, just as he'd said.

But she could see weeds poking up between the bars of the cattle grid, and one of the gates was hanging at a jaunty angle because the gatepost was falling down, making the faded grandeur somehow less intimidating than it might otherwise have been.

His ridiculous house, as Emily had described it, falling to bits and shabby-chic without the chic? There was certainly nothing chic about the weeds.

She fought down another hysterical laugh and drove through the gates, the cattle grid making her teeth rattle, and then up the drive between the trees. There was a light in the distance and, as she emerged from the trees, the tarmac gave way to a wide gravel sweep in front of a beautiful old Georgian house draped in wisteria, and her jaw sagged.

The white-pillared portico was bracketed by long, elegant windows, and through a lovely curved fanlight over the huge front door welcoming light spilt out into the dusk.

It was beautiful. OK, the drive needed weeding, like the cattle grid, but the paint on the windows was fresh and the brass on the front door was gleaming. And as she stared at it, a little open-mouthed, the door opened, and more of that warm golden light flowed out onto the gravel and brought tears to her eyes.

It looked so welcoming, so *safe*.

And suddenly it seemed as if it was the only thing in her world that was.

That and Sam, who came round and opened her car door and smiled down at her with concern in those really rather beautiful slate-blue eyes.

'Hi, there. You found me OK, then?'

'Yes.'

Oh, she needed a hug, but he didn't give her one and if he had, it would have crumpled her like a wet tissue, so perhaps it was just as well. She really didn't want to cry. She had a horrible feeling that once she started, she wouldn't be able to stop.

'Come on in. You look shattered. I've made you up a bed in the guest room.'

His simple act of thoughtfulness and generosity brought tears to her eyes anyway, and she swallowed hard. 'Oh, Sam, you didn't need to do that.'

'Didn't I? So where were you going?'

She followed his eyes and saw them focused on her suitcase where she'd thrown it on the back seat. She shrugged. 'I don't know. I didn't really have a plan. I just walked out. And I am so *angry*.'

'With the clinic?'

'No. With my in-laws.'

His brow creased briefly, and he held out his hand, firm and warm and like a rock in the midst of all the chaos, and helped her out of the car. 'Come on. This needs a big steaming mug of hot chocolate and a comfy chair by the fire. Have you eaten?'

She shook her head. 'I've got a sandwich,' she said, pulling it out of her bag to prove it, and he tutted and led her inside, hefting her case as if it weighed nothing. He dumped it in the gracious and elegant hallway with its black-and-white-chequered marble floor, and led her through to the much more basic kitchen beyond the stairs.

'This is Daisy,' he said, introducing her to the sleepy and gentle black Labrador who ambled to her feet and came towards her, tail wagging, and while she said hello he put some milk to heat on the ancient range. She could feel its warmth, and if he hadn't been standing beside it she would have gone over to it, leant on the rail on the front and let it thaw the ice that seemed to be encasing her. But he was there, so she just stood where she was and tried to hold it all together while Daisy nuzzled her hand and pressed against her.

'Sit down and eat that sandwich before you keel over,' he instructed firmly, and so she sat at the old pine table and ate, the dog leaning on her leg and watching her carefully in case she dropped a bit, while he melted chocolate and whisked milk and filled the mugs with more calories than she usually ate in a week.

She fed Daisy the crusts, making Sam tut gently, and then he took her through to another room where, even though it was April, there was a log fire blazing in the grate.

The fireplace was bracketed by a pair of battered leather sofas, homely and welcoming, and Daisy hopped up on one and snuggled down in the corner, so she sat on the other, and Sam threw another log on the fire, sat next to Daisy and propped his feet on the old pine box between the sofas, next to the tray of hot chocolate and scrumptious golden oat cookies, and lifted a brow.

'So—I take it things didn't go too well?' he said as she settled back to take her first sip.

She gave a slightly strangled laugh and licked froth off her top lip. 'You could say that,' she agreed after a moment. 'They were devastated, of course. Julia was wondering how much it would cost to get the other woman to give up James' baby. When I told her there wasn't one, she fell apart, and I went to pack up the annexe, and when I went back to tell them I was leaving, they were arguing. It seems Julia had talked James into signing the consent form for posthumous IVF while he was on morphine. They lied to him, told him it was what I wanted.'

He frowned, her words shocking him and dragging his mind back from the inappropriate fantasy he'd been plunged into when she'd licked her lip. 'But surely you'd talked about it with him?'

She shook her head. 'No. I only knew about it after he'd died. They'd told me he'd been desperate for me to have his child, but he couldn't speak to me about it because he knew it would distress me to think about what I'd be doing after he was gone.'

Sam frowned again. 'Did you think that was likely, that he wouldn't have talked to you about something so significant?'

'No. Not at all, and there was no mention of it in his diary. He put everything in his diary. But I was so shocked I just believed them, and it was there in black and white, giving his consent. And it was definitely his signature, for all that it was shaky. It never occurred to me that they'd coerced him—he was their son. They adored him. Why would they do that?'

Her voice cracked, and he felt a surge of anger on her

behalf—and for James. The anger deepened. He hated duplicity, with good reason. 'So they tricked you both?'

'It would seem so.'

'And you'd never talked about it with James?'

She shook her head. 'Not this aspect. The idea was to freeze some sperm so that if he survived and was left sterile by the treatment, we could still have children. Once we knew he wasn't going to make it, nothing more was ever said. Until Julia broached it after the funeral.'

*After the funeral?* Surely not right after? Although looking at her, Sam had a sickening feeling it was what she meant. He leant back, cradling his hot chocolate and studying her bleak expression. She looked awful. Shocked and exhausted and utterly lost. She'd dragged a cushion onto her lap and was hugging it as she sipped her drink, and he wanted to take the cushion away and pull her onto his lap and hug her himself. And there was more froth on her lip—

Stupid. So, so stupid! This was complicated enough as it was and the last thing he needed was to get involved with a grieving widow. He didn't do emotion—avoided it whenever possible. And she was carrying his child. That was emotion enough for him to cope with—too much. And anyway, it was just a misplaced sexual attraction. Usually pregnant women simply brought out the nurturer in him.

But not Emelia. Oh, no. There was just something about her, about the luscious ripeness of her body that did crazy things to his libido too. Because she was carrying his child? No. He'd felt like it when he'd hugged her in the car park at the clinic earlier today, before he'd known it was his baby. It was just that she was pregnant, he told himself, and conveniently ignored the fact that he'd felt this way about Emelia since the first time he'd seen her...

'So what did they say when you told them you were leaving?' he asked, getting back to the point in a hurry.

She shrugged. 'Very little. I think to be honest I saved them the bother of asking me to go.'

'So—if you hadn't got hold of me, where *were* you going to stay tonight?'

She shrugged again, her slight shoulders lifting in another helpless little gesture that tugged at his heartstrings. 'I have no idea. As I said, I didn't really give it any thought, I just knew I had to get out. I'd have found somewhere. And I didn't have any choice, so it doesn't really matter, does it, where else I might have gone?'

Oddly, he discovered, it mattered to him. It mattered far more than was comfortable, but he told himself it was because she was Emily's friend—and a vulnerable pregnant woman. That again. Of course that was all it was. Anybody would care about her, it was nothing to do with the fact that this delicate, fragile-looking woman, with the bruised look in her olive green eyes and a mouth that kept trying to firm itself to stop that little tremor, was swollen with his child. That was just a technicality. It had to be. He couldn't allow it to be anything else—and he certainly wasn't following up on the bizarre attraction he was feeling for her right this minute.

'You're done in,' he said gruffly, getting to his feet. 'Come on, I'll show you to your room. We can talk tomorrow.'

He led her up the broad, easing-rising staircase with its graceful curved banister rail, across the landing and into a bedroom.

Not just any bedroom, though. It had silk curtains at the windows, a beautiful old rug on the floor, and a cream-painted iron and brass bed straight out of her fantasies, piled high with pillows and looking so inviting she could have wept.

Well, she could have wept anyway, what with one thing and another, but the bed was just the last straw.

He put her case on a padded ottoman at the foot of the bed, and opened a door and showed her the bathroom on the other side.

'It communicates with the room I'm using at the moment, but there's a lock on each door. Just remember to undo it when you leave.'

'I will.'

'And if there's anything you need, just yell. I won't be far away.'

Not far at all, she thought, her eyes flicking to the bathroom door.

'I'll be fine. Thank you, Sam. For everything.'

He gave a curt nod and left her alone then, the door closing with a soft click, and she hugged her arms and stared at the room. It was beautiful, the furnishings expensive and yet welcoming. Not in the least intimidating, and as the sound of his footfalls died away, the peace of the countryside enveloped her.

She felt a sob rising in her throat and squashed it down. She wouldn't cry. She couldn't. She was going to be fine. It might take a little time, but she was going to be fine.

She washed, a little nervous of the Jack-and-Jill doors in the bathroom, then unlocked his side before she left, turning the key in her side of the door—which was ludicrous, because there was no key in the bedroom door and he was hardly going to come in and make a pass at her in her condition anyway.

She climbed into the lovely, lovely bed and snuggled down, enveloped by the cloud-like quilt and the softest pure cotton bedding she'd ever felt in her life, and turning out the light, she closed her eyes and waited.

Fruitlessly.

She couldn't sleep. Her mind was still whirling, her thoughts chaotic, her emotions in turmoil. After a while she heard his footsteps returning, and a sliver of light appeared under the bathroom door. She lay and watched it, heard water running, then the scrape of the lock on her door as he opened it, the click of the light switch as the sliver of light disappeared, and then silence.

How strange.

The father of her child was going to bed in the room next to hers, and she knew almost nothing about him except that he'd cared enough for his brother to offer him the gift of a child.

A gift that had been misdirected—lost in the post, so to speak. A gift that by default now seemed to be hers.

And now he was caring for her, keeping her safe, giving her time to decide what she should do next.

Something, obviously, but she had no idea what, and fear clawed at her throat. Her hand slid down over the baby, cradling it protectively as if to shield it from all the chaos that was to follow. What would become of them? Where would they go? How would she provide for them? And where would they live? Without Sam, she had no idea where she would have slept tonight, and she was grateful for the breathing space, but her problem wasn't solved, by any means.

'I love you, baby,' she whispered. 'It'll be all right. You'll see. I'll take care of you, there's nothing to be afraid of. We'll find a way.'

A sob fought its way out of her chest, and another, and then, with her defences down and nothing left to hide behind, the tears began to fall.

* * *

He heard her crying, but there was nothing he could do.

She was grieving for the child she'd never have, the man she'd lost forever with this last devastating blow, and there was no place for him in that. All he could do was make sure she didn't come to any harm.

He didn't know how he could protect her, or what she'd let him offer in the way of protection.

His name?

His gut clenched at the thought and he backed away from it hastily.

Not that. Anything but that. He'd been there, done that, and it had been the most painful and humiliating mistake of his life. He couldn't do it again, couldn't offer the protection of his name to another pregnant woman. The first time had nearly shredded him alive and he had no intention of revisiting the situation.

But there was a vital difference. He *knew* this child was his. There was no escaping that fact, however shocking and unexpected, and he couldn't walk away. Didn't want to. Not from the child. He'd do the right thing, and somehow it would all work out. He'd make sure of it. But Emelia—hell, that was a whole different ball game. He'd have to help her, whatever it cost him, because he couldn't see a pregnant woman suffer. It just wasn't in him to do so. But his feelings for her were entirely inappropriate.

He nearly laughed. Inappropriate, to be attracted to a woman who was carrying his child? Under normal circumstances nobody would think twice about it, but these circumstances were anything but normal, and he couldn't let himself be lured into this. It would be too easy to let himself fall for her, for the whole seductive and entrancing package.

Dangerously, terrifyingly easy, and he wasn't going there again. Even if she would have had him.

So he lay there, tormented by the muffled sobs coming from her bedroom, wanting to go to her and yet knowing he couldn't because she wasn't crying for him, she was crying for James, and there was nothing he could do about that.

And when finally the sobs died away, he turned onto his side, punched the pillow into shape and closed his eyes.

She must have slept.

Overslept, she realised as she struggled free of the sumptuous embrace of the bedding and sat up.

Sun was pouring through a chink in the curtains, and she slipped out of bed and padded over, parting them and looking out onto an absolutely glorious day. Everything was bathed in the warm and gentle sunshine of spring, and in the distance, past the once-formal knot garden on the terrace below with its straggling, overgrown little hedges, and past the sweeping lawn beyond, she could see gently rolling fields bordered by ancient hedgerows, and here and there a little stand of trees huddled together on a rise.

It was beautiful, in a rather run-down and delightfully bucolic way, and she wanted to explore it. Especially the walled garden over to her right, which drew her eyes now and lured her with the promise of long-forgotten gems hidden by years of neglect.

However it wasn't hers to explore and she reminded herself she had other priorities, as if she needed reminding. She had nowhere to live, no clear idea of her future, and that had to come first. That, and food.

She was starving, her stomach rumbling, her body in mutiny after yesterday's miserable diet of junk food and caffeine, and she bit her lip and wondered where Sam was and how she could find him, and if not, if it would be too rude to raid his fridge and find herself something to eat.

Clothes first, she told herself, and went into the bath-room, tapping on the door just in case. It was empty, but the bathmat was damp, and she realised she must have slept through his shower. She had no idea what the time was, but her stomach told her it was late, so she showered in record time, looked in her suitcase for a pretty jumper and some clean jeans with a really sexy stretch panel in the front to accommodate the baby—just the thing for reminding her of all the good reasons why it didn't matter what she looked like—and then in a moment of self-preservation she dabbed concealer under her eyes, added a quick swipe of mascara and lip gloss and made her way down to the kitchen.

Daisy was there, thumping her tail against the cupboard doors in greeting, and as she straightened up from patting the dog she saw Sam lounging against the front of the range with a mug cradled in his large, capable hands.

His rather grubby hands, to go with the worn, sexy jeans and the battered rugby shirt. He looked light years from the suave and sophisticated man of yesterday—and even more attractive. He smiled at her, and her heart gave a little lurch of recognition.

'Hi. How did you sleep?' he asked, his voice a little gruff.

'Well. Amazingly well. The bedding's blissful.'

'It is good, isn't it? I can't stand rubbish bedding. Hungry?'

'Mmm. Have you got anything healthy?'

His mouth twitched. 'Such as?'

She shrugged. 'Anything. Yesterday I had chocolate, cheese and caffeine!'

'So—does healthy rule out local free-range eggs?'

'How local?'

'Mine.' Her eyes widened, and Sam laughed at her. 'Everyone around here has chickens.'

'There *is* no one round here,' she pointed out, but he shook his head.

'There are lots, and it's only a mile or two to the village. I've got local home-cured bacon from pigs that grub around in the woods, sausages ditto, mushrooms, tomatoes—'

'Whoa!' she said, laughing now, and he felt his gut clench. 'I said healthy!'

'It is. The bread's local, too, so's the butter.'

'You're going to tell me next that you grow the coffee, and I'll know you're lying.'

He felt his mouth tilt into a grin. 'The coffee's Colombian. So—are you up for it? Frankly, as it's three hours since I had breakfast, I'd happily join you and we can call it brunch, if it helps.'

She gave in. He watched it happen, saw the brief internal tussle and the moment she surrendered, her body relaxing as the fight went out of her and a smile bloomed on her lips, making his body clench.

'Thank you. That would be lovely.'

Not nearly as lovely as you, he thought, his eyes feasting on her as she stooped again to talk to Daisy. Her hair, the colour of toffee, swung down across her face, and when she hooked it back behind her ear he could see that smile again.

God, she was gorgeous, and he had no business eyeing up a pregnant woman he'd given sanctuary to! Especially not one he was locked in a complicated relationship with for the next twenty-odd years. And anyway, she was still grieving, he reminded himself firmly. Definitely out of bounds.

He scrubbed the grease and dirt from the lawnmower off his hands, pulled out the frying pan, stuck it on the hot plate and started cooking.

'Thank you. That was amazing.'

'Good. You looked as if you needed it. And there were vegetables.'

'Yeah—fried.'

'Barely, in olive oil. And fats carry vitamins.'

'Yes, Mum,' she said teasingly, and he wondered if he could be arrested for his thoughts, because her smile was having a distinctly unplatonic effect on him. And that was a disaster, because he didn't do this. Didn't get involved with nice women. Any women. Especially ones who were carrying his child.

These days he only engaged in the kind of relationship where everyone knew the rules, where there were no expectations or hurt feelings.

No broken hearts, his or anyone else's.

Been there, done that, he reminded himself, as if he needed reminding.

'More coffee?'

'No, thanks.'

He shoved the chair back and walked over to the stove, and Emelia watched him thoughtfully. Something had happened—some kind of sizzly, magnetic thing that left her feeling breathless and light-headed.

Hormones, she told herself sternly, and hauled her eyes off his jeans.

'No, thanks, I'm fine,' she answered, a little on the drag and sounding just as breathless as she felt. She cleared her throat silently and sighed as she realised she was staring at his shoulders now—those broad, solid shoulders that would feel so good to lean on—

No! No, no, no! He was being kind to her, it didn't mean anything, and she had to keep this relationship firmly on track, because if he wanted to keep in touch with his child—and for its sake she desperately hoped he would—she'd be stuck with him for the next however many years.

'Sam, I need to make some decisions,' she said firmly, and he glanced at her over his shoulder.

'About?'

'Where I go next.'

He sat down again, mug in hand, and searched her eyes, his own expressionless. 'There's no hurry.'

'Well, there is. I have to get settled somewhere and register with a doctor and a maternity unit for my antenatal care, and I need to find a house, and a job.'

'Any ideas?'

She gave a brittle little laugh and wished she had. 'Not one—but I can't stay here indefinitely. I ought to make a few phone calls. My mother, for one—not that I can stay with her. She lives in Cheshire, in a tiny little cottage with my stepfather who wouldn't take kindly to me rocking up with a baby on the horizon and shattering their peaceful existence. And anyway, I'm too old to go and live with my mother.'

Sam frowned slightly, his brow pleating as he studied the grain on the table top, tracing it with his finger. 'Don't rush into anything, Emelia. You can stay here as long as you need to. There are lots of things to consider, and maybe we should consider them together, under the circumstances.'

She felt her eyes fill, and looked away before he saw the tears gathering in them. 'You're right. We should be thinking about this together. I just hate imposing...'

'You're not imposing,' he said flatly. 'And you're welcome.'

'Am I?'

He frowned again and met her eyes, his thoughtful. 'Yes,' he said after too long a pause. 'Yes, you are. The situation isn't ideal, but we have to make it work, for the sake of the baby and our sanity. So, yes, Emelia. You're welcome—you and the baby, for as long as you need.'

'Thanks,' she said gruffly, emotion welling up and threatening to suffocate her, and as if he realised that, he moved on.

'So—do you have any ideas at all? Any thoughts, long or short term?'

She shook her head. 'No. Well, plenty of thoughts, but no constructive ones. They talked about compensation, but I don't know how much or when it'll come through, so I'll have to find a job in the meantime—supply teaching's the obvious one. I can always do that.'

He frowned slightly. 'You're pregnant.'

'Well, heavens, so I am. I hadn't noticed.' She rolled her eyes and he sighed softly.

'Emelia, it will make it harder. When did you last teach? You'll probably need a police check, and they take weeks. By the time it's done you'll be on maternity leave and it'll be the summer holidays anyway. And the ordinary job market is a real scrum these days, never mind in your condition.'

She shut her eyes briefly. She really didn't need him pointing this out to her, she was well aware of the paucity of her options.

'It's not a *condition*, Sam. I'm fit and strong. I can do anything. I'm only nineteen weeks pregnant. Lots of women work right up to the end if they have to.'

'But you don't, so you could just stay here and be sensible.'

She stared at him blankly. 'What—till the compensation's agreed? It could be weeks. Months, more likely.'

'Even more reason. I'm sure we'll all survive,' he said drily.

She wasn't. Not if he kept on wearing those jeans—no! She mustn't think about them. About him. Not like that, it was crazy. She met his eyes. 'Not without money—and before you say it, I can't just sponge off you, Sam—and even if I could, what would I do all day?' she argued, trying to be logical in the face of rising panic. 'I can't just sit about. How is that sensible? I've got over four months before the baby comes. I have to do *something* to earn my keep.' *Even if I am unemployable...*

Sam scanned her face, saw the flicker of anxiety that she tried to mask, and knew before he opened his mouth that he'd regret this.

'Can you cook?'

'*Cook?* Why?'

He shrugged, regretting it already and backpedalling. 'Just an idea. I thought you could pay your way by taking that over, if you really feel you have to, but it's not very exciting. Forget it.'

Her brow pleated. 'Cooking for you? A few minutes a day? No, you're right, it's not especially exciting and it's not much of a deal for you, I'm a rubbish cook. And anyway, I've done a bit of supply teaching recently to stop me going crazy, so my police checks are up to date. Maybe I'll contact the local education authority and ask them if I can go on the supply list. There must be schools around here. Maybe one of them needs some cover.'

She wouldn't be underfoot. He felt relief like a physical wave—and as the wave ebbed, regret. Ridiculous. He was being ridiculous. He didn't want her here.

But he wanted the baby. He'd said so, in as many words,

yesterday, and she seemed to be taking it on board. And of course that meant she'd be around, and he'd have to live with the consequences—

'Tell me about the garden,' she said now, cutting through his troubling train of thought. 'Who looks after it?'

He laughed, more than happy to change the subject for a minute. 'Nobody. Couldn't you tell by the weeds in the cattle grid?'

'Have you tried to find someone?'

He shrugged. 'There's a lad from the village who's done a bit. He helps from time to time when it gets too bad. And I cut the grass—hence the dirty hands. I had to rebuild the mower again this morning. I hit something.'

'Something?'

He shrugged again. 'A branch? Who knows. It was out in the wilds a bit, and I was cracking on, because it's a heck of a task, even with a ride-on mower. There's a lot of it.'

'How much?'

He shrugged. 'Fifteen acres? Not all cultivated,' he added hastily as her eyes widened. 'There's the old knot garden on the terrace, the kitchen garden and the walled garden by the house. That's my favourite—it opens off my study and the sitting room we were in last night, but it's a real mess. And then there's the laburnum walk and the crumbling old orangery which is way down the list, sadly. The rest is just parkland—or it used to be. None of it's been managed for years and it's all just run wild.'

'Can we look?'

'Yes. Come on, I'll show you around, if you're interested. Daisy's always game for a walk.' He pushed back his chair and led her out of the front door into the sunshine, Daisy trotting at his heels, and they strolled along the weedy path at the top of the terrace, past the knot garden that desperately needed clipping back into shape, to a crooked, elderly door in a high brick wall at the end.

It yielded to his shoulder and creaked out of the way, and ducking under the arms of an old rambling rose, he led her through into the most wonderful garden she'd ever seen in her life…

# CHAPTER THREE

IT WAS a mess, of course—overgrown, with climbers hanging off the walls and the old gravelled paths swamped with weeds and grass, but under the chaos she could see it had once been beautiful.

Old shrub roses in the wide borders were smothered in buds, and she could see some already starting to open. There was a lilac on the point of bursting, and amongst the weeds, perennials were struggling towards the sun.

She closed her eyes and let her other senses take over. The low hum of bees, the growl of a tractor in the distance, a dog barking, the pure, sweet song of a blackbird. Somewhere fairly close, a cockerel crowed. Sam's? Probably. She'd heard one this morning at some ungodly hour.

Her eyes still closed, she breathed in deeply through her nose and caught the scent of new-mown grass and the heady sweetness of a spring-flowering viburnum. And it was warm—so much warmer than outside, the sheltering embrace of the walls making a micro-climate where tender plants would thrive.

All it needed was some loving care.

'It's lovely,' she sighed wistfully, looking around again and trying to take it all in. 'A real secret garden.'

'Exactly—it's a mess,' he said with a wry laugh, but she shook her head.

'It's full of treasures, Sam. Some of these roses are ancient, and they just need careful pruning and a bit of a feed, and they'll be wonderful again.'

'But it all takes time and I've been concentrating on the house. It seemed fairly important as the roof was falling in.'

'Oops.' She smiled and met his eyes, wondering yet again if their baby would inherit them. Beautiful, beautiful eyes... 'Emily said you were a bit mad buying it,' she said, bringing her mind back to order, and his mouth twitched.

'Did she?' He looked around, taking in the faded beauty of the house and garden—not nearly so bad if you half closed your eyes so it went into soft focus. 'She's probably right,' he admitted slowly, 'but I love it here. I bought it at auction. I was trawling the net, looking at property, feeling restless—it wasn't a good time in my life and I just wanted—well, whatever, I saw it, and it was being auctioned that day, so I got in the car and drove out here and had a quick walk through the ground floor and the outside of the house and bid for it.'

'And you got it?'

He knew his smile would be wry. 'There was a bit of a tussle.'

'I'm not surprised,' she said with a little chuckle. 'It's gorgeous. So—you didn't have a survey first?'

'No. No time. Literally. I had ten minutes to decide if I was going to bid or not, but they say you make up your mind about a house in the first eleven seconds or some such ridiculous thing. It didn't even take me that long. I'd decided before I set foot in the house, after I stuck my head in here on the way round. That was enough to convince me. And there was dry rot in the roof, and the bedrooms underneath were trashed because the weather had been coming in, and it was a mess. But that was fine. Nothing that couldn't be sorted by throwing money and a lot of effort at it, so that's what I've been doing. There's a cottage that was sort of habitable, and I lived in that and started getting the house sorted out, bit by bit, and then once the kitchen was useable and I had a bathroom and a couple of bedrooms and somewhere to sit in the evening by a fire, I moved in here and started work on the cottage.'

'On the *cottage*?' she said, puzzled that he hadn't finished off the house first. They were strolling along the paths between the beds, and she could see the structure of the garden, the little lavender hedges that had escaped and run wild…

'I needed guest accommodation, but it'll make a lovely holiday cottage eventually, so I've been fixing it up, but it's just about done and then I need to turn my attention back to the house. There's still loads that needs doing, but it'll take a while.'

She looked up at the house and blanched at the thought of the maintenance and repair bills—never mind a major renovation.

'The cost must be horrendous. Do you have a really good job or are you just naturally wealthy?'

He gave a hollow, slightly cynical laugh. 'No, I'm not naturally wealthy, but I've worked hard. I used to buy and sell companies. I kept a few and I've got a steady income, but to be honest I've lost interest in that way of life. It's not all it's cracked up to be and I can't be bothered to chase it any more.'

'So you threw everything you had at this place and ran away to the country?'

His smile didn't quite reach his eyes, for some reason.

'Pretty much. Not quite everything, but I've stepped back from the front line, as it were, and I'm taking time out and fixing the house. That's a task and a half, but I'm enjoying the challenge. I know every nook and cranny of the house now, and it's becoming part of me. It's damned hard work, but you know the saying, what doesn't kill you makes you stronger. And I'm only doing what I can. There's a specialist team waiting to come in once the planners are happy.'

Well, of course there was. It was a huge task, even her inexperienced eyes could see that, and there was no way one man could do it alone.

He paused at the gate. 'Want to meet the chickens?'

She laughed softly, and he felt his guts curl at the musical sound. Crazy. She was pregnant! How could he want her like this?

*Because it's your baby? Or just because she's beautiful?*

'Do they need meeting?' And then, when he stared at her blankly, she added, 'The chickens?'

He gave her a smile that was probably a little off kilter. 'You might be less resentful when they wake you up at stupid o'clock.'

'You could have a point.' She chuckled again, and yet again his guts curled up and whimpered.

'Come on, Daisy,' he said, slapping his leg and trying not to think about Emelia.

'So—why chickens?' she asked as they walked. 'Isn't it easier to buy eggs from the shops?'

Sam laughed. 'Much, especially since they hardly ever lay anything, but I inherited them with the house and in a moment of weakness I gave them names so I guess they're with me till the fox gets them or they fall off their perches,' he admitted ruefully, making her smile so that her nose crinkled in a scarily sexy way that just took his breath away.

She felt her smile waver as he frowned at her for some reason. Or at himself for his sentimentality? She wasn't sure.

'Come on, we'll go and introduce you,' he said, and abruptly led the way to the kitchen garden. It was separate from the house, the empty beds arranged in a grid pattern between the gravel paths.

'I want to have a go at growing vegetables again this year,' he told her. 'I know it sounds like a load of old romantic nonsense, but I love it. It's just a case of time, though—and I don't have enough,' he said honestly.

She watched the chickens happily scratching in the beds, and hoped the vegetables and eggs weren't a significant contribution to the household budget. The veg didn't stand a chance and it would take a heck of a lot of eggs to pay the builders.

She looked back at the house thoughtfully. 'It must have been amazing in its hey-day,' she said softly, and he nodded, his expression gentling as he looked up at it.

'Yes. And I want to bring it back to life. I've got so many plans for it, but there just aren't enough hours in the day and everything seems to take twice as long as you think, but one day I'll get there and it'll be a fantastic home again.' There was a tension in him, a kind of pent-up excitement in his eyes that reminded her of James. He'd been like this—full of wild plans and crazy schemes. They'd been going to do so much, had so many plans, all now turned to dust.

And as Sam finished speaking, she saw the light go out of his eyes before he turned away, and she wondered what had happened to send him into retreat. Because that was what he was doing—pulling up the drawbridge, going into some kind of bucolic trance.

*It wasn't a good time in my life.*

He walked on, and after a moment she followed him. Emily had hinted at something in his past, but she hadn't given away any secrets. Secrets there were, though, of that Emelia was sure, and she found herself reassessing her opinion of him.

He'd always seemed so confident, so assured, so grounded on their previous meetings. And maybe he was, but it was as if some thread in his life had snapped and left him changed from the man he'd been.

*I've lost interest in that way of life. It's not all it's cracked up to be.*

What had happened? He seemed—maybe not lonely, exactly, but there was a sense of isolation that didn't quite gel, as if he was building this wonderful family home and knew there would only ever be him in it.

It's nothing to do with you, she told herself firmly, and followed him as he left the kitchen garden and took her on a guided tour of the rest of the house.

It was beautiful, but there was much still left to do, and as he talked about it, telling her his plans, she felt a twinge of regret that she would never be part of them, never share his dream, and from the way he was talking, neither would anyone else. He never said 'we', only 'I' or 'me'. A loner, for whatever reason. But maybe their child would be the one to share it with him, would bring warmth and joy into his life and make him happy again.

And as for her…

He'd offered her his friendship. That was all. Grudgingly. No, not grudgingly, but reluctantly. His friendship and a safe place to stay until she'd sorted out her options. And building pipe dreams about some rosy future with him, even for a second, was completely and utterly ridiculous…

'I ought to make a few phone calls, work out what I'm going to do, where I'm going to go,' she said pensively.

They were back at the kitchen table, and Sam felt himself frown. One minute she'd been talking about finding work locally, the next she was talking about leaving. He frankly wasn't sure which was worse—staying, probably, and he was beginning to think that was a generally thoroughly lousy idea. But he'd offered, so he'd thought he'd just have to shut up and cope with it. But now—now she was talking about leaving, and he suddenly felt uneasy that she might settle miles away and he'd lose sight of the baby.

That was worse. Definitely. But only because of the baby. That was all he was worried about, he told himself firmly. Well, not quite all, if he was going to be brutally honest, but it was only the baby he'd allow himself to care about.

'Why don't you go down into the village and find the primary school and talk to them about the possibility of doing some supply teaching?' he said, hoping there would be something that would keep her and the baby close, because otherwise his life would get even more complicated. 'They might need someone for the odd day, and maybe you could earn enough to tide you over till the compensation comes through.'

'It's an idea,' she said slowly. 'Maybe I could find a little cottage or something to rent close by, just until after the baby's born. It would give us a chance to get to know each other, and if we're going to share this baby in any meaningful way—not that I know if we are, but *if* we are—then we ought to know each other, don't you think?'

'Yes,' he said, wondering if knowing her better would make it easier or just a damn sight harder. 'And we are.'

'We are?'

'Going to be sharing the baby in a meaningful way. I meant what I said. I don't walk away from commitment.'

'But you didn't want this, Sam. It was never part of the plan for you to have a child—not like this.'

He sighed softly. 'Neither of us wanted this, Emelia, but it's happening and we have to find a way to deal with it. And I think you living close by is a good idea, at least until after the baby's born. So—sure, go down to the primary school and have a chat to them, and maybe they'll have something for you, and then we'll start to think about where you should live.'

She nodded and got slowly to her feet. 'Do you know where it is?'

'Out of the gates, turn left and go down to the village. It's got road signs and things. You can't miss it.'

They didn't have anything.

The head was lovely and very welcoming, but they had no need for a supply teacher at the moment.

'I'll take your number, but I don't expect there will be anything,' she warned.

Defeated at the first hurdle, Emelia drove back to the house, realising as she did so just what a huge and sprawling place it was. Not the house. The house was quite neat and tidy, really, although only someone truly overindulged would describe it as small in any way, but the grounds and other buildings that went with it must be a constant drain on his resources, and not just financial.

And he was doing a lot of the work himself.

She admired him for that. He was clearly successful, and yet he'd turned his back on the high-flying world of big-city finance and was concentrating on a dream. She could see him now, driving the little lawn tractor, and she pulled over and waited for him as he changed direction and headed towards her.

'Hi. How did you get on?' he asked, cutting the engine and propping his arms on the steering wheel so he could see her through the car window.

'OK. She was very nice—but they haven't got anything at the moment.'

'Anything in the pipeline?'

She shook her head, wishing she could give him some other news, because he was right, they needed to be near each other to sort out their relationship. If you could call it that. She supposed it was.

'I tell you what, I'm nearly done. Why don't you go and put the kettle on and I'll be there in a minute or two. We can talk about it over a cup of tea. The back door's unlocked.'

She nodded, went back to the house and gave Daisy a hug, then put the kettle on and waited. True to his word— something she was beginning to realise was typical of Sam Hunter—he was there in a very few minutes, by which time she'd discovered she couldn't find anything in his kitchen.

'Tea or coffee?' he asked.

'Coffee, please, if there's a choice. I was going to make it but I couldn't find it, only decaf tea.'

'It's in the freezer,' he said, 'but it's decaf, too. That's all I have—can you cope with that?' he asked, and she laughed softly.

'Decaf is fine. I don't want the baby buzzing.'

'No, you don't. I had to give it up. I hardly ever have caffeine now—I put myself in hospital once, and never again. That was one of the reasons I quit the City.'

'Caffeine?' she asked, intrigued.

'The way I was using it, to keep me awake and counteract jetlag and overwork. I was drinking several jugs of strong coffee a day, sleeping about three hours a night, working all over the world—at one point the companies I owned were responsible for an international workforce of over a hundred thousand. I was ridiculously busy, and I realised while I was lying in hospital on a heart monitor that I was killing myself and I wasn't even sure why.'

'So you looked on the internet and found this house.'

He smiled wryly. 'Exactly,' he murmured. 'They'd discharged me once they realised I wasn't having a heart attack, and I was at home in my apartment chewing the walls for caffeine and letting my system recover, and I started to look for an alternative. This was it. And now I work as hard physically as do mentally, I get at least six hours' sleep a night and, except in extreme circumstances, I don't drink caffeine.'

But he'd had a double espresso yesterday.

Extreme circumstances? Oh, yes…

'Sam, why aren't you married?' she asked suddenly, her mouth moving without her permission, and he went utterly still, his hand poised on the kettle while she kicked herself.

'Should I be?'

'I don't know,' she said carefully. 'You've got a big house that's crying out for a family, you obviously don't hate children or you wouldn't have offered to help your brother have one, it's not that you can't have them, that's pretty obvious, and you're not exactly hideous—I just wondered why you weren't married yet, that's all. Or maybe you were. Maybe it didn't work. I just— You're my baby's father. Maybe I should know?' she suggested tentatively.

He didn't answer at first, just poured water into the

cafetière and reached for two mugs while she wished she'd kept her mouth shut, and then at last he spoke.

'I nearly was,' he said eventually. 'Very nearly. But—things didn't work out. She'd lied to me, told me she was having my baby.'

'And she wasn't pregnant?'

'Oh, she was pregnant all right, but it wasn't my child, she wasn't what I thought she was, and I lost it all—the wife, the child, the family thing—the whole lot of it all just lies.'

She felt her eyes prickle. 'That must have been awful,' she said softly, and he gave a hollow laugh.

'It wasn't much fun. So let's just say I'm a little more cautious now and don't take things on trust any more. It's better that way.'

'I'm sorry,' she murmured. 'I shouldn't have asked. This huge place—it just seems odd, you living in it on your own.'

'It's fine, I like it that way. Elbow room,' he said, and turned round, his eyes curiously blank. 'So—enough about me, what about you, Emelia?' he asked as he sat down, sliding a mug towards her and straddling a chair backwards as he shifted the subject firmly back to her. 'What are you going to do next?'

'I don't know,' she said quietly, trying to think about that instead of him being so cruelly deceived. No wonder he seemed remote sometimes. 'I suppose I'll have to look further away. It's very rural here, there aren't many schools. I might be better in a town.'

'There isn't a town for miles.'

'So I'll have to go miles. Maybe back to Cheshire—'

'No! You were going to live around here until after the baby was born—the first year or so. Emelia, we'd agreed.'

The first year? 'No, we hadn't, Sam, we'd just talked about it. And if there's no work, I'll have to go, or I won't be able to pay my rent.'

'Unless you have the cottage.'

She frowned. 'The cottage you're doing up?'

'Yes.'

'But it's your guest cottage.'

'I think this takes priority,' he said drily. 'And you've got to live somewhere, so why not there?'

She shook her head, suddenly feeling panicky. It was too cosy, too easy, too convenient. Too claustrophobic, after Julia and Brian. 'No. And anyway, maybe I want to be near my mother.'

'No! I can't see the baby if you're living on the other side of the country. Visiting you at weekends and so on won't work at all. It's not fair on any of us. I want to be part of every day, pick it up from school, babysit, share all the milestones. It means a lot to me. I want to be hands on with this, Emelia. I *have* to be.'

'Do you? What if I don't want that?' she said stubbornly, feeling the net closing. 'What if my lifestyle and independence are more important to me than your convenience? I'm sorry you lost your dreams of a family, Sam, but I wasn't part of that dream, and this is me we're talking about as well as you. You'll be taking over my life, and I'll be taking over yours.'

'Nonsense.'

'Sounds like it, if you have your way.'

He sighed sharply and rammed his hands through his hair. 'Look, I'm sorry, I'm not trying to take over your life, and I know you aren't trying to take over mine, but in a way the baby's taken them both over. So let's work with what we've got, and try and find a solution.'

'Such as? Because I'm fresh out of ideas, Sam, and I

have to live. And I don't do charity. Brian and Julia kept me, and I hated it. I'm not going there again because you have some misplaced sense of responsibility.'

'It's not misplaced, and it's not charity,' he said firmly. 'The cottage is sitting there, empty. It's just common sense.'

'Are you saying I don't have any?' she growled, and he could see she was getting angry now, working herself into a corner where there was no room for compromise.

So he stood up and put his mug in the sink. 'Time out,' he said flatly. 'You look tired. Go and have a rest while I make some phone calls, and we'll talk again later.'

'Phone calls to who?'

He felt his eyebrow twitch. 'You want to vet my phone calls?'

'No. I don't want you pulling strings for me.'

'I wasn't. I have a conference call booked in ten minutes, so I'll be in the study, and I don't want to be disturbed.'

She coloured slightly, and he could see the wind go out of her sails as if he'd punctured them. 'I'm sorry. You're right, we need a breather. I'll keep out of your way,' she muttered, and disappeared towards the little sitting room.

Damn. Now he felt guilty. He detoured into the study next door, pulled out a book he'd found in the house when he'd moved in, then took it to her as a peace offering. 'Here—the original planting plans for the rose garden and the knot garden,' he told her. 'I thought you might like to see them, since you seem to be interested.'

She met his eyes, studying him in silence for a moment, then she reached out her hand and took the book.

'Thank you,' she murmured politely, and then turning her back on him, she settled into the corner of the sofa and opened the book.

He was dismissed.

Sam retreated to his study and his conference call, leaving Emelia to browse through the old garden plans. He was sure from the look on her face when he'd glanced back at her that she'd be occupied for hours.

Which suited him just fine, because spending time with her was harder than he could possibly have imagined.

It wasn't just that he found her insanely, ridiculously attractive, he thought as the call ended and he realised he'd hardly registered a word. It was the insane, ridiculously attractive idea of spending much more time with her—maybe even pottering out there with her in the rose garden while their child puggled about making little mud pies, and in the corner, under the shade of a tree, would be a pram—

'No!'

He slammed on the brakes and closed his eyes, ramming his fingers into his eye sockets and trying to blot out the image. Crazy! He wasn't letting his imagination run away with him. He'd done that before, and it had turned to dust before his eyes. He wasn't doing it again. This was *his* house, *his* dream, and he wasn't sharing it with anyone. That way, he couldn't lose it.

He'd have her close, but not that close. He couldn't afford to let her that close. It would be too easy to fall into the honey trap.

A cold, wet nose nuzzled his wrist, and he lifted his hand and fondled Daisy's ears gently. 'It's all right, sweetheart, I didn't mean you,' he said softly. 'I'm just going slightly mad here.'

She gave a low wuff and ran to the French doors, her eyes pleading, and he gave up the unequal struggle. Emelia would be busy with the book, curled up in the sitting room where he'd left her, so he and the dog could go out in the rest of the garden and stretch their legs and play a game without fear of interruption.

He went through to the kitchen and grabbed her ball on a rope, and opened the back door. Maybe after an hour or so of brisk walking with the odd ball game chucked in for good measure, he'd be back in control of his mind—

Or not. Emelia was standing on the path by the knot garden, staring at the scruffy little hedges with a frown furrowing her brow, and he wanted to press his thumbs against it and wipe away the frown, to touch his lips to the tiny creases and soothe them. And then he'd tilt her head and kiss her—

'We're just going for a walk,' he said, as Daisy ran up to her and licked her hand.

She met his eyes warily. 'Can I come?'

He stared at her, wondering how to tell her, politely, that he was trying to get away from her before he went mad.

He couldn't.

'Sure,' he said, and her mouth tipped in a smile that sent his guts into free-fall.

He walked like a man possessed!

They'd hardly gone ten steps before she realised what she'd let herself in for, but she kept up without a murmur, and then he stopped her, finger to his lips, as the deer had come out of the woods, and they stood motionless and watched until something spooked them and they melted into the trees like shadows.

'They're beautiful,' she murmured, and he gave a wry grin.

'They're immensely destructive, and they make a heck of a racket at night, especially in the autumn with the rutting season. Everyone thinks the countryside's quiet, but between the deer, the foxes, the badgers and the owls it can all get a bit much. Then the birds start at four o'clock, not to mention the cockerel, and once I'm awake I tend not to go back to sleep, so I'll apologise in advance if I disturb you at five in the morning in the shower. I just get up when I wake up and get on with the day.'

She wondered what on earth he found to do at five in the morning, but maybe that was when he kept tabs on his business. Whatever, it sounded horribly early.

'Don't worry about me, I think it must be the hormones but I can sleep through anything at the moment,' she told him, and then in the second before he looked away, she caught a flash of something in his eyes.

Something she'd seen before. Something he didn't like and was trying to deny.

*Desire?*

No way. She was pregnant, for heaven's sake! Why on earth would he be interested in a pregnant woman?

He wouldn't, she told herself firmly, and followed him, concentrating on putting one foot in front of the other until they were back at the house, and then she retreated to the sitting room and curled up on a sofa with Daisy and the garden plans and waited for her legs to stop aching.

She was sitting there now, her hand idly stroking the dog, when Sam came in.

'Fancy a cup of tea?'

'I'll make it,' she said, starting to get up, but he just frowned.

'No, you won't. I must have nearly walked you off your feet—you look shattered. You should have said something.'

And he walked out again before she could answer, coming back moments later with a tray laden with tea and biscuits—more cookies, only chocolate this time. She was going to be like a house.

He sat down, picked up his tea and stared at it for a moment. 'I've been meaning to ask about your things,' he said abruptly, without any preamble. 'Do you want to get them sent here, or do you want to go back and collect them?'

She chewed her lip thoughtfully, and Sam saw a flicker of uncertainty on her face. 'I ought to do it myself—if you're sure it's all right? I could put them in store but there isn't much, really, other than my clothes. I just feel I ought to get them out sooner rather than later.'

'It's fine.' His mouth firmed. Damn them for putting her through this! 'Of course I'm sure. I wouldn't have offered if I wasn't and heaven knows the house is big enough, whatever you've got. I'll come with you. I've got an estate car, it'll be easier, and we can always take the trailer,' he added, before he could think better of it, and the relief on her face was almost comical.

'Sam, would you? We won't need the trailer, everything'll fit easily in a biggish car, and I'll tell them you're a friend. It might be a bit much if they realise you're the baby's father.'

It hadn't even occurred to him to worry about them, but of course Emelia was worrying. She was the sort of woman who'd worry about everyone, no matter how unkind they'd been to her. She'd be a great teacher, kindly but firmly sorting out the bullies. He could picture her with children clustered around her, snuggled up and hanging on her every word.

He could quite easily do that…

'That's fine,' he said hastily. 'Any time will do. Just arrange it.'

'OK. Have you told Emily and Andrew yet? About the baby?'

He shook his head. 'No. They're flying back tomorrow. I might have to do it after they're home. In fact it'd probably be better. Do you want another cookie?'

She gave him a good-natured, indulgent smile. 'No, but you go ahead. You've got a way to go before you look as fat as me.'

'You don't look fat, you look—'

He broke off. He'd been going to say gorgeous, but it was inappropriate and dangerous and would get him into all sorts of hot water. And he wasn't going there.

'Pregnant. Yes, I know. It takes a bit of getting used to...' She trailed off, her hand on the baby, and that tiny frown was back.

'What's wrong?' A slow smile dawned on her face, and she looked up and met his eyes, her tender expression bringing a lump to his throat.

'Nothing's wrong,' she said softly. 'It's starting to get really active, and it—it just stops me in my tracks sometimes.' She coloured slightly, and then held out a hand to him. 'Do you want to feel it?'

Did he? He'd been desperate to at first, but now he wasn't sure. There was a part of him that was longing to lay his hand over his child, but another part that was afraid of such intimate contact with Emelia, because he knew it would complicate things even further. But he got up, on legs that felt suddenly rubbery and uncooperative, and sat down beside her. She took his hand and pressed it to the smooth little curve, and he felt something move under his palm. Almost a fluttering, barely discernible and yet unmistakeable.

His baby. His baby, growing inside her, and there was something shockingly intimate about it, shockingly *right*.

He let his breath out on a huff of amazement and met her eyes, and something happened then, some incredible sense of connection, of belonging, and he leant in closer, drawing her wordlessly against him and pressing his lips to her hair.

The baby shifted again, and he chuckled softly, amazed at the sensation. 'That must be so weird,' he murmured a little gruffly.

'It is. It's really strange at first, but wonderful.'

'It's incredible. So strong for something so tiny.'

His fingers were splayed over her bump, his thumb almost grazing the underside of her breast, his fingers perilously close to forbidden territory. He shifted his hand again, and she nearly whimpered. It would be so easy to pretend this was real, to fall into the cosy little trap and let him take over, let him look after her as he was obviously wanting to do.

And maybe—she'd seen the way he looked at her from time to time. She'd thought it was because of the baby, but thinking about it, he'd looked at her like that before, when they'd met on other occasions at the clinic. So maybe she hadn't misread it at all. Maybe he did want her, for herself and not just for the child. Could she trust it? Could it really be so simple?

Probably not. He'd already told her he was more cautious now, and she was about to pull back when he lifted his hand and eased away, saving her the trouble.

'It seems to have gone back to sleep,' he said, his voice scratchy and strange, and he retreated before he did something really, really stupid like kiss her.

Because he'd been *this close*…

'It's amazing, isn't it?' she said softly, her eyes slightly unfocused. 'It feels so *real* now! It's sort of been a bit theoretical, you know? A bit—I don't know, almost as if it was happening to somebody else, but now—now it really feels like mine.'

Her eyes filled with tears, and he closed his own, her face too painful to watch.

She was thinking of James. He was sure she was, thinking of the man who should have been here with her, feeling the baby move, sharing the moment. Not a random stranger linked to her forever by an inadvertent error which had cost her more than anyone could ever know.

There was no amount of compensation that could make up for what she'd lost, and nothing he could do to make up for the fact that the baby would be his and not James'. But he could make her life easier, and he could care for her, and he would love his child—because it was his, too, as much as hers—to the end of his days.

But not Emelia. She was off limits, and she was staying that way. He'd given up dreaming.

'I'm going to do some paperwork,' he said brusquely, and getting to his feet, he walked out, leaving Daisy torn between her new friend who was sitting by a plateful of biscuits, or the man who'd fed her and walked her and played with her since she was tiny.

No contest.

She stayed with the biscuits, and he went alone.

Alone, the way he wanted it, the way he liked it.

It was safer that way.

# CHAPTER FOUR

THEY went the next morning to collect her things, in the big four-wheel-drive estate car he'd bought when he'd moved to the house. It had been used for any number of things, but this was one he'd never anticipated—collecting the possessions of a woman who was carrying his child.

He glanced across at her, and she gave him a fleeting smile. She looked tense, a little uneasy. Not hard to work out why.

It was about thirty-five miles to her in-laws', and as the miles rolled by, she became more tense and withdrawn. And he was concerned. He could see how much she was dreading it, but she'd insisted on doing it herself. He wondered now if she'd changed her mind.

'Are you OK with this?' he asked quietly, as he pulled up in the street close to the house she indicated.

'I have to be. I'll just say as little as possible, because if I open my mouth, I'm afraid I may not shut it.'

He hesitated for a second, then reached out and squeezed her hand. Just briefly, but she turned her head and met his eyes, and he felt as if she'd shown him the deepest, most intimate recesses of her soul. And it robbed his breath.

'Emelia—stay here,' he urged, shocked at the pain and anger and betrayal he'd seen there. 'Let me get the stuff.

You can go for a walk or something. Just tell me where it is, so I know what I'm looking for, and I'll deal with them.'

She looked away, so, so tempted by his offer, but knowing she had to do this herself. 'I never have to see them again,' she said. 'I can manage.'

Although she wasn't sure she could. And the first step was to let go of Sam's warm, strong hand which she seemed to be holding again, so he could turn into the drive.

She freed her fingers and unclipped her seat belt, then got out and walked towards the front door. They were expecting her, but it was still a few moments before Brian opened the door, and she was grateful for Sam's strong, silent presence behind her when he did.

'Julia's out,' he said, looking uncomfortable. 'She couldn't face seeing you.'

'And you could?' she said softly, knowing he'd been complicit, even if it hadn't been his idea, but then she cut herself off with a little shake of her head. 'Look, I don't want to talk about it. I've just come to collect my things, and then I'll go. This is Sam, by the way. He's a friend of a friend. He's got an estate car and he said he'd give me a hand.'

It was all true, but not the blatant, most glaring truth which she was reluctant to reveal. Brian swallowed it, anyway, and offered his help, but Sam refused.

'That's all right, I'm sure we can manage.'

'Don't let her lift anything.'

She caught the icy look Sam gave her father-in-law, saw him pale and step back. 'I'll leave you to it,' he muttered, and went off in the direction of the kitchen. Relieved, Emelia led Sam through to the annexe bedroom and looked around. Nothing had been touched—except the diary. It was missing. And his watch and pen, but not his wedding ring, she realised.

It was as if Julia had wanted to cut Emelia out of their lives by choosing to ignore their son's marriage, and in a moment of defiance, she picked up the ring and slipped it into her pocket. It was hers, after all. She'd bought it, she'd given it to him. And she had no intention of forgetting the man she'd loved with all her heart.

She opened the wardrobe, and Sam watched her thoughtfully as she studied the contents. He'd seen her hesitate, seen her pick up the ring and lift her chin defiantly as she'd put it in her pocket.

And he'd seen the pain in her eyes as she'd turned.

'OK, is this it?' he asked, breaking the endless silence, and she nodded.

'Yes. Everything at this end. There's a side door we can use to take it out.'

'OK. You go and sit in the car, I'll do this.'

'No, I'm OK,' she said, but she sat down, anyway, on the bed, her fingers absently pleating the cover as he carried the bags and boxes and hangers of clothes out to the car. The packing was a bit haphazard, to say the least, but it didn't take long to load. It probably would have fitted in her car, at a pinch, he thought. There was something incredibly sad about that small pile of her possessions, and he stood back and looked at it and wondered how after a lengthy relationship she had so little to show for it.

Shaking his head slowly, he went back into the house and found her sitting where he'd left her. 'All done.'

'Thank you,' she said, but she didn't move, just looked around, her eyes empty.

'I'll be in the car,' he said, giving her space to make her farewells, and she nodded.

'I should say goodbye.'

She locked the door after him, and walked slowly back

to the kitchen. Brian was sitting at the table waiting, his face drawn.

'Got everything?' he asked, and she nodded.

Then, despite her best intentions, found herself unable to ignore the elephant in the room.

'She had no right to do that, either to me or to him, and neither did you,' she said softly. 'You've put me through hell, Brian. It was bad enough losing James. To know you and Julia deceived us both like that—it's beyond immoral. You should be ashamed.'

He ducked his head. 'I am. We are. But we thought, a child—'

'You thought a child would replace your son, which shows how little you really knew him, because you could never replace him. He was unique. We're all unique. You should have respected that and concentrated on loving him instead of scheming to keep a bit of him alive for your own selfish ends.'

She turned, to find that Julia had come in and was standing behind her, ashen-faced and trembling. 'Emelia, I'm so sorry, I wasn't thinking properly,' she said brokenly. 'Please forgive me.'

Emelia hesitated. It would be so easy to walk away and leave it like this, but Julia was right, they'd been out of their minds with grief and under those circumstances judgement could become skewed.

'I'll try,' she promised, too hurt for anything but honesty. 'You may have more trouble forgiving yourself.'

Julia nodded, sniffing to hold back the tears. 'I left his ring for you,' she said then. 'I thought—you might have left it by mistake.'

She could feel it in her pocket, pressing into her thigh, and she slid her hand in and pulled it out and handed it to Julia.

'You keep it. I don't need it now,' she said gently, and squeezed her hand. It tightened convulsively for a moment, then let her go.

Sam was waiting for her in the car, and as she closed the front door behind her, he got out and came round and opened the car door for her, his hand touching her shoulder gently.

'All right?' he asked, and she felt a tear slip down her cheek.

'Yes, I'm fine,' she lied, trying to hold it together at least until they were off the drive. 'Can we go?'

'Sure.'

He slid behind the wheel, fired up the engine and pulled smoothly away without another word, as if he realised how hard she was finding it.

She blinked a few times, glanced back in the wing mirror at the receding house, and then fixed her eyes firmly ahead. That was what she should be concentrating on—the future. Not the past. The past was gone. Over.

'Want a coffee?'

'Not here. Let's get right away first.'

He nodded and concentrated on the road, and as they cleared the town boundaries, she turned her head towards him and gave him a fleeting and probably rather wobbly smile.

'Sorry. End of an era.'

His eyes were gentle and concerned, and he nodded. 'I saw a woman go in. She looked a little upset. Was that Julia?'

'Yes. I—um—I said more than I meant to, but maybe it was as well. We cleared the air. She asked me to forgive her.'

'And did you?'

She gave a tiny shrug. 'I said I'd try. I don't know. I have to let go, and to do that I have to forgive her, don't I? You can forgive without excusing.'

'I don't know,' he said quietly. 'Sometimes you just have to move on in whatever way you can.'

*It wasn't a good time in my life.*

Was that what he'd been doing when he'd bought the house? Moving on, in whatever way he could? Poor Sam—but he seemed confident he was doing the right thing now, so maybe she shouldn't feel sorry for him, even if he had lost his dream…

When they got back he carried her things up to her bedroom for her, refusing to let her lift any of them, and when she started to put them away, he stopped her.

'Leave that for now. I'm starving and we never did get coffee.'

'Oh. Well, you go ahead, I'm not really hungry.'

'Emelia—'

'Please, Sam,' she said, and then her voice cracked and the tears she'd been holding down for hours now spilt over and coursed down her face.

'Oh, sweetheart,' he murmured, and she felt him gather her up into his arms, cradling her face against his chest as he led her to the ottoman and sat down with his arms round her, rocking her gently as she cried.

It felt so good to be held by him, so safe. And today had been such an awful day…

'I'm sorry,' she whispered unevenly. 'It was just really hard. There were so many memories—'

'I'm sure there were. You don't need to apologise,' he murmured gruffly, smoothing her hair with his hand and wishing there was something he could do to ease the pain she was feeling. But there wasn't, because he was the cause of it, in a way, or at least the facilitator that had enabled the clinic to make the mistake. Without him, she wouldn't have become pregnant, and she and Julia and Brian would have parted company in a much more gentle way, without this tearing grief that was threatening to destroy them all.

All he could do was be there for her.

'I'm sorry. I'm OK now,' she said, easing away and swiping the tears from her cheeks. He pulled a tissue out of the box beside the bed and handed it to her, and watched with a frown as she mopped herself up. 'What an idiot,' she mumbled, feeling stupidly self-conscious now as he studied her.

'You're not an idiot,' he said gruffly, dropping down onto his haunches in front of her and taking her hands in his. 'You're a brave and wonderful woman, and I'm immensely proud of the way you conducted yourself today. You were gracious and dignified, and it can't have been easy.'

She felt her eyes fill again, and she gave a little laugh that was half-sob. 'Would you stop being nice to me for a minute?' she protested, and he chuckled and straightened up.

'Sure. I'm starving. Stop snivelling and let's go and find something to eat. There's a little café near here. They do the best carrot cake in the world.'

'That's just empty calories.'

'Rubbish. It has carrots,' he said.

'Oh, well, that's all right, then. What are we waiting for?' she said, and without even bothering to look at her blotchy, tear-stained face, she headed for the stairs.

'So, have you thought any more about the cottage?'

She put another little forkful of cream topping in her mouth and shook her head. 'No,' she said eventually. 'It just all seems too tidy. Too easy.'

'Maybe easy's OK just this once. Things don't have to be hard for the sake of it, you know.'

She gave a short laugh and met his eyes, and he could see the wariness in their red-rimmed depths. 'Oh, they do, Sam. Why would anything be easy when it could be difficult—even if it seems it at first?'

She was right. Sometimes when things appeared easy, they were anything but. Take Alice.

On second thought, don't bother. This was nothing like the situation he'd found himself in with Alice, and he knew that, although there were similarities. But they were superficial, and the reality was light years apart. Emelia was warm-hearted and kind and considerate, and Alice was a cold, calculating bitch and he'd had an extremely lucky escape.

'So—you were saying you needed to sign on with a doctor and sort out your antenatal care, so wouldn't it make sense just to settle here and then you can get all that under way? You've got enough going on without making it all harder for the sake of it.'

'But—Sam, I'll make friends at the antenatal class. I know people who've done that and they and their families have been friends for years. My mother's still friends with someone she met at her antenatal class, and I'm still in touch with her daughter. So I want to know where I'm going to be long term before I sign up for everything.'

'And it can't be here?'

She sighed. 'I need a good reason.'

And he wasn't good enough. Of course not. They didn't have a relationship—not like that. But it was gradually dawning on him that he wanted them to. That he wanted to give it a try, to see if this attraction he felt for her might be reciprocated, or if it was just him falling—yet again—for a mirage.

Probably.

But the baby would still be there.

'The baby's a good reason,' he said, latching on to fact and ignoring the variables. 'I meant what I said about being involved in its daily life. And it's a great part of the world. Just think about it. You could do worse than to live around here. Promise me you'll think about it.'

'On one condition,' she said, making him instantly suspicious. Alice had been a great one for conditions.

'What?' he asked warily.

'I want another coffee.'

He gave a huff of laughter, called the waitress over with a twitch of his eyebrow, and to her relief he let the subject of the cottage drop.

They finished their coffee and headed back to the house, and she went straight upstairs to sort her room out.

'Are you OK doing this, or do you need a hand?' Sam asked, making her pause on the stairs and look back down at him. He was being so kind, but she'd taken enough of his time today—and oddly, she felt she could cope now.

'I'll be fine,' she assured him gently. 'Thank you.'

'You're welcome. Shout if you need me.'

Hmm. She wouldn't think about that.

As soon as she'd finished she went out into the rose garden to enjoy the last of the afternoon sun and study the garden. Or at least she'd meant to, but she got a little distracted.

Sam found her there a little while later, resting on the bench, and came and sat down beside her.

'I wondered where you were. I've had a phone call from Emily and Andrew. They're coming over now.'

'Oh. They're back safely, I take it.'

'Yes. They got back earlier but they've only just opened

their post. They had a letter from the clinic, and they rang me about it.'

'Did you tell them about the baby?'

'Yes—was that all right?'

'Of course.' She stood up, a little stiff from sitting on the hard bench. 'So when will they be here?'

'About half an hour? Less, probably.'

'I'd better wash my hands and put on some clean jeans.'

He smiled and reached out a blunt, strong finger and stroked her cheek. 'You might need to get the mud off your face, too,' he teased gently, 'unless it's a new beauty treatment?'

'Of course,' she retorted. 'Very good for the complexion.'

'I must try it some time.' His lips quirked and he looked at the weeds on the ground, then took one of her hands in his and studied it with a little frown. 'You've been busy.'

'I've been clearing round the roses. It can't have been done for years.'

'It hasn't. Don't overdo it.'

She shot him a look and brushed her hands off on her jeans. 'Don't worry, I'm not being stupid.'

'Good. I've put the kettle on. They shouldn't be long now, it took me a while to find you.'

'I'm sorry, I should have told you what I was doing, but I just got carried away,' she confessed with a smile.

He searched her face, saw the strain of the morning had gone, replaced by a tranquil peace that suited her far better.

'Don't worry about it,' he said with a smile, and ushered her towards the French doors that led to his study. 'Come on, you need to spruce up a bit. You've got vegetation in your hair.'

'It's my woodland look. I thought I'd audition for

*A Midsummer Night's Dream*,' she told him mischievously, and he felt a tightening in his gut. God, she was gorgeous. Her skin was kissed by the sun, and her eyes were shining and she looked—

She looked out of bounds.

He closed the French door firmly. 'I'll see you in the kitchen when you're ready,' he said, and strode off, leaving her to tidy up while he took himself back into the kitchen and gave himself a serious talking to.

Andrew and Emily arrived just as she was coming down the stairs, and Emily hurried over and hugged her, her eyes filling with tears.

'Oh, Emelia, are you all right?'

'Yes, I'm fine,' she said, her heart fluttering a little, guilt and other mixed emotions tumbling through her as she hugged Emily back.

'Oh, gosh, look at you! I haven't seen you for ages, and it really shows now!' Her eyes welled over, and Emelia bit her lip and hugged her again.

'Don't. Please don't cry. I'm so sorry.' She could feel her own tears welling, and tried hard to blink them away, but she'd been dreading this conversation and Emily was sobbing and it was more than she could cope with.

'Don't be sorry. It wasn't your fault. I'm just so sorry it's not James' baby—'

'No. Don't be. I've got things to tell you about that, things I've only just found out myself, but I just feel so gutted for you.'

'For me?' Emily led her over to the stairs and they sat down on the bottom step together, still hanging on. 'Why would you feel gutted for me?'

'Because it could have worked this time! There's obviously nothing wrong with Sam, and this should have been your baby—'

'Don't. Don't beat yourself up, Emelia. It's happened, and OK, I didn't get pregnant this time, but you lost your chance forever—'

'They lied,' she said, cutting in, and told her what she'd discovered about James' consent.

'Oh, that's dreadful!' Emily said, her face going pale. 'Oh, thank God I didn't get pregnant. That would have been so awful. They would have wanted the baby and I couldn't have—' Her eyes filled again, and Emelia hugged her as she collapsed in another bout of tears.

'Shh, it's all right,' she murmured, hoping it was true, and as she lifted her head she met Sam's concerned eyes.

'Are you OK?' he mouthed, and she nodded and tried to smile. It was a brave effort, but he was glad to see it, and he took Andrew into the kitchen, leaving the two women alone together while he filled his brother in on the recent events.

'So what the hell are you going to do now?' Andrew asked. 'I mean—you're having a child, Sam, and I know how seriously you take that. We've talked about it enough times. Are you going to ask her to marry you?'

'Don't be stupid,' he snapped, and then rammed a hand through his hair and apologised. 'Sorry, I didn't mean to bite your head off. It's been a difficult couple of days. But—no, of course I'm not. We don't know each other, and anyway, she's still grieving for James.'

'But even so, she'll still need help and support, Sam.'

'Of course she will. And I'll give it to her.'

'And the child?'

'Of course the child!' he snapped, and Andrew arched a brow reprovingly.

He gave a heavy sigh and leant back against the range,

pushing the kettle back onto the hotplate to boil. 'Sorry. I'm sorry. Yes, of course I'll support the child. I want to be involved with its life. I need to be. So she can't go far away. I've offered her the cottage.'

'And will you be all right with that?'

'I'll have to be, won't I? It's happening, Andrew, we're having a baby. I can't duck out of it, and I don't want to. Anyway, what about you guys? Did you have a good holiday?'

Andrew's smile was sad and twisted something deep inside Sam. 'Actually, we did. We talked a lot—something we've not really been doing, and we came to the conclusion we'd give it a year or so before we try again—but that was before we knew about this. And you may feel differently now. In fact, we think you have been, for a while.'

His brother's words shocked him slightly, but as he opened his mouth to deny it, he realised there was an element of truth in what he'd said. He had been having reservations, and he certainly didn't know how he'd feel now about being a donor for them. About giving them a child who would be half-brother or -sister to this child Emelia was carrying. His own child. A child who'd call him Daddy.

Hell. He swallowed hard. Did that change anything? He wasn't sure, but he realised now that he needed to think it through again, and he was deeply grateful to his brother for making that so easy for him, for opening the way to him to back down if he felt he needed to.

'Can I think about it?' he asked slowly.

Andrew sighed and laid a hand on his shoulder. 'Of course you can. It was only ever your choice, Sam. We don't want you to feel under pressure. And to be fair, we aren't sure about trying again. We're considering adoption.'

He nodded, glad they were giving him time, because

that aspect hadn't even occurred to him. And he realised it should have, because this could signal the end of the line for Emily and Andrew's dreams.

'I'm sorry. I've been so busy coming to terms with what's happened I didn't see the bigger picture.'

'Hey, it's OK, bro, it's a lot to take in. You worry about Emelia and the baby, let me worry about us.' He propped himself against the wall and met Sam's eyes again. 'So how's Emelia taken it?'

'OK, I think, but we're taking it pretty much hour by hour at the moment. She's trying to decide what she wants to do when the compensation comes through, and we're still…' He hesitated, 'arguing' on the tip of his tongue, gave Emelia a wry smile as she walked into the kitchen with Emily and went on, '*discussing* where she's going to live.'

Weren't they just, Emelia thought.

'She can come to us,' Emily said, picking up a biscuit off the plate on the table. 'Can't she, Andrew?'

'Yes, of course she can, if she wants to,' he said, but Emelia could see reluctance in his eyes, and she thought of the upheaval a house guest could cause under normal circumstances, never mind a house guest who was having a baby that by rights should have been theirs!

'I don't—sweet of you though it is. It wouldn't be fair on any of us.'

'I've offered her the cottage,' Sam said, and Emily jumped on it, her eyes lighting up.

'Oh, Sam, what a marvellous idea!' she said, going over to him and hugging him. 'I'd forgotten all about it, but you'd be close to the baby, and you'll be able to see it all the time! It's the most perfect solution. Oh, Emelia, you'll love living there! It's so pretty—is it ready yet?'

She shook her head, still resisting. 'I have no idea. And besides, I'm not sure if I want to be that close.'

'Whyever not? And anyway, where else would you go—unless you *do* come and live with us? Would you rather do that? Because you can. You don't have to be noble.'

'No, Emily, I'm not being noble,' she said gently. 'You're only being kind. You don't want me—truly.'

Emily opened her mouth to deny it, then smiled a little sadly. 'It might be hard.'

'Of course it would. Don't be silly, I'll be fine. I'll find somewhere.'

'But—the cottage—'

'Leave it, Em,' Andrew said softly, and she floundered to a halt and nodded.

'So—are you letting that kettle boil dry, or are you going to make some tea?' Emelia said with a wry smile, and Sam returned the smile and shrugged away from the front of the range and made the tea as instructed, wondering how she could behave with such grace and dignity in the face of all this mayhem.

'So—about the cottage.'

Emelia put the last of the biscuits back into the tin and snapped the lid back on before she answered him.

'What about it?'

'I thought I could take you to look at it.'

She bit her lip and hesitated. 'I'm not sure. I can't afford to pay you rent, Sam, and you were going to use it.'

'Only so it's occupied, and to be honest I'd much rather have you. At least I know you're housetrained. And you'll be better off there than anywhere else because it's properly maintained, if anything goes wrong it'll be fixed instantly and—well, you'll be close by. I'll be able to help you with things.'

'Things?'

He shrugged. 'Walking up and down in the night with a colicky baby?'

'Planning ahead?' she said drily. 'It might not have colic.'

'Hopefully not. I like my sleep and there's enough going on to compromise it, but the offer's there, and it'll remain on the table whatever happens.'

'So—where is it?' she asked, feeling herself weaken. 'The cottage?'

'On the other side of the rose garden. It used to be the shooting lodge. Come on, I'll show you, it's still just about light enough. Emily's right, it's really pretty.'

And it was very close, she realised as they walked round the corner of the rose garden and past a small copse of birch and hazel. Single storey, it was built of red brick, with roses tumbling over the porch and glorious views across the parkland from the pretty arch-topped windows, and as he opened the front door she could imagine being there with the door open, letting the light and air flood in and fill the house.

She followed him in and looked around at what might be about to become her new home.

It was simply furnished, with comfortable sofas, a wood-burning stove, a well-fitted modern kitchen and bathroom and two bedrooms. Just enough for her on her own with the baby, she realised, and to do anything other than take it would be foolish.

'We need to agree the rent,' she said, and he sighed patiently.

'Emelia, there is no rent. This is my baby, too, and I have as much of a duty towards it as you do. I'm in this for life now, like it or not, and there's no need for you to be grateful, it's just the way it is. You're having my child, I'm supporting you. That's all.'

'And you'd do this for any woman? If the clinic had mixed this up in any other way, if it was someone you'd never met, a total stranger instead of someone only a little bit strange—would you offer her your cottage?'

He opened his mouth to say yes, and shut it again. 'I don't know. But it isn't a total stranger, it's you, and as you said before, you're not that strange.' He smiled fleetingly, and she shook her head and smiled back, feeling a little overwhelmed still by the speed of all this. Just forty-eight hours ago she'd been packing up her things and breaking the news to Brian and Julia.

'Sam—I don't know what to say.'

'Try yes.'

'Really?'

'Really. It's just standing here, Emelia. A few tweaks and it's done. You can move in in a couple of days. Think about it.' He handed her the key. 'Here, you can lock it up when you leave. Have a good look around, see how you feel about it. I'll be in my study.'

And patting his leg for Daisy, he left her there, standing in the middle of the sitting room, with the endless views over rolling countryside in front of her, and the key in her hand.

The key to her new life?

Maybe. She went around the cottage again, checking out the storage, the furniture, the bathroom and kitchen; she sat on the sofas and realised one was a sofa bed for guests, and then she went out of the back door into the garden.

It was overgrown, as she might have expected, but given time and a little effort it could be lovely. It wasn't formal like the ones at the house, but a proper cottage garden, and she could see lupins and hollyhocks and foxgloves all coming up, little cushions of campanula between the paving stones that by June would be a blaze of brilliant blue—it would be gorgeous.

An absolute haven for the soul, she realised, and exactly what she needed. Even if it was only for a while, she'd be a fool to turn it down.

Smiling, and with the weight of worry slipping off her shoulders, she walked back to the house, her tread lighter, her spirits lifting. Maybe, after all, it was going to be all right…

# CHAPTER FIVE

'WELL?'

'I'll take it—but there are rules,' she said firmly, perching on the edge of his desk just inches away from him, and he sat back in his chair to give himself space, twiddling his pen between his fingers and searching her face thoughtfully.

'Such as?'

'I pay rent. We keep a tally, and when I get the compensation, I'll pay you back. I'll need living expenses, as well, because I've got nothing for food or electricity or gas—'

'No gas. It's heated with electricity or the woodburner,' he told her.

'OK, fuel, then. I've got nothing for food or fuel, no way of taxing my car, which I'll have to do in the next few weeks, and I can't afford to buy any baby equipment—'

'I'll buy the baby equipment.'

'No! Sam, these are the rules!'

'Yes. And you don't get to make them all. You want to be self-sufficient, that's fine. I admire your independence and I'd feel the same way. But the baby's mine as well as yours, and if it needs equipment, I'll buy it equipment. And I'll provide you with a car—'

'I have a car.'

'So sell it and bank the cash. I've got a safe, sensible car here doing nothing, and I'll pay the running costs.'

'What car?' she asked, ready to dismiss it. He could see it in her eyes.

'The Volvo,' he said, and her eyes widened.

'That great big four-wheel-drive thing? You must be crazy. It's huge!'

'No, it's just safe, all the baby equipment will fit easily in it, and it's doing nothing most of the time so you might as well use it.'

So what would he drive? His BMW, of course, she realised. He drove a BMW with a folding hard-top—she knew that because she'd seen him putting the top up in the café car park on the first day of this fiasco. And it looked pretty darned new.

But that wasn't the point.

'I don't want it,' she said flatly. 'I've never driven a car that size, and I don't intend to start now when I'm pregnant.'

'But it's easy!' he said. 'Really, Emelia, it's just a car! Do we have to fight about everything?'

'Apparently! I can tell you haven't got a wife. You remind me so much of James when we first got married.'

He tilted his head slightly. 'That didn't sound like a compliment,' he said warily, and she snorted.

'It wasn't,' she retorted. 'Just for the record, I don't like being told what to do. I don't like being told how to do things. I don't like being told I shouldn't do things. I don't like being told what I like.'

'Ouch,' he said slowly, wincing. 'That's a little harsh. I'm only trying to help, but you're not making it easy.'

'Because it *isn't* easy!' she wailed in exasperation. 'None of this is easy! I feel as if a bomb's gone off in my life, and it's blown away a whole lot of things that were hemming me in and I thought I was finally free, but now—now I look around and there's another fence, a more attractive fence, admittedly, but it's still a fence, still containing me, ruling my actions, my movements— Sam, what if I don't want to live round here just so you can see your child? This isn't where I come from. It's not where my friends are!'

'So where are they, Emelia?' he asked softly. 'Why didn't you go to them after you walked out? Why did you come to me?'

She couldn't answer for a moment, face to face with a truth she didn't want to acknowledge.

'Tell me,' he ordered softly.

She felt her shoulders slump. 'Because you were the only person who would really understand,' she admitted slowly. 'Or I thought you would, but sometimes I don't think you do.'

His smile was wry and a little bitter. 'Oh, I do. I understand more than you know. But think about it logically. This is where I live, but it's also a great place to bring up children. Look at the grounds—it's like an adventure playground! Trees to climb, paths to cycle on, a little stream to splash in—and then there are all the places in the house to hide. It's amazing. I would have loved to be a child here. And I own it, and there's room here for you—more than enough. So if not here, then where else? We've got this fabulous resource. Why on earth not use it?'

'No. *You've* got this fabulous resource,' she reminded him. 'I, as you very well know, have nothing at all. So I have very little choice, and I know that, but I need to be able to manage that choice if I'm not going to end up feeling every bit as trapped as I did by Brian and Julia! They suffocated me, Sam, and I won't let it happen again. It's *my life*! OK, our lives are going to be linked by this child, but I still demand the right to have a life of my own, to be more than a mother. And if I want a relationship, I don't want you breathing down my neck and vetting the man of the moment.'

Man of the moment? *Man of the moment?* He felt sick suddenly, and he shut his mouth with a snap and turned his head away, staring out of the window and seeing her in the arms of another man.

*You're mad*, he told himself. *Utterly mad. She's not yours to be jealous over! And there is no man—*

'Is there a man of the moment at the moment?' he found himself asking, and then could have kicked himself for revealing interest in her love life.

'It's none of your business, but of course there isn't. How would there be? Look at me, Sam! I'm pregnant, and getting more pregnant by the minute! Who the hell would want me?'

He would—since she'd asked. And since she'd asked, he looked at her. He looked and he wanted, but there was no way he was sharing that. Instead he made a joke of it.

'I didn't think you could get *more* pregnant. I thought either you were or you weren't.'

She laughed, a little reluctantly, he thought, and then sighed and scraped her hair back off her face and shook it out behind her. He closed his eyes and bit back the groan. When he opened them again she was looking at him a little oddly.

'So—where do we go from here?'

'How about into the kitchen to find something to eat?' he suggested hastily, and wondered how on earth he was going to survive the next twenty years with this temperamental, fiery, gutsy and incredibly lovely woman hovering just out of reach…

'How hungry are you?'

'Starving,' she said honestly, because it seemed a long

time since they'd had the carrot cake and she'd somehow missed out on the biscuits when Emily and Andrew were there, but he was frowning into the fridge as if he didn't like what he saw, and then he shut it and turned to her.

'Look, it's eight o'clock, I'm famished and I can't be bothered to cook. D'you fancy going out? We could go to the pub in the village. The food's OK, I've eaten there a few times, and you can always have something light. Or there's a really nice little restaurant, but we're talking about driving a few miles for that. Up to you.'

She hesitated. The pub sounded more casual, less like a date, really, but he'd be known there, and everyone would start talking if he rocked up with a pregnant woman—

What on earth was she thinking about? If she was going to be living here, and he really meant what he said about being involved with the baby, then everyone was going to know soon anyway, surely?

'Are you ready to go public?' she asked, and she saw the realisation of what it meant flicker in his eyes.

He gave a reluctant grin. 'We're going to have to do it some time,' he said. 'We might as well get it over with.'

'It's a pity Andrew and Emily aren't still here so we're more of a group.'

He didn't think so. In fact he was glad they weren't, glad he was finally going to have time to talk to her one to one, to get to know her, the mother of his child. The woman who didn't like to be told what to do, etcetera.

'The restaurant's nicer,' he said, trying to tempt her. 'The food's amazing. It's got a Michelin star but it's not ridiculously experimental. And the puddings are fantastic,' he added, going for her Achilles' heel, and she crumbled.

'How dressy is it? Because I'm a bit short of decent things that still fit.'

'Not dressy at all, you'll be fine as you are. It's all about the food.' He smiled at her. 'I should go and grab a cardigan, though, it might get cold later. I'll wait for you down here.'

She nodded and went up to her room, opening the wardrobe and searching through the clothes. Perversely, even though it wasn't dressy, she wanted to change into something nice, but there was very little that still fitted her and although Brian and Julia had been more than generous with the baby things, they'd only given her a small allowance for herself.

So, with her options pretty limited, she pulled out a fine silk and linen mix cardi with a waterfall front that framed her bump nicely, and just because she had pride, she put on a little make-up—not much, just enough to boost her confidence a little and cover the tinge of red still around her eyes that gave away the emotional afternoon—then she added a set of chunky beads to dress it up a bit and checked in the mirror again.

Stupid. It was only for her, she wasn't trying to impress him—and if she told herself enough times, maybe she'd start to believe it. She shut her eyes and sighed sharply at the nonsense, and went downstairs to Sam.

He was just coming out of the kitchen, still in the crisp shirt, well-cut jeans and casual shoes he'd had on earlier, but he'd knotted a soft-as-thistledown cashmere sweater the colour of his eyes over his shoulders, and one look at him and she knew she'd been lying to herself.

He glanced up at her and hesitated for a second, then smiled, holding out his arm to usher her through the door, and it felt suddenly, ludicrously, as if this was all real, as if he was taking her on a proper date, and she was his—what? His wife? His partner? Girlfriend?

Or just the accidental incubator of his child.

They were stuck with each other, she reminded herself

sharply, and if it wasn't for the baby, there was no way he'd be taking her anywhere, so allowing herself to think about him like that would just add another complication to a situation that was already complicated enough.

And she needed to keep reminding herself of that…

He was right, the menu was amazing, and she stared at it in despair. 'There are too many lovely things!' she wailed, and he chuckled.

'We can come again,' he told her, and she felt her heart hitch a little.

Really? That sounded like another date.

'Will you think I'm throwing my weight around if I make a suggestion?'

She blinked, and then the day caught up with her and she started to laugh. 'You? Throwing your weight around? Surely not?'

He smiled. 'Try the fillet steak in pepper sauce. It's absolutely amazing. Or if that's too heavy, the sea bream is fabulous.'

'Whatever. Surprise me.'

He ordered both. 'You can try them and have the one you fancy,' he told her. 'Just remember to save room for the pudding.'

She grinned. 'Oh, believe me, I will.'

The waiter came and took their order, and Sam propped his elbows on the table and studied her thoughtfully.

'Tell me about yourself.'

Emelia blinked at him, as if he'd said something really weird. 'Me?'

'Well—I wasn't talking to the waiter,' he murmured.

She coloured softly. 'Oh. Well—what do you want to know?'

'I don't know. What is there to know?'

She gave a little thoughtful sigh. 'Not a lot. I'm twenty-seven, nearly twenty-eight, I was born and brought up in Oxford until I was nine, then my father moved to Edinburgh University and we were about to relocate up there when he died, so my mother and I went to Lancashire, where her family are from, and we lived just north of Manchester for six years, then she met Gordon and we moved to Cheshire. I stayed with them until I went to university in Bristol, and I met James in my second year. He was reading maths, I was reading English, and I stayed on and did a fourth-year post-grad teaching certificate and he did a Master's. We got married at the end of that year, when we were twenty-two, and then two years later we discovered he'd got testicular cancer. And two years after that, he was dead.'

There didn't seem to be anything he could say that wouldn't be trite or patronising, so he didn't say anything. And after a moment she lifted her head and smiled gently at him.

'So, your turn.'

'What do you want to know?'

'Whatever you want to tell me.'

Nothing. Nothing at all that would open him up to her and make him any more vulnerable than he already was, but he found himself doing it anyway.

'I'm thirty-three, I was born in Esher, in Surrey, and by the time I was twenty-one I'd started my first company and bought another one. I was still at uni—I did an MBA, kept trading on the side and it snowballed from there. Then—'

He broke off.

'Then?' she prompted, her voice soft, and he sighed. The next bit wasn't so nice, and he really didn't want to go there, so he gave her a severely—severely!—edited version of the truth.

'Someone cheated me,' he said bluntly. 'It left a bad taste in my mouth, and I threw myself into work, and then I ended up in hospital and realised I wasn't enjoying it any more so I walked away from it. That was when I saw the house. It's taken the last two and a half years to reach this point in the restoration, but once the local planning people and English Heritage make up their minds about what I can and can't do with the inside, I'll be able to finish it off.'

He ground to a halt and shrugged. 'So, that's me.'

'Was it her?'

'Pardon?'

'The person who cheated you. Was it the woman you were going to marry? The one who wasn't having your child?'

Hell. He thought he'd been vague just now, but Emelia was just too good at joining up the dots. He stuck to facts. 'Yes. But there were two of them—a couple. Professionals. I'm older and wiser now.'

'And a lot more cynical, I would imagine.'

He just smiled, a bitter smile, probably, because he still felt bitter and always would. There were some things that you couldn't forgive, some lies that were too cruel. You just had to move on. And he had. He was.

Sort of.

'Sea bream?'

They sat back, the plates were put in front of them and they dropped the subject and turned their attention to the food.

She couldn't decide, so they swapped halfway, and then he had to endure watching her struggling with the dessert menu.

'The melting middle chocolate pud is amazing,' he told her helpfully. 'So's the apple crumble. Or they do a selection to share that sounds interesting.'

She nibbled her lip thoughtfully and he felt his guts clench again.

'Let's try that,' she suggested.

Oh, Lord. It suddenly seemed ludicrously intimate and he wanted to kick himself for suggesting it. He did it, though, holding out a spoonful of rhubarb crumble to her, stifling a groan as she closed her lips around his spoon and sighed sensuously before dipping her spoon into the tiny chocolate pudding and reaching over to feed it to him. They squabbled over the last bit of rice pudding, and she ended up victorious, then held it out to him, her eyes teasing.

It was a wonder he didn't choke on it.

Emelia felt crazily full, but it had been worth every bite.

Especially the bites from Sam's spoon. And his eyes—

She wouldn't think about his eyes, she told herself, heading upstairs. It was too dangerous. She was falling for him, she realised, and it was altogether too easy.

He was charming, funny, sexy—a lethal cocktail of masculinity mixed with a surprising sensitivity.

Very dangerous. Dangerous because she couldn't trust it. He was trying to convince her to stay so he'd be near the baby, sweet-talking her into thinking it would be a good idea. And it probably would, but she mustn't let herself be lured by his charm. She had to make the right decisions for herself and the baby based on common sense. The trouble was, she didn't seem to have any left, she thought in despair. Not where Sam Hunter was concerned.

He was in the study—he had work to do, he'd said, and so she went to bed and fell asleep thinking about his eyes...

Two days later, she moved into the cottage.

Sam brought all her things down again, put them in the

car and drove them round, and she unpacked them and stood back and thought of all the things she'd left behind, all the things she hadn't thought to bring—like vases.

She'd had some lovely vases, tall slender ones for lilies, and a lovely round tulip bowl that had been a wedding present—but she hadn't thought of it, and now she looked around and it seemed barren. Cold and empty and soulless.

'It'll soon be home,' he said, as if he'd read her mind—or more probably her face. James had always told her she'd be a lousy poker player.

She gave a soft sigh. It seemed years since she'd had a home she could really call her own. Not since she and James had bought their little house in Bristol and furnished it on a shoestring. They'd stretched themselves to the limit, but it had been home, and they'd been happy there.

It seemed so very, very long ago. She could scarcely remember it.

'Hey, it'll be all right,' Sam said, rubbing her shoulder gently, and she gave a sharp sigh and nodded, and he dropped his hand, as if he'd only touched her because he'd felt he had to. And it would have been so nice to lean on him, to put her arms round him and rest her head on that broad shoulder.

'Look, I know it's small, and it's probably not what you were used to with James, but it's got lovely views, the garden could be really pretty and it's very private, and there's an outhouse that could possibly be turned into another bedroom if you felt it was necessary. Just—see how it goes, OK? If there's anything you want decorated differently or changed, just say. I want you to think of it as your home.'

The short, disbelieving huff of laughter was out before

she could stop it, and he frowned and pressed his lips together.

'I'm sorry. It's just that I've heard those words before, and when the chips are down, they mean nothing,' she told him frankly. 'So—thank you for the offer, but I'll just settle in and we'll see. I may want to move to something else, maybe something in the village.'

Something not quite so disturbingly close. He was standing just a foot or so away, and she could smell the scent of his aftershave, clean and sharp and tangy, and beneath it the subtle undertones of warm, spicy musk from his body. She could so easily have taken that one small step and laid her head against his chest, her cheek against the fine, smooth cotton of his shirt, her ear tuned to the beating of his heart.

She could almost feel the warmth, the solidity, the coiled masculine power of his body—

'Do whatever you want. It's not a prison, Emelia. There is no fence, imagined or otherwise. If it's what you want, you're free to go, but I'll have to follow, in some degree. I can't ignore this child, and I won't. I take my responsibilities seriously.'

She nodded.

'I know. I'm sorry. You probably think I'm being unreasonable and ungrateful—'

'I don't need your gratitude,' he said softly. 'I just need you to feel safe and secure and at home. If that isn't here, then we'll find somewhere that is.'

He tossed the key in his hand for a moment, then put it down on the windowsill. 'I'll leave you to it. The phone's connected—if you need anything, just call me.'

'Sam?'

He stopped in the doorway and turned to her, his eyes unreadable with the light behind him. 'Yes?'

'Thank you.'

The smile was fleeting and she couldn't tell if it reached his eyes, but he gave a brief nod and left, closing the door softly. Seconds later she heard the car start and he drove away, and she stared at the door for a moment before turning back to look at the house.

And listen.

It was so quiet! Utterly silent, really. She walked through it, her footfalls muffled on the new carpets, and it seemed so strange. She trailed her fingers over the woodwork, up the door frame, along the edge of the wooden worktop. Her home?

A shiver ran over her, and she opened the back door and went out into the garden, just as the sun came out again.

And she stood there, basking in the warmth of the sun's rays, drinking in the peace of the garden, and gradually her heart settled to a steady, even rhythm and she felt her body relax.

The baby stirred, stretching, and she felt a little foot sweep across the wall of her abdomen. At least she thought it was a foot. Maybe it was just her imagination, but it seemed reasonable. Whatever, it settled again, clearly content, and with a lingering smile on her face, she turned and went back inside her home.

The kitchen, she discovered to her relief, was fully equipped. It even had the luxury of a dishwasher, only a small one, but it was enough. She'd appreciate it, she thought, when her bump got so big she couldn't reach the sink.

She opened the fridge to see if it was on, and blinked.

Food? Real food. Milk and bread and eggs, and spreadable butter and bags of salad and fresh salmon and mini chicken breasts and baby new potatoes, and in the freezer section there were peas and beans and a whole host of other things, including a few ready meals. Simple, wholesome ones, not salt-laden greasy curries. Healthy, nutritious food for her and the baby. And there was even a box of chocolates in the fridge.

Her eyes filled, and she blinked the tears away and looked around again. There was an envelope propped up against the kettle—a card from Sam with a picture of a cottage on the front, and inside, 'Wishing you happiness in your new home.' Beneath it, he'd written, 'Good luck settling in. Shout if you need anything at all. Sam X'

She stared at the X. And then the anything at all.

A hug would be nice, she thought, and fought down the stupid urge to cry.

When she'd looked around it had just seemed like a haven. Now that it had actually happened, it just seemed somehow wrong. So lonely on her own. So lonely without Sam—

No! She wasn't going there, and she wasn't going to wallow in self-pity. She was going to get on with it, to settle in, to make it how she wanted it, and anyway there wasn't time to be lonely, because she had to earn her keep.

And she'd had an idea about that, an idea she still had to run past Sam, but she was hoping he'd go for it. It would be hard, but it would be worth it.

And if she still had time to feel lonely after that, she clearly hadn't done enough!

He stood at the window at the end of the landing and stared at the cottage through the trees.

Was she all right? He hadn't heard a word, and he'd been standing by all day for her to call to say she couldn't find the immersion heater switch or a light bulb had blown or the dishwasher wasn't working, but there had been nothing.

He'd been deafened by the silence, and the urge to go over there and check up on her was overwhelming.

Oh, for heaven's sake, he was going insane! He'd go over there now and talk to her, he decided, heading down the stairs and out of the front door. She might have slipped and fallen, or had a haemorrhage or any one of a million things—

He stopped on the path and frowned. The gate of the rose garden was open. Just a touch, but enough to let a rabbit in, and he went to close it and heard the unmistakeable sound of digging.

Digging, for heaven's sake! There was only one person who could be doing it, and she had no business doing anything so strenuous in her condition. He pushed the door open and went in, and saw her standing there with one hand on a garden fork, her cheeks rosy with effort, her eyes bright, a huge weed dangling from the other hand.

And she was grinning victoriously.

'What on earth are you doing?' he asked softly, and Emelia felt her colour deepen as she dropped the weed on the pile like a hot potato.

'I'm sorry. I couldn't resist it. I brought the book out here the other day, and most of the plants are still here! It's amazing. Some of them must be over a hundred years old. I think this one's Celestial; it's the most exquisite old shrub rose. And there are several musk and gallica roses, and I think that one's Old Blush China...'

She trailed to a halt. He was cross. She could see he was cross, even though his lips were pressed firmly together and he wasn't saying anything. He walked over to her and took the fork out of her hand, hooking it out of the ground easily and leaning on it as he studied her.

'You're really enjoying this, aren't you?' he said thoughtfully, trying to banish the picture of the puggling, muddy child and the pram under the tree that was still haunting him days later, and she nodded.

'Yes, I am, but it's going to take a while, and I thought—I don't want to cook for you. That's never been my strong point, and supply teaching doesn't seem to be a likely option, but I can garden,' she went on, her eyes alight as she made her pitch. 'And goodness knows this place needs it. I could earn my keep, Sam. Pay my rent, my running costs, so I don't feel I owe you anything. And you'd get your garden.'

He hesitated, horribly tempted because it was a mess and all his spare time at the moment was channelled into the house. In the face of that, the garden was way down the list of his priorities, and in any case he had no idea where to start with restoring it. But apparently Emelia did, and she was looking at him expectantly, her eyes bright, enthusiasm shining from her eyes, and he almost buckled. Almost.

He sighed. She was tiny, a good head shorter than him and fine-boned and—dammit, thoroughly pregnant, even if it wasn't a *condition*!

'It would be too hard for you,' he said flatly, but she shook her head.

'No. It would be a labour of love. I could do it, Sam—I could rescue it,' she told him earnestly, feeling the surge of enthusiasm, the prickle of excitement at the prospect. 'I'd love to do it. At least let me try. Please?'

'What if I get someone to help you?' he offered, before he knew what he was going to say. 'There's a lad in the village—he cleared the kitchen garden for me. Want me to give him a ring? It's either that or I get in someone much more expensive, and they'll have their own ideas, of course,' he added, taunting her deliberately when she still hesitated.

She chewed her lip, and he felt a twinge of guilt, but he wasn't going to let her hurt herself, and at the same time he couldn't bring himself to deny her the pleasure it was obviously bringing her. Never mind denying himself the pleasure of watching her...

'It might be helpful,' she conceded. 'Just to do the heavy stuff—'

'I'll call him,' he said, grabbing the advantage while he had it, and changed the subject. 'How's the cottage?'

She smiled again, her eyes—such expressive, beautiful eyes, he thought distractedly—softening. 'Lovely, thank you. And thank you for the food. You even thought of chocolates.'

'I'm learning.'

Her mouth twitched, and he felt his joining in. He shook his head and let himself smile. 'Fancy a cup of tea?'

'Actually, that would be lovely.'

'I'll go and make it. Why don't you pack up for today and come and find me in the kitchen? Daisy's missed you.' It was a lie. He didn't even know where Daisy was, until she emerged from the undergrowth wagging her tail and smiling at him, and Emelia bit her lip and looked guilty.

'I don't think so. She's been with me most of the day. Sorry. I should have told you.'

He shook his head at the dog. 'You faithless hound,' he said softly, and scratched her ears. 'So—tea in ten minutes?'

'Tea in ten minutes would be lovely,' she agreed, and smiled again.

She'd caught the sun, and there was a streak of dirt across her brow and down one cheek, and she looked happier than he'd ever seen her. Happy and beautiful, and he had to drag himself away.

So she was beautiful. So what? There was no way he

could let himself act on this. Not with the baby complicating it so much. It would be a complete and utter emotional minefield, and he was never going there again.

# CHAPTER SIX

EMELIA slept like a log.

She woke up the following morning for the first time in her little cottage, blissfully comfortable—until she tried to move. She was so stiff she could hardly get out of bed, and she vowed to take it a bit easier in the garden in future.

But he'd agreed to her suggestion! She was delighted by that, not only so she wouldn't be beholden, but also because she was excited by the challenge, and she got up and made herself tea and sat at the table in the window overlooking the rolling parkland and fields in the distance, and planned how she was going to tackle the garden.

Only a rough idea. She'd need more time to work it out properly. Then she showered—a power shower that drenched her and eased some of the aches, and she realised she felt better than she had in ages. Since before James had died, in fact.

The last three years had been hard—desperately hard, in so many ways—but they were over, and her life was entering a new phase. And for the first time since she'd been given the shocking and life-changing news that she was having Sam's baby, she was looking forward to the future with real enthusiasm.

She decided not to overdo it, though, that morning, and so after she'd dressed and had breakfast, she went and enrolled with a doctor and a midwife, and got her next scan booked at the local hospital, then changed, ate one of the bananas Sam had bought for her and tackled the garden gently.

And Sam appeared, just after she'd just started work, and brought her a cup of tea.

'How's it going?' he asked.

She brushed off her hands and smiled. 'OK. I've only just started. I'm sorry I wasn't here first thing but I had other things to do, and I'm going to have to skive on Monday, too, I'm afraid. I've got my twenty-week scan.'

His eyes tracked down and hesitated, then he lifted his head and searched her face. 'I don't suppose—'

'Would you like—?' she asked, speaking at the same time, and he gave a quiet laugh.

'Please—if you won't find it intrusive?'

Intrusive? The father of her child being present? Odd word, but somehow appropriate under the circumstances. She thought about it for a second, then shook her head.

'No, I won't find it intrusive, Sam,' she said gently. 'You're more than welcome to come. In fact, you can help me. It's at the local hospital and I have no idea where to go.'

'I'll take you. Just tell me when. And I don't expect you to be here nine to five, Emelia,' he added, a slight frown pleating his brow. 'Do as much or as little as you want. I'm just grateful for your input because this has been niggling at me for years.'

'OK.' She eyed his hands and smiled. 'So—is that for us, or are you just taunting me with the biscuits?'

He chuckled and sat down on the arbour seat, put the tea and biscuits down, and then vanished through the French doors into the sitting room, returning seconds later with a cushion.

'Here,' he said, shoving it behind her with a little frown, and she leant back on it and smiled.

'Thanks. You're a star,' she murmured. 'It seems ages since anyone spoilt me.'

'James?' he asked, wondering if she'd tell him to butt out, but she nodded, and she didn't look put out, so he went further. 'Tell me about him,' he suggested quietly, and then waited.

She smiled—that told him a lot, for a start. 'He was crazy. Clever, interesting, but he had some wacky ideas. We didn't always see eye to eye, but living with him was never boring. He always wanted to travel, to work his way round the world. We were going to save some money and go.' Her smile faded. 'We never got there. He found the lump the day after he brought the brochures home, and he was in hospital a fortnight later having surgery. We didn't get another chance.'

'You must miss him.'

She smiled again, a gentle smile that really got to him. 'I do,' she said honestly. 'He was my best friend. We had so much fun together, and we had so many plans—not just for travelling. He wanted to live in Clifton one day, he said, in one of the tall town houses overlooking the suspension bridge, and fill it with children. We argued about that.'

Sam frowned. 'The children?'

'Oh, no, the town house. We both wanted children,' she said, and then gave a wry little laugh. 'Ironically, I wanted to live in the country and teach in the local primary school.'

'You could do that here, maybe, one day,' he suggested quietly, and he watched what could have been hope, and then caution, flicker through her oh-so-expressive eyes.

'If I'm still here.'

He didn't like that. The idea of her leaving seemed

wrong, somehow, and he thought they'd got past that, but maybe not. He could ask her to marry him, of course— except it wasn't that easy. She still missed James—and he wasn't sure he'd want to marry her anyway. He didn't. Of course he didn't—but anyway it was out of the question. They'd be doing it for all the wrong reasons, and that was a thoroughly lousy idea. And anyway, she'd probably say no.

He drained his tea and stood up. 'I have to go—I've got a call coming in. Have you had lunch?'

'I don't need lunch,' she said, standing up too and handing him the mug. 'I had a banana earlier and I've just had three biscuits. I'll carry on for a while, then I'll stop. Don't worry about me.'

Easy to say, not so easy to do. Especially when he could see her from his desk struggling with a recalcitrant rose bush. She pricked herself and sucked her finger, and he had to shut his eyes and fight off the mental images.

It was yet another phone call he scarcely got the gist of.

She slept well again that night, and she found after a couple of days that she was used to her little cottage. Not only used to it, but loved it. She didn't even close the curtains now. Who was to see? She was woken every morning by the sun on her face, and as she went to bed at night, the last rays of the sun would streak through the other window and paint the room in pinks and golds.

It was, as Emily had said, a beautiful place to be, and she'd settled in surprisingly well, even though it was a little lonely. She could cope with that, though. After the claustrophic atmosphere with Brian and especially Julia, to be alone was precious, and goodness knows she saw enough of Sam in the day, fussing over her like a mother hen.

He was picking her up on Monday morning to take her to the hospital for her scan, and she found herself studying the contents of her wardrobe. Silly. She needed trousers and a top that would pull out of the way. Not pretty, impractical clothes that in any case she didn't own!

She sat on the bed with a short, defeated sigh. She really, really needed an income. Doing the garden for Sam was all very well, but she had to buy clothes, and it wasn't a case of want, it was a case of need. Her bump was growing rapidly, her bras didn't fit properly and she simply had to address it.

But how? There was no way she was asking Sam for help, he'd done more than enough.

Shaking her head, she stood up, pulled out the only pair of decent trousers that still went round her and a top that still more or less fitted, and put them on. She'd have to ask Sam to take her to a shop on the way home. Somewhere cheap.

There was a knock at her door, and she tugged the top straight and went to open it. Sam was standing with his back to the door, studying the area outside the cottage, and he turned to her with a smile.

'Morning. All set?'

'Just about. Let me find my shoes and grab my bag and I'll be with you.'

She was back in seconds, and he waved his arm at the bit of wall beside the front door.

'You could do with a bench here, couldn't you?' he said. 'Somewhere to sit and have a cup of tea in the sun first thing in the morning. And a table and chairs for the garden, so you can eat outside if you want. I meant to get them, but I just haven't got round to it.'

'Are you sure? It would be really nice,' she said, imagining that early-morning cup of tea in the company of the squirrels.

'Of course I'm sure,' he said easily, opening the door of the BMW for her. 'OK with the hood down?'

'Fine. It's a perfect day for it,' she said, scraping her hair back and twisting a band round it to hold it as they set off, then went on, 'On the subject of furniture, you could do with something in the rose garden, as well. On that bit of flagstone paving outside the French doors. It's crying out for a nice table and chairs.'

He nodded slowly. 'It is. I've thought that in the past but there didn't seem to be any point until now. I could sit there and have breakfast and read the papers over a coffee.'

'Is that your decaf coffee?' she teased and he shot her a wry grin.

'That'd be the one. So shall we do that after your scan? And we can have lunch out somewhere. There's a pub by the river that does the best scampi and chips.'

'Sam, I'll be like a house!' she protested, and then bit her lip as she remembered she'd been going to ask about clothes shopping.

'What?' he said, tipping his head on one side and studying her briefly as they paused at the gate.

'I *am* like a house,' she said frankly. 'I need clothes. I'm—sort of growing.'

His eyes dropped to her bump, and she felt her cheeks warm at his thoughtful stare. 'I suppose it goes with the territory,' he said with a slight smile. 'I'm sure I've seen a mother and baby place close to a garden centre that sells really nice outdoor furniture. We can do it all at once.'

He pulled away, problem apparently solved to his satisfaction, and she rested her head back and closed her eyes and enjoyed the feel of the sun on her face and the wind ruffling gently around her as they meandered slowly along the lanes. Magical. Perfect.

For a while he said nothing, then he broke the silence.

'About the scan,' he said, and she opened her eyes and turned her head to look at him.

'What about it?'

'Will they be able to tell the sex of the baby?'

It was something she'd been pondering on—not whether or not they could tell, because she knew they could, but if she wanted to know. 'Yes,' she said. 'They should be able to.'

'So—do you want to know?'

She nibbled her lip thoughtfully. 'I'm not sure. On the one hand it makes it easier to buy things, but it doesn't really matter unless you're going to indulge in a mega-fest of pink or blue, but maybe—I don't know,' she sighed. 'It'll make it much more real if it has a sex, much more of a person. A son or daughter, instead of just a baby. And then if anything went wrong…'

'Nothing's going to go wrong,' he said, shocked at how much that thought disturbed him. 'Why should it? People have babies without any problems all the time.'

'But if it did—'

'If it did,' he said gently, 'it would break your heart, Emelia, whether you knew the sex or not. It's obvious how much you love it.'

He was right, she realised, but there was still a bit of her that thought it might be tempting fate—which was silly, and the baby *was* very real to her already. Of course it would break her heart if anything happened. Knowing the sex wouldn't make the pain any worse.

'I take it you want to know?' she asked, and he turned his head and gave her a wry smile.

'It's not really my place to dictate it,' he said, but she could see from his eyes that he would rather know.

'Can we see how I feel at the time?'

'Of course.'

But it was a moot point, because it was a 3D scan, and by the time the sonographer had focused in on the baby, it was blindingly obvious.

'Oh! It's a boy!' Emelia gave a little gasp and put her hand over her mouth, and she felt Sam's fingers tighten on hers.

A son, he thought numbly as the reality of it hit him like an express train. I'm having a son—a mischievous little boy to climb the trees and race headlong down the slopes and fall and skin his knees, so I have to pick him up and carry him to Emelia so she can kiss it better, because it has to be her—

'Sam?'

He blinked, suddenly aware of the hot prickling sensation behind his lids and a lump in his throat the size of a house.

He turned to her, and found tears welling from her eyes. 'It's a boy,' she said again, her voice unsteady. 'We're going to have a boy!'

He hugged her. He couldn't help himself. He gathered her up in his arms, cradled her to his chest for a breathless, emotional second, then with his arms still round her, they watched the rest of the scan together. The fingers and toes, the heart, the eyes—it was incredible. His son—their son.

He felt a tear slide down his cheek, but so what? Seeing his son like this was the most incredible experience of his life, and if he couldn't let his emotions show—well, it was just wrong.

He hugged her again, his arm tightening round her

shoulders, and she looked up and gave him an emotional smile. 'Oh, Sam,' she whispered, stroking away the tear with a gentle hand, her fingers lingering on his cheek. 'I'm so glad you're here.'

*We're going to have a boy!*

'Me, too,' he murmured, his eyes back on the screen, fascinated by the image of his son's face. 'Me, too.'

They were given a DVD of the scan, and a couple of photos, and as they left the hospital he still had his arm round her.

'Coffee or shopping?' he asked.

'Shopping. I'm saving myself for scampi and chips,' she told him with a grin, so he drove through the town to the outskirts and pulled up in a retail park. Outside a shockingly expensive baby shop.

Damn. She was going to have to buy something, but this really wasn't the place she had in mind—

'OK, before you argue,' he said, cutting the engine and turning to her with a stern look, 'you'll need a certain amount of money to live on every month, and you'll need to work out your budget, so if I give you what I feel is reasonable for the restoration of the rose garden and the knot garden, you can do it in your own time, you'll have the money to see you through and you can budget accordingly. Fair?'

She swallowed and nodded. 'Very fair. How about the rent?'

'Forget the rent. The place was standing empty and probably would have done for months.' And he named a figure for the garden restoration that made her mouth drop open in shock.

'Sam, that's—'

'Fair,' he said firmly. 'It's that or nothing and it's less

than one of the quotes I've had. If you don't like it, I'll get someone else to do the garden. Take your pick.'

'I'll pay you back—'

'No. And I'm buying your clothes today. What you do after that is up to you—and would you for goodness' sake let it go!' he growled as she began to protest, but he was sort of smiling and she leant over to kiss his cheek, giving in because after all he could afford it and he really seemed to want to.

But the kiss was a mistake. His jaw was firm, and his cheek, slightly roughened by stubble, grazed her lips and left them wanting more. She straightened up and pulled away.

'Thank you,' she said, a little breathlessly, and he nodded, smiled tightly and got out of the car.

'Come on, let's shop.'

She was nothing like Alice.

He knew that, but watching her flick through the racks of clothes, checking the pricetags and wincing slightly, was a revelation. She chose carefully—things that would last, things that would see her through to the end, now. Not nearly enough, he thought, but there was always another time. And there was one dress she'd hesitated over, and he'd seen the indecision in her eyes before she'd taken a deep breath and added it to the inadequate pile.

He watched her run her fingers longingly over the end of a cot, then move on to a much more economical version. Not that there was anything particularly economical in the shop, but the quality was good. They'd come here for the baby equipment nearer the time, he decided, giving her space while she checked out the underwear and went to try things on. And he wouldn't let her argue.

But he could still feel her lips against his cheek, see her

fingers trailing over the cot, and he wondered what they'd feel like trailing over him…

He pretended interest in a sort of pram thing that changed into a chair and a car seat and a carry cot, and an obliging assistant came and told him all about it. Not that he cared, but it took his mind off Emelia…

She headed for the changing room with the bare minimum to tide her over until she went shopping herself. He'd said he was paying for these things, so she'd selected a few, but only just enough to look convincing.

They were lovely, though. She'd tried to be practical, but there was one pretty dress she'd just had to have. She'd pay him back when he'd given her the—utterly ridiculous—payment for the garden restoration. But it would be worth it. It was gorgeous, and she felt beautiful in it. Elegant and sophisticated and feminine, instead of first cousin to a heffalump.

She took it off, reluctantly, and put it with the underwear and tops and trousers that she was having, and he paid without a flicker of hesitation, ushered her out of the door and took her to the garden centre across the car park.

An eyewatering amount of money later, he'd chosen the furniture, paid for it and arranged delivery, and they were heading for lunch.

And about time, because her stomach was grumbling and she was beginning to feel a little light-headed.

Or, maybe, she acknowledged, that was just being with Sam!

'We ought to think of names,' she said, when they finished eating.

'Max,' he said instantly.

'Max? Why Max?'

He shrugged. 'It goes well with Hunter.'

'Or Eastwood.'

He felt himself frown. 'Eastwood?'

'Well, it's my name.'

'To be strictly accurate, it's James' name,' he reminded her softly, and her eyes clouded.

'I know. But I don't want the baby having a different name to me. It makes things so difficult at school.'

'Was that what you found after your mother remarried?'

'A little. I was older, of course. Max is going to start out with his parents having two names.'

'You said Max.'

She smiled. 'So I did. OK, I like Max. He looks like a Max. What would you have wanted if he'd been a girl?'

'Esme,' he said without hesitation.

'Esme?' she said, laughing. 'That's awful. Esme Eastwood.'

'I think it's pretty.'

'I don't. I rather liked Alice.'

She watched the laughter die in his eyes, and he put his empty glass down and stood up.

'It's a good thing it's a boy, then,' he said, and strode off towards the car park. She drained her glass, stood up and followed him thoughtfully.

Who on earth was Alice?

She got into the car, opened her mouth to ask and thought better of it. He was staring straight ahead, and she'd pretty much worked it out anyway.

So she said nothing, and he drove her home, dropped her off and disappeared for the rest of the day.

Nothing more was said, and anyway, it was none of her business.

He'd tell her when he was ready, she thought, and just

got on with her life. The weeks went past, and she settled into a routine of working, resting and pottering happily in her home, and she sorted out her life.

She was booked for her delivery in the hospital where she'd had the scan, and the midwife had recommended an antenatal class, so she'd signed up, starting in a few weeks.

The bench outside her cottage was delivered, and it was a master stroke by Sam. She drank her tea on it every morning, and got to know the squirrels that played up and down the beautiful ancient oak tree nearby.

And she saw the badgers, after she'd been there about six weeks. She was disturbed in the night by shrieking and squabbling outside her bedroom window, and when she sat up in bed, slowly so as not to alarm them, she saw three youngsters tussling with each other on the grass in front of the cottage.

They were just feet away, and she watched them for several minutes, fascinated, until in the end they shambled off and left her in peace. She was still smiling when she fell asleep again, and she smiled now, thinking about it, as she told Sam in one of their impromptu little breaks in the shade.

'You're lucky. I've heard them, but I've never seen them,' he told her, and it was on the tip of her tongue to suggest he should come over and watch for them when she thought better of it. Sam sitting up with her in the dark seemed like a bad idea. Too cosy. Too intimate. Too dangerous. It was hard enough in daylight while she was working in the garden and he'd come and sit with her for a few minutes— sometimes at the new table, sometimes in the shade under the old apple tree or in the rose arbour, depending on the time of day and the strength of the sun—and fed her treats. Wicked cookies or tiny sandwiches or sometimes, if it was very hot, slices of watermelon or crisp, juicy pear, washed down with tea. Iced green tea with lemon on the hot days, piping hot normal tea otherwise.

It made her rest, and it made her feel cared for, and he took a real interest in her work. He knew more about the plants than she'd imagined, and not only that, he wanted to learn. He cared, both about the history of the garden and its future, and sometimes he even came and worked alongside her for a while, if he was at a loose end or she was struggling with something particularly tough.

And now, because there was only so much he could do in the house until the English Heritage people had made their recommendations, he'd turned his attention to the grounds.

'So what are you doing today?' she asked him.

'I'm going to rebuild the gatepost,' he announced. 'I'm sick of seeing it like that, with the gate hanging. I might even get Dan to take the ivy off the wall so we can read the name of the house.'

Just in case we need the ambulance in a hurry, he thought, but didn't say so. She would only have ripped his head off if he had.

'Why's it called Flaxfield Place?' she asked curiously.

He shrugged. 'They must have grown flax around here in the past, I suppose. It's the site of a much older house, probably a farm. I keep meaning to research the history, but I haven't got round to it yet. No time, as usual.'

His grin was wry, and he drained his glass and stood up. 'Right, I'm going to the builders' merchants. Do you want anything while I'm out?'

'No, I'm fine.'

'OK. Will you be all right while I'm gone?'

She frowned. What a stupid question, she thought, and nodded. 'Of course.'

'OK. Back soon.'

He wasn't long. An hour, at the most, but the first thing he did when he returned was check on her.

'What's the matter?' she asked drily. 'Making sure I haven't run off with the family silver?'

He frowned. 'Don't be ridiculous. There is no family silver. How are you doing? Have you stopped for lunch?'

'Hardly, it's only twelve. Dan's here, by the way. He was looking for you.'

'Yes, I saw him, he's cutting the ivy back on the wall as we speak. Once he's done that I'll send him up here to you.'

'What, so he can keep an eye on me?' she asked, only half joking, and he frowned again.

'I thought you wanted a hand?'

Emelia nodded. 'I do. This elder needs digging out.'

'Don't overdo it. It's taken years to get like this. It can hardly be recovered in a minute.'

'I know, I know,' she grumbled, and got awkwardly to her feet. He was right, of course, she *was* overdoing it again, and her bump was starting to get in the way a little. She arched her back and he scowled, so she scowled back.

'Stop it. If you want to make a fuss, you can bring me lunch.'

He rolled his eyes. 'Anything that stops you killing yourself,' he growled, and stalked off in the direction of the house, leaving her smiling.

She went and sat in the rose arbour, on the ancient teak seat which had probably been there for fifty or more years, and waited for the ache in her back to ease. It was looking better, she thought, eyeing the garden critically. Much better. Or at least the part she'd tackled was. There was still a lot more to do, and then the knot garden needed clipping and shaping, and as for her own garden, she hadn't even set foot in it with a tool yet.

She'd meant to. She'd thought she could put in an hour in the evenings after she finished in the rose garden, but by the end of the day she was exhausted, even though she'd taken to having a lie-down after lunch when the sun was at its height.

And it wasn't going to get better the further on she was in her pregnancy, she realised.

She bit her lip. She had to keep going. She was massively conscious of the huge amount of money Sam had paid her for this restoration, and the terrifying thing was it wouldn't last long. Her car had failed its MOT test last week and she'd had to fork out hundreds of pounds to get her suspension sorted. That had been totally unexpected— although maybe the little creak should have warned her.

She dropped her head back and closed her eyes, shoving the sunglasses up to hold her hair off her face so the air could cool her skin. The blackbird was singing in the apple tree, and if she opened her eyes she knew she'd see the robin scratching in the freshly turned soil.

Bliss.


She was asleep.

Sam put the tray down quietly on one end of the long arbour seat and lowered himself carefully onto the slats. She had a tiny smile on her lips, and there was a little streak of sunscreen across her nose. He was pleased to see it. She didn't always bother and then she burned.

And why should he care? he asked himself. She was an adult woman.

He gave a silent grunt of laughter. As if he hadn't noticed that. His eyes traced the growing curve of her abdomen, her hands linked loosely round it and resting on her thighs, and as he watched, the bump shifted and jerked.

Her hand lifted and slid over it soothingly, caressing their baby, and he felt a huge lump lodge in his throat. Even in sleep—

'Why are you watching me?' she murmured, and he gave a guilty start.

'I wasn't,' he lied. 'I thought you were asleep.'

'Just resting and listening. It's so beautiful in here. I can see why you bought the house on the strength of it.'

'Talking of which, I've had a call from English Heritage,' he told her. 'They're sending someone to check a few final details, and then I can get the specialist team in to start work.'

She opened her eyes and turned her head towards him, sitting up again. 'That's great,' she said, and picked up a sandwich. 'What's in this?'

'Chicken and pesto. OK?'

'Lovely, thanks,' she murmured distractedly. The talk of the specialist team had reminded her, as if she'd needed reminding, just how out of her league Sam Hunter was. Flaxfield Place must have cost over a million even falling apart, and the specialist restoration would undoubtedly double it.

But it wasn't just about money. She owed him far more than simple cash. She owed him her sanity and her peace of mind, and there was no way one could put a price on that.

So she'd persevere, bit by bit, and she'd give him what she could in recompense.

She'd give him his rose garden.


The builders were in by the end of the next week—and perhaps foolishly, she'd imagined she'd see no less of him.

But she hardly saw him. They were working in the bedrooms overlooking the rose garden, and sometimes if she glanced up at a window, he'd wave to her. When he was getting the builders a drink he'd bring her one, but that was all. And she missed him.

The slow, leisurely breaks seemed to have stopped, and when she did see him, he seemed preoccupied.

'Problems?' she asked one day, as he was poring over plans in the kitchen when she went in to get a drink.

'Not really. I'm just juggling things in the master bedroom suite.'

'Want me to help?'

'No, it's fine,' he said, folding the plan up again and straightening. 'How are you getting on?'

Well, he didn't have to show her the plan. 'OK. It's hot today.'

'Go and rest—have a lie-down or something.'

'We haven't had lunch yet. I thought I'd make something.'

He shot her a guilty look. 'Ah. I grabbed a sandwich. Sorry. I've been up since before five, I ran out of steam.'

'You're as bad as the blackbird outside my bedroom window,' she said mildly, trying not to be hurt that he hadn't brought her a sandwich, too. Or at least made one and left it in the fridge for her. 'I'll pop home, then, and get myself something, and have a rest and a shower. Freshen up.'

He nodded, then frowned and vanished, leaving her there wondering what she'd said to send him away. Because it must have been something.

You're getting paranoid, she told herself as she walked back to her cottage with Daisy at her side. You didn't say anything. He's just preoccupied with the builders. You simply aren't that important. And that's why he didn't ask you for your advice, either. It's none of your business, nothing to do with you. And you aren't ever going to be in the master bedroom suite, so why on earth would you care?

But it still hurt.

*I'll pop home, then.*

Home?

Hell, he wanted her to think of the cottage as home, and yet...

He stared down at the folded plan in his hand—the plan of the master suite. He'd been trying to incorporate a nursery into it, but it was tricky.

So why hadn't he shown her the plan and asked her advice?

Because he'd been imagining them in it together when she'd walked through the door, that was why. Imagining her getting up in the middle of the night and going through to the baby. Lifting him from his cot and bringing him back to bed to breastfeed him. And ultimately the baby would move into the room beyond the nursery to make way for the next one—

'Idiot!' he growled. He was going crazy. He didn't need a nursery off his bedroom, because there was no way this was going to happen! She was still getting over the loss of her husband, and he—he would never forget Alice's lies and the pain they'd caused him. It had destroyed his dreams of being a father and a husband, and he wasn't going to risk that happening again. He was trying to move on, but only in a direction he considered to be failsafe and foolproof. And Emelia was not in that direction.

Oh, no. She was right in the other direction, leading him headlong into trouble, and it didn't matter how much he wanted her, how much she stirred something deep and elemental inside him, he wasn't going there in a million years.

So why the *hell* was he looking at the plans and building stupid, dangerous, incredibly tempting pipe dreams?

'Everything OK, boss?'

He gave the foreman a distracted smile. 'Yes, fine. I was wondering about putting the wardrobes in the bedroom instead of here, to leave it free.'

The foreman nodded. 'It would make a nice little nursery, perfect for the little one.'

He felt his neck heat. Stupid. There were plenty of rooms his son could have down the line.

'Forget it, it's fine as it is. Just carry on as you are.'

'Well, you've got a few days to think about it,' he said cheerfully, and carried on, as instructed, whistling softly.

Sam stared out of the window. It overlooked the rose garden, and working on the bedroom suite had given him a perfect excuse to watch Emelia without her knowing.

He frowned. There'd been far too much of that, and not enough concentrating on the core business. And fantasising about their baby in a nursery was certainly not the core business!

'I'm going to finish the gatepost,' he said abruptly, and turning on his heel, he ran down the stairs two at a time and left the house. A few hours' hard work should burn off some of the pointless and crazy images his mind was conjuring up, and maybe by nightfall he'd be tired enough to sleep.

# CHAPTER SEVEN

HER antenatal classes started a week later, and it just underlined what a strange situation she was in.

Everyone else had a birth partner, the father of the baby or a mother, sister, friend. She was the only one there alone, and she felt conspicuous and uncertain.

They were all friendly, but there was a limit to what she wanted to volunteer.

'Hi, I'm Emelia, and I'm only pregnant because the IVF clinic made a dreadful mistake and so instead of my dead husband, the father of my baby is a total stranger' didn't seem to be quite the thing. So what was? 'I'm a widow/single mother/elected to have a baby alone/the victim of a monumental mix-up'? If he'd been there, of course, she could say, 'This is Sam, he's the baby's father but we aren't together.' That was probably the most accurate and economical.

But he wasn't there, and he wasn't going to be, was he? Why should he? The pregnancy, the labour, the birth—they were hers alone. It was only the child he was involved or concerned with, until and unless there was a problem.

And then the second week Judith, the coach, asked if she had anyone who could come with her the following week as they were doing a series of activities that needed two people to work together.

No, not really.

It wouldn't have been so bad if she'd had a woman friend she could ask, but she could hardly ask Emily, could she? That would be beyond cruel. Her mother was on the other side of the country, she worked full time and although she was supportive and interested and offered sage advice on the phone, she wasn't in a position to drop everything and come and help.

Which left no one.

She was working in the rose garden the following day and mulling it over in her mind when Sam appeared with a tray of watermelon slices, glasses clinking with ice and beaded with tiny droplets, and some sandwiches.

'Here. Come and sit down and have something to eat,' he said. 'You've been working non-stop for hours.'

She stood up awkwardly, wincing at the pins and needles and a twinge in her side, and he frowned at her. 'Don't start,' she warned, and he smiled wryly, but he still watched her walk to the arbour and sit down beside him, and there was something that could have been concern in his eyes.

'Have you been watching me again?' she mumbled round a sandwich, and he looked a little guilty.

'The bedroom's just above here, and I was painting. All I had to do was glance down.'

She hmphed, and he gave a soft chuckle.

'OK, fair cop, I was watching you—but only because I thought you looked a bit glum. Everything OK?'

'Fine,' she began, but then sighed. 'Well, not really fine,' she admitted. 'I went to my antenatal class last night, the second one, and everyone's birth partner was there.'

'And you didn't have one,' he finished softly.

'Mmm—well, not for the classes. Not that that's really a problem most of the time, but—well, it's next week. They're doing activities that need two people, and I don't have anyone to take. And the only person really is Emily, and I couldn't ask her.'

'No, you couldn't. But you could ask me.'

She blinked and stared at him, her mouth open. Only slightly, and she shut it as soon as she realised, but—

'You?' she squeaked.

He looked slightly offended, and she backpedalled hastily.

'I didn't mean— Sam, I *couldn't* ask you. It's too much. I know you didn't sign up for this level of involvement—'

He shook his head. 'Emelia, I'm his father. Who better?'

Someone who loves me? Someone who wants to be there, who doesn't look as if they're going to the dentist for root canal work?

'Are you sure?' she asked, and he nodded.

'Absolutely. What time?'

'Tuesday evening, seven o'clock. We'll need to leave just after six-thirty.'

'No problem—I'll drive. Here, have some watermelon.'

She took a slice, and was lifting it to her lips when he said, 'Actually, I've got a favour to ask you, too.'

'Go on, then, fire away,' she said, biting into the cool pink flesh and swiping the juice from her chin with a grubby hand. 'What is it?'

'It's the nursery. I wanted to ask your advice on furniture.'

She stared at him. 'What furniture? What nursery?'

'The nursery here. I'll need to get a cot and all sorts of other things, I suppose—you'd better tell me what I need.'

She held up her hand. 'Whoa, there. Hang on. Need? Here?'

'For when he comes to stay,' he explained, as if it was obvious.

Not to her, it wasn't. 'He can't come and stay here for ages!' she said, fighting down the panic. 'Months—years, probably.'

He frowned again. 'Why not?' he asked, as if it had never occurred to him, and the panic escalated.

'Because he'll be too small for sleepovers without me!'

'Not without you. I don't mean him to come without you, but—well, I thought it would be a good idea for him to get used to me and the house right from the beginning.'

'So you're just assuming I'll come and stay? Like—what, like a *nanny*?' she asked, her voice deadly soft, and there must have been something in her tone that warned him, because he met her eyes a little warily.

'I'm not suggesting that at all,' he began, but she was cross now. Cross enough to rip into him, because he could have thought this through and obviously hadn't, and scared that it was the thin end of the wedge that would end with her losing custody of her child.

'No,' she said flatly, jumping to her feet and glaring down at him. 'This is my baby, Sam, and he lives with me, in my house. You want to play happy families, you come to me and do it. And when the baby's old enough to need it, then we'll talk about furnishing the nursery, and not before.'

He met her eyes in stony silence, then with a curt nod he stood up, too, and leaving their little picnic lying there on the bench, he walked out of the garden, taking Daisy with him, and shut the door behind him with a little more force than was strictly necessary.

He'd looked hurt, she realised belatedly. Hurt and puzzled by her reaction.

And then she remembered he'd offered to come with her to antenatal classes. Because he was trying to take over? Or just because she'd needed someone to support her?

The latter, she realised in dismay. He'd volunteered to give up his time to be her partner at the class, even though he'd looked appalled at the prospect, and then he'd asked for her help and advice—the very thing she'd been miffed about him not doing just a few days before, and now, just when they were making some progress, she'd shot it all down in flames.

It was Tuesday again, and as Emelia got ready for her antenatal class, she was still feeling sad and confused because of the way she'd reacted to Sam.

She would have apologised, but he'd been away over the weekend so there hadn't been a chance, and it had been really weird without him. She'd been here on her own working on the last section of the border, which had given her altogether too much time to think.

And she didn't think much of herself.

He hadn't needed to do any of this, she reminded herself for the hundredth time as she sat on the bed and looked around the safe and comfortable home he'd provided for her and the baby. He could have washed his hands of it, told her to do what she liked, sued the clinic for compensation and walked away. He might even have insisted she have the pregnancy terminated, she thought, her mind recoiling at the thought. Did he have the power? She had no idea, but he hadn't suggested it. Quite the opposite. Instead he'd been amazing, and all she'd done was hold him at arm's length and defend her corner.

But she'd had good reason, she reminded herself in justification. Julia and Brian had slowly and insidiously taken over almost every area of her life in the past few months, and just the thought of him taking over where they'd left off filled her with dread.

No chance, though. He'd walked away. Taken himself off the next day, and it was only by chance she'd seen the car return this afternoon, and then Daisy had reappeared, running to greet her as she walked back to her cottage after finishing work in the garden. But Sam hadn't come, which meant he was still angry.

She'd stopped a little earlier today, because she'd needed to shower and change for the class, but now it was six-thirty, and she had to leave in a few minutes, and if she hadn't been so stupid Sam would have been with her and she wouldn't be facing the class alone again—

There was a soft knock at the door.

'Emelia? It's Sam.'

She sat motionless for a second, unable to believe her ears, and then she heard him knock again.

'Emelia?'

She opened the front door to find him standing there, looking good enough to eat in soft, battered jeans and a clean white T-shirt that fitted him just right—not tightly, nothing so blatant, but closely enough to show off his flat, toned abdomen and broad, solid chest. His hands were rammed in his back pockets, his face unsmiling, and his eyes were expressionless.

'Are we still on for tonight?' he asked, and she felt her eyes filling with tears.

She tried to speak, but the tears welled up and choked her, and she turned away, stumbling back inside and pressing her hand to her mouth, all the emotions of the weekend rising up at once to swamp her. She'd thought he wasn't coming—thought he was angry with her, and she'd felt so ashamed—

'Hey, hey, come here,' he said, and she felt his hands,

warm and hard and safe on her shoulders, turning her into his arms and wrapping her against the solid and utterly reassuring bulk of his chest.

She slid her arms round him and hung on. 'I'm so sorry,' she began, but he shushed her and hugged her again.

'That's my line,' he said. 'I didn't mean to take over, I just thought if the baby was going to be staying regularly, it made sense to have the house equipped for him. I didn't even think about how you might feel about him staying with me. I just made all sorts of stupid assumptions, and I'm sorry. I'm new to this, you'll have to tell me how it goes.'

'Like I know!' she said as she let him go, trying to laugh and hiccupping with another sob instead.

She found a tissue in her hand, still neatly folded as if he'd come prepared for waterworks, and when she'd got herself under control again, she realised she'd left a dribble of mascara on his shoulder.

'I'm sorry, I've messed up your T-shirt,' she said, but he didn't even look at it.

'It doesn't matter. Are you OK?'

She nodded, and without warning he tilted up her chin with his fingers and brushed a fleeting kiss over her lips. 'Let's go, then,' he murmured, and she followed him out, her lips tingling, her heart skipping crazily because he'd kissed her.

Sam had no idea how he'd ended up escorting the mother of his child into an antenatal class.

It was so far off his radar it was laughable, but there he was, surrounded by all the happy mothers- and fathers-to-be, introducing himself to them as Sam. Nothing else, but it seemed nothing else was needed.

Pretty obviously, they all assumed he was the father—

which shouldn't really have been a problem, given that it was the truth, except that he was trying to work up to telling people and he hadn't quite got a handle on how to do it yet. But here, of course, he didn't have to, because the birth partners were either the babies' fathers, or they were women themselves.

There was some introductory chat and a graphic discussion of labour that made his blood run cold, and then they did some breathing exercises for working through contractions.

Fine, he thought. Easy. Think of something distracting—ride the wave. Simple. Next time he hit himself with a hammer, he'd try it. It would make an interesting change from swearing and whimpering.

They talked about drugs for pain relief—presumably for when riding the wave ceased to be effective—and positions for labour. And the more he heard, the more relieved he was that her mother would be there.

But then as the class ended, the tutor looked him in the eye and said, 'So, see you next week again, Sam,' and he found himself agreeing.

'Did you mean that?' she asked as walked out to the car.

Did he? Maybe. He had no idea why, and there was no way she'd ask him to be there for the birth, but the classes? That was different. He could do that.

'Yes—if you'd like.'

She looked as if she was going to say something for a second, but then she nodded and got into the car. 'Thanks.'

He slid behind the wheel and took the buckle of the seatbelt from her, clipping it home. 'Your mother's coming for the birth, isn't she?' he asked, checking.

'She should be. I've got to report back the substance of

the classes so she can keep up, and she's aiming to come down the week before my due date.'

'And if you're early?' he asked, glancing across at her as they paused at a junction.

She turned and met his eyes. 'Then I guess if the worst comes to the worst and my mother can't get here in time, I'll be on my own.'

Oh, hell. He was about to offer—he was opening his mouth to say so, when he thought better of it. He couldn't be her birth partner. It was all getting too close for comfort, and he was getting so emotionally involved with Emelia it was going to be really hard to keep his distance.

So he said nothing, and they travelled the rest of the way in silence.

She finished the rose garden by lunchtime on Friday, and went home to rest.

The little hedges round the central beds were clipped, the grass was cut and edged, the gravel paths were hoed, the roses were blooming their heads off. No thanks to Sam. He'd been fussing again—probably because of something Judith had said about not overdoing things and making sure exercise was appropriate for the stage of the pregnancy.

She'd seen his eyes narrow and known he was filing it for later, and she'd been right. Every time she stretched, he was there with a drink, or asking her about something trivial. Not the nursery—he'd learned his lesson on that one—but other things. The knot garden. The vine in the kitchen garden. Anything to stop her working, but it was finished, at last, and now it was time to enjoy it.

And enjoy it she would, with Sam, because it was a beautiful garden, a wonderful, sensual feast of scent and colour, and after she'd showered and put on the gorgeous dress she'd succumbed to on the day of her scan, she went back in there to check everything, and sat down in the arbour for a moment to soak up the atmosphere.

She'd made some nibbles and put a bottle of bubbly on ice in his fridge—nothing fantastic, but she felt a few bubbles were in order—and as she sat there, taking time out and waiting for Sam to come, she ran her hands slowly backwards and forwards over her bump. The baby stretched, and she arched her back to make room, and laughed softly as he took advantage and kicked her in the ribs.

He was restless, stretching and squirming, and she spoke softly to him, settling him with her voice. Odd, how she'd learned that her voice could soothe him. Or make him agitated, if she was arguing with Sam. Their baby seemed to hate that.

She saw Sam at the window of the bedroom, and waved. The builders had gone for the day, the place was theirs alone. And it was time to celebrate the garden.

'Come down,' she called, and he left the window.

Moments later, he emerged from the house via the French doors from the sitting room, and crossed to her. He'd showered and changed, washing away the building dust and detritus from his hair, and it was still damp, just towelled dry and raked back with his fingers, but he hadn't shaved, the stubble fascinating her. She so wanted to touch it…

'Are you all right?' he asked, and she frowned.

'Of course I'm all right. I wanted to show you the garden, that's all. It's finished.'

He looked around it, and she shielded her eyes as she turned towards the sun, pointing out the old rambling rose that had scrambled through an apple tree and burst into life.

His brows drew together in a frown. 'You should have

your sunglasses on,' he told her gently. 'You're screwing up your eyes.'

She tilted her head, a little cross that he wasn't paying attention to his garden after all her hard work on it. 'Why are you so worried about my wrinkles?' she demanded.

'I'm not worried about your wrinkles, I'm worried about your eyes.'

'Really? Why? They're my eyes. I'm perfectly capable of looking after them myself.'

Sam gave a short huff of disbelief, unconvinced. 'Is that right? So if you're so good at looking after yourself, why are you rubbing your back?' he asked with another frown. 'You've overdone it again, haven't you?'

Her eyes turned to fire, and she threw her hands up in the air in exasperation. 'For goodness' sake, what is it about this whole thing that's turned you into a caveman? First my eyes, now my back. Are you like this with all women, or is it because of the baby?'

'It's nothing to do with the baby—'

'Well, what, then?' she cried. 'You watch my every move, you fuss and interfere and crowd me until I'm ready to scream, and then I catch you looking at me as if—'

She broke off, breathing hard, and his eyes dropped to her breasts, rising and falling with every breath, taunting him with the ripe, sweet flesh that he ached to touch.

He lifted his eyes to hers again. 'As if I want to pick you up and carry you into my cave and make love to you?' he said softly, his voice raw with need.

Her eyes flared, darkened, and her mouth formed a silent O of surprise. Her lips quivered, and she flicked out her tongue to moisten them and he was lost.

'Really?' she whispered.

He tried to laugh, but it came out strangled. 'Yes, really,' he said. 'I know it's crazy, I know it's inappropriate, but—I want you, Emelia. And I've wanted you, if I'm honest with myself, from the day I met you.'

She sucked in a breath. 'Oh, Sam.'

She reached up a hand, her knuckles brushing lightly over his cheek. He could feel the drag on his stubble, where he hadn't had time to shave, and he could hardly hear for the blood pounding in his ears. Her thumb trailed over his bottom lip, tugging it, and he sucked in a sharp breath and closed the gap.

Their lips touched, tentatively at first, then with a hunger and urgency that should have frightened her, but simply seemed to fuel her passion.

'Emelia,' he groaned, and then her legs buckled and he caught her, sweeping her up into his arms and carrying her in through the French doors and up to his bedroom. He kicked the door shut, the last functioning piece of his mind aware that Daisy was following, and set her gently down on her feet.

Her dress—that lovely dress she'd bought after so much deliberation—had ridden up, exposing her legs, and the top had twisted, showing off her cleavage. So ripe. So lush.

'So beautiful,' he whispered hoarsely, his breath snagging in his throat and almost choking him. He reached out a trembling hand and touched her, a lone finger trailing down her cheek, her throat, over the hollow above her collar bone, down over the soft, tender skin he'd ached to touch for so long now.

He cupped her breast in his palm, his fingers closing over it and squeezing gently, and she dropped back her head and gasped, her pupils flaring and driving him over the edge.

He tore his clothes off, stripping off his shirt over his head, kicking his jeans aside, shucking his boxers. He needed her—needed her now, and, oh, he had to slow down… He knelt at her feet and slid his hands up her legs, his fingers finding a tiny scrap of lace and elastic that almost sent him into meltdown.

He nearly lost it. He'd thought— Hell, he didn't know what he'd thought. Big maternity pants? Not this tiny little scrap of nothing that came away in his hands, pale turquoise with little pink bows. He swallowed hard and closed his eyes, counting to ten.

Maybe a hundred would be better. A thousand—

'Sam?'

He opened his eyes and looked into hers, and she reached out a trembling hand and laid it against his heart.

'Make love to me?'

Emelia woke slowly, her limbs languorous, her eyes heavy-lidded.

Sam was beside her, his legs tangled with hers, his palm warm and gentle against their child. She turned her head to look at him, and met his watchful eyes.

'Hi,' she said softly, and he smiled, but the smile didn't quite seem to reach his eyes. Those shadows she'd seen lurking there from time to time seemed darker now, more troublesome than before, and she reached out a hand and cradled his cheek.

'It's OK, Sam,' she whispered. 'I know you don't want this.'

Didn't he? Hell, he didn't know any more what he did want, but making love to Emelia had been one of the defining moments of his life, and he hated the wave of doubt that lashed him now. If only he could trust her— Oh, that was so stupid, of course he could trust her. She wasn't Alice—and yet…

'Can we just take it a day at a time?' he asked, and she smiled sadly, her eyes gentle.

'Sure.'

The baby kicked, and his hand jerked, then settled again against the imprint of a hard little foot. 'Hey, steady, you, that's your mum,' he murmured, and dropped a kiss on her bump, then stroked his hand over the smooth swell, amazed at how it had grown in the few short weeks she'd been there. Shocked at the thought of how much bigger it would grow. More shocked still at what was to come.

And for the first time, he realised he wanted to be there for the birth, wanted to be part of the beginning of his son's life, his first breath, his first sight of the world. He wanted to hear that first cry, to be there when the midwife laid him on her breast. And he wanted to be there for Emelia.

He wanted it so much it scared him.

'You were going to show me the garden,' he said gently, and she searched his eyes, then smiled tenderly and kissed him.

'I was.'

He got up and held out his hand. 'Come on, then—let's have a quick shower and you can show me what you've done, and then we'll go out for dinner.'

'I've made some food,' she told him. 'And I put a bottle of fizz in the fridge. I thought we ought to celebrate it being finished.'

'Sounds good. We'll have a picnic.' He turned on the shower and pushed her into it. 'Go on, we'd better not share or it'll be dark by the time we get back outside.'

Shame. She'd quite been looking forward to it…

'Where's the fizz?'

'In your fridge. I put it in there earlier.'

'Let's take it out with us,' he said, and they carried it out and put it his new table, and he opened the wine and poured two glasses, and they strolled along the paths and drank to the garden.

'It's gorgeous,' he said with an awed smile, pausing by the arbour. 'You've done a fantastic job. Thank you.'

'It's been a pleasure.'

She took a deep breath, and went on, her voice curiously fervent, 'I owe you so much, Sam, and I can never repay you. There's no way you can put a price on the peace of mind and security you've given me, for the time to find my feet and decide what to do, but then I realised how much you love this garden. For some reason, it has a significance beyond price. I don't know why, I just know it was important enough to you that you bought the house on the strength of it.'

She lifted her hand and touched his face tenderly. 'I don't really know what happened to you, Sam. You've never told me all of it, and I don't really like to ask, but I know it hurt you deeply. And I can't make you whole again, but maybe the garden can. That was why I wanted to do it for you, to give you somewhere where you can heal, somewhere you can sit whenever you need to be at peace.'

Her words choked him. He realised for the first time what she'd been doing, why she'd been so driven, so focused. And he looked around, seeing for the first time everything she'd done for him, with so much love, and he felt his eyes burn.

She was wrong, he realised. She could make him whole again, if only he could dare to trust that they could make something real and lasting out of this ridiculous situation.

'It's beautiful, Emelia,' he said quietly. 'And you've worked so hard. I never meant you to work so hard, but I promise you, it won't ever go in vain. Even if I get a gardener in the future, this will always be mine, and I'll care for it and keep it just as it is now. Thank you. Thank you so much.'

'Oh, Sam, it was a pleasure,' she said, going up on tiptoe and pressing a kiss to his cheek, her eyes glittering. 'And I could help you, if I'm still living here, in the cottage.'

If? Did she mean she was thinking of moving away still? His gut clenched. For a brief moment of madness, he'd imagined her in the house with him, sharing his life in a much greater way, but if she was thinking of going...

'You've done enough. I couldn't ask you to do more.'

'I'd love to. And I can tackle the rest, bit by bit. So long as you aren't in a hurry, because the baby's getting in the way a little now and it's harder to bend over.'

'There's no hurry,' he said, and slipping his arm round her shoulders, he hugged her to his side. 'It really is beautiful,' he murmured, absorbing the scents and sounds as well as the colours. 'Beautiful.'

'It was always beautiful underneath. You knew that.'

'But I didn't know how to set it free. You've done that, let it breathe again, and I'll treasure it forever.'

He bent his head and touched his lips to hers, his kiss gentle, a kiss of gratitude for her kindness and understanding. 'Thank you, Emelia. Thank you for my garden.'

She rested against him for a moment, then together they strolled back to the table and sat down facing it, the last of the sun warming them as Sam fed her the tiny morsels—smoked salmon curls, on blinis with soured cream and herbs, fingers of cucumber and carrot dipped into humus—and then he brought out the bowl of strawberries and cream and fed her those, until they couldn't take it any more.

Every time his fingers touched her lips, he groaned. Every time his lips closed on her fingers, she inhaled softly.

Then a strawberry slipped from her fingers, and she

leant in and licked the juice from his chin, the stubble rough against her tongue, and she couldn't hold back the tiny whimper of need.

His breathing ragged, he tilted her face to his and took her mouth in a kiss so fiercely tender and yet so possessive that it robbed her of her breath.

'Emelia,' he said on an uneven sigh, and scooping her into his arms, he carried her up to his room.

They woke in the morning in a tangle of arms and legs, and he made love to her again, savouring every moment.

It was amazing. She was amazing. Her body was beautiful, smooth and firm and utterly feminine. He couldn't get enough of her, and she was so responsive, demanding everything and yet giving so much more.

That was so like her, though. She'd given him more than he could ever have imagined, and he'd given her so little in return. There was one thing he owed her, though. One thing he had to do, and he couldn't put it off any longer.

# CHAPTER EIGHT

'I'M GOING to feed Daisy and let her out,' he said, getting reluctantly out of bed. He showered, dressed and went down, and she followed more slowly, her hair towelled but still dripping, and found the back door open and no sign of him.

'No eggs,' he said disgustedly, coming back in empty-handed with Daisy at his heels. 'I was relying on them, there's nothing else. They truly are the most useless chickens. Maybe I should just admit defeat and get rid of them.'

'That's such an empty threat.'

He grinned. 'Teach me to give them names.'

And she'd bet her life none of them were called Alice...

'There must be something else,' she said, and opened the fridge.

Nothing. Well, nothing suitable for breakfast.

'Humus?' he said, looking over her shoulder, and she gave a little chuckle.

'For breakfast?'

'Whatever. It's about all there is to put on toast. I ran out of marmalade the other day. And butter. I meant to shop. I've been busy.'

'Oh, Sam, you are hopeless. You need—'

She broke off, and the smile died as his mouth firmed to a hard, uncompromising line.

'What?' he asked, his voice flat. 'What do I *need*? Finish the sentence, Emelia.'

She looked at him, registering the change in his voice, knowing this was a tipping point. She gave a resigned sigh. 'It was a joke, Sam. I was teasing you. I know you've been busy. But I also think you're lonely, you're rattling around in this great place—you're nesting, Sam. That's what you're doing, and you don't even seem to realise it.'

'I'm happy,' he said firmly. 'I don't need a wife. I don't need anything.'

'Well, I do,' she said, just as firmly. 'I need breakfast, and I'm obviously not going to get any here, so why don't we go over to my place and I'll cook for you? Truce?'

He nodded slowly, the tension gradually leaving him, and he gave her what had to be a half-hearted smile. But at least he was trying. 'Truce,' he agreed, and followed her, Daisy at his heels.

He was being stupid. For a second there he'd thought she was offering herself for the job, but why would she? She was still grieving for James, he'd seen the grief at first hand when she'd picked up her things—but she'd slept with him last night, made love with him again and again. Was that the act of a grieving widow? Or a woman alone in the world and afraid for her future? A woman desperate to secure a future for herself and her child. He could hardly blame her, but he was damned if he was going to fall for that one twice.

But her eyes had held such reproach, and for the umpteenth time, he reminded himself she wasn't Alice.

'Emelia—'

'Bacon and eggs?'

He put his thoughts on hold. For now. He knew damn

well he was in the wrong and owed her an apology. An apology, and an explanation. But breakfast first.

'How about a bacon sandwich and a cup of tea on the bench?' he suggested. And then he could talk to her.

About Alice.

He felt his throat close, but there was no choice. It was time.

'I need to tell you about Alice.'

Emelia glanced at him, sitting beside her on the bench in the sunshine. 'Is she the woman who told you she was pregnant with your baby?'

A muscle bunched in his jaw, and he glanced away, then met her eyes again and nodded briefly.

'It isn't pretty,' he warned.

'I didn't imagine it would be.'

'She worked for me. She was an accountant, and we started seeing each other. Stupid, really. It was nothing serious but she was a beautiful woman and it was no hardship. I took her out for a meal one night, and she had to leave early because her mother wasn't well. She had Alzheimer's, apparently. We went out for the odd drink after that, and I kissed her, but nothing more. I've always made it a rule not to mix business and pleasure, and I was sort of sticking to it. Then she told me there was someone taking money from the firm. The auditors were coming in, and she'd been doing a little work in preparation, and something didn't quite add up.

'I left her to deal with it. It was nothing major, she said, only petty fraud, but she wanted to get the evidence before we contacted the police. I went abroad—I was working all over the world at the time, a night in New York, a night in Sydney, a night in Singapore. I was sick of it, ready to settle down, and on the last morning I woke up and didn't know where the hell I was. I had to check my BlackBerry to find out. And when I got off the plane, she was there to meet me. She said she had good news—she'd got the evidence to nail the employee but she hadn't called the police. She took me out for dinner to celebrate, and then she took me home and stayed the night. Two weeks later, she told me she was pregnant.'

Emelia closed her eyes, shaking her head in disbelief. Oh, poor Sam. It was the oldest scam in the world, and he'd fallen for it. No wonder he was so damned wary. 'And?' she prompted, knowing there was more to this—much more. He'd said it was a professional couple. So who—?

'I didn't know how she could be. I was always very careful—I don't do unsafe sex.' He frowned, and she realised he hadn't used a condom last night, not once. And there were more reasons than pregnancy for using them, so had it been his way of showing her he trusted her?

'Anyway, she was definitely pregnant, and as I said, I was tired of jetting all over the world and suddenly there it all was on a plate—a wife, a child, a real home. It didn't hurt that she was clever and beautiful as well. You were absolutely right about me. I was ready to settle down. And I fell right into her trap. I asked her to marry me, and within seconds, it seemed she had a shortlist of houses for us to look at. "We can't bring up a baby in your apartment," she told me, and promptly found a house overlooking Richmond Park that was apparently perfect. Then of course she needed an engagement ring—a stonking great diamond nearly as big as the house—and the wedding was booked. Nothing lavish, oddly, just a quiet registry office do with dinner out for a few close friends and family.

'That was fine. I didn't want a huge wedding, but I was surprised she didn't. And then, just a week before the wedding, when the house was bought and the nursery furniture was on order and the interior designers were in, I asked her what she wanted as a wedding present.'

'What, on top of all that?'

He smiled wryly. 'Everyone was doing it, she told me. The big house, the diamonds. All her friends. So when she asked me what I wanted, I said she'd given me all I could possibly want. I was getting excited about the baby, really beginning to look forward to the birth. She'd started to show, and I was absurdly proud. It was ridiculous.'

'It wasn't ridiculous,' she said, having a horrible feeling she knew where this was going and aching for him, because she'd seen how tenderly he'd touched their baby, his hand caressing him, smiling as he felt the movements, and she could feel his love for Max coming off him in waves.

'Anyway, even though I'd already got her the matching diamond earrings, I asked her what she wanted, and she said if I really loved her, I could prove it by making her a partner in the company.'

Emelia felt her eyes widen. 'Just a little present, then.'

His mouth twisted. 'Indeed. And I finally, belatedly, smelled a rat. I smiled and stalled her, made some vague comment that basically suggested she'd have to wait and see. She'd had a text while we were having dinner, and she went to the ladies' and left her phone on the bench seat. It must have fallen out of her bag, and I checked the text. "Did he fall for it? X" So I made a call, and had her followed. She wasn't staying at mine that night—her mother needed her, she'd told me. And she went home to a man who had a conviction for fraud.'

Of course. 'So—did you call the police?'

'Yes. She was convicted of fraud and given a suspended sentence and struck off. She'll never work as an accountant again. I also found and apologised to the man she'd framed to get close to me, but when I told her there was no way she was bringing up my child, she just laughed in my face and said it wasn't my child anyway. I'd lost it all, as if I'd woken up and realised it had only been a dream. Only it was a nightmare, and it was real.'

A spasm of pain crossed his face, and she reached out a hand and placed it over his where it lay on his thigh. 'Oh, Sam, I'm sorry.'

'Yeah. Me, too. She'd been going to marry me and take half the company. The house and the diamonds were just icing on the cake. And there was no mother with Alzheimer's.'

'Was that when you ended up in hospital?'

He turned his hand over, threaded their fingers together and stroked his thumb idly over hers. 'No. I threw myself into work and spent nearly a year trying to kill myself with caffeine-induced tachycardia and chronic insomnia before I'd admit I was hating every minute of it. So I sold the company, retained another one which I'd started years before and which has always looked after me nicely, and bought the house. I was ready to settle down, ready to take time out, and then I saw the rose garden.'

'And you were lost.'

He smiled a little sadly. 'I was lost. There was something inside me that needed to be here, something about this place which I just knew would make it all right again.'

'And has it now? Is it working?'

The smile faded. 'I'm getting there. Slowly. But—' He broke off, his brow pleating as he held her eyes. 'I don't know if I can do this bit, Emelia. Us. You and me and the baby. I don't know if I trust it, it seems so…tidy, and I don't know if I trust my own reaction to you both. I'll be a father to Max, gladly. I could never walk away from that and I'm more than happy to accept as much responsibility as you like. But I don't know if I can give you more. I know you aren't like Alice, but there's no way on earth I want to make myself that vulnerable again.'

She held his eyes, then swallowed, retrieving her hand from his. 'So—why did you make love to me? If you couldn't do "us", then why—?'

'I don't know. I'm sorry. I shouldn't have.'

'No, you shouldn't,' she said softly, hugging her upper arms and looking away. 'If you didn't want me, then you should have left me alone. Left us as we were, Sam. You shouldn't have touched me if you didn't want me.'

'I wanted you,' he said, the words dragged out of him against his will, and she turned back to him, her eyes pools of betrayal and pain.

'Not like that. There's a difference between wanting my body and wanting the whole package, the sleepless nights, the colic, the morning sickness, the labour, the arthritis and incontinence pads—that's wanting me, Sam. Wanting me when I'm old and grey, just because you love me. Wanting me when the bad stuff happens, as well as the good, being there to hold my hand—that's wanting me. Not a little recreational sex to pass the time until the baby arrives.'

'It was more than that,' he said, his words a harsh denial.

'Was it? How much more, Sam?'

He swallowed and turned away, uncrossing his ankles and standing up, hands rammed in his back pockets.

'How much more?' she repeated.

He turned back, his eyes black with the shadows of Alice's deception. 'Much more, but—'

'But?'

'I'm sorry, Emelia—more sorry than I can tell you, but—I just can't do it.'

'So where does that leave us?' she asked quietly. 'Am I staying, or am I going?'

For a long time he said nothing, and she was so, so afraid he'd say go. But he didn't.

'Stay,' he said, the word a plea. 'If you feel you can. And I'll support you and the baby, pay all your bills, give you your own bank account so you don't have to ask for anything. I'll buy the baby equipment—either pay for it or come with you to choose it, and when you're ready we'll talk about the nursery here, but in the meantime if there's anything you need that I can give, it's yours.'

Fine words. And sincere enough. Honest.

The only trouble was, she wanted the very thing he couldn't give. She wanted Sam.

And he was off the menu.

She spent the next few days licking her wounds.

She felt tired and listless, the adrenaline high of finishing the rose garden wiped away by the realisation that Sam could never let himself love her.

She pottered in the house, resting more than usual, thinking about the baby and drawing up a list of equipment she'd need. The cottage had broadband, and he'd lent her a spare laptop so she could go online and look for goodies.

She couldn't summon any enthusiasm, though, and on Tuesday, when the sun came out, she went out into the cottage garden and started to clear it. She'd been meaning to for ages, and somehow it was only when her fingers were connected to the soil that she felt grounded and secure. And she needed that. Missed it.

It reminded her of the rose garden, though, which she'd put so much love into for Sam, and she found her eyes filling up from time to time.

She didn't do long. Half an hour at a time, because there was no pressure, and anyway this garden was easier to clear. Smaller, for a start. And in between her weeding sprees, she would make a cup of tea and sit in the shade at the back of the house with her eyes closed and listen to the birds.

It was her antenatal class that night, and she wasn't sure if Sam would come. He hadn't said he wouldn't, and he'd been round every day to check on her, putting her bin out this morning, cutting the grass in front of the house last night, but he'd refused her offer of a coffee.

So that was over the boundary, then, she thought, and wondered why she hadn't kept her mouth shut. It had been so much easier before. She should have pushed him away in the garden instead of kissing him back. Instead of pleading with him...

She wondered, as she worked, if he would turn up. And she wondered how she'd feel about it. Much more shy, curiously, she thought. Crazy, because the other night he'd investigated every inch of her body, as she'd investigated his, and there were no secrets left.

She knew he'd had his appendix out, and that he'd slipped out of a tree as a boy and sliced his leg on a metal gatepost. There was a faint scar under the springy, wiry hair that covered his thigh, and he'd told her the story of how Andrew had run for help and left him hanging there by his ripped jeans. He'd been eleven, and too adventurous for his own good, and she wondered if Max would be as wild and free.

She was about to leave for the class when she heard his car pull up outside, and there was a knock on the door. He was dressed in jeans and a T-shirt again, but black this time—in case she cried?

'I didn't know if you'd still want me,' he said, and she had to swallow hard.

Want him? She'd never stop wanting him. Somewhere between discovering he was the father of her child and handing over the rose garden to him, she'd fallen in love with Sam Hunter, and even though she'd thought she'd never love again after James, she'd been proved wrong.

'It's up to you,' she said. 'I don't want you to feel uncomfortable.'

'Don't worry about that,' he said, worryingly not denying it. 'I said I'd come, and if you want me to, I'm still willing.'

'Then—yes, please,' she said, and tried to smile, but it was a pretty pathetic effort and he pressed his mouth into a hard line and closed the door after her, turning the key and slipping it into his jeans pocket.

He was obviously finding it hard being around her, and she almost wished she hadn't asked him to come, but she hadn't wanted to exclude him. So long as there was the slightest chance he'd come round, she wanted that door left open for him, and if that meant putting up with a little awkwardness from time to time, so be it.

They talked about baby equipment at the class, amongst other things.

Cots, buggies, prams, gadgets that performed all three functions and turned into bouncy chairs and car seats and all manner of other things besides, and they had the great nappy debate, real versus disposable.

He should have found it all immensely dull and irrelevant. To his astonishment, he was riveted—because this was his baby they were talking about, his and Emelia's baby...

Not only would there be a person in the world that owed his life to him, but he would, at least, have a practical and useful role in that person's life.

Starting very early with changing nappies, if the class was anything to go by!

They spent a few hilarious minutes trying to get a nappy on a doll, and he found himself hoping that Emelia opted for disposables, because sticky tabs looked like the way forward to him. Sticky tabs he could cope with. Maybe.

There were things that weren't relevant to him—things like massage and using oils and preparing the body for birth—some really quite intimate things. He tuned them out, trying not to think of her body in that way, trying to forget what it had been like, for those few short hours, to have been granted the licence to touch her in such intimate and personal ways, to learn the secrets of her body.

The body of a woman was a miracle, he was discovering, and he felt oddly dislocated by his role simply as father of the baby and not as her partner. Excluded. He wanted to share that miracle, to have the right and the privilege to see this thing through with her, to be there when the child was born.

Even though it terrified him.

But, fortunately or unfortunately, it wouldn't happen, because he wasn't going to be there. Her mother would have that privilege, and no doubt she'd be far better at it than him.

But he felt a real sense of regret.

They talked about nursery equipment on the way home.

'We ought to start thinking about this,' she said. 'I'm getting closer—only another eight weeks to go. And it could be early.'

She thought his fingers tightened on the steering wheel. She could understand that. It filled her with an element of panic, too.

'Want to go shopping tomorrow?' he offered.

'Can you? How about the builders?'

'I can bunk off.'

\* \* \*

They shopped for hours.

He left Daisy in the care of the builders, and they went to the retail park where they'd shopped for the garden furniture and her clothes.

There was a huge choice. Bewildering, Emelia thought. So much stuff, and it was so horrendously expensive. With Alice in the back of her mind, she was wary about running down her fantasy wish list and ticking all the boxes, but after an hour of studying the various ways of moving babies around the world in safety, Sam ground to a halt.

'What's your ideal?' he asked. 'Of what we've seen, which would do the job best for you?'

She thought, and pointed one out. 'It looks well made, it's easy to operate and switch from one mode to another, it's light enough to lift—'

'So what's the problem? Don't you like the colour?'

She laughed softly. 'I don't like the price.'

'Don't look at the price. Look at the safety, look at the ease of use. Those are the key things.'

It was much, much easier after that.

They chose the bulky, expensive items of kit, arranged for them to be delivered and then moved on to the accessories. And on. And on.

They'd stopped for lunch, but by three-thirty she'd had enough.

'I need to go and rest,' she told him, and he frowned and ran his eyes over her, his mouth in a hard line.

'Why didn't you say something?'

'I just did.'

'You look shattered.'

'It's just come on suddenly. It does that.'

'Does it?' he growled, looking unconvinced. 'Stay here, I'll get the car.' And he strode off, pulling up alongside her just a minute or two later. 'Right, home—unless there's anything else you want to do today?'

She shook her head and fastened her seatbelt. 'I'm fine.'

'You'd better be,' he muttered, and set off at a nice steady pace. Daisy was waiting for them, lying down on the step by the front door and watching, and she ran over, tongue lolling, and greeted them as they pulled up outside the little shooting lodge.

'You need to sleep.'

'Actually, I'm fine,' she told him, for the second time. 'I thought maybe we could sit here and talk about the other things we'll need while we trawl the net and drink tea?'

He eyed her searchingly. 'OK. I ought to go and check on the builders, and feed Daisy, and at some point I need to order more food or I won't get a delivery tomorrow. Why don't I go and do that and you can wander over when you're ready and we'll sit in the rose garden and do it.'

She crumpled. They'd spent hours sitting in the rose garden. It was where she'd grown to love him, and the temptation to go back there, to sit with Sam surrounded by the scent of the roses and the sound of the birds, just overwhelmed her.

'OK. You go and I'll join you in a while.'

He nodded and drove off, and she walked into her little house and closed the door and leant against it. She'd lied. Well, not really, she *was* fine. But she was also emotional. It had been hard shopping with Sam, doing all the things that normal couples do, getting ready for their first baby.

But they weren't a normal couple, and they never would be, and today had just rammed it home. Not that it needed ramming. She was more than aware of it, more than conscious of the gulf between them, and she wondered now if she could do this, if she could live so close to him, alone, loving him, wanting him, needing him, with him wanting and needing her but refusing to love her, and neither of them able to walk away because of Max.

She plopped down onto the sofa and picked up a cushion, hugging it. It felt so inviting. Too inviting. She snuggled down on her side, tucking the cushion under her head, and closed her eyes. She'd just lie here quietly for ten minutes, gathering her thoughts, and then she'd go over…

# CHAPTER NINE

SHE was lying on the sofa, curled on her side, her head resting on her hand, and he stood there for a moment by the window, watching her.

Wanting her, in so many ways, and yet so unsure of the way forward. He thought of all the things she'd said, all the ways in which he should want her. He wanted her in all of them, but this—this was so hard. Could he do it? Keep a safe distance, be there for his child, offer Emelia support and yet still feel as if he was locked in an emotional wasteland, so near and yet so far?

He closed his eyes and rested his head against the glass. He didn't know. Sleeping with her had been a huge mistake. Even so, he'd do it again, just for the memories that haunted him now day and night.

The feel of her skin, like silk beneath his hands. Her body, soft yet firm, supple, warm, welcoming him. The soft cries. The gentle touch of her hand against his skin, the urgency, and then the boneless relaxation, the utter contentment of repletion.

Never before had it been like that, and with an instinct born of bitter experience, he knew it never would be again.

And there was guilt, now. Guilt that he'd taken something

that hadn't belonged to him, and overlaid her memories of her beloved husband with a lie.

Was it a lie? It had felt more true, more honest than anything in his life before, but behind the door he dared not open was a deep, dark void of bitterness and regret that had stopped him from believing in it.

Still stopped him believing in it.

He tapped lightly on the window, and she opened her eyes and struggled upright. She'd been asleep, he realised, and wished he'd left her there. His cowardice would have been happy at that.

'Come in, the door's not locked,' she said, and he went in, pausing in the doorway.

'I'm sorry, I didn't realise you were asleep. The builders have gone, and I've put the kettle on. I wondered where you were.'

'Worrying about me again, Sam?' She shook her head and gave him a smile that twisted something inside him. 'You don't need to.'

Oh, I do, he thought, but he didn't say so. Instead he said, 'Do you want to do this another time?'

She shook her head again and got to her feet. 'No. Let's do it now. In fact—while we're ordering stuff, why don't we have a look for things for the nursery in the house? It would make sense, and you never know, I might want the odd night off.'

Her smile was gentle this time, and he realised she was holding out an olive branch. Desperate for a way forward, at a loss to achieve it alone, he took it.

'Sounds good to me. Shall we?'

Daisy came running up to Emelia as they left the cottage, and she bent to stroke her and caught a look on Sam's face—a look that puzzled her.

'Faithless hound,' he said, and she frowned.

'Are you jealous?' she asked, and he chuckled, feeling some of the tension leaving him.

'I might be. She's supposed to be my dog, but she just adores you. I don't know if I want to share her.'

She stopped walking and looked at him seriously. 'We're going to have to share the baby,' she said, and he felt the tension coming back and tightening his chest.

'It's not the same, Emelia. I don't care if Daisy loves you. I could easily love you if things were different. But the baby—it's not so much a timeshare as each of us having an opportunity to give something to him. It's different.'

He could easily love her? She smiled, her brow smoothing. 'Yes, it is. We'll get there, Sam. We have to.'

He nodded, and pushed open the kitchen door. The room was full of steam. 'I think the kettle's boiled,' he said wryly, and made the tea. There were biscuits on the table on a tray, and a cake, and he put the teapot there with the mugs and milk jug.

'Are you trying to fatten me up?' she murmured, and he chuckled.

'Don't think I need to. I think nature's got her own way of doing that.'

She tilted her head and gave him a funny look. 'Do you think I'm fat?'

He thought of her body, sleek and smooth, the firm swell of her pregnancy extraordinarily beautiful. Mother Earth.

'No,' he said firmly. 'I don't think you're fat. I think you're perfect.'

Their eyes clashed, and he felt his throat tighten with emotion.

'Right, you bring the laptop, I'll bring the tray,' he said hastily. 'Daisy, come on.'

* * *

They sat under the arbour, Sam trawling comparison websites and checking out all sorts of equipment she hadn't even thought of getting, and she ate cake and drank tea and let him play.

He was getting into it, she thought, but wondered if he was latching on to this with such enthusiasm because it was something he could safely get involved in. Maybe that was all she needed to do—let him do the things he could, and not fret for the things he couldn't. She didn't need a man in her life. She'd been planning to bring this baby up alone, with the support of relatives. This, in a way, was exactly the same—except, of course, the relationship was closer, massively complicated by its accidental nature and further complicated by her own emotional involvement.

'Finished your tea?'

She nodded.

'Come and see the nursery.'

They went in through the French doors, and up to the newly finished suite of rooms which overlooked the rose garden. She hadn't been in here since the day he'd shown her around, and it had changed hugely.

'It's lovely,' she said approvingly, looking round his new bedroom. 'Oh, Sam, you've done a fabulous job. I love the colour.'

'I wanted something soft that reflected the rose garden,' he said, 'but not pink. I thought the creams and blues would pick up the lavender.'

They did, the gentle blue grey and cream restful and calm, and she loved it.

Her eyes were drawn to the beautiful old mahogany half-tester bed, huge and solid and inviting. It was the bed in which he'd made love to her just a few days ago, moved into here now, and it seemed like a lifetime since that night. She dragged her eyes away.

'So what have you done in the nursery?'

He gave a wry smile. 'Blue. Sorry.'

'I'm sure Max won't mind blue,' she teased.

He gave a short laugh and led her through a doorway into a small room that must have been at one time the dressing room for the master bedroom.

'So, what do you think?' he asked.

She looked around the empty, freshly decorated room and her eyes filled. He'd started painting a frieze. Not like Brian's smudged, stencilled little train, but a row of alphabet letters with animals climbing through them—an anteater, a bear, a ginger cat, a black Labrador like Daisy, an elephant—all exquisitely hand drawn and painted in soft pastel shades for his baby. She turned to him, swallowing down the lump in her throat. 'You're going to struggle with the X,' she said, and he smiled wryly.

'Yes. I thought of that the other day. The only X I could think of was extinct. I think he'll be a bit young for the issues of deforestation and global warming.' He shrugged. 'Oh, well, it was just an idea, I probably won't get round to finishing it,' he said dismissively, and then took a deep breath and looked around. 'So—equipment. What do we need?'

They were building bridges.

Slowly, day by day, as the birth approached and the equipment they'd ordered appeared, they prepared the two houses for the baby's arrival.

He missed a couple of the classes because he was away in London attending business meetings, but he asked her about them and she found a book on pregnancy and childbirth lying on the coffee table in the sitting room a few days later, open at a relevant page.

Interesting, but not surprising. He'd researched old roses

when she'd told him a little about the ones in the garden, and it seemed he tackled everything in his life in the same way.

She spent a few days in her own garden, when there were just two weeks to go, doing a little tidying. It was hard, though. The ground was just too far away, and she was glad when in the middle of the week Sam said he'd come and cut the grass for her, because she was beginning to realise that it was all too much for her at this stage in her pregnancy.

She'd wanted it tidy, though, before the baby was born, and now it was, but she was paying the price. Her back had been aching ferociously all day, and even lying down hadn't eased it.

So while he cut the grass, she went into the baby's room and looked around. Just checking, for the umpteenth time, that everything was ready. Her mother would be sleeping in there because the baby would be in with her at first, of course, but the bed was made, the room was squeaky-clean and she should really shut the door on it and stop fussing.

She leant over to tug a minuscule crease out of the quilt cover, and her back started to ache again. Damn. She'd been overdoing it, she realised, but there was no way she'd admit it to Sam.

She opened the back door and leant against the frame to ease the ache. 'Fancy a cup of tea?' she asked, and he nodded.

'That would be good. I'll just finish this. Two minutes.'

She left him in the garden and went back to the kitchen, leaning on the worktop and breathing slowly and deeply. That was better. Focus on something else. Distraction. It would be good practice for labour—

'Ahhh!'

She sagged against the units, her eyes flying open and her lips parted, taking little panting breaths and trying to find that safe place they'd talked about in class.

It was nowhere to be seen, and she felt a tide of panic sweep over her. It wasn't supposed to happen like this! Her mother wasn't coming until the weekend, and it was only Wednesday! She couldn't be in labour—

Another wave hit her, and she slumped forward, crossing her arms on the worktop and resting her head on them, trying to find the zone. Ride the wave—think about something else. Anything else! Think about the fridge. What's in the fridge that'll go bad while I'm in hospital? And where's my bag? Half-packed. 'Oh, rats!'

It wasn't helping. She was supposed to be thinking about lying on a palm beach, her skin fanned by soft, warm breezes, her feet washed by the slow lap of the sea...

Better. Better because it was easing off. She straightened up, stared at her watch and checked the time, then she felt the tightening again. Three minutes. Three minutes? Already?

But she'd had backache all day...

'Stupid, stupid woman.'

'Who's a stupid woman?'

'I am,' she gritted, and dropped her head forward again onto her arms.

She was in labour.

Sam felt the blood drain from his head and leave him cold with fear. She couldn't be in labour! Her mother wasn't due for another three days, and that meant he'd have to help her.

If she'd have him. He laid a hand on her back, the heel of his hand rubbing firmly over her sacrum where she'd been pressing her fingers.

She groaned softly, and he stopped.

'Don't stop!' she ordered, so he started again, slow, rhythmic circles, and gradually he felt her relax.

'OK,' she said, straightening. 'I need to ring the midwife and talk to her. I think I need to go in.'

'Already?'

She looked up at him, her soft green eyes shadowed with uncertainty. 'They're every three minutes.'

Hell.

'I'll get the car,' he said, and ran.

Her waters broke on the way in, but luckily Sam had had the foresight to scoop up some towels on his way, so she didn't have to feel guilty about his upholstery.

Just as well. She didn't have the energy or reserves for guilt. Her world had narrowed right down, her focus absolute. As if he understood, Sam said nothing, just drove her to the hospital, took her in and left her in the care of a midwife and went to park the car. Within a very few minutes, they'd examined her and she was settled in a side room.

'You shouldn't be too long now, you're almost there,' the midwife told her.

Almost there, but no sign of him, she thought with a flutter of nerves, and she needed him.

But he wouldn't be with her. He'd had umpteen opportunities to offer, if for any reason her mother hadn't been able to make it, and he hadn't. He didn't want to be there for the birth.

Sam arrived back as she had another contraction, and she rolled to her side with a tiny noise of distress.

He swallowed. He had no idea how he was going to do this, but he couldn't leave her. He went round to her side, crouched down and watched her face as she concentrated.

Incredible. He could almost feel the power of her thoughts, the tight focus, and his admiration for her soared.

She opened her eyes, let out a long, slow breath and smiled at him. 'You're back.'

And she sounded pleased. Hugely pleased—relieved, in fact. Nearly as relieved as him, because there was no way he was leaving her.

'Is there anything I can get you? Ice chips? A cold flannel?'

'Ice would be lovely. And I might want to walk around.'

She didn't. A few steps in and she sagged against the wall. He caught her, hooking his arms under hers and taking her weight, as he'd been taught in the class, and she panted lightly through it and then lifted her head as she straightened.

'Maybe not,' she said with a little smile, and he led her back to bed and went to find ice.

'Sam, you don't have to be here,' she said after another hour or two. She wasn't sure, she'd lost track of the time, but she was coping. Maybe it was because he was there, maybe it was because she was doing OK, but she was concerned about him. He hadn't wanted to be there, and as he protested now, she shook her head.

'Sam, I know you don't want to be here,' she told him gently. 'You're only being nice to me.'

'When was I ever nice to you?'

She tried to smile, but another contraction was coming and she felt herself zeroing in on it. When it was over, she opened her eyes and found him just where she'd left him, his eyes on her, his concentration on her absolute.

'OK now?'

She nodded. The midwife came and examined her, and Sam turned his back and stared out of the window, giving her privacy and yet still not leaving. He hadn't left her side once except to get ice, and when the midwife went he fed her another ice chip and wiped her head with the cool compress.

'What about Daisy?' she asked, belatedly.

'Daisy's fine. She's gone home with the builder.'

Emelia frowned. 'Will she be all right?'

'He'll feed her—what do you think?' he said drily, and she laughed.

'OK.' She glanced at the window and realised the sun was setting. It was late evening, and he hadn't eaten. 'Why don't you go and get something to eat? I'm fine, really. This could go on for ages.'

They were moving her when he got back from his hasty sandwich and coffee, and his heart jammed in his throat. She was linked up to a monitor, and he could see the baby's heartbeat. Or was it hers? He wasn't sure.

The midwife kicked the brakes off the bed and looked at him.

'We're moving her to the delivery room but she might need a C-section. There's a problem with the cord. Are you in or out?' she asked.

Emelia's face was glazed with perspiration, her eyes unfocused as she concentrated on her breathing. And then the monitor went off and she started to panic.

Her eyes sought his and clung, and he swallowed.

'I'm in,' he said, and stepped into the abyss.

He was glad he'd been to the classes.

He'd thought it would all be calm and slow and to do

with finding the zone, but the baby's cord had got twisted round its neck and the only zone he could find was one filled with chaos.

People were everywhere, there was talk of Theatre, and the baby's heartbeat was crashing with every contraction and taking an age to come back up again as they struggled to free the cord.

Emelia clung to him, his hand crushed agonisingly in her surprisingly fierce grip. She'd been gardening, of course, day after day, and her hands were strong. Very strong.

'OK, it's free, you have to push now, as hard as you can,' they told her, and from somewhere inside him he found the words to encourage her, not letting her give up, bullying her to keep going, praising her when she did, and all the time his heart was racing and he was shaking with fear.

She couldn't do it any more. She was exhausted, shocked and afraid, and it was all too hard, but then his face swam into focus and she locked on to his eyes. Slate-blue eyes, utterly calm, his smile encouraging. 'Come on, sweetheart, do it for me. One more push.'

She gave him one more push, and then another, and another, and then there was a mewling cry, a hiccuping sob and a full-blown yell of rage, and everyone was smiling and laughing and they were lying the baby on her, pushing her T-shirt out of the way and putting the baby against her skin.

'He's a gorgeous, bonny boy,' someone said, but all he could think of was Emelia and how incredibly brave she'd been.

'Well done,' he said, and stepped back out of the way so they could get to her. He could feel tears tracking down his cheeks, and he scrubbed them away and tried to smile, but it was too hard so he gave up and just stared at the baby lying there on her chest.

She was smiling down at him, her hands caressing him with a tenderness that brought a smile back to his eyes once more.

'Does he have a name?'

'Max,' they said together, and shared a smile that threatened to push him over the edge again.

'Congratulations, Dad!' someone said, and he felt the floor dissolve beneath his feet.

He was a father. He'd never thought he'd be a father, not since Alice. Well, only to Emily and Andrew's baby, and that wouldn't really be a father. That would be an uncle, nothing more, really.

But this…

They took the baby from Emelia while the midwives busied themselves with her, and he was wrapped in a soft white blanket and handed to Sam.

'I'll drop him!' he said in panic, but they just smiled.

'Of course you won't. He's the most precious thing you'll ever hold. There's not a chance you'll drop him.'

He stared down at Max, streaked with blood, a shock of black hair plastered against his head, and thought, She's right. You're the most precious thing I'll ever hold. More precious by far than anything in my life has ever been.

Except Emelia—and she wasn't in his life. Not really, not in the way she should have been, the way he wanted her to be.

But he could love his son.

The dark blue eyes stared back at him, filled with the wisdom of the ancients, and he felt humbled and incredibly honoured to have been granted this gift.

'Here, Sam, sit down,' someone said, and pushed a chair behind his knees. So he sat, and he stared down into his son's eyes, and fell head over heels in love.

# CHAPTER TEN

'SHE's had the baby.'

'Sam—that's great! How are they?'

He could hear Emily shrieking in the background, and there was a stupid smile on his face that he couldn't seem to get rid of.

'She's fine, Andrew. They're both fine—'

There was a clatter and Emily came on the line. 'Sam, tell me all about it—is she OK? How did it go?'

He felt the shock of it all come back and hit him. 'Um— well, there was a bit of a panic at the end with the cord, but everything was OK. She was amazing. I don't know how you women do it.'

And then he remembered that this woman couldn't do it, that this was the baby they might have been having, but for the monumental mix-up, and guilt hit him in the solar plexus.

'Emily, I'm sorry, that was crass,' he said, but she cut him off.

'Sam, don't be daft, we're both thrilled for you. So how long's she going to be in there?'

'They said she can come home tomorrow, but her mother's not here till the weekend, so I'm a bit wary about them discharging her.'

'Want me to come?' Emily said, after the tiniest

hesitation, and he thought of the hurt it would bring—and, selfishly, that he wanted to be the one there for her.

'I can do it.'

'Can you? There might be lots of personal stuff, Sam.'

Of course. He hadn't thought of that. He had no idea what might be needed, but although he would have done it all, he had the sense to realise that for Emelia, the presence of a woman would be preferable.

'Do you mind?'

There was another tiny hesitation, then she said, 'Of course I don't mind! We'll come tomorrow night. If you can bring her home and settle her, we'll come as soon as we can.'

'What about Friday?'

'We'll take a day off. That's fine, Sam. This is family.'

Emelia wasn't family, he thought, and then it struck him that she was, of course she was. She was the mother of his child. How much more 'family' could she get?

'Thanks,' he said, massively grateful for the offer and deeply aware of what it must have cost her. Cost them both. 'Bless you. I'll get your room ready.'

He couldn't sleep. Wouldn't have known how to, after the tumult of the day. There was so much to think about, so much going on in his head, in his heart.

He contemplated opening a bottle of champagne, but he didn't want to drink it alone, so he made a cup of tea—about the hundredth he'd had that day—and then threw it down the sink, poured a small measure of malt whisky and went out into the rose garden.

It smelt amazing. He'd taken to sitting here in the evenings, when the builders had gone home and Emelia was ensconced in her cottage, and he crossed to the arbour and settled on the old teak bench, drenched in the scent of the garden and surrounded by Emelia's gift to him, and closed his eyes.

He was a father.

Not a husband, not really a lover, but he was a father.

'Welcome to the world, little Max,' he said softly, and then because his lids were prickling and his throat was tight, he drained the glass. It made him choke slightly, made his eyes water. He closed them, and saw the baby's face, the serious eyes staring up at him.

The eyes of his precious, beautiful son.


Daisy came back with the builders in the morning, utterly delighted to see him again but just as happy to follow the builder in case he gave her any more treats.

'I think you might have been spoiling my dog,' he said mildly, and the man laughed.

'I don't know what you mean. So, how are things?'

'Great. Excellent. It's a boy—'

His voice cracked, and the builder slapped him on the shoulder.

'Well, congratulations, Sam. Welcome to the world of sleepless nights and baby sick.'

Except they wouldn't be his sleepless nights.

'Cheers. You're all heart,' he said drily, and went to phone his parents. He hadn't told them last night, not after his conversation with Andrew and Emily, and it had been very late to call them, but he called them now, realising that for them this was a very big deal.

Alice hadn't only hurt him, she'd hurt them, taking away the grandchild they'd been longing for, and for the first time he felt sympathy for Julia and Brian Eastwood. They must have felt just like his parents had, only for them there would be no other chances. No wonder Emelia had been so forgiving of their deceit.

His mother cried. His father sounded choked and was a little forced. He guessed they'd be over to see the baby just as soon as they could find someone to look after the animals.

'Give her our love,' they said, although they'd never met Emelia before, and he said he would.

Even though he couldn't give her his.


He came to get her at midday, after she'd seen the midwife and the consultant who'd been there in the end at the birth. She didn't remember him, but that wasn't surprising. She hadn't really been aware of anything but her body—except Sam. She'd been aware of Sam for every single moment.

He'd been amazing—an absolute rock, even though she knew he'd found it hard. His reluctance had been obvious from the first, but he'd stayed with her, stayed calm, kept her focused. She couldn't have done it without him.

He walked in, looking a little wary and out of place, and she held out her hand to him and pulled him close for a hug.

'Sam, thank you so much for yesterday,' she murmured into his shoulder, and he perched on the edge of the bed beside her and hugged her back, his arms gentle.

'You're welcome. How are you? Did you have a good night?'

'OK.' It hadn't been, really, and yet it had been the most amazing night of her life. She'd been sore and tired, but so wired, somehow, that she couldn't sleep, and she'd spent half the night lying staring at baby Max so that now her eyes were gritty and she felt like death warmed up. 'I could do with a nap.'

'I'll take you home,' he said, and looked into the crib. Max was wearing a tiny little sleep-suit, but even so the cuffs had been turned back and the legs were empty where he'd drawn his up inside it.

'Could you call the midwife? She'll take me down, they have to,' she told him, and so he went to find her, still marvelling at the sight of those tiny little hands lying utterly relaxed on the ends of his skinny arms. So frail, so delicate, and yet tough enough to endure what must have been difficult for him, too.

'Emelia's ready to go,' he told them, and they were escorted down to the car park. The baby seat was lashed into the back of the car, and they installed him in it, looking like a doll in the confines of the straps, tucked up in a blanket with his tiny little hat sliding over one eye.

Hard to imagine him playing football or climbing trees, and with a little stab of fear came the realisation of what his parents had gone through when he'd been a child, wild and free and reckless with the scars to prove it. The very thought made his blood run cold.

'You did a good job of that gatepost,' she said as they turned into the drive and rattled slowly over the weeded cattle grid between the properly suspended gates.

'Not just a pretty face,' he said, and she looked at him. He wasn't. There were depths to Sam that fascinated her, so many facets to his personality to discover—if only she ever had the chance.

'Emily and Andrew are coming tonight,' he said as they made their way up the drive. 'I wasn't happy about you coming home without your mother here yet, and Emily offered. She thought—well, that I shouldn't really have to do some of the things that might need to be done, and I thought you might prefer it.'

'Oh, Sam, that's kind of her. Thank you.'

'I also thought you should be in the house until your mother comes.'

She hesitated. The cottage was all set up—but so, too, was the house. If she had one room with the baby, and Andrew and Emily had the other, sharing the Jack and Jill bathroom, then Emily would be near her if necessary. But Sam was ahead of her.

'I've put a single bed in the nursery for now. I thought I could sleep in there and you could have my bed,' he said. 'But if you'd rather go to the cottage, I'm sure we can rearrange ourselves.'

It would be easier for all of them at the house, of course, and also more room. But—Sam's bed, where he'd made love to her with so much tenderness and passion?

'It's only for a night,' he told her. 'Then when your mother comes, you can go back to the cottage with her and it'll all be clean and tidy and ready.'

Of course it would. It made absolute sense, and it would be pointless and stupid to argue when she agreed with him. But—his bed?

'You're right,' she said. And hopefully she'd be so tired tonight that she'd sleep wherever she was.

There were flowers in his bedroom—roses and lavender, from the garden.

They weren't so much arranged as jammed in a vase, but Emelia thought she'd never seen anything more lovely and for the umpteenth time that day, her eyes filled.

'Oh, Sam, thank you,' she murmured, touching the rose petals.

'Pleasure. You look bushed. Have you had lunch?'

'No. I just want to rest.'

'OK. There's water here, or I can get you tea or coffee or fruit juice—'

'Water's fine. Thank you, Sam.'

'I'll leave the door open—yell if you need anything,

or bang on the floor. I'll be downstairs. And don't worry about Daisy coming up, she's banished to the kitchen.'

'OK.' She listened to him go, to the steady rhythm of his feet on the stairs as he ran lightly down. Then there was silence.

Absolute silence, and she realised the builders weren't there. Either that or they'd been moved to another part of the house, because she could hear nothing.

No radio, no tuneless whistling, no hammering or drilling or shovelling—just the sound of the birds in the rose garden below the open window.

Sam, she realised, giving her quiet to rest after the birth. Sam, who'd picked her favourite roses.

She undressed, went to the bathroom and then looked at Max, tiny in his cot. He was lying on his side, eyes shut, out cold, and she guessed that yesterday must have been hard for him, too. He'd probably wake soon for a feed, but she had to sleep.

Maybe he'd last an hour or so. If she could just get an hour...

She snuggled into Sam's bed, sniffing the sheets and feeling ridiculously disappointed to smell the fresh scent of laundry. Of course he'd changed them. He'd done everything.

Everything except love her—

Don't start, she told herself firmly. Just go to sleep.

Max woke for a feed over an hour later, and Sam heard him cry and came up.

'Stay there, I'll bring him to you,' he said, and ridiculously, after all that had taken place the day before, she felt shy.

He took himself out of range, though, sitting by the window and staring out while she pulled her top out of the way and undid her bra, and she coped quite well, she thought, thrilled that feeding Max had come so naturally to her, fascinated by the sight of his tiny rosebud mouth beaded with milk, the fragile fingers curled against her breast.

She swapped sides, resting him against her shoulder to burp him, but he just cried, his little legs drawn up to his tummy.

Sam turned his head and frowned. 'Can I help?'

'I don't know. Could you try and get his wind up?'

What the hell did he know about winding babies? Nothing! But he took his son, rested him against his shoulder and rubbed gently, and was rewarded with a shocking belch that made them both laugh in surprise.

'OK! I think he might be ready for Mum again,' Sam said with a smile, and handed him back, still a little awkward. Emelia held her arms out, and he lowered Max into them, his fingers brushing her breast as he did so.

It was covered, but he still felt the impact of it all the way down to his toes, and he backed away and retreated to the window seat again, studying the garden as if his life depended on it.

It was so silly, Emelia thought, watching him. They could have had it all, if only he'd been able to accept her love. She felt her eyes prickle, but held herself together and finished feeding Max, then together they changed his nappy. His skin was so soft, so tender, the little legs bowed and mottled, almost transparent.

'He's incredible,' Sam said reverently, running a finger gently over his downy cheek as she put him in his cot. 'I can't believe he's mine. I can't believe I've done anything good enough in my life to deserve him.'

'Oh, Sam—'

'Sorry. It's just a bit of a rollercoaster.'

It was. A rollercoaster, an emotional minefield, and Emelia was struggling, too. Her own feelings were enough to deal with, but Sam's as well just overloaded her.

Still, she coped—more or less. Sam brought her something to eat, then she rested some more, fed Max again and began to feel like an old hand. She could do this, she thought. She could cope.

She was OK till she saw Emily.

They arrived at six, and her friend came straight upstairs, tapping on the door and tiptoeing in just as Emelia put Max down again.

'Hiya,' she said softly, peering into the cot and pressing her fingers to her lips. 'Oh, he's so like Sam!'

'I know. If there was ever any doubt about what the clinic had done, it went the second I saw him. He really is his daddy's boy—'

Her voice cracked, and Emily gave a tiny sob and gathered her into her arms, hugging her and rocking her gently. She led her to the bed and sat her down on the edge, perching beside her as she tried to pull herself together, and then she tucked her up in bed and sat up beside her, holding her hand and plucking at her fingers absently.

'Are you OK, Emelia? Really OK?'

'I'm fine. It wasn't that bad. A bit scary, that's all.'

'I meant about Sam.'

Oh. 'No, not really,' she said honestly, starting to cry again, and Emily shushed her as she rolled into her shoulder and let go of all the tumult of emotions that had built up over the past few weeks.

'Oh, Emelia. Have you fallen in love with him? I was so afraid you would.'

'I was OK until he—' She broke off, but Emily stared at her searchingly.

'Until he…?'

She shook her head. 'I spent the night with him. It was crazy, I shouldn't have done it, but it just felt so right, and then in the morning there was nothing in the fridge and I told him he needed a wife. And he told me about Alice.'

Emily's sharply indrawn breath was followed by a soft sound of sympathy. 'Oh, Emelia. How was he?'

'I don't know, really. Distant, removed, shut down—she really did a number on him, didn't she? It sounded awful.'

'It was. We were so worried about him. I didn't know him all that well, Andrew and I had only been together a year and Sam was always so busy I'd only met him a few times, but I'd always really liked him and I didn't like Alice one bit when we met her. I was shocked that his judgement was so skewed, that he'd slept with someone with such dead eyes. She just—she wasn't there, behind her eyes. Does that sound strange?'

'No. If she was lying, maybe it was the only way she could do it. Shut herself away so you couldn't see it.'

'Maybe. Andrew was shocked when she chose the Richmond Park house, but in fact Sam did well because he sold it for more and bought this place instead, which was the best thing he's ever done. Or it would be, if only he hadn't come here to hide.'

'Well, it's not really working,' is it?' Emelia said softly. 'The very thing that scares him rigid has followed him here. And I don't know if I can do it, Em. He was amazing yesterday—absolutely fantastic. He did everything so calmly, so solidly—he was a rock, and yet today—he's gone again, retreated back into himself.'

'Is he scared of the baby?'

'No. He's scared of me. Scared of loving me.'

'But he does love you. You've only got to listen to him

talking about you. He was so proud of you yesterday—he hardly talked about the baby, it was all about you.' She sighed shortly. 'I can't believe he's so blind, he just can't see what's under his nose, but he'll come round, Emelia. I'm sure he will. Just give him time.'

She gave a tiny, humourless laugh. 'He's had nearly five months, Em. He's still not come round, not even slightly. If anything it's worse. And he's very honest about it. He admits he can't do it—he even told me he could easily love me if things were different.'

'Oh, the idiot! Of course he can do it,' Emily muttered. 'The man's a fool.'

'Anyway,' Emelia went on, 'I'm not sure I dare trust him. He's so wary, so busy not giving anything away that if he did, I wouldn't be sure he wouldn't take it back. She's hurt him too badly, Em. She's torn his heart out, betrayed his trust. I don't know if he'll ever get over it, and I'm certainly not holding my breath. Life's too short. I can't wait for him.'

'So what are you going to do?'

'I don't know. Live here, share Max with him, try and get a job in a local school in a year or so, and make some friends, I suppose. I don't need a man in my life. Sam's taking care of the practical stuff, and I can live without the emotional upheaval. I never thought there'd be anyone else after James anyway, and I'm not sure I want anyone.'

'Not Sam?'

She gave a shaky sigh. 'Of course Sam. I love him. But there won't ever be anyone else. Loving two men and losing them is enough for any woman. I might take up knitting.'

Emily laughed, a strained little sound at first, but then they both started, and ended up doubled over and leaning on each other.

'Are you girls OK?'

'We're fine,' Emelia said, smiling at Andrew and kissing him on the cheek. 'Go and see your nephew. He's in the cot.'

His face, so like Sam's in many ways, showed a flicker of emotion as he bent over the crib and introduced himself to his sleeping nephew.

'He's so like Sam,' Andrew said softly, staring at him in amazement. 'There's a photograph of him in the pram at a few days old, and he looks just like that. There's no doubt, is there?'

'No doubt at all,' Sam said from the doorway. 'He's got my eyes.'

'Just so long as he doesn't have your ability to fall out of trees.'

Sam shrugged away from the doorpost and joined his brother. 'I've already had horrors over that. Watching him grow up is going to be nailbiting, I can tell already.'

He straightened up and gave Emelia a slightly strained smile. 'OK?'

She nodded. 'I'm fine,' she lied. 'A bit tired. I could do with another nap.'

'We'll leave you to sleep. I'll bring you some supper up later.'

'I can come down. I'm not an invalid,' she said, and he gave a curt nod and went out, followed by Andrew. Em gave her a hug and slipped off the bed, pausing.

'Are you really all right?' she murmured, and Emelia nodded.

'I'm fine,' she lied again. 'Go on, go and talk to Sam. He needs some normality.'

And she needed—she didn't know what she needed. For them to go? It was lovely to see them, but really she didn't need any help to do anything, and she just wanted time alone with the baby.

She wished she'd insisted on going to the cottage, but events had got in the way and she was powerless to change it now, so she lay down, closed her eyes and thought of sandy beaches and the rustle of palm trees in a tropic breeze.

It didn't work.

'So what are you going to do next?'

'About what?' he asked, although he was horribly sure he knew the answer.

'Emelia, living in the cottage, so close and yet so far away. Keeping your distance.'

He stared out of the window. She was sitting at the far end of the rose garden, under the arbour, and Max was lying in his little chair in the sitting room at Sam's feet, guarded by Daisy. The baby was fast asleep, and she'd gone outside for a breath of fresh air. Keeping her distance, as he was?

'I don't have a choice. She's not really interested in me. It'd just be too tidy, wouldn't it? Why does everybody want to make everything so tidy? Maybe we're happy like this.'

'Are you?'

He couldn't answer that, not without lying, so he didn't bother.

'I hope you know what you're doing, Sam,' Andrew said softly. 'For both your sakes.'

He frowned. 'We're trying to do the best for our child.'

'Are you? I think you're both so busy protecting yourselves you can't see what the best thing is. I just hope you find out before it's too late.'

'I don't know what you're talking about—'

'I know you don't. You can't see what's right in front

of you. You love her, Sam. And she loves you. Why don't you just go and tell her?'

His heart crashed against his ribs.

'I don't love her—'

'Oh, tell it to the fairies, Sam! Of course you love her. You haven't taken your eyes off her since she went out there. And she loves you, too, but she's afraid to show it because she can't cope with any more pain in her life. But this is hurting her, Sam, and it's hurting you, and it's all so unnecessary.'

He stood up. 'You don't need us here. I'm going to take Emily home and leave you two alone.'

'But Emelia—'

'Is fine. There's nothing she's going to need you can't do for her. You were there for the birth, you've slept with her—'

He jerked his head up and stared at Andrew. 'What makes you say that?'

'She told Emily.'

He shut his eyes and swore. 'It was a mistake.'

'No. I don't think it was. I think for once your guard was down and your heart sneaked past it. Sam, she loves you. She's waiting for you, but she won't wait forever. Trust her.'

Trust her? How? And how to trust himself? What if he failed her?

'You won't let her down.'

He stared at his brother hard. 'How the hell do you know what I'm thinking?'

'Because I love you. And she does, too. Do it, Sam. For all your sakes, take a deep breath and do it.'

*Take a deep breath and do it.*

Andrew had gone, taking Emily with him, but they'd

said goodbye to Emelia in the garden and she was still out there.

And Max was sleeping soundly, his little rosebud mouth working from time to time.

Sam looked down the garden, his eyes searching for her in the gloom. There was a light on the wall, enough to see your way along the paths, but he couldn't see her in the shadows of the arbour. He knew she'd be there, though.

His heart pounding, he stood up and walked out of the French doors and down the garden to the woman he loved.

She saw him coming.

There was something about the slow, measured stride that made her heart beat faster, something about the look on his face in the dim light that stalled the breath in her throat.

Andrew and Emily had gone, she had no real idea why. She hoped they weren't upset by the baby, but they might have been.

But that wasn't what this was about. She could tell that— could feel it, deep inside her, in the lonely, aching void where her love for him lay bleeding.

'Everything all right?' she asked, and he said yes, but then shook his head.

'Not really. Mind if I join you?'

'Of course not.'

She fell silent, waiting, hardly daring to breathe, and after a long moment Sam looked up and met her eyes.

'I don't know if I can do this,' he said softly, 'but it isn't just about me, is it? It's about you, and Max. And yesterday—you were amazing, Emelia. I was so proud of you, and so scared for you, so worried that something would go horribly wrong.'

'It was OK, Sam.'

'It could have been worse. Much worse. And I realised, in that moment, just what you meant to me. I think I already knew, to be fair, but I wasn't ready to acknowledge it, and I'm not sure I'm ready now. I'm not sure I'll ever be ready, but it can't hurt any more if you leave me than it hurts right now, wanting you and not being with you.'

He took a breath, looked around. 'When you did the garden for me, it wasn't really about the garden, was it—or am I wrong?'

'No,' she told him softly. 'You're not wrong. I knew your heart was broken. I thought, if I put my heart into the garden, then my love might heal you.'

A tear spilt down her cheek, and he lifted a hand and smoothed it away with his thumb.

'Emelia,' he said, his voice hardly more than a sigh of the wind. 'I love you. I can't promise not to let you down, I can't promise to live forever, but I can promise that I won't hurt you deliberately, or lie to you, or cheat on you. I'll do everything I can to be a good father to Max, but I need more than that. I need your love. I need you beside me every day. You said once that if I truly wanted you, I'd want you when you were old and grey and toothless—'

'I think I said incontinent,' she said with a smile, hope flourishing in her heart like an opening rose.

He laughed softly. 'Maybe you did—but you were right. And I do love you like that, and I will love you whatever happens.'

He took her hand in his, and knelt in front of her on the fallen rose petals, his eyes burning in the darkness.

'Emelia, I know I can't measure up to James, and I know you'll always love him, but if you could find it in you to share your life with me, to raise our children together as a real family—Emelia, will you marry me? Will you do me the honour of being my wife?'

'Oh, Sam, I don't know what to say.'

She was too choked to speak, too tired and overwrought and emotional to come up with anything as beautiful as his words, but it seemed she didn't need to.

'A simple yes would do,' he said unsteadily, and she laughed and threw her arms around his neck.

'Oh, yes—Sam, yes, yes, yes.'

He shifted so he was sitting on the bench again and gathered her up against his side, and then tenderly, with so much love, he kissed her.

'I love you,' he whispered. 'I'm sorry it's taken me so long to trust you enough to tell you.'

'Oh, Sam, I love you, too. I love you so much. I've known for ages, but yesterday—yesterday you were just—there for me. I couldn't have done it without you, and you just knew exactly what to do.'

'I had no idea. I just winged it.'

'Well, remind me to have you with me next time, then,' she said with a smile, and he blanched.

'Next time?'

'Of course. I want more babies—lots more.'

'How can you even think about it?' he groaned, and she laughed.

'I might need a few months,' she told him. 'And a ring on my finger.'

'I haven't got you an engagement ring.'

'I don't want one. I just want shares.'

'Shares?' he said, his voice wary.

She smiled and kissed him. 'In your heart.'

'No shares,' he said, kissing her back tenderly, his eyes filled with love. 'It's all yours. Forever.' He lifted his head after a second, listening, then smiled wryly. 'Yours and our children's—and talking of which, I think that's our son demanding his mother's attention.'

He stood up and drew her to her feet, and arm in arm they walked back down the rose garden to Max—and the rest of their lives. Together…

# THE MUMMY MIRACLE

## BY
## LILIAN DARCY

**Lilian Darcy** has written nearly eighty books. Happily married, with four active children and a very patient cat, she enjoys keeping busy and could probably fill several more lifetimes with the things she likes to do—including cooking, gardening, quilting, drawing and travelling. She currently lives in Australia, but travels to the United States as often as possible to visit family. Lilian loves to hear from readers. You can write to her at PO Box 532, Jamison PO, Macquarie ACT 2614, Australia, or e-mail her at lilian@liliandarcy.com.

## Chapter One

"I don't think she's ready yet." The words floated up through Jodie's open bedroom window from the back deck.

"Oh, I agree! She's not!"

No one in the Palmer family ever thought Jodie was ready. She sat on her bed, struggling to raise her left arm high enough to push her hand through the strap on her summery, sparkly, brand-new tank top. The hand wouldn't go, which meant she couldn't start the long journey down the stairs to join the Fourth of July family barbecue as the—not her idea—guest of honor.

She pushed again, the feeble muscle refusing to obey the muddy signal from her brain. It was noon; time for everyone to start arriving. "So I guess they're right. I'm not ready," she muttered, but she knew this wasn't what her sister Lisa's comment had meant.

It had meant Not Ready, capital *N,* capital *R,* and

during Jodie's twenty-nine years had covered everything from her learning the shocking truth about the Easter Bunny at the age of seven, to going out on her first date at fifteen. She vaguely remembered from last summer, about a hundred years ago, that Elin had even questioned her readiness to see Orlando Bloom's wedding photos in a magazine—and, admittedly, she had been a little envious of the bride.

What wasn't she ready for this time?

It could be anything. Going back to work?

Well, yes, she knew she wouldn't be doing that for a while, since she managed and taught at a riding barn for a living and spent hours in the saddle every week at Oakbank Stables.

Reading the police report on the accident scene? Might never be ready for that one. Fixing her own coffee? Wrong, sisters. She'd been practicing in rehab and, not to sound arrogant or anything, she was *dynamite* when it came to spooning the granules out of the jar.

"Guys?" she called out to her sisters. "Can I have some help up here?"

From down on the deck she heard an exclamation, voices, the scrape of chairs. Lisa and Elin both appeared half a minute later, flinging the bedroom door back on its hinges with a slam, wearing frightened looks to complement their red-white-and-blue patriotic earrings.

"It's okay," she told them. "You can put the defibrillator down and cancel the 911 call. I just can't get my arm into this top, that's all, and I know people will start arriving any second."

"Maddy and John just drove up," Lisa confirmed. "And Devlin was right behind them."

"Devlin's coming?" Jodie's heart bumped sideways against her ribs. Dev. Every time she saw Dev…

There was an odd little silence. Possibly there was. It ended so quickly that she wasn't even sure if it had happened.

"He's been so great, hasn't he?" Lisa said brightly. "How many times did he go in to see you, while you were in the hospital?"

"You tell me," Jodie joked. "I was unconscious for most of them."

"Do you remember anything from that time?" Elin asked, hesitant. At forty, she was the eldest of the four Palmer girls, and managed to be both the bossiest and the most nurturing at the same time. "The doctors said you might retain some memories, even from when you weren't responsive."

She and Lisa both stood there waiting for her reply, each almost holding their breath. Jodie fought a bad-tempered impulse to yell at them to stop the heck worrying about her so much!

Instead she said carefully, "I wouldn't call them memories...."

"No...?" prompted Lisa.

"But let's not talk about it now. Help me downstairs. I'm so slow. My brain sends the instructions but bits of my body don't respond. I'm thrilled I managed to get into the jeans."

Thirty-eight-year-old Lisa, sister number two, hugged Jodie suddenly with a warm, tight squeeze, and planted a smacking kiss on her cheek. Of the four Palmer girls, she and Jodie were physically the most alike, blonde and athletic, outdoorsy and lean. Lisa liked tennis and the beach and it had started to show in her tanned skin. She didn't take care of it the way she should. Hugging her back, Jodie decided she'd have

to give Lisa a sisterly lecture about that, soon, because
Palmer overprotectiveness could cut both ways.

The slight, strange tension in the room seemed to
have gone, chased by the hug. "Honey, forget slow,
we're just so happy you're okay," Lisa said. "Talking.
Walking. Getting better every day. *Home.*"

"I know." Jodie blinked back sudden tears as they
let each other go. "Me, too."

Devlin Browne was standing on the deck when she
reached it, his dark hair showing reddish glints in the
sun, his body tall and strong; there was no evidence of
the accident that had injured the two of them in such
different ways, nine months ago. He grinned at the sight
of her, from behind his sunglasses. "Look at you!" She
wished she could see the expression in his blue eyes.
He ran his life with such quiet confidence and certainty.
She loved that about him, wished right now that some
of his qualities would rub off on her.

"Yeah," she drawled in reply, "all the grace of a ballerina."

With a walking frame for a dance partner. The doctors and therapists had promised that if she worked hard,
she'd be rid of it soon. She planned to astonish them
with her progress.

"Don't knock it," Dev said. "Compared to how you
were even a week ago."

"I know. I'm not knocking it, believe me." She felt so
self-conscious in his presence, so aware of the strong
length of his body. Nine months and more since those
three explosive nights of lovemaking, but to her they
felt like yesterday. The way their bodies seemed to fit
together so perfectly. The smell of him, warm and fresh
and male. The words he'd whispered to her in the dark,

naked and blunt and charged with sensual heat. Did he ever think about it?

Lisa helped her to sit down and took away the frame, while Elin handed her an ice-cold glass of tropical juice. The deck was dappled with sun and shade, and there was a breeze. It was a perfect day. Dev pulled up an Adirondack chair to sit beside her. He leaned against the wooden seat-back, casually stretched his arms. But his mood wasn't as casual as he wanted her to think. His gaze seemed intently focused behind those concealing sunglasses, and she didn't know if his sitting so close was significant.

Were they dating?

Could she ask?

*Um, excuse me, Dev, I was in a coma for nearly eight months, and rehab since. Can you just catch me up on the current status of our relationship?*

A thought struck her. That Not Ready comment of Lisa's a few minutes ago...

Not Ready to hear that Dev had moved on to someone else?

But she didn't have time to examine the cold pit that opened deep in her stomach at this idea. There shouldn't be a pit! He'd been up front with her nine months ago. "I have nothing to offer, Jodie," he'd said. "I'm only here until Dad is ready to go back to work. My career is in New York, it's pretty full-on, no room for commitment, and I'm not looking for it. I really like being with you, but if you're interested in something long-term, it's not with me."

How did a woman respond to something like that? She knew Dev had said it out of innate honesty and goodness of heart. He wasn't the kind of man who promised what he couldn't deliver, or tricked a woman into bed with sweet-talking lies. He called it how he saw it, and when he laid his cards on the table, he laid them straight.

Nine months ago he'd been all about the short term, about saying goodbye when it was over, with a big grin, warm wishes and no regrets for either of them, yet now he was sitting beside her, searching her face, examining the set of her shoulders as if he cared that she might not be coping.

Which she wasn't, fully.

Everything was happening too fast. Dev stood up to greet Lisa's husband. Mom and Dad came out from the kitchen, Dad in full male barbecue armor, with plastic apron and an impressive weaponry of implements. The front doorbell rang and Elin went to answer it.

And sister number three—Maddy—and her husband, John, were here, having at last managed to negotiate the trip from their car. They'd come around the side of the house and climbed the steps to the deck carrying two bulging diaper bags, some kind of squishy portable baby gym and a baby in a carrier.

Their baby. Their little girl. Tiny. Just a few weeks old. Jodie hadn't even known Maddy was pregnant. She'd only been told about baby Lucy after she was born—another questionable instance of Not Ready—and hadn't seen her yet, because Maddy and John lived in Cincinnati, two hours from Leighville, the Palmer family's Southern Ohio hometown.

"Oh, she's asleep!" Mom crooned. "Oh, what an angel! She already looks so much bigger than she did two weeks ago."

"Can we put her somewhere quiet?" Maddy asked.

But it was too late. The baby began to waken, stretch-

ing her little body in the cramped space of the car carrier and letting out a keening cry.

"Oh, she needs a feed," Maddy said. "Where shall I
go?"

"Not here," Dad said. He was a traditional man, with
a passion for woodworking and gadgetry. In his world,
feeding and diaper changes didn't belong in the same
space as a barbecue.

"You wouldn't believe how difficult it was just to get
here, all the gear we had to bring. John, can you set up
some pillows for me in…? Oh, where!"

"My room," Jodie said quickly. "There's a heap of
pillows, and fresh flowers, and a rocking chair."

"Oops, I'm going to have to change her first.…" But
John had already gone to ready the room. Maddy held
Lucy with the baby's legs awkwardly dangling and
her little face screwed up as she screamed, and looked
around for the diaper bag. "She's in a mess. Oh, I'm not
good at any of this yet! Where's the monitor? We'll need
it if she naps. I have no idea if she will. And when she
cries like this… First baby at thirty-six, people do say
it's harder."

"Here, don't worry, it's fine." Of all people, it was
Dev who stepped forward and took the crying baby. He
cradled her against his shoulder and commenced a kind
of rocking sway and a rhythmic soothing sound. "Shh-
sh, shh-sh, it's okay, Mommy's coming in a minute, shh-
sh, shh-sh." Jodie felt a strange, unwanted tingling in
her breasts and a familiar yearning in her heart. Why
did he do this to her when she tried so hard to stay sensible? How could he possibly look so confident and so
good, holding a poop-stained baby? Why was he still
in Ohio, and not back in New York?

She had a vivid flashback, suddenly, to the first night

they'd made love. Bed on the first date. You weren't supposed to do that, if you were a female with a warm heart, but of course it hadn't felt like the first date. She'd known Dev since she was sixteen, and she'd responded to him with half a lifetime of pent-up feeling—to his hands so right on her body, to his voice so familiar in her ear.

"Thank you, Dev!" Maddy unzipped the diaper bag and rummaged around inside. She didn't seem surprised that Devlin had taken control, but Jodie was.

Not about the control, but about the thing he was in control *of.* If you were talking legal contracts or high finance or building plans, team sports, political wrangling, then, yes, Devlin Browne could take control in a heartbeat. Would always take control. But when it was a *baby?*

What did he know about babies?

*He doesn't even want kids.*

The thought came out of nowhere, one of the memories from before the accident that her brain threw out apparently at random. "Did I have amnesia?" Jodie had asked at one point.

"Not like in the movies," they—her doctors and therapists—had said. "But of course there are some gaps. Many of them you'll eventually fill in. Some you never will."

"Like the accident itself?"

"Yes, it's quite probable you'll never remember that."

But she remembered that Dev didn't want kids.

*How* did she remember that?

She searched her mind, watching him as he gently bounced the baby on his shoulder. He wore jeans and a gray polo shirt with black trim, filling the clothing with a body honed by running and wilderness sports. The fabric of the jeans pulled tightly across his thighs, and the sleeve-band of the polo shirt was tight, too. There was some impressive muscle mass there, and Jodie's fingers remembered it, even while she was trying to remember the other thing—the thing about him not wanting kids.

If he didn't want kids, how could he school all that male strength into the tender touch and soft rhythm needed to soothe a newborn baby? When Maddy was ready, he handed Lucy over to her, and casually warned, "Watch the wet patch on her back."

But he didn't want any of his own…

Okay, it was over dinner, she remembered. They'd been out together—and slept together, heaven help her—three times since his temporary return to Leighville. As far as Jodie's family were concerned, she and Dev had only been dipping their toes in the waters of the great big dating lake.

To her, though, it immediately felt deeper. She'd had a major crush on him at sixteen when he'd briefly dated one of her good friends before he—Dev—had left for college in Chicago a couple of months later. Turned out the crush had never really gone away.

She couldn't track back to how the subject of kids had come up that night. Maybe something to do with his restless lifestyle. He was based in New York these days, but his work in international law took him all over the world—three months in London, a summer in Prague. He'd only come home for a couple of months last fall to take over his father's small-town legal practice on a temporary basis while Mac Browne had heart surgery.

Okay, so she might possibly have asked Dev, over their meal, if he ever intended to settle down.

He'd probably said no, he didn't. The I-have-nothing-to-offer thing, again.

And then he'd definitely—twenty seconds or five minutes later—said that he didn't want kids. Fatherhood didn't fit with his plans.

Which was fine, she'd thought, because he was only in town for a short while, and she'd only gone into this dating thing so she could finally get a thirteen-year crush well and truly out of her system and then wave him goodbye. A big grin, and no regrets.

Or not.

*If I sleep with him, he'll break my heart when he leaves,* she'd thought back then. *And if I don't sleep with him, he'll* still *break my heart when he leaves....*

But that was last October, and he was still here. The accident would explain part of it. October eighth, the two of them driving home after dark from date number four, a fall hike in Hocking Hills followed by dinner, when a driver in an oncoming car had lost control around a bend. Devlin had broken his leg in three places and had a permanent metal plate in there, but he didn't even walk with a limp at this point, so shouldn't he be safely back in New York or in a hotel room in Geneva by now?

Instead he was standing here on her parents' summer deck sharing a joke with her dad, throwing up his head when he laughed, shirt fabric pulling across his broad shoulders when he raised a beer can to his lips, reminding her far too strongly that she hadn't remotely gotten the crush out of her system last fall, or during the nine months of coma and rehab since.

He'd come to visit her in the hospital five times since she'd woken up, seen her at her most vulnerable, in tears and struggling to move and speak, fighting her own uncooperative body. He'd been so supportive, but cautious at the same time, never talking about anything too personal, and she had no idea what it all meant. Her brain still felt scrambled, tired, and life was a jigsaw puzzle with too many pieces missing.

"Is she out here? How is she?" This was Jodie's Aunt Stephanie, following Elin out to the deck. Seemed as if *everyone* had been invited today. Jodie began to feel overwhelmed and more than a little tired. She'd been discharged from the nearby rehab unit yesterday, and would still be attending day therapy sessions there for a while. She'd spent just one night, so far, in her own precious bed.

"Jodie…!" Aunt Stephanie said, and leaned down to hug her.

Dad put hot dogs and burgers and steaks onto the barbecue grill. Lisa brought out bowls of salad. Lisa's husband, Chris, took a soccer ball onto the grass beyond the deck and began kicking it back and forth with a handful of kids. Everyone talked and laughed and caught up on family news.

Maddy came down with Lucy wide awake and contentedly milk-filled in her arms, and Jodie asked her on an impulse, "Can I have a hold? If you put a pillow under my left arm, so I don't have to use any muscle?"

She felt a strange yearning and a rush of emotion that she didn't remember feeling for her other nieces and nephews when they were newborn. Well, she'd only been in her early twenties then, not ready to think about babies. Lisa's youngest was seven years old.

"Do you want to, honey?" Mom asked, in a slightly odd voice. "Hold her?"

"Yes, didn't I just ask?"

"Quick, someone grab a pillow from the couch,"

Mom ordered urgently, as if baby Lucy were a grenade with the pin pulled and would explode if Jodie didn't have her nestled on a pillow in the next five seconds.

"John?" Maddy said, in the same tone.

"Coming right up." He ran so fast for the pillow Jodie expected him to come back breathless.

*Sheesh*, she thought, *I could probably ask for a metallic gold European sports car convertible with red leather seats right now, and there'd be one in the driveway by the end of the afternoon. You know, I should definitely go for that...*

Maddy stuffed the pillow between the arm of the chair and Jodie's elbow. "Now, just cradle her head here, Jodie. If you're not sure about this..."

"C'mon, Maddy, lighten up. I've held babies before. I've been holding them for years." Elin's eldest two were in their midteens.

"Yeah, but this is *my* baby," Maddy joked, in a slightly wobbly voice.

Okay, so it was a new-mother thing. Fair enough.

But there was that feeling in the air again, everyone seeming to hold their breath, everyone watching Jodie a little too closely. Mom, Lisa, Dev. Dev, especially, his body held so still he could have been made of bronze.

The accident. The coma. That was why.

When she was one hundred percent fit and well, would they finally stop?

"Shouldn't be such a fuss, should it?" Dad muttered from behind the barrier of the barbecue grill. No one took any notice.

Jodie held the baby, smelled the sweet, milky smell of her breath, the nutty scent of her pink baby scalp covered in a swirl of downy dark hair, and the hint of lavender in her stretchy cotton dress, from the special baby laundry detergent. Oh, she was so sweet, just adorable, and if everyone was staring at the two of them, well, that was fine and normal. It was one of the *rightest* sights in the world, a person tenderly holding a newborn child.

"Oh, you sweet, precious thing," she crooned. "Thank you for not crying for your auntie, little darling."

She bent forward and planted a kiss on the silky hair, and took in those sweet scents again, close to tears. As she straightened again, she could smell onions frying, too, the aroma unusually intense and satisfying, as if she'd never smelled frying onions before. Sometimes her brain reacted this way, since coming out of the coma. It was as if all her senses had been reborn.

And then suddenly they hit overload, like little Lucy hitting overload when she was due for her nap.

"Can you have her, Maddy? My arms are getting tired."

"You did great," Maddy said, and too many people echoed the praise. Dev growled it half under his breath.

But maybe they were right. She felt wiped. Dev leaned toward her. "Are you okay?"

"Need some lunch."

"Just that?"

"Well, tired…"

Baby Lucy yawned on her behalf, and Maddy murmured something about taking her upstairs.

"To Jodie's room," Mom said quickly. "Not in—"

"No, I know," Maddy answered, already halfway inside.

"But I definitely need lunch," Jodie admitted.

"Sit," Dev ordered. "I'll grab whatever you want." There was a tiny beat of hesitation. "You did great with the baby."

"So did you."

"Uh, yeah." A quick breath. "Hot dog with everything?"

"Please!" She managed the hot dog, covered in bright red ketchup and heaped with those delicious onions, managed replies to various questions from family members, and to a comment on the kids' soccer game from Dev, managed probably another half hour of sitting there—Maddy had come back downstairs with the baby monitor in her hand—and then she just couldn't hold it together, couldn't pretend anymore, guest of honor or not, and Dev said, "You need to rest. Right now."

Mom didn't quite get it. "Oh, but Devlin, it's her party! We've barely started!"

"Take a look at her."

Jodie tried to say, "I'm fine," but it came out on a croak.

"You're right, Devlin," Mom said. "Jodie, let's take you upstairs."

"But Lucy's asleep on her bed," Maddy said.

"Couch is okay," Jodie replied. "Nice to hear everyone talking." She joked, "I mean, it is my party."

"Here," said Dev, the way he'd said it to Maddy over an hour ago, about baby Lucy. He helped her up and she leaned on him, and he smelled to her baby-new nose like pine woods and warm grain and sizzling steak. He didn't pass her the walking frame, just said, "Don't worry, I've got you," and she found that he did. He was so much better than the frame, so much more solid and warm, with his chest shoring up her shoulder and his chin grazing her hair. Her heart wanted to stay this close to him for hours, but the rest of her body wouldn't co-operate.

They reached the couch and he plumped up the

silk-covered cushions, grabbed the unfinished hand-stitched quilt top her mother was working on, tucked it around her like a three-hundred thread-count cotton sheet and ordered, "Rest."

"I will."

"I'll leave your frame here within reach, if you need to get up."

"Thank you, Dev." She'd already closed her eyes, so she wasn't sure that he'd touched her. She thought he had, with the brush of his fingertips over her hair, but maybe it was just a drift of air from his movement. She didn't want to open her eyes to find out, or to discover he'd gone. Touch or air, she could feel it to her bones.

He must have gone. She hadn't heard his footsteps on the carpet, but now there was that sense of quiet.

*Sleepy* quiet.

In the kitchen, making coffee and cutting cake, Elin said, in a voice that wasn't nearly as soft as she thought, "I don't think she was ready for this many people so soon."

"It's just family," answered Lisa.

"It's a big family," Maddy pointed out.

"Mom wanted a celebration for her coming home." Lisa again.

"We should have waited a week or two for that." Elin.

"But by then…" Maddy.

"I know. I know." Elin sighed.

Jodie shut all of it out, the way she'd learned to shut out the noise and the interruptions in the hospital and rehab unit, and drifted into sleep. When she woke up again, her sisters were still in the kitchen.

No, she amended to herself, in the kitchen *again*.

They were cleaning up this time, and the way they were talking made it clear that most people had gone, including Maddy, Lucy and John. She must have slept for a couple of hours, and the house had grown hotter with windows and deck doors open. Was Dev still here? She could hear the vigorous, metallic sound of Dad cleaning off the barbecue out on the deck, and Elin and Chris's kids still playing in the yard, but no Dev.

She felt refreshed but stiff-limbed. Here was the walking frame within reach, just as Dev had promised. She twisted to a sitting position, inched forward on the couch and pulled herself up, automatically comparing her strength to yesterday, and a week ago, and a week before that.

Better.

*I'm getting better.*

Her therapists had told her it would come with work and so far today she hadn't done any work, just a few range of motion exercises for her hands and arms this morning.

Time for a walk.

She called out to her sisters in the kitchen, to tell them what she was doing, and Elin appeared. "You're sure?"

"I'm supposed to, now, as much as I feel like. I'll only go around the block."

"Need company?"

"No!" It came out a little more sharply than she'd intended.

The Not Ready stuff drove her crazy. It had been driving her crazy for years.

Not ready to go for a walk on her own, in her own street, at three-thirty in the afternoon on the Fourth of July? Come on!

She'd once said to her three big sisters, long ago, "I'm littler 'n you *now,* but watch out 'cause I'm getting bigger!" and somehow she was still insisting on that message, twenty-something years later, even though, thanks to a serious childhood illness at the age of five that had apparently scared the pants off of the entire family permanently, she never had caught up to them size-wise and was the smallest and shortest at size 4 and five foot three. But she didn't need the level of protectiveness they and her mother gave her. Why couldn't they see it?

Dad seemed to have an inkling, but he rarely interfered. She remembered just a handful of times. "Let her have horse-riding lessons, Barbara, for heck's sake!" he'd said to Mom when Jodie was seven. "It'll make her stronger." And then ten years later, "If she wants to work with horses as a career, then she should. She should follow her heart."

"No, thanks," she repeated to Elin more gently, because anger wasn't the way to go. "Send out a search party if I'm not back in forty-five minutes or so, okay? And I have my phone. You think anyone in Leighville is going to look the other way if they find someone collapsed on the sidewalk in front of their house?"

"You sure?"

"I'm sure, Elin. You can help me down the front steps, is all."

It felt so good, once Elin had gone back inside. To be on her own, but not alone in a hospital rehab bed. To be out in the warm, fresh day, with no one watching over her, or telling her, "Yes! You can do it!" with far too much encouragement and enthusiasm, every time she put one step in front of another.

*I could walk for miles!*

No, okay, not *miles*, let's be realistic, here.

But maybe more than just around the block. She had

the frame for support. It would be slow going, concentration still required for every step, and the afternoon heat had grown sticky, but she'd never been a quitter. There'd be a garden wall or park bench to sit on if she was tired. There were all those neighbors looking out for her, knowing about the accident and that she had just come home.

She could walk to Dev's.

Or rather, Dev's parents'. He'd mentioned today that he was living there for the time being, just a throwaway line that she hadn't thought about at the time because she'd been fighting the sense of fatigue and overload, but now it came back to her.

And it didn't make sense.

Why was Dev living at his parents' place, even as a temporary thing? Jodie was living with hers because of the accident, but that was different. Why was he still here in Leighville at all, when she had such a strong memory from nine months ago, of his insistence that he planned to return to New York as soon as he could?

It had something to do with her, with the accident, she was sure of it, and if her family had somehow roped him into the whole let's-protect-Jodie-till-she-can't-breathe-on-her-own scenario, then damn it, he had to be stopped. He had to be told.

*I don't need it, Devlin. I don't want it. Not from you or from anyone else.*

She was definitely walking to Dev's, and they were going to talk.

## Chapter Two

"Shh-sh," Dev crooned, bouncing the baby gently against his shoulder. "Shh-sh."

It did no good. His rhythmic sway and soothing sounds had had more success with baby Lucy today than they were having now with his own child, in his own house. He'd heard her screaming as he came up the front path, and the sitter had met him at the door, looking harassed and more than ready to go home.

"I'm sorry, Mr. Browne, she just won't settle."

He'd taken the baby, paid the sitter, tried everything he knew in the hour since, but DJ was still crying. He knew from experience—over two months of it, since she'd come home from the hospital—that she would settle eventually, that it wasn't anything serious or horrible, just colic, but it wasn't fun to hear her crying and to feel so helpless.

Dev didn't *do* helpless.

He'd sent his parents off to their vacation condo in Florida three weeks ago with a sigh of relief. Both the Brownes and the Palmers were acting way too protective of everyone involved, since his and Jodie's accident nine months ago. He often suspected that the Palmers would take DJ from him completely, if they could. Maybe he should take them up on that, relinquish custody and go back to New York.

But his heart rebelled at this idea, the way it often rebelled at the suffocating level of Palmer helpfulness. Jodie's mother and her two sisters here in Leighville seized on his need for babysitting too eagerly, he felt, trading on their combined experience of child-raising and his own helplessness. His parents had been taking a hand at it, too, but seemed suspicious that he was somehow being exploited, that Jodie had trapped him into this situation.

Which was ridiculous, since she didn't even know about it.

Today, despite his misgivings about the attitudes of both Palmers and Brownes, he could have done with some family help, but it wasn't possible, the way things stood. He was supposed to keep the baby safely away from the Palmer house.

Keep her away until Tuesday, the day after tomorrow, when Jodie had her appointment with doctors and therapists and counselors.

Zero hour.

His stomach kicked.

How did you prepare for something like that? He and the Palmers had been politely fighting about it for several weeks. The Palmers thought she still wasn't ready, while Dev couldn't handle the covering up, the distortions, the silence, even though he often dreaded what might happen once Jodie knew.

Doctor-patient ethics had become more of a concern with every step forward in Jodie's difficult recovery. There was an insistence now that she had the right to be told, and that she was strong enough, so the moment of revelation had been fixed for ten o'clock Tuesday morning.

What would she want? Where would he fit? Would she understand how much he loved this baby girl, this surprise package in both their lives? He felt an increasing need to know how it would all pan out—he hated uncertainty, and not knowing where he stood—but there was a lot to get through first. For a start, how did you say it?

*Jodie, you need to know at this point that while you were in the coma state...*

DJ wailed and shuddered in his ear, but maybe it was easing now. Was she too hot? Dev preferred open windows and the chance of a breeze to the shut-in feeling of an air-conditioned cocoon, but what would be best for the baby? He rocked her a little harder and she seemed to relax into his shoulder, her sweet, milky breath soft on his neck.

He loved her more than he'd imagined possible, and he had no idea what this was going to mean, once Jodie was told.

"Stop crying, sweetheart. That's right. Settle down, it's okay. Is your tummy still hurting? Not so much now, hey? Not so much…"

*How did this happen to me?*

Nine months ago he'd been enjoying a hot fling, ground rules fully in place, with a warm, funny and surprisingly gutsy woman, who'd turned his temporary return to Southern Ohio from an act of duty into an unexpected pleasure.

Thanks to Jodie, he'd stopped seeing a slow-paced backwater town and started seeing the beauty of the changing landscape in the fall. Instead of feeling the suffocation of routine, he'd felt the sinewy strength of family ties. He'd rediscovered the pleasure of a good laugh, of collecting the morning newspaper from the front yard while the grass was wet with dew, of hearing rain or birdsong outside his window instead of city noise.

But it was just an interlude. They both knew it. He'd said it to her direct, because he didn't want the risk of her getting hurt.

Even after the accident, he'd at first only planned to stay until his leg was put back together and healed. Jodie had family here. She wouldn't be on her own, whether she stayed in a coma state or made a full recovery. He didn't belong at her bedside, keeping vigil, the way her parents and sisters had.

But then…

DJ went through another spasm of pain and stiffened and screamed harder in his arms. "Ah, sweetheart, ah, honey-girl, it'll stop soon." He rocked her and massaged her little gut with the pad of his thumb.

*How did this happen to me?*

And what would change, come Tuesday?

Everything.

"Everything, baby girl," he murmured. Hell, he was so scared about it!

The knock at his front door startled him a few minutes later, the brass rapper hitting the plate unevenly, a couple of strong, jerky taps and then a weaker one. With DJ still in his arms, her crying beginning to settle to a kind of shuddery grumble, he went to see who was there, and when he saw Jodie standing there, he knew he didn't have until ten o'clock Tuesday anymore.

Zero hour was now.

The baby wasn't Lucy.

Jodie worked that out in around forty seconds, as she and Dev both stood frozen on either side of the threshold.

The baby wasn't Lucy, because Lucy belonged to Maddy and John, and had gone home with them to Cincinnati, and was smaller and newer than this little thing.

This little thing clearly belonged to Dev, and explained exactly why his crooning and shushing and swaying on Mom and Dad's back deck had been so effective earlier today. He'd had practice. Recent practice, and a lot of it.

"You'd better come in," he said heavily, after standing there in what appeared to be a frozen moment of shock. Jodie was pretty shocked herself. "I think she's going to sleep," he added. "You're not catching her at the best time. I wish you could see her smiling, the way she's been doing the past month."

"It's a girl?"

"Yes."

"What's her name?"

"I…uh…I call her DJ."

"DJ," she echoed blankly. He *called* her DJ. But it wasn't her name?

"You look like you need to sit. Shoot, of course you need to sit."

"Yes. I do." She hadn't realized it herself until now, despite her shaky hand on the heavy door knocker, but, yes, her legs had turned pretty shaky, too, and the frame wasn't giving enough support. She had no idea what was happening, here.

Dev had a baby.

He absolutely, one hundred percent *had...a...baby.*

He had a cloth thrown over his shoulder to catch the spit-up, and a hand cradling the baby's little diaper-padded butt as if it grew there, and a puffy rectangle of baby quilt in the middle of the floor, with a baby gym arched over it, like the one Maddy and John had brought to Mom and Dad's today for Lucy, even though their three-week-old infant could hardly be expected to play with such a thing.

This baby was definitely older. Dev had just mentioned she'd been smiling for the past month, and Jodie had enough nieces and nephews, thanks to all of Elin and Lisa's kids, that she knew when smiling happened—six weeks or so. This baby, small though she was, had to be getting on for about ten weeks old.

Do the math, Jodie, do the math. Nine months plus two and a half equals almost a year. When you were busy "getting the old crush out of your system," last fall, the mother of Dev's baby must already have been pregnant....

But where was the mother now? *Who* was the mother?

"Here. Sit here," Dev said, after she'd made her way inside. It was a pretty house, but the décor was too frilly and fussy for a man like Dev, with lace and florals and porcelain knickknacks everywhere. His mother's taste. "I'll take the frame. Do you want coffee, or something?"

"No. I— No, I'm fine."

"Look, it's obvious we need to talk. Let me get you something."

"Is—? Who else is around?"

"No one. My parents are in Florida. They have a condo there. I made them go."

"You *made* them?"

"Don't you sometimes feel…haven't you felt, these past few weeks, as if sometimes there's just too much family?"

"Ohh, yeah!"

*That* she could relate to.

But the baby…

DJ had fallen asleep on Dev's shoulder. "Hang on a sec," he muttered, and picked up a roomy piece of cloth that turned out to be a baby sling. He draped it across his shoulder, tucked the baby inside and stood there, still swaying gently. "If I put her down now, she'll just wake up again," he explained. "She needs to go a little deeper before it's safe."

"You're very good at it."

"Yeah…not really. I'm getting there. I have a who-o-ole heap of help."

A heavy silence fell, during which the obvious reference to DJ's mother wasn't made.

Dev said nothing about her.

Jodie didn't want to ask.

"She's adorable," she said instead, feeling woolly and wooden about it, wondering if she should be angry. Or hurt. Or just cheerful. *Wow, you have a baby, congratulations. You said you didn't want kids, but whoever the mom is obviously didn't get the memo.*

Unless of course…

Well, accidents happened. Baby-producing accidents, as well as ones that break legs in three places and put people into comas and necessitate the removal of spleens. Dev and some unknown woman had had a contraceptive "oops" roughly eleven months ago, and here was a baby, and her mom had probably just run to the store for diapers and milk. She and Jodie would meet each other any minute now.

"I can't take this in," she blurted.

"I don't blame you. Jodie, this was all set up for Tuesday. Does your family know you're here? They couldn't!"

"Oh, my family... Didn't you just ask me if I felt there was too much family? Well, there is! I said I was going for a walk and I didn't need company. I just told them around the block, and that if I wasn't back in forty-five minutes, send a search party. Coming here was an impulse."

"I'd better call your folks." He rocked the baby in his arms instinctively.

"It hasn't been forty-five minutes."

"You're going to be here for a while." He'd already picked up the phone and hit speed dial, as if the matter was urgent.

*He has my parents on speed dial,* she registered. But she liked his directness, the decisive way he moved. It was reassuring, somehow. Dependable.

He spoke a moment later. "Hi, Barb?" Barb was Mom. "Just letting you know, Jodie's here.... Nope, not my idea... No choice, at this point... I can't argue it now, you have to trust me.... Of course I will... No. Just me. Please... Yep, okay, talk soon."

"What was that about, Dev?" She tried to stand up, but her legs wouldn't cooperate. The walk had tired her more than she wanted.

"We've both said it. Too much family."

"Right."

"First, tell me why you came. I mean, what made you

think—? What gave you the idea—?" He broke off and swore beneath his breath. "Just tell me what made you come."

His difficulty in finding the right words made her flounder a little, and struggle for words herself. "I wanted to ask you…or to thank you, too, for coming to see me in the hospital those times."

"Just that?" He sounded cautious, looked watchful, as if waiting for a heck of a lot more.

"Well, and for—I don't know if I'm even the reason for this, or even *part* of the reason, but…not going back to New York when you planned."

"Hell, of course I wasn't going back to New York!"

She looked at him blankly and he understood something—something that *she* didn't understand at all, but she could see the dawn of realization in his face, while her body stopped belonging to her and belonged…somewhere else, to someone else.

It was a familiar feeling. Just the accident and her slow recovery? Or something more?

He was muttering under his breath. Curse words, some of them. And coaching. He was coaching himself. He sat down suddenly, in the armchair just across from the couch, with the sling-wrapped baby cradled in his arms, as if his legs had drained of their strength just like Jodie's had.

"*Pretend* I've just been in a coma for nearly nine months, Devlin," she said slowly. "Tell me anything you think I might not know. *Pretend* my family has a habit of shielding me from the most pointless things. And from the serious things, too. And tell me even the things you think I already do know. What did you mean, *set up for Tuesday?* What did you mean, *no choice at this point?* And this might be totally off-topic, but how is there a baby? And where is her mom?"

## Chapter Three

She doesn't know. She doesn't understand.

The realization kept cycling through Dev's head, paralyzing him. Hell, he hadn't wanted it to happen like this! He'd been so scared of the moment, sometimes—scared about what it would mean for his own bond with his baby girl. What if Jodie wanted the baby all to herself? What if he was suddenly shut out? He wasn't prepared to let that happen, but how tough would he be willing to get about custody and access, when Jodie's recovery was still so far from complete? What would be best for DJ?

He'd wanted to get the revelation over with, so that at least he would begin to know where he and DJ stood, but the timing had to be right. It had to be done in the right way.

With all the talk, the questions, the arguments back and forth between pretty much every member of the

Browne and Palmer families for weeks, the conjectures that maybe at some level she knew, and that some tiny thing might easily jog a memory, no one had considered that Jodie herself might be the one to determine when they broke the news.

Devlin had wanted her told sooner, and his parents had been on his side. The Palmers had wanted to wait, insisting she wasn't ready for such a massive revelation. The doctors, therapists and counselors wanted to respect the family's wishes, but had been growing more insistent with each stage in Jodie's improvement, after the setback of the serious infection she'd had just after DJ was born.

This was part of the problem. It had all happened in stages. It wasn't as if she'd just opened her eyes one day and said, "I'm back. Catch me up on what I've missed!"

All through the coma there had been signs of lightening awareness, giving hope for an eventual return to consciousness, but it had been so gradual. First, she followed movement around the room with her eyes, but couldn't speak. It seemed so strange that she could have her eyes open without real awareness, but apparently this was quite common, the doctors said.

Then her level of consciousness changed from "coma" to "minimally conscious state." She began to vocalize vague sounds, but had no words. She started to use words but not sentences. She began to move, but with no strength or control. For several days she cried a lot, asking repeatedly, "Where am I? What happened to me?"

Once she'd understood and accepted the accident and the need for therapy, she'd become utterly determined to make a full recovery and had worked incredibly hard. Every day, over and over, in her hospital room, in the occupational therapy room, or the rehab gym, they all heard, "Don't bother me with talking now, I'm working!"

Barbara Palmer began to say, about the baby, "Not until she's home," and her therapists cautiously agreed that, emotionally, this might be the right way to go. Let her focus on one thing at a time. Don't risk setting back her physical recovery with such a shock of news.

How did you say it?

How the hell was he going to say it now?

*You were five weeks pregnant at the time of the accident, it turns out, although we're almost certain you didn't know. You gave birth, a normal delivery, at thirty-three weeks of gestation, when your state was still defined as coma, just a week after you first opened your eyes. This is your beautiful, healthy baby girl.*

He said it.

Somehow.

Not anywhere near as fluently as it sounded in his head.

"Sh-she's yours…Jodie," he finally said, stumbling over every word. Yours? No! He wasn't going to sabotage his own involvement. "She's *ours*," he corrected quickly. "I didn't know what to call her. I thought you'd want to decide. So she's been DJ till now, because those are our two initials. Is that okay? Are you okay? This was supposed to happen on Tuesday, at your appointment, with your doctors and therapists and people on hand to answer all your questions. To—to help you deal with it."

The words sounded stupid to his own ears. *Deal with it.* Doctors and counselors could help someone *deal with* a cancer diagnosis, but this was in a whole different league.

Her eyes were huge in her face. She couldn't speak. She was slightly built, which made a stark show of her current shock and vulnerability. He remembered thinking her funny and gawky and oddly impressive when she was sixteen and he was eighteen, and dating her friend. Impressive because she looked as if a breath of wind would blow her away, but, boy, did she get on your case if you treated her that way.

She'd been just the same in the hospital and during rehab, once she could speak and move. She'd insisted on her own strength and her own will, and proved with every step that she was as strong and determined as she claimed. She fought her family on it all the time, because she was seven years younger than her next sister and she'd had a serious brush with meningitis as a child, and the whole clan had babied her ever since.

Well, for once she wasn't fighting or insisting. She was too shocked. He'd half expected a protest or a denial. *You're messing with my head. It can't be true.* But she didn't say anything like that. She believed him at once, which made him wonder if there was a tiny, elusive part of her brain, or a lacing of chemicals—hormones—in her body that had known the truth.

Her conscious mind, though, and her sense of self, had been completely in the dark.

"I have a thousand questions," she blurted out.

"Of course. Ask them. I'll tell you everything as straight as I can."

"I can't."

"Ask them?"

"Do this." She tried to stand up, but her legs wouldn't carry her.

"Sit," he insisted. "You don't have to say anything. Or do anything. Let me talk, if you want."

"Okay."

So he talked, keeping it a little impersonal because that felt safe, and leaving out a few things, because he couldn't hit her with all of it at once.

He told her about the signs of labor, the quick delivery they'd all been praying for, to ease the stress on her body. Told her DJ's length and birth weight and head circumference. Told her proudly that the baby had Jodie's own strength. Despite her premature birth, DJ had been stepped down from the NICU into the lower-level special-care unit within a couple of days, and had come home from the hospital in less than two weeks.

"Home?" Jodie croaked.

"Here. And your parents' place. She spends a lot of time there." More than he was happy with, to be honest, but he hadn't wanted to fight them on that at a point when Jodie's full recovery had still been very much in doubt, and when his own future wasn't fully resolved. Would she ever be able to take care of a child? If she could, did that mean he'd go back to New York?

"Why are you here? In Leighville?"

She was asking the wrong questions, wasn't she? He took in a breath to suggest this to her, but then changed his mind.

Ah, hell, there was no script for this! She should ask whatever she wanted to, in whatever order it came. And if she didn't have an instant, overpowering need to hold DJ in her arms, he should be glad of the reprieve. He couldn't stand the idea of losing his daughter, not even with generous custody and access, when the bond between them had grown so strong.

"I'm still working at Dad's law practice," he explained, trying to stay practical and calm. "He's in no hurry to get back into harness. I expect he'll decide to retire. I'll head back to New York… Well, that's open-ended at the moment. All decisions on hold, I guess. My apartment is rented out. I have a conference coming up in Sweden in early October, followed by a couple of months consulting in London."

"You were supposed to be back in New York by last Christmas. Was it your dad's health that changed your plans?"

Shoot, didn't she understand?

"They found out you were pregnant before I even had the plates put in my leg."

"How?"

"Blood tests, part of assessing your condition. When they told me…" Again, how to say it?

"You knew you had no other choice," she supplied for him.

He couldn't argue. Not the words, anyway. Maybe the edge of—what?—bitterness, or anger, in her tone. He *hadn't* had any other choice. Not then. He wasn't going to abandon his child before it was even born. He wasn't going to deprive her of a father, when she might never have a mom. But it was different now. "I don't want another choice," he said. "This all needs time to work out, and that's okay."

"You said you didn't plan on ever having kids."

"You remember that?"

"Over dinner. You had steak with pepper sauce. I had strawberry mousse cake for dessert."

"Shoot, you do remember!"

"Yes. It's like yesterday, that mousse cake." The sub-text of *explain yourself, Dev* was very clear. She wasn't really talking about dessert.

He said slowly, "What was it John Lennon once said?

'Life is what happens to you while you're busy making other plans.'"

"Or while you're in a coma," she drawled.

"Yeah, then, too."

Tentatively, they both smiled, and something kicked inside him. He had a couple of memories that were like yesterday to him, too. Her passion in bed, almost fierce, as if in lovemaking, too, she had to prove her own strength, had to fight against the wrong preconceptions. Her saucy grin when she undressed. And his ambivalence.

He really, seriously, hadn't known if it was a good idea to take her to bed that first time, even though she said she wanted it, and said she understood there was no long-term, and no promises, and that was fine. He'd told himself a couple of times their first night that he would stop kissing her soon, that he would reach out and still her hands if she went to pull off her clothes.

But then she'd done it. Crossed her arms over her chest and lifted her top to show a hot-pink bra and neat, tight breasts. Shimmied her way out of her skirt. Grinned at him.

And there'd been no question of stopping after that point. He'd used protection, but—not to get technical, or anything—maybe applied it just a little too late.

"But the dates don't fit," she said suddenly. "She's too old. She's smiling. Lucy isn't."

"Because DJ was premature," he explained again. "Healthy preemies learn to smile at the same age after birth as full-term babies, even if they're smaller and a little slower in other areas. DJ and Lucy would have been born within a week or two of each other, if DJ had come at the right time. The doctors say it's good that she didn't. It was easier on your body that she was little, and early. Would you like to hold her?"

He asked it before he thought. Blame Lucy for that. Jodie had looked so happy and comfortable holding her tiny niece today.

DJ was different. DJ had baggage.

Jodie stiffened and stammered. "No, she's—she's—N-not yet, when she's asleep. If I disturbed her and she cried…"

"It's fine. We'll transfer her in the sling. It'll be easy, I promise." Listen to him! Five minutes ago, he'd been scared about the strength of her maternal feelings and what they might do to his own connection with his child. Now he was trying to rush her into them. He didn't know what he wanted anymore.

Which was weird and unpleasant, because he *always* knew what he wanted.

Her weakened left hand made a claw shape on her thigh. "No. No, I can't. I just can't."

Jodie heard the note of panic in her own voice, but there was nothing she could do about it. The panic was there. She couldn't explain it to Dev. Couldn't even explain it to herself. But there was a huge, massive chasm of a difference between holding and clucking over Maddy's little Lucy and holding this baby.

*My baby. Half an hour ago, I didn't know she existed. But she's mine.*

It was overwhelming.

It should have been wonderful. A miracle.

*Dev loves her. I can see it.*

But it didn't feel wonderful, it felt terrifying.

*Thank heaven Dev loves her, because I don't.*

No. No! She had to love her own child! She did. Of course she did.

But why couldn't she feel it? Why wasn't it kicking in at once, the way it had with Elin and Lisa and Maddy and all the other normal mothers in the world, the very first moment they looked at their babies? Dev clearly expected it to, with his urging that DJ would be safe in her arms. It wasn't a question of safety. Why could she feel so tender toward Lucy today, and yet so distant and scared about this baby?

*Scared?* A surge of strength hit her. She wasn't in the habit of giving in to *scared*. She took in a breath to tell him that she would hold the baby after all. And she would have reached out her hands before the words came, except they were a little slow to respond to her brain's signal and she had to make an extra effort.

But before either the movement or the words could happen, Dev accepted her refusal, gave her an easy excuse. "You're tired," he said. He let out a breath that might have been partly relief, as if maybe he'd doubted the strength and coordination in her arms more than he'd let on. "We should wait a little."

She almost argued.

Almost.

But, oh, he was right, she was tired, and she'd tried so hard to stay on top of everything today. She let it go, and watched him tiptoe to the infant car carrier sitting in the corner of the living room and lay the baby down, easing his forearm out from beneath her little head with a movement so practiced and gentle it almost broke her heart.

"Very tired," she managed to respond. "I'm sorry."

*I'm so sorry, DJ.*

"Don't beat yourself up." The baby stirred a little, but didn't waken.

"I—I—" Did he know? Did he understand the extent of her panic?

"Let's take it slow. It's okay."

"Thanks. Yes."

She heard a car in the driveway, and footsteps and the voices of Elin and Mom. Dev lunged for the door before they could knock. He held it open and stood with the width of his body shielding the room from their view.

Mom said, "Is she still here?"

"Yes, but why are *you* here, Barb? I asked you very clearly to—"

"I'm sorry, we just couldn't— I'm sorry." This was Elin, clearly reading his anger. "We have a right to be involved in this, too, don't we? DJ is ours, too. We all care so much."

"You'd better come in."

"Thank you," said Mom, in a crisp voice.

"I really think it's best, Devlin." This was Elin, in a softer tone.

"We are as involved in all of this as you are." Mom again.

They dropped at once to sit on either side of Jodie on the couch, their voices running over her along with their hands, all of it a jumble that she heard at two steps removed, like recorded voices or lines from a half-remembered play. *Honey, are you okay? Obviously you know. Obviously there's so much to talk through. That's why we wanted to wait until you were ready. What has Dev said, so far?*

"You barely gave me time to say anything," he said.

"Listen, it's not as if any of us have had any experience with a situation like this, Devlin," Elin said.

"Shh…keep your voice down, can you?"

"Sorry…sorry." Elin glanced over at the baby and looked surprised. "You have her in the car carrier?"

"She seems to sleep better in there, during the day."

"Well, then, I guess…" *But I never did that with my babies,* was the implication.

"She's fine. She wouldn't sleep so peacefully if she was uncomfortable there."

"If you say so."

Both Devlin and Elin were holding it together with difficulty, and Mom looked trapped and unhappy, her mouth open as if she wanted to speak, although no words came.

Jodie slumped against the back of the couch. She'd started to shake. Could they feel it? She felt more tired than she'd ever felt in her life, and her lips had gone dry. She closed her eyes, willing this chaos of family and tension and questioning to…just…stop.

"Should we take her? Jodie, are you ready to go home?"

She opened her eyes. "Yes, take her."

*I mean, who is she? How can she even exist?*

"I—I don't know what I want to do," she blurted. "I think I need some space. Another nap." Her own bed seemed like the safest haven in the world.

There was a small silence, while Elin and Mom and Devlin all looked at each other, shrugged and raised eyebrows and gestured—body language that was beyond Jodie's ability to interpret right now.

"I guess that's an option," Dev said slowly to Elin and Mom. "For you to take her and Jodie to stay here."

"That's not—" *What I meant.* But the rest of it wouldn't come, and the first bit had come almost on a whisper, and they were too busy making plans to hear her.

"She should transfer to the car without waking," Dev said. "I have a couple of bottles made up in the fridge."

"We have bottles. We have diapers, clothes, everything. You know that. She's due for her bath."

"I'll drop Jodie home when she's ready. She's right. We need to talk. Have some space."

They'd worked it all out between the three of them, while Jodie was still struggling to lift an arm to brush a strand of damp hair from her eyes. She was staying here with Dev to talk. The baby was going back with Mom and Elin. Going back before she, the mother, had even touched her.

She wanted to argue the plan, but the words wouldn't come, so in the end she let it happen, and when the baby carrier was buckled into the car and Mom and Elin had driven away, she felt so relieved, and so ashamed of the relief, and so horribly, horribly tired. "I can't—" she said to Dev.

"I know you can't talk yet. Sleep first."

"Two naps a day. I'm like—" She stopped.

A baby.

*My baby.*

"Just rest."

"Why aren't you in New York? Tell me why. In simple words. Because it seems to me that you didn't have to still be here. Obviously DJ is being taken care of. Obviously she's loved. Obviously I have the support. So why?"

He looked at her steadily, with some of the anger he'd clearly felt toward Elin and Mom still simmering below the surface. He seemed to be thinking hard before he chose his words.

"Because she's my daughter." The last two words came out with a simmering intensity. "Because we're a family. You and me and DJ. Three of us. That's not negotiable. Three of us, not two."

"A family…" Jodie echoed foolishly, tasting the word and not feeling sure of how it felt in her mouth.

"Not a regular family, for sure."

"No…"

"But DJ needs a family of some kind.…" He paused for a moment, and she filled in the words he didn't say, in her head. *And not necessarily a whole cluster of over-involved grandparents and aunts.* "I'm right here in the picture and I'm not going to go away. And we have a heck of a lot to do and talk and think about, to decide how that's going to work."

## Chapter Four

Jodie woke to the smell of something delicious coming from Dev's kitchen. The daylight had begun to fade, which meant she must have slept a good three hours this time. She felt disoriented and not in full possession of either her body or her brain. It was just the way she'd felt coming out of the coma. It was like being in the eye of a hurricane—eerily quiet, with a sense of danger all around.

She gave herself a couple of minutes to regroup, then sat up and eventually stood, steadier on her feet than she would have expected. As before, Dev had left her walking frame within reach, and the quiet, considerate nature of this small gesture almost brought her to tears.

She could hear him in the kitchen, chopping something on a wooden board. The delicious aroma announced itself as beef sizzled in a pan. She'd had a crush on him thirteen years ago, she'd slept with him three times, and she'd had no idea until now that he could cook. It didn't surprise her, though. When Devlin Browne put his mind to something…

He heard her—the rubbery tap of the frame on the floor—as she reached the kitchen doorway, and he turned. "Hi. Better?"

"Think so. It's crazy. To need all that sleep."

"Your brain is still healing."

"So I've been told."

"I'm making brain food. A beef-and-vegetable stir-fry, full of iron and vitamins."

"It smells great."

"Ready in a couple of minutes. Sit down." He nodded at the wooden kitchen table, then moved to pull out a chair for her.

"No, don't," she said quickly, taking one hand off the frame to reach for the chair herself. "I'm fine. I hate—" *my family hovering over me* "—too much help."

"Duly noted." He turned back to the stove, tossed in slivers of onion and red bell pepper, sticks of carrot and celery, lengths of green bean. The pan hissed and made a cloud of aromatic steam, filling the silence made by their lack of conversation.

He seemed to understand instinctively that she didn't want to talk yet—or not about anything important, anyway—and to her surprise the interlude of silence between them felt easy and right. She didn't have that uncomfortable itch to break the quiet with a rush of words that people often experience in the company of someone new.

Not that Dev was new.

But this felt new.

Untested.

*Three of us. We're a family,* he'd said.

Anything but the usual kind.

She watched him. Just couldn't help it. The way his neat, jeans-clad butt moved as he tossed the contents of the pan. The way his elbow stuck out and his shoulder lifted. He added the cooked meat and leaned back a little as another cloud of hissing steam came up. There was rice in a steamer on the countertop, and a jug of orange juice clinking with a thick layer of cubed ice.

Nine months ago, he hadn't wanted a serious relationship, but now it was as if she'd simply blinked and woken up to find herself here, in his kitchen, and the mother of his child.

Connected.

Yet not.

*Are we dating?*

She felt they needed to talk about it—for *hours* surely—but had no idea what to say, what to suggest. He was the one who'd had time to think. The surge of chemistry she'd felt earlier at the family barbecue couldn't compete with her shock and disorientation. It hummed in the background of her awareness, but she didn't know what to do with it, just wished it would go away.

"Is there a schedule?" she blurted out.

"A schedule?"

"Of who takes care of—of DJ."

*DJ. That's my baby's name. Well, it's not her name. It's what we're calling her in the interim.*

A crazy litany of baby names began to scroll in her head, the ones she'd vaguely thought, over the years, that she liked. Caroline, Amanda, Genevieve, Laura, Jessica, Megan, Anna… The idea that it might be up to her to make a decision, replace temporary DJ with something different and permanent that would belong to the baby her whole life, was daunting. A huge, confusing responsibility that she didn't feel equipped to handle.

"Your family has her when I'm at work," Devlin answered. "Mainly your mom. She's set up Elin's room for a nursery."

"That's why Lucy had to sleep in my room today." An image flashed in her head of her sister's old room with the door firmly closed. Even if she had seen inside, she would have assumed it had been set up for Maddy's baby girl.

"But Elin and Lisa have her sometimes, too. And then I pick her up on my way home."

"The night shift."

"That's right. I expect she'll spend more nights at your parents' place now." *Now that you're home,* he meant.

"That's why you look tired." A rush of tenderness and guilt ran through her. Those creases around his eyes, and she hadn't been here to help. Crazy to feel that it was her fault, and yet at some level she did. What kind of a mother slept through her whole pregnancy and didn't even waken to give birth? What kind of a mother had an eleven-week-old baby that she'd never touched and held?

He made a wry face. "Yeah, she's not exactly sleeping through. Your sisters have been great with that. They've stayed over here three or four times to give me a good night. Your whole family has been—" He stopped, as if the word he'd originally intended to say was wrong. "Amazing. They have. I was a little short with them before, and I shouldn't have been. The boundaries—the roles—are complicated."

"It's okay. I know how you feel. Just be thankful they're not trying to cut up your food."

He laughed and she smiled at him and then her breath caught, and the question she'd been asking in her head even before she'd found out about DJ came blurting out, "Are we dating, Dev?"

He went still. She just knew he was going to say no. It was there in his body language so clearly, and she wondered why on earth she'd thought it necessary to ask. Well. She hadn't thought. Her brain didn't seem to control either her body or her words anymore.

Eventually answered in a slow, careful way, "That's a question, isn't it?"

"I mean, I'm not suggesting you have a thing for unconscious women." The humor didn't work. It was too dark for a moment like this. It didn't evaporate the tension, as intended. She apologized. Seemed as if she might be doing a lot of that. "I'm sorry. I was just—"

"It's okay. Lightening the mood. You had a right to ask. I talked about making a family, just now."

"When you came to see me in the hospital, I didn't know why you were there. Because I didn't know about DJ. And last fall we…"

"I know." He was still so uncomfortable. They both were.

"I don't think we're dating," she said, before he could say it. "It would be crazy. It's not what we need. It would just be a complication. We have enough of those."

He nodded, and looked relieved. "You're right. I guess that's what I've felt. First things first. Take care of DJ. Take care of you. Take all of it slow. You're not strong enough to do much with a baby right now. We want to find a way to share her and love her. There's no hostility or conflict. I want to keep it that way. We *have* to keep it that way. I want as much involvement as I can have."

"But she'll be with me most of the time." Was it a question, or a statement? She didn't even know.

"Once you know her," he said. "Once you can take care of her. You're her mother and most of the time the baby stays with the mom. I'm accepting that."

*But am I?*

She saw herself stranded with baby DJ in her parents' house for weeks at a stretch with barely a break. She imagined the winter days closing in, keeping her and the baby inside the house, when normally even in the cold weather she loved to be outdoors.

These weren't the pictures she wanted to have of herself and her baby, but they were the ones that came. She heard herself wrangling and bickering with Mom about when to introduce solid food and whether to dress her in pink.

Dress her in pink…

She tried to picture it, and couldn't. At all. With a stab of horror she realized, *I don't remember what she looks like.* All she had were two vague images of a little face distorted with crying and then peaceful in sleep. Would she recognize her, beyond the familiarity of Dev's arms, or Mom's? Could she pull her own daughter out of a lineup?

Another bizarre image came to her. Police station. One-way glass. "Now, Ms, Palmer, look carefully at the numbered cribs. Do you see your baby here? It's very important that you make a correct identification."

But she couldn't…

"Dinner's up," Dev said. "I think we're— I'm glad we said this."

She tried to stand, to go over to the bench and help

him dish out the food, but her feet caught and she al-most fell. He was there just in time.

"He-e-ey. Who-o-oa." He caught her and folded his arms around her. "You didn't have to get up. I'm bring-ing it to you."

She felt his breath fanning her hair and his chin rest-ing on her shoulder, and could have stayed like this forever. She loved the way they fit together despite their mismatched size. She loved the smell of him, the strength of him, the honor and humor and decisiveness and brains. She loved the fact that he could hug her like this so soon after they'd agreed—the only thing they *could* agree on, in this situation—that they weren't dat-ing anymore.

It was just a hug, and yet if she just turned her face up, she was sure he would kiss her. The chemistry was still there, a deep pool of it, secret and still, magical and unspoken.

She wanted him to kiss her.

Desperately.

*Just kiss me, Dev, so I don't have to think. Just kiss me, so I know that part is okay, even if everything else isn't.*

*I don't care what we decided.*

*I don't care about sensible.*

*Kiss me and say, "Let's get married, and I'll take care of whatever you need," so that we can play by the rules and be a normal mommy and daddy and then maybe I'll feel as if I belong in my own life, instead of being just a visitor.*

"This is the most insane situation," he muttered. "I don't know what to tell you. Just take your time. That's all. We all need to give this time."

*Kiss me. Say it.*

*Shoot!*

This neediness, this wasn't *her!* *Jodie Palmer, don't you remember who you are? You've been fighting your whole life to show how strong you are, and now you're clinging to Dev as if he has all the answers and so you can just go with the flow?*

The familiar stubbornness kicked in. Maybe a little off-center, but at least it was there, and the feeling came as a huge relief. She pulled out of his arms and crisply said, "Thanks. You're right. We'll give it time. We'll work it out. Thank you. Mmm, that smells good!"

He steered her the few steps back to her seat then turned toward the stove, blinking as if he'd opened his eyes in bright light, and she was so happy that she'd held herself together. What if she had clung to him and expressed all that neediness?

He spooned rice into wide bowls and added a ladle of the hearty stir-fry, then placed the bowls on the table, and as they began to eat—it tasted so good!—she found something she wanted to ask him that didn't have the sense of dependency and need she so wanted to fight in herself. "The other driver, Dev. I—I haven't felt ready to ask until now. And you know my family wouldn't bring it up without direct questions."

"No, they wouldn't. We've had a couple of discussions about that, too."

"I bet you have!" She folded her mouth into an upside-down smile. "Who was it? Were they injured, too? He? She?"

"He."

"What happened?"

Dev put down his fork. "He wasn't badly hurt. You don't need to know anything about him."

"You don't sound too sympathetic. What went wrong?"

"He was driving over the limit."

"Speed or alcohol?"

"Both."

"Ah, okay. All bases covered, then. A fine upstanding citizen." She gave another twisted smile.

He shrugged and opened his palms. "Exactly."

"And where is he now?"

"Tried and convicted. All you need to know."

"It happened and it's over, and now we just live our lives. That's it, isn't it?"

"Is that what you really think?"

She paused with the fork halfway to her mouth. Most of the food fell off. She was still a little wobbly with her silverware control. "Yes. Don't you?"

"Yes, I do. I was a little concerned that you might feel differently."

"That I'd want a vendetta? Or that I'd brood and feel bitter?"

"Many people would." He was leaning toward her over the table, studying her the way he'd studied her several times today. She knew why. How was this going to work? How would baby DJ connect or divide them? What did they both want? Could they manage to keep this free of conflict and misunderstanding and hurt? Everything came back to that. Everything they said to each other gave a potential clue.

"Well, not me," she told him. "I just like to get back on the horse."

"Mmm," was all he said.

But she could see something in his face. Relief and approval. It was something they shared, this attitude to the accident and how to process it, and that was a plus.

In life, you have to play the hand you're dealt. She believed this, and so did he. You can't waste energy in "if only" and regret. You can't go looking for bitterness and revenge.

Especially when she had other things to think about.

Like a baby she didn't know she'd had.

Like a baby she wouldn't recognize in the street.

Too hard. Way too hard.

She felt a surge of restlessness and fight, a need for the physical movement that was still so challenging, and told him suddenly, "I seriously do want to get back on the horse."

"The real horse?" She'd caught his attention again. "You want to ride your horse again?" They were both making slow progress with their meal. "Your thoroughbred? He's leased out, since the accident, isn't he?"

"Leased out, to another rider, Bec, who's a good friend and who would give him back in a heartbeat. She lives out near Pictonville, on forty acres. I could go see him anytime. He's not sold."

She'd been so happy to discover this. Elin had told her, "Even though Mom's never been a fan of your riding, even in the darkest hours when we questioned how much you'd recover, she wouldn't hear of Irish being sold."

But now Dev said, "A spirited thoroughbred, Jodie? Twelve hundred pounds of muscle with a back higher than your shoulder?"

"Of course not yet," she said quickly. "Not him. I'd ride Snowy or Bess."

"Who are they? Are they quieter?"

"They're our hippotherapy horses, at Oakbank. They're trained for people like me, disabled riders and riders with special needs. You wouldn't believe how patient and understanding they are. They seem to know exactly what a rider is capable of, whether they have cerebral palsy or a missing limb or autism. I want to ride again. I need to ride. My life just can't change that much." She had to blink back tears, and was shocked at the way her emotions had shifted so fast. "Dev, I know this isn't what we should be talking about. We should be talking about…about DJ, but that's too big for me right now."

He reached across the table and covered her hand with his. "Nobody said we had to work everything out in one night."

"No. Okay. Good."

"Just eat. Talk about horses, if you want."

"I think I should go home after we eat."

"So I'll take you home."

"Thank you." She was tired of saying the words, but it seemed as if there were a thousand thank-yous she needed to give, and at least half of them belonged to Dev.

Jodie was quiet in the car, and Dev didn't push. It had been a huge day, for both of them.

Certain things stood out from the mess of conflicting emotions. First, the fact that she had never been given a real chance to hold DJ. He didn't know if that was his fault, if he should have made space for it—*forced* it—in the highly charged atmosphere between himself, Elin and Barb. Second, her wobbly little question about whether they were dating. Last fall seemed so long ago to him, but to her it must be so much fresher.

Those nights together. They were vivid and real for him if he thought about them, but too much had been overlaid since, and he didn't think about them often. He hadn't been in love with her last fall, and he couldn't have fallen in love with her during her long sleep. This wasn't Sleeping Beauty or Snow White.

There'd been desire in their relationship, yes…a ton of it. Care, even. But "in love" meant forever, and he couldn't see it, he wasn't open to it, not with anyone. It didn't fit with the way he saw himself and his life, and it never had.

He loved his parents. He admired them. They were good people. But marriage had made them so slow and staid. They never left their comfort zone. They never seemed to want newness or adventure or zest. His mother said it to him sometimes, with a combination of smugness and resignation. "You'll feel differently when you're married.… You won't care about those things when you're married with a family."

He'd seen it with most of his married friends, too. They began eating at the same restaurant every week. "They do such a good veal parmigiano." They didn't renew their passport when it expired. "We won't really travel until the kids are in college. Well, Orlando, of course, for the theme parks."

If marriage meant losing the capacity for curiosity and courage and adventure, he didn't want it. He'd decided this at twenty and nothing had yet happened to make him change his mind.

Not even DJ, because how would it be good for her, to submit to an institution he didn't want to belong to, purely for her sake?

All he wanted was to know that she was loved, so he could get his own life back on track and stop existing in this limbo of uncertainty.

He wondered what would be happening at the Palmer house. When he pulled into the driveway there was no visible light in DJ's room. The night-light would be too dim to show from the street. Was she down for the night? Should he take her home?

Jodie hadn't even touched her yet. Had he been wrong to let Barb and Elin whisk the baby back here? Should he have just ordered them to leave? He didn't want the conflict that came with their differing interpretations of what Jodie needed. He wanted to see the bond between Jodie and DJ, but he was scared of it, too.

Scared of its potential power.

He jumped out of the car and came around to open her door and help her out. For a moment, she looked as if she might protest, but she was clearly too tired to manage on her own. The doctors and therapists had said it would be like this. The difference between what she could manage when she was fresh and what she could manage when she was fatigued might be huge at first.

Sure enough, her body looked heartbreakingly awkward and frail in the passenger seat, and after several seconds of intense, futile effort, she told him, "I can't."

He bent down. Slid his arm beneath hers and around her shoulders. "Hold on."

But she couldn't do that, either.

"I'll carry you."

"Dev, no, I'm—"

"You're wiped."

He shifted position, one arm coming beneath her thighs. It was incredibly awkward, and if she hadn't been such a featherweight, he couldn't have managed it. Once he'd straightened, it was much easier. She laid her head against his shoulder, with her hip pressing into his stomach, and he felt this surge of tenderness and confusion and determination.

Somehow… *Somehow…*

Somehow, what?

What did he have the power to do? To make her get better? To make her come to the right decisions about her future? What were they?

"You can put me down now."

"I'm fine. You don't weigh much."

"Please." There was an insistence to it, the old stubbornness about her size and strength that had made him smile and piqued his interest at eighteen. How did such a small body house such a strong spirit?

Gently, he let her down, still holding her firmly until they both knew that her feet would carry her weight. They did, but there wasn't a whole lot of margin for error. "I'll need to lean," she said.

"Leaning is fine." Leaning was *too* fine, really. He liked touching her too much, felt too connected to the scent and softness of her skin. He had to fight to keep his awareness under control, with the slight weight of her breasts just above his hand and her silky fall of blond hair in kissing distance.

They'd agreed on this. They weren't dating. There was no place for this helpless attraction. Just imagine if they had a flaming purely-for-the-sex affair and then parted in conflict and anger. It happened all too often. Sex didn't solve anything. It had too much of an agenda of its own.

And where would that leave him? Shut out of DJ's life forever? Or limited to a hard-won weekend visit every three months, exchanging her back and forth in the parking lot of a service-plaza fast-food restaurant halfway between here and New York as if she were a packet of cocaine? Meeting her at the airport, once she was old enough, and discovering she'd become a school kid or an adolescent or an adult since they'd last met?

No. It wouldn't be enough. No!

He wasn't going to be forced back to New York by the sheer strength of Palmer will.

Barbara Palmer stood in the open doorway, having heard the car. She looked watchful and anxious, as if expecting them to have covered major mileage tonight in their talks about the future.

They hadn't.

They'd barely talked about DJ at all. More about horses, in fact. And no matter how much Dev told himself to go with what Jodie needed, to give her time and space, it worried him a little. He didn't want to lose his daughter to her mother, but he wanted her mother to love her. Anything else was unthinkable.

"Did you have a good evening, honey?" Barb said to Jodie.

She thumbed cheekily in his direction. "I never knew he could cook."

"Are you okay? You look—"

"Tired. Of course. But I'm fine." She managed the steps into the house. In some ways she was better on steps than on the flat ground. "I think I'll go up right away."

"She's asleep," Barb said.

But Jodie hadn't been talking about seeing DJ. From the side, Dev saw the little look of fright and reluctance on her face and said quickly, "We'll take a look at her, though, Barb." He still had his arm around Jodie's body and could feel her stiffen and flinch.

Barb had seen nothing, it seemed. She began, "You're not going to—?"

"No, I'll leave her here for the night," he reassured her, "if that's okay."

"Of course it is! Of course you shouldn't wake her and move her!"

"But we'll take a look, make sure she hasn't kicked off her covers." He pretended he couldn't tell that Jodie didn't want to.

Why didn't she?

Well, the hugeness of it. It made sense, maybe. She just needed that first bit of ice broken, that first sense of confidence in her new role, that was all. Maybe right now, if they just went into the baby's room together and watched her sleeping, something in her heart would open and settle.

He didn't give her a choice, just took her with him, helping her up the stairs, opening the door of Elin's old room, which was as familiar to him now as if it had once been his. Beside him, he heard Jodie's quick, shaky intake of breath, as if Elin's door was the gateway to a whole new kingdom.

## Chapter Five

Mom had used Elin's room as a sewing den for years but hadn't redecorated since Elin moved out. In Jodie's memory, the walls were still painted a defiant, brooding purple and were covered in posters of Elin's teen heartthrobs—John Cusack, Michael J. Fox and Johnny Depp. Actually, Elin in her teens had had pretty good taste.

Now, though…

There was a ballerina night-light plugged into the socket low on the wall beside the crib, Jodie saw. It gave off a quiet, pinkish light, revealing a room utterly different to the one she'd always known. Gone were the purple and posters, to be replaced by walls of a soft golden yellow with a theme of ducks and daisies in the scattered groupings of toys and decorations. There was a crib made of blond wood, with linens of white *broderie anglaise* cotton, a white closet, chest of drawers and shelves, and in just a couple of places there were color accents in a light sage-green.

On the chest of drawers sat the baby monitor, its glowing light showing that it was switched on. But there was nothing to hear. Baby DJ was fast asleep.

Dev went across to her as if drawn like a magnet, his feet incredibly soft on the polished hardwood floor, a grin breaking onto his face in a way that told Jodie he didn't even know it was there. He had Jodie's hand trapped—not trapped, *held*—in his, so she had no choice but to go with him. He leaned over the crib and didn't say a word, just gazed, and Jodie's heart began to thump and her throat tightened, and the baby...the baby...

Didn't belong to her.

Was gorgeous, an angel, a sweetheart, a darling.

A stranger, when she should have been Jodie's whole world.

She knew this, because she'd seen it just today with Maddy and Lucy. Beyond the new-mother panic, or as a *part* of the new-mother panic, Maddy had been utterly mesmerized by Lucy, utterly in love with her. The way Elin had been with her firstborn, and her second and third. The way Lisa had been with hers.

Transformed.

Mothers to their bones.

The way Dev was already a father to his bones. A daddy. DJ's daddy. "Isn't she beautiful?" he whispered, as if he couldn't keep back the words.

"Yes. Yes, she is." She learned the baby's little face off by heart—the button of a nose, the plump cheeks—and thought, *at least I'll recognize her now...*

"I'm sure she won't wake up if you touch her."

"How? Where? I mean, I really don't want to wake her up."

"You won't. Anywhere."

*Where would I touch her if she belonged to me?*

Jodie didn't know. She reached out her hand, and felt Dev holding her tight as if he knew she might otherwise fall. She thought she might put her hand on DJ's head, to see if her hair felt as silky as Lucy's, but it didn't feel right. It felt...

Not her head.

She laid her palm on the baby's back, instead. She was sleeping on her side, propped in that position with two little baby quilts rolled up, so Jodie had to slip her fingers between the roll and the stretchy fabric of DJ's miniature pink sleep suit.

"She's breathing, I promise," Dev said.

"Oh, I wasn't— I was just—"

"It's okay. I didn't mean— It's okay. I check that she's breathing all the time."

But she didn't feel as if it was okay, and took her hand away. She wasn't strong enough to keep her arm in that position for long anyhow. It would start to disobey the signal from her brain pretty soon and just flop.

Flop onto DJ and wake her up.

Mom was hovering outside, peering around the door, which Dev had left ajar. "I thought about putting the monitor in your room, honey, but that's probably not a good idea just yet," she said in a kind of stage whisper as Jodie and Dev came out. "It would be hard for you to get out of bed quick enough to go to her."

*Would I need to go to her that fast?* Jodie wondered. Do all normal moms leap out of bed the second they hear the first tiny cry? What about in the dark, ancient days before baby monitors were invented? How fast did moms get to their babies back then?

She could argue the issue. She could insist on Mom letting her have the monitor.

Dev had gone watchful again, but she hid her panic, made it about common sense instead. "Yes, you'd better have it, Mom. I'd hate to…you know…" She indicated the common-sense issues with a flap of her fingers.

*I'd hate to only reach her after that big spotty monster hiding under her crib had already drooled all over her. I'd hate no one to get there in time to catch her reciting Shakespeare in her sleep.*

"I know. I think you're right. I'm sure that's the best decision," Mom said, as if it were momentous, like deciding on risky corrective surgery, or what college DJ would attend. "We can keep it that way as long as you want. Well, when she's sleeping here, of course."

Dev said nothing.

"I've done a spreadsheet," Barb announced when Dev arrived back at the Palmers' house the next morning.

"A spreadsheet?"

"I can do one every week. Here's a copy I printed out for you. The schedule has gotten more complicated now that Jodie is home, but see the color coding?"

Dev took the page. Yes, indeedy, he could see the color coding. Yellow for Jodie's hours at day rehab, blue for DJ's naps, even though she wasn't nearly as predictable in that department as the spreadsheet suggested. Green apparently meant DJ at Devlin's and he didn't like the scattered nature of those color blocks. So he was only having her two nights this week? Whose idea was that?

Barb had said to him some weeks ago, when Jodie's recovery began to unfold with such positive signs, "Now you'll be able to go back to New York," and he couldn't get those words out of his head. Did the Palmers want him to go? Did he?

Meanwhile, where was pink for Dev, Jodie and DJ go to the park? Or, better, lilac for Barb, Elin and Lisa get the hell out of town for a few hours so Jodie can make up her own mind about what she wants to do with the baby?

In fact, he couldn't see one color block or notation in the schedule that gave Jodie any time with DJ on her own.

"I mean, it's just a draft, obviously," Barb said, reading the disapproval in his face.

He said in apology, "I'm not a huge fan of spreadsheets, to be honest."

"But you must use them all the time, in your work."

"People put them together on my behalf. And I file them in the cylindrical file." He mimed balling a sheet of paper and tossing it in the trash.

"You throw them *out?*"

"Spreadsheets can make you feel like you're organized when really you're not, don't you think? Like bullet-point presentations. I'm not a fan of bullet points, either." He dropped the flippant tone and spoke gently, because despite everything, he was becoming fond of his daughter's grandmother. He knew she meant well. "You know DJ won't nap to a schedule, Barb, so why pretend about it on paper? We don't know how much time Jodie's going to be spending with her at this stage. Can't we keep it flexible?"

Barbara pressed her fingertips to her temples. "I'm just trying to manage this situation."

"I know. And I appreciate it. But I don't think a spreadsheet is the answer. Where are they, anyhow?"

"DJ is in her bassinet on the deck. I just gave her a bottle. Elin was helping Jodie in the shower, but I think they're done."

"So Jodie's upstairs?"

"Let me call her. I'm sure she hasn't come down."

He hesitated. It bothered him that Jodie wasn't with the baby, and yet why should it? What did he expect? He'd been so afraid of the opposite happening, of the love kicking in too fiercely and possessively and shutting him out, and now he'd done a full turn-around and wanted to push the other way.

It wasn't logical. *He* wasn't logical. He was a mess of conflicting wants—to go back to his real career in international law, yet keep the strongest possible bond with DJ, to see Jodie discover her love, yet for that love to be generous when it came to his own needs.

Jodie had huge needs of her own. She still struggled to manage dressing and showering and the most ordinary day-to-day things. She was so brave about it. Brave and funny and stubborn. She couldn't have taken over all of DJ's care even if she wanted to.

Did she want to? This was the crunch, the big question. Was she holding back from DJ in order to work harder on her own recovery, or because she couldn't cope with suddenly being a mom?

"I'll go up," he told Barb.

"I'll be in the kitchen, if you need me," she said. "You'll…say the right things, won't you?" Her face twisted with worry and he felt his frustration build. What did Barb want from him? It would help so much if she could just relax a little.

He found Jodie in her room doing some range-of-motion exercises for her arms and legs. She wore calf-length black leggings and a strappy white tank, little more than a scrap of stretch fabric and lace. The swell of her breasts peeked above the neckline of the tank, and the leggings made her tight, round butt seem even tighter and rounder. Dev had trouble keeping his gaze where it belonged.

But there was a serious point to the stretchy clothing. She was working hard. There was a sheen of sweat across her forehead and her collarbone, and she lifted her top away from her stomach to let in some air. "Nothing's working this morning," she said, slightly breathless. "Starting to come back a little."

"How about doing them on the deck?" He didn't like the way she was shut in her room like this, with DJ out of sight and out of mind.

"I guess that would be okay."

She managed the stairs on her own, while he went a few steps ahead of her, ready to brace her if she fell. When they reached the deck and she saw the bassinet with its lacy white canopy, she froze for a moment. She hadn't known until now that DJ was out here. "Oh, right," she murmured, then began to grab the air with her hand as if seeking something solid for support. Dev helped her get comfortable on the built-in wooden bench that ran along the railing and went to peek at his daughter.

She'd woken up. The wicker of the bassinet creaked a little as she tensed her body and let out a whimpering cry. She writhed, as if her digestion was bothering her, but then her gut settled and she blinked a few times and looked up at the view. Dappled leaves. Dev had learned that small babies, when awake, just lo-o-ove to look at dappled leaves with a background of sky.

Ooh, and here's something else they love to look at—their daddy. She caught sight of him and her face broke into the darlingest smile in the world. "That's right, sweetheart," he whispered, and smiled back. He was pitifully in love with her, and "in love" meant forever, and he didn't even care.

Jodie was watching him, he could see, distracted from the exercises she'd been so dedicated about up in her room. He felt a thud of sudden vulnerability—all that fear of the unknown where DJ's future was concerned.

He had to bite the bullet.

They both did.

Jodie had to have her first hold.

He didn't give her a choice today, just picked DJ up—she was wearing a stretch-cotton smock dress with tiny blue flowers on a white background, and matching bloomers—and brought her across. "Here, why don't you take her for a bit?"

"I—I— Now?" Jodie stammered.

"Yes, but you need a couple of cushions, right?"

"I think so."

"I'll grab some." He was more than capable of managing a baby and two cushions at once. He'd recently managed a baby, a poopy diaper and a handful of wipes with a phone pressed to his ear at the same time, talking international law. He settled the cushions on either side of her.

"Can you…? I'm leaning, I think."

She was right. Her body had slipped a little on the bench. He sat down beside her and nudged her bare, pale shoulder with his.

"I hate this," she said.

"*Hate* it?"

"No… No!" she corrected quickly. "Not the baby! Not her. My body. The fact that sometimes I'm not co-ordinated enough to sit straight, by myself."

"Right. You'll get there."

"I know. But it's frustrating." She sounded wobbly. Scared. Maybe she didn't hate the idea of holding the baby, but she definitely had issues with it. Because she didn't trust her body?

"I would never let her fall," he said, and lifted the baby across.

*This is my baby.* To Jodie it still didn't seem real. *This is my baby, in my arms.*

DJ didn't seem to consider this event to be miraculous in any way. She looked up at Jodie, fixing her gaze just below her hairline. She didn't smile. Her eyes were a dark, swimmy blue and she had translucent blisters on her lips from sucking on her bottle. The neckline of her tiny dress was still a little damp from where some of the formula had leaked from the corners of her mouth. She felt heavy.

No, it wasn't the weight, it was the tension in Jodie's muscles. "I didn't feel this tired, holding Lucy yesterday," she said.

Dev had risen and moved away. He stood on the far side of the deck, beneath the thickest shade from the black-cherry tree, watching her to check that she was all right. "You were in a chair with armrests for that," he said. "And Lucy's a little lighter than DJ. Can you not manage it? Let me know if—"

"No, I want to." Something kicked inside her, a stirring of tenderness and love. But it wasn't strong enough. It wasn't the overwhelming certainty Jodie wanted it to be.

*I love her,* she said inside her head.

No, that wasn't quite right.

She tried again. *I love you!*

It was true. She knew it was. But she couldn't *feel* it. She looked down at the baby, smiled at her and learned by heart every crease in her little arms, every strand of her hair, but she couldn't *feel* her love.

Those swimmy blue eyes looked up at her, so serious and unsmiling and somehow so wise and *old.*

*She'll see it. She'll feel it. She'll know.*

She still wasn't smiling. Jodie tried to coax it out of her by showing her how. She stretched her lips, crinkled her eyes. *This is your mommy smiling at you, DJ.* But it didn't work. DJ didn't smile back, and Jodie knew why.

You couldn't tell lies with your own body. You couldn't fake love coming out of every pore of your skin. Lying here in her arms, DJ would soon know that this person, this mommy person who was supposed to have such a total skin-to-skin bond and connection, didn't yet love her in the right way, and she absolutely *must not* be allowed to know that.

Jodie broke into a sweat. "Can you take her, Dev?"

"Or I could give your arm some more support."

"No, take her. I don't think more support would be enough."

"Here…" he said, and sat down beside her again, twisting around so that his left arm cradled hers and his chest shored up her shoulder. His strength and warmth and clean male smell slammed into her, seeming far more *right* than the feel of a baby in her arms. More real. Stronger. Could he feel it, too? She thought so. His breathing had changed, growing shallower.

She felt weak and shaky and tingling with need, all at the same time. Her body was far better at remembering familiar things than learning new ones, it seemed. Every cell and all her senses remembered last year so vividly. The way his touch and his laughter had set her alight, the way she'd felt strong and alive yet safe in his arms. The feel of his mouth making a hot trail from her neck to her breasts. The sureness in the way he caressed her, slipping his hand between her thighs, curving his palms over her butt.

Last year, he would have pressed his lips to her neck and teased her and set her on fire. She would have turned her face toward him and kissed him back, brushing her mouth against his and sliding it away, making him go after her and coax her lips into parting and drinking him in, and it would have lasted for minutes on end. She would have gloried in the feel of those hard muscles covered in satiny skin.

Their physical connection was magic and wonderful and made her dizzy.

Still.

But the new thing, the magic and wonder and dizziness of being a mother, her body couldn't learn. She couldn't even *fake* a smile now. No wonder DJ wasn't smiling back.

"I really think you need to take her now, Dev," she said shakily.

Mom appeared in the doorway to the deck. She was wearing a flour-spattered apron, and was brushing her hands against it, as if dusting them off in readiness to be of help. She must have heard the note of panic in Jodie's voice, the panic that Dev had ignored.

"No, see?" he said quietly. "You're fine."

"I—I think I'm not. I think I need a break. Can you please take her?"

He still wouldn't. Instead, he pressed his body more

tightly against her, curved his other arm over her shoulder to support her on the opposite side. Her back wasn't touching the bench at all now, it was only touching him, and she began to take calming breaths, giving in to his insistence and certainty.

Maybe she could do it, after all. Maybe with him here, loving his baby girl so much, the love would filter into Jodie as well, filter through her into DJ so that wise DJ wouldn't guess who it really came from. She could smell the mingled scents of both of them, Dev and DJ. Baby powder and milkiness and aftershave and warm male skin.

Mom stepped forward. "Dev, she says she's tired. Don't push it, please, until after we've talked to her doctors and therapists on Tuesday."

"Does that make a difference?" He slid his hand around the bundle of baby.

"Well, yes, doesn't it? They may have very specific guidelines about how much she's allowed to do."

"How much baby holding?"

"How much child care. How much of anything. She has a heap of exercises to get through every day. Just brushing her teeth…" She bent down, and Jodie could smell that, too—flour and vanilla and peaches. Mom must be making a pie.

She picked up the baby, cradling DJ's head against her shoulder. Dev loosened his supporting grip and she saw him rake his lower teeth across his top lip in a gesture of unspoken frustration. There were so many pairs of arms in this little baby's life, reaching out to her.

"Let's bring her bassinet inside," Mom said. "It's getting too hot out here now. Maybe she could lie on her blanket on the lounge-room floor and have a kick. She loves that. I'll get her baby gym, too. She was really hitting those rattles the other day."

"Thank you, Mom," Jodie said.

Just as had happened last night, Dev didn't say a word.

## Chapter Six

"Is there anything more you want to talk about at this stage, Jodie?" asked Dr. Reuben on Tuesday morning.

Everyone waited for her response. Mom, Dad, Elin, Jodie's physical and occupational therapists, the neurologist and the obstetrician who'd delivered DJ nearly twelve weeks ago.

And Dev.

DJ herself was at home with Lisa. She and Elin were both schoolteachers, with the summer off, which Mom had pronounced to be a blessing. Jodie wasn't so sure. Dev seemed restless about the baby's absence, moving as if his empty arms needed filling, although Jodie herself had agreed there was no point in bringing the baby in for this meeting.

"No, I think I'm fine. For now," she said brightly. "I mean, you've all said I can call, talk to anyone about anything at any time. You've said—" she turned to the obstetrician, Dr. Forbes "—that my body recovered very well from the birth itself, and that there's no reason why I shouldn't conceive again in the future."

She bit her lip. Why parrot this back to him, this reassurance about her future fertility, when she hadn't even begun to deal with the baby she already had? She couldn't think of the right things to say. She couldn't think of *anything* to say.

"You're doing very well indeed," the man said.

He was older and a little distant, somehow exactly the kind of man you would expect to have delivered a baby you'd had no knowledge of until two days ago. The kind of man who would have looked after Jodie's physical well-being perfectly and professionally during and after the birth, but who would be rather glad that her emotional adjustment now was an issue for other professionals, such as Dr. Reuben, to deal with.

She felt stubborn and protective and private about it, suddenly. She didn't want professionals helping her to learn to love and take care of her baby, she wanted to do it, like a three-year-old, All By Herself.

Even though she'd already proved to herself that she didn't know where to start.

Trish and Lesley, the therapists, began to speak, stressing the importance of keeping her rehab on track in other areas. It couldn't all be about the baby. Jodie would have to put her own needs first. "It's what they say on airplanes," Trish said. "First, fit your own oxygen mask, then assist your child. If you're not taking care of yourself, how are you going to look after a baby?"

They all seemed to feel that this was a huge risk, that Jodie's own therapy would be derailed by her tiring herself out with her child, attempting one hundred and ten percent.

"I have plenty of help," she managed to say. "I think I'm going to be sensible about it. I know how much love DJ already has, even without me."

Trish and Lesley seemed to approve. Then Trish repeated, "But is there anything more you need? Anything you want?"

*Anything I want? Anything I need? I want to love my baby. I want to be the one who knows when she's hungry or tired or hurting. I want to be the one who can soothe her to sleep. I want her to know in her bones that I'm her mom, but she doesn't know it and I don't know how to teach her. She responds to Dev and Lisa and Elin and Mom but not to me, and I'm scared about that.*

So scared, she couldn't begin to express it, especially not with all these eyes fixed on her face—the professional gaze of the therapist, the more personal ones belonging to Dev and Mom, trying to hide their concern but without success. Her whole life felt wrong and mixed-up, compared to last fall, before the accident. She remembered one of her last horseback rides, a trail ride through the woods belonging to Oakbank Stables with some intermediate riding students, the hooves of the horses soft on the carpets of newly fallen leaves.

That day, everything had seemed right with the world. The sweet secret of Dev and their plans to see each other that night. The fresh, peaty smell of the woods. The clink of stirrups and bridles in time to the rhythmic movements of the horses.

"I need to see my horses," she said.

It wasn't what Trish or Lesley had expected. Dev and Mom, maybe, but even they didn't understand, she could tell. They thought she had her priorities all wrong. Horses, when she had so much work to do on her body? Horses, when she had a baby to learn to love and care for?

Dad shifted in his seat, and made a gruff sound, but said nothing. He could take her side sometimes, but when he stayed silent, she never knew what he was keeping back. Approval? Or the reverse?

So she backpedalled, ashamed and guilty and scared. "Not yet, of course. I mean, I know that. It's not a priority. But when it happens, it'll do me a world of good, I know it."

"We'll certainly work toward it," Trish promised. "Hippotherapy is a definite possibility for you, given your background." She looked at Dev and Mom, who both nodded. "But that's not what we're here to talk about today."

Jodie understood that she'd gone off-topic, that her therapists and doctors were focused on her adjustment to the baby and the fact that she'd given birth. "I—I really can't think of anything else for now," she told them lamely.

Dr. Reuben and Dr. Forbes both shifted in their seats just the way Dad had, busy schedules dictating that they make a move to the next patients on their lists.

"Thank you," Jodie said to them, and everyone stood up.

*Thank you* was incredibly useful, she'd begun to discover. You could make it mean so many different things. You could fob people off with it and they never guessed. She thanked Mom for the spreadsheet she'd printed out, even though they weren't sticking to it. She thanked Lisa for her words of experience regarding diaper rash, even though she—Jodie—hadn't done a diaper change yet. You could use it as a piece of very effective camouflage against revealing what you really felt.

The fear.

The doubt.

The distance.

The shame.

She said it again, just to make sure. "Thank you." And everyone nodded and smiled and murmured and told her she was doing incredibly well.

For the next three weeks and more, *thank you* worked like a charm.

She said it to Dev when he picked her up and took her to the park with DJ and did all the carrying in the baby swing and the strapping in and out of the stroller so that Jodie barely needed to touch the baby—or Dev himself—at all. She said it to Mom and Lisa and Elin when one of them took her to rehab while another took care of DJ at home. She said it to Dad when he carried DJ in her car seat or filled her little plastic bath.

Maddy called from Cincinnati to suggest coming up with Lucy for a mommies-and-babies play date, and Jodie said that rehab didn't leave enough space in the schedule right now, but thank you for thinking of it, it was a great idea for sometime down the track. Trish said that Jodie could have the baby at rehab sometimes and they could work on some strategies for taking care of her safely within Jodie's current limitations. Again Jodie hid behind "thank you" and "down the track."

If anyone noticed that she'd only actually held DJ in her arms twice since that first time on the deck, they didn't comment. DJ commented, in her own way. She didn't smile. If anyone noticed that both those smile-less times Jodie had to fight an overwhelming feeling of distance and inadequacy and panic, they didn't comment on this, either.

Or not to her face, anyhow.

Three weeks and four days after her discharge from the hospital, a Wednesday, she caught them commenting behind her back. She'd been taking a nap—this napping business was getting old fast—after a tiring but encouraging day at rehab, when she heard the front door open and the voices of Dev, Lisa and Mom. Moving with the necessary slow precision across her bedroom rug and into the carpeted corridor, she was too quiet and they didn't hear her. She'd only been asleep half an hour, a shorter time than usual. They wouldn't expect her to surface for another hour.

It was the same old line, from Lisa. "I just don't think she's ready, that's all."

"But what's going to make her ready, Lisa?" Dev's voice, low and intense, an emotional, threatening growl that did something to Jodie's insides every time she heard it. "Do you think I was ready, when DJ was newborn? I'd never held a baby in my life. Isn't it only doing it, doing the hands-on with no one to step in the moment you have the slightest episode of not coping, that makes you ready as a parent? You do it, you have to do it and you learn. You live it, you can't imagine life without it and the love kicks in."

"The love?" This was Mom. "She loves DJ! Of course she does! You can't be seriously suggesting she doesn't love her own baby, Devlin!"

"I'm not sure that you're letting her love her, Barb."

"That's not true!"

"I appreciate that she mustn't be overloaded, but do you ever let her feed DJ? Or hold her in the bath?"

"That's not the point!"

Jodie stood with her hands on the stair rail for support, hearing it all. She wanted to tell Dev that it wasn't

Mom's fault. She wanted to say, "Hey, I'm here! Let's discuss this face-to-face, not when you think I'm asleep because you think I can't handle it."

But maybe they were right. She couldn't handle it. She wasn't handling it. The love hadn't kicked in.

"She's working too hard on her rehab, for one thing," Lisa said. "You know what she's like. One of her riding instructors, when she was about twelve, said she had more guts than a slaughterhouse."

"Oh, Lisa!" Barb wailed.

"Yeah, graphic image, but I'll never forget that and it's true. She's an incredibly brave person, and she's exhausting herself with work on her exercises."

"Because she wants to be strong enough to take care of DJ," Mom argued. "Which she isn't, right now. She's told me. She's afraid of letting her fall."

"She's too tired to take care of DJ." Lisa again. "She needs a break, just some time out. From everything."

"I think you're right," said Mom. "Time out. How can we do this?"

"Dev, leave the baby here and just take her out tonight, or something," Lisa said. "Take her to dinner. Take the pressure off. You want her to take more of the load off your hands—"

"It's not about the load," he interrupted. "Do you think that's what this is about? That I want to be able to hand DJ over to her and get the hell out? Shoot, that's the opposite of what I want!"

"I'm not saying that." Lisa stopped, then added in an abrupt tone, "Well. I don't know. You're going back to New York, aren't you?"

"Look, that's a decision I can't make yet."

"You had made it, I thought."

"When we weren't certain she'd ever come out of

the coma. When she was so sick. Of course I wasn't going back to New York if I had a daughter to raise on my own. The situation's changed now, hasn't it? Everything's negotiable. All I know is, I'm not going to be shut out."

"Okay, but I'm assuming—" She cut herself off again. "I don't want to pressure you about the status of your relationship when it's none of my business."

Dad passed through the hall at that moment, and offered, "You got that right!" before he kept right on going, on his way out to mow the lawn.

"It is our business!" Mom said. "It's about DJ's future, and Jodie's well-being. Is there a relationship, Dev?"

"Of course there is. We're the parents of a child."

"You know that's not what I mean."

"Yes, I know it, but that's the only answer I can give you right now."

"We're going around in circles." Lisa gave a sigh that traveled all the way up the stairs to Jodie on the top landing.

"We are," Dev said. "But taking her to dinner is a good idea, and I'm happy to do it."

Lisa kicked into action at once. "I'll make a reservation. How far are you willing to drive? There's that gorgeous new French place in Fairfield—La Brasserie. If you cut across through the back roads, it's not too far."

"And I'll run DJ's bath," Mom said. "By the time Jodie wakes up, she can have the bathroom to herself to take a shower and get ready. It's still early. If you make the reservation for seven, Lisa. That way Jodie's not out too late."

"Isn't La Brasserie a little too—?"

But they didn't let Dev finish. "Make it special,"

Lisa insisted. "Make it a milestone. A new start. She's off the walking frame. She's already so much stronger and better than she was a few weeks ago. She knows we're here for her. And she's always fought so hard to be independent and to achieve her goals. If she's not fighting us for more hands-on with DJ, it's because she doesn't feel it would be safe. When she's ready, I know my baby sister, she'll say so! She'll absolutely insist!"

*Thank you, Lisa.*

Was it true, though? It would have been true, before the accident, Jodie knew. Now, though... Would she absolutely insist?

"You're right," Mom decreed. "She will."

Jodie started carefully down the stairs. "Are you guys making plans for me?"

Mom looked up at her. "Oh, you're awake already?"

"Just now. It's great, isn't it? Down to one nap, most days, and it's getting shorter."

"We're sending you and Dev out to dinner," Lisa said. "DJ's staying here."

"Can I help with her bath?" She caught the covert, meaningful looks Mom and Lisa exchanged that seemed to say, "See? Jodie's absolutely insisting."

"Of course, honey," Mom said.

But they didn't let her, not really. Dev went home to shower and change. Lisa made the restaurant reservation. "La Brasserie, Jodie, it's gorgeous. You wouldn't have been there, since it's new." Mom ran the water, testing it expertly with her elbow to make sure it wasn't too hot.

"Let me get her undressed," she said, "because that's tricky."

Jodie stood back and watched as the little wriggly arms came out of the stretch cotton dress, looking so fragile and small and wobbly it seemed as if one wrong move from Mom's expert hands and the arms might break.

Jodie hissed in a horrified breath at the mental image and Mom turned to her with a question in her face.

"It's okay," Jodie said quickly. "Just glad you're doing this bit."

But then Mom did the next bit as well, sliding DJ into the bath and scooping the warm water over her perfect, satiny, slippery skin.

"Doesn't she ever smile in the bath?"

"Ooh, no, bath is way too serious for that," Mom cooed, gazing down at DJ, her own smile as gooey as a marshmallow. "She used to shriek, at first, but she likes it now. Don't you, sweetheart precious?"

"H-how can you tell, without her smiling?"

"Look at her splashing her little arms and wriggling around." Mom was still beaming, her hair damp around her face, a damp patch on the front of her blouse and two pink spots on her cheeks. She looked as happy as a young girl, but she also looked deeply tired. She was sixty-five years old, with forty years as a parent and seventeen years as a grandmother already under her belt. How much longer could she keep this up?

*I have to start learning.*

"Could I shampoo her hair?"

"Of course." Mom took a step to the side. She kept hold of DJ, while Jodie pooled a tiny amount of baby shampoo onto the round head with its water-slicked hair. She massaged it in, her coordination still jerky. Mom cradled the little head in her cupped palm to keep it steady.

"I don't think I'd better rinse it off," Jodie decided. "I might get shampoo in her eyes."

So Mom did that part, also, then picked her up and wrapped DJ in a towel and sent Jodie for a clean outfit and a fresh diaper. "Just one of her little playsuits, in the second drawer. This is what Maddy used to do for you when you were newborn and she was seven, choose your outfits after your bath."

*Great,* Jodie thought. *My child-care capabilities are those of a seven-year-old. I'm so proud.*

But it wasn't funny. It hurt. It shook her up. And she couldn't talk about it because that would only shake her up more.

Dev appeared at six-thirty, because Fairfield was a half-hour drive away. Jodie had spent nearly an hour getting ready, and in this area there was genuinely something to celebrate because she didn't need help with any of it now. She could get her arms into both sleeves. She could manage the whole shower. Lipstick and mascara were another story, but this was easily solved. Her face was cleansed, exfoliated and moisturized, but makeup-free.

She met him at the front door and his expression seemed to approve the swirly print dress and tiered jacket, which she had teamed with flat shoes in basic black because managing killer heels at this stage would have made managing lipstick seem easy. He looked so good himself, in dark pants and a lightly patterned button-down shirt, freshly shaven and his hair still a little damp around his neck from the shower.

They'd both dressed as if it were a date, she realized.

Was it a date?

But no, they'd answered that one already.

"How's DJ?" was the first thing he said to her.

"Oh, great. Asleep. I gave her her bath. Well, helped."

"Did you?" She could tell he was pleased, and felt

guilty that she'd overstated her involvement. What was that really about? Wanting to make him happy? Or hiding her own distance and fear?

He put his arm around her back as they walked to the car. To an outsider they would have looked like a standard pair of new parents, taking a well-earned break for couple time while Grandma babysat. It was such a long way from the truth. Such a long, long way.

Dev had a glass of red wine with his meal but Jodie kept to plain water. "I'm not putting anything into my body that's going to interfere with my control."

It made sense, yet still he told her, "You can let go a little, can't you?"

The idea of this evening had been to relax her, but so far it hadn't worked. He could see her intense concentration on managing the meal, to the point of twisting the pepper grinder over her chicken all by herself when the waiter was eager to do it for her.

He could see her making the right kind of conversation, too, refusing to rehash today's milestones in rehab and instead dragging in current events and politics and celebrity gossip as if this were a neurological examination. Could she remember the name of Scarlett Johansson's latest film? Could she keep track of this summer's star players in baseball and golf?

"I want to progress," she answered.

"You won't, if you push too hard. You'll get overloaded and go backward. Was this dinner a mistake?"

"No, it's great." She squeezed out a smile.

"It's not what you need," he said on her behalf, because he could suddenly see this, and knew she wouldn't say it herself.

"No, you're right, it's not." Her face fell. "I thought maybe it was, but—"

"I'm sorry. It was Lisa's idea, and I know how much she cares about you and wants you to get strong."

"They all care about me. It seems to blind them, sometimes. It's always been this way, and it's so hard to fight it when I'm fighting with everything I have just to use a damned fork without messing up!"

She blinked back tears of anger and frustration and all he could think was *Hell! Hell!* Out loud he said, "But that's them. Your family. This is me. You can tell *me* what you really want and need, can't you?"

There was a pause and he could see her struggling, pushing things back deep inside. A familiar fear surged inside him. What might she say? What would he do if she wanted him out of her life completely?

She had no right to insist on it, since he was DJ's father, but how much of a battle did he want, with his innocent daughter as the winner's prize? Would he take her to family court over it? Hell, he dreaded anything like that. He knew that the law could make custody issues worse as well as solving them, especially when the matter crossed state lines.

She pressed her lips together and he knew she'd decided to keep something back, and yet when she spoke, he could see it was going to be important and honest, even if it wasn't the whole truth. "I want to go to Oakbank. I want to see the horses. And ride. People are acting as if that's something trivial, something to think about down the track, but it's not, it's something I want now. It was so much a part of my life. Way more a part of my life than—" She stopped, flooded with color and pressed her lips together again.

He understood and said it for her. "Than being a mom. Because you weren't one."

"I l-love her."

"I know you do. Of course you do." How could she not? He loved her to pieces.

"I want to take care of her, but I'm scared, and Mom and my sisters… They're so experienced with babies. I need to go back to something I used to do well. Even if I can't do it well anymore, I just need to…be a tiny bit of that person again, for a while, or else I can't learn— I won't learn to be the new— This doesn't make any sense."

Oh, but it did. Shoot, it did. Dev felt he'd been blind, and fallen into the same trap as her family. Not really listening. Not seeing her real needs. "I'll take you tomorrow," he said.

"It doesn't have to be—"

"Tomorrow," he insisted. "We can spend the whole day there, if you want."

"Rehab—"

"Rehab can wait. This is rehab. I'll call Trish and tell her what's happening. I'll call my office and have Marcia cancel my appointments for the whole morning. No arguments, okay, Jodie?"

But she wasn't planning to argue. Her face had lit up. Her eyes were shining. "Thank you, Dev. Thank you so much for not being like my mother and my sisters." She had some color back in her cheeks now that she'd been able to spend a little time outside and the contrast of that smile and that skin and that blond hair took his breath away.

He remembered the way she'd felt leaning against him a few weeks ago, the first time she'd held their baby, so warm, so focused, yet shaky and uncertain, bringing out a kind of tenderness in him he'd barely known could exist. If he could have cut off his own leg to have her fully healed and complete and strong the way she used to be, he would have done it.

"You're welcome," he said, and she must have heard the huskiness in his voice.

## Chapter Seven

Driving to the restaurant, the summer evening had still been bright and hot, but now it was dark, a kind of misty blue darkness with a big yellow moon rising in the east. The last time she'd been out driving with Dev in open country in the dark, Jodie realized, was the night of the accident. Oddly, she wasn't scared about it. Maybe because she had no memory of the accident or the drive.

They came around a swoopy bend, the same kind of bend they must have come around that night, with forest on both sides. An oncoming car swept past them, going fast. She heard Dev swear beneath his breath. He was thinking of that night, also.

"Do you remember it?" she asked him. "I mean the—"

"I know what you mean. Yes, I remember it. I was conscious the whole time. Let's not talk about it."

"You were thinking about it."

"Can't help it, sometimes."

"Like now, when someone speeds past the other way."

"Yes." Gritted teeth.

Oh, Dev. It shocked her to think of how much he'd been through. She hadn't thought of it this way before— that her long sleep had been a protection, in many ways, while Dev had suffered through the accident, suffered the agony in his leg echoing the agony of uncertainty, not just for that one terrible night, but for months afterward. Would there be a healthy baby? Would the baby's mom ever wake up?

She put her hand on his arm. Ole Lefty, which wasn't always fully responsible for its actions. She pressed and gripped too hard, and he took his eyes off the road to look at her, and slowed the car. She could see the suffering in his face, the surge of memory. His hands were clenched and shaking on the wheel.

A turning appeared just ahead, a side road with a sign that shone brightly when the car headlights hit it. *Deer Pond Park*. He took it without a word and slowed even more, taking his foot off the gas pedal as if he didn't trust himself with the vehicle's power.

The parking area was deserted. The car rolled to a stop in the farthest corner, with Dev's arms slumped over the wheel. The engine died. "I'm sorry," he said, his voice thick as if he was fighting nausea. "It just…hit me. Hell, I'm shaking. And when that car just now— It wasn't even really speeding. It was a family minivan, for heck's sake."

"I shouldn't have talked about it."

"It wasn't your fault. I was thinking about it already. It's the first time I've driven on a dark country road."

"In so long?"

"Couldn't drive at all for the first few months, because of my leg. Since then, I've been pretty busy sticking close to town." Taking care of a baby. Watching her mom wake up.

"I'm an idiot."

"No." He shook his head, ran a still-unsteady hand down his face as if to wipe the emotion away.

"I am. 'It's not always about you, Jodie,'" she said out loud, with bitterness, mocking herself.

Dev opened the car door. "I need some air. For a minute. But this is not your fault. Let's not do that to each other."

He slid out into the fresh night air, walking away from the vehicle, lacing his fingers behind his head so that his elbows stuck out. She heard him breathing, big whooshes of air blown out through rounded lips. He circled back and leaned his thighs against the hood of the car, looking out over the moonlit pond just yards away, still blowing those careful breaths.

She scrambled out of the vehicle and went to him. "Dev…"

"You were lying there," he said, the words torn from him as if by a force he couldn't control. "I could barely reach you to touch. Just my fingertips. Couldn't do anything for you. I could see blood in the dark. I could hear the other driver yelling and moaning. Crying on the phone when he got himself together enough to call 911. I didn't know… I thought you were breathing but I wasn't sure. And my leg was trapped. And shattered. They had to cut us out. It took three hours."

"Oh, Dev…"

"I'm sorry." He pressed his fingers into his eyes. "Your family didn't want me to tell you all that."

"No. They wouldn't."

"I'm sorry."

"Don't do that to me, Dev, don't treat me like a child, the way they do. I'm not. I'm a grown woman. A strong woman. And I'm— I'm—" She didn't know how to finish.

*In your debt, forever.*

*Here for you, forever.*

Words weren't strong enough.

Touch just might be.

She reached for him, running her stronger right hand—the one that she might actually be able to control—up his arm. She rested it on his shoulder, beside his warm neck, and leaned her body close. "You're amazing," she said. "You've carried this load of memory all on your own, while I've been free."

"I guess I did need to talk about it." He was still shaking a little, not from weakness, she guessed, but from the effort of holding everything in. She didn't want him to hold it in. Such tightness and control would surely kill him.

*Let go, Dev, let go.*

Not fully aware of what she was doing, she began to soothe his muscles with her touch, the way her own muscles had been massaged back into life with physical therapy. She knew all those movements so well, by now.

That's better. That's good. Let go, Dev.

He let out another shuddering sigh and wrapped his arms around her. She felt the warmth of the car hood from the hot engine, and heard it begin to tick as it cooled.

"When the paramedics arrived and confirmed you were alive, this rush of relief, I can't describe…" His voice rumbled against her chest, his breath making a heated caress in her ear. "And then they gave me drugs for the pain and I had this hallucination. I thought we were in a shipwreck, floating in a lifeboat with sharks circling in the water, the only two people left in the whole world. All I could reach was your hair. I held on to it...."

He showed her, taking a soft handful in his fist. She could feel his thumb resting, light and warm, on the back of her neck. He moved a little, bringing his cheek against hers. It was a little rough, so familiar, so good. She turned her head and pressed her lips there, because she couldn't stop herself. He sighed and she felt his mouth against hers, kind of soft and absentminded as if he weren't really here. He was still back in that horrible night.

"That was all I could reach," he repeated. "And then they cut you free and took you away. And it was just me and the sharks." He laughed.

"Wasn't funny at the time," she whispered.

"Nope."

"Wish I'd been there."

"I'm glad you weren't."

"Well, I'm here now." She took his face in her hands, and her hands did what they were told as if they wanted this, too. She pressed her lips to his forehead and then—because she couldn't help it, she was so overwhelmed with feeling for him, with a sense of all the power that connected them—to his mouth.

*Oh, Dev. Oh, Dev.*

He kissed her back, hungry about it, desperate. His mouth was almost too hard against hers, and he crushed the breath out of her lungs, leaning into her. She had to ease him away, but, oh, not too far.

*Yes, Dev, if kissing you helps to let go...*

*I'll kiss you for whatever reason you want, for every
reason there is.*

Their two mouths melted together once more, sweet
with the chocolate that had finished off their meal. He
let go of her hair and moved his hands down to cradle
her backside and pull her closer, the swirly skirt of her
dress falling against his legs.

She could feel his arousal and he didn't try to hide
it. He wanted her to know what was happening, and
he couldn't be in any doubt, himself, about what this
was doing to her. Her body came alive, her senses reborn. Even the texture of his shirt seemed magical.
The woodsy male smell of him. The dark fan of lashes
against his cheek that she glimpsed when her eyes
drifted open.

She touched him, her hands not fully controlled so
that sometimes her grip wouldn't let go or her hand
would land in the wrong place. There weren't any wrong
places, really. Everywhere felt right. His hip, the top of
his thigh, his shoulder blade.

And then it got serious.

He slid his hands beneath her top to touch her bare
skin and she wanted those hands on her breasts. He
must have known. He dragged his mouth away from
hers and trailed it down, pulled her summery jacket
from her shoulders and traced the neckline beneath it
with his lips. The straps of her top and cream lace bra
fell against her upper arms.

He lifted her breast in his cupped palm and breathed
a warm breath against her peaked nipple, ran his tongue
around it and sucked, released, kissed, sucked again. A
fire of pleasure and need stabbed down into her groin,
and her body told him *keep going, we are so good at
this, both of us.*

She reached for the fastening of his pants, but couldn't make her fingers work. They scrambled help-lessly and in the end she just left them there, curled against his stomach, while she kissed her way down his chest then pushed her forehead into the hard, flat place between his hips. Through the textured fabric of his pants, she felt the push of his erection against her mouth.

"No…" he groaned, pulling her up. "I want you closer."

"That's not close?"

"I want you like this.…" He pressed himself into her, kissed her mouth again.

"Yes, oh, yes." She tried his fly again and did better this time. The button came through the hole, the zipper eased down.

"We can't do this," he muttered, but he didn't mean it.

"I want to." She always did, when it was Dev. Al-ways. Something about him. No explanation. Just chem-istry. "Do you?"

"Hell, do I? How can you ask?" He straightened from his lean against the car hood and flipped her around in one twirl of a movement so that she was the one lean-ing. The engine was still warm. He cupped her bottom again and lifted her higher until she sat on the smooth metal. "It's not going to be pretty."

"I don't care."

"Good. Neither do I."

Maybe it wasn't pretty, but it was beautiful—dark and moonlit and beautiful. He grew patient, as if there were no hurry in the world now that they'd agreed on what they wanted, and just kissed her for a long, long time. Her mouth. Her shoulders. Her breasts. Touching her everywhere. Teasing her deliberately until she was almost whimpering, wanting him so badly, swollen with it, more than ready.

Of his own readiness, there was no doubt. His erection nudged at the apex of her spread thighs, hard and hot. She wrapped her legs around him and he slid her skirt until it bunched at her waist, then pushed aside the triangle of fabric at her crotch. They were doing this fully clothed, and that was just fine.

*Fully* clothed.

He had his wallet in his back pocket and it carried protection. She held him while he rolled it in place, running her fingers over the taut skin across his lower stomach, brushing the small, tight buds of his nipples through his shirt.

When he entered her, she was as smooth as silk around him, tight with her own need and he filled her so completely that she gasped at the first thrust. Oh, Dev. Oh, Dev. Yes. She clung to him, legs and arms shaking with effort, and he guessed it would have to be quick or not at all.

The car rocked and Jodie sobbed. He pinned her with his hands, stroked her with his hardness until the night exploded. She was a little ahead of him and took him with her, shuddering with gut-deep sound.

Yes. Oh, yes.

They were both breathless. He laughed and held her hard, and maybe she should say something. *That was amazing.* But it seemed trite and so obvious. Hell, yes, it was amazing. When had it not been amazing with Dev? So she just laughed with him and kissed him clumsily. He was just as clumsy, kissing her back.

"You can make a man forget, can't you?" he said.

"That wasn't the reason for it."

"No, I know, but it helped. It was good, Jodie."

"Good?"

"Amazing."

He sounded humble, which was how she felt, too. Humble because she didn't know what happened next. Didn't know how to ask. Didn't know *what* to ask.

*Are we dating?*

They weren't. They'd agreed.

And yet there was this. Stronger than ever.

He'd gone very quiet, very still.

"I'm not allowed to drive yet," she said, even though he knew this perfectly well.

"Are you asking if I'm okay to drive?"

"Don't particularly want to have to call one of my sisters to come with her husband and ferry us home."

"We won't have to do that. Just give me a minute."

"Have lots of them. As many as you like."

"Not too many, or we'll get a phone call asking where we are."

"Mmm, true, and Deer Pond Park probably wouldn't be a good answer."

"No."

They giggled like teenagers, and she thought, just as she'd thought last year, *don't spoil this, Jodie, don't try to nail exactly what he thinks and feels. Life is so precious. You almost had it taken away. Don't spoil this, when it's been...*

*Amazing.*

Dev made it back to the Palmer home without cracking up at the wheel. His whole body tightened and went on high alert, heart racing and sweat breaking out, every time a car went past, but he made it, breathing out a sigh of gratitude when they left the dark country road and came beneath Leighville's street lighting. He sighed again when he turned into Barb and Bill's driveway.

Jodie fell against him a little as he helped her out of the car. She often did. It was nothing new, something she couldn't help because of that weakened left side of her body. This time, though, he pulled her against him and kissed her sweetly, because he didn't want her to think he'd just closed the book after one quickie on the car hood in a deserted nighttime parking lot.

It wasn't supposed to be a long kiss, but he couldn't help himself. Lied to himself about it, in fact. Told himself it would be just one more moment of sensing her sweetness and grace, just one more moment of smelling her clean skin, tasting her peachy mouth. He didn't intended it to last long. Just one more sweet touch, that was all it would be.

But he couldn't stop. He tried. Took his mouth away in a brushing movement that only made him want to go back again, and go deeper this time.

Oh, so much deeper, the way he had twenty minutes ago in Deer Pond Park.

He ran his hands over her neat, sweet backside, made into the perfect rounded shape from her years of riding. He brushed the undersides of her breasts with his fingers. He slid his thigh between her legs and felt the silky swish of her dress fold around him in a way that mimicked the much more intimate kind of folding he'd so recently known.

It seemed incredible that his need could mount again so fast.

And she kissed him back. There was no doubt in the world about that. She lifted her face, parted her lips, shaped her body to fit against his so perfectly that she could be in no doubt about what his was doing to him. Again.

"One thing my body can still do," she whispered.

"Yes, oh, yes," he whispered back, his voice raspy with need. "You hadn't been scared about that before tonight, had you? Scared that it couldn't?"

"I hadn't thought. I hadn't considered—"

"Of course you hadn't." He brushed her mouth again, teased her lips with his tongue, cupped her head in his hands.

But the moment had changed. The whole Palmer family was inside the house, and Jodie had remembered the fact. She hadn't asked Dev what it all meant, back at the park, and he was glad about that because he wouldn't have known what to tell her.

"This isn't a good idea right now," she said.

"I'm sorry."

"It wasn't just you."

"I started it."

"I let you."

"You're not really strong enough yet to push me away."

"Oh, you think?" She did it with a cheeky smile, a nice shove to his chest—a little clumsy but very well-directed—and began to steer herself firmly toward the house, the shoe sole on her weaker side brushing the paving with a light rasping sound.

The front door opened, and Barbara appeared. For a moment, Dev wondered if she might have seen that steaming kiss. Lord, he shouldn't have let himself! It should never have happened! It hadn't *needed* to happen when he'd kissed her so thoroughly—and done so much more—in the moonlit park.

But Barb's face seemed untroubled, and he had no

doubt that she would have looked and behaved differently if she'd been watching them from the window. "Elin said you were home. You're a little later than we expected. How did it go, honey?"

"Major victory with the pepper grinder. Slightly challenging drive home in the dark, on the country roads. That's why we're home late. We took it slow."

Some of it they took slow, Dev amended to himself, fighting back his awareness of everything she hadn't said. Some of it they took at magical, erotic speed.

"And I'm cutting class tomorrow," Jodie finished.

"Cutting class?"

"Dev's taking me—" She stopped and corrected herself. "Dev's taking *us* to Oakbank."

"Us?"

"Me and DJ." Her voice wobbled a little at the end, and there was a little note of triumph in it, too. Dev heard it, and was so happy she wanted to bring the baby, too.

Barb looked at him. "Dev?"

"I think it's a great idea," he said firmly. But he knew from Barb's face that she wasn't going to let him off the hook that easily.

## *Chapter Eight*

Elin appeared at Dev's front door just as he was about to head upstairs to bed, after some mindless TV to wind himself down. For the first three seconds, he thought it was about DJ and the strength drained from his legs. It was after eleven at night. His little daughter had been fast asleep an hour ago when he'd left the Palmers, just a few blocks away.

But this was anger on Elin's face, not panic. "We need to talk," she said.

She was a strong woman, a good six inches taller than Jodie and more heavily built, with the weight of her three children starting to gather around her hips. She had Jodie's blue eyes, blond hair and wide smile and Dev liked her a lot, but he didn't particularly want her here on his doorstep with such a hostile look on her face, and arms folded in a way that said she meant business.

"Come in." What else could he say?

She launched in before she'd even crossed the threshold. "I heard your car in the driveway. I was in DJ's room picking up a load of laundry. I looked out the window to see how Jodie was managing the climb from the car. And I saw what happened." The accusation was crystal clear.

"Right," he answered. What would she say if she knew what had happened half an hour before that? He shuddered to think. "Would you like coffee, or something?"

"No, I wouldn't. I'd like to know what the hell you think you're doing with my sister."

Pretty obvious, wasn't it?

Unfortunately, however, Elin was right. He knew it as he'd known it all along. He hadn't absorbed a second of the TV murder mystery he'd just watched, because he'd been thinking about tonight instead. He should never have kissed her, let alone sat her on the hood of his car, pushed her pretty skirt up to her hips and—

Yeah.

Had that shattering episode of flashback to the accident done so much to destroy his good sense? Or was that only an excuse?

He sighed between his teeth. "Okay, you don't have to tell me."

But Elin told him anyhow. "She is so vulnerable right now! She has so much to deal with and to work out."

"Don't I get a share in that?"

"A share in what?"

"The vulnerability, the stuff to deal with."

"All the more reason I shouldn't have to say this, Dev. You have no right to add any kind of complication whatsoever, and especially not that kind. Can you honestly tell me she's in the same place she was in last year—or that you're in the same place—when it was okay for both of you to have a no-strings-attached relationship with a use-by date of three months? Can you honestly tell me DJ doesn't make a massive difference to the equation?"

"No, I can't. You're right."

"Are you going back to New York?"

"You'd like me to, wouldn't you?"

"What makes you say that? Is that an accusation?"

"I guess it is, Elin. I think you and Barb would sometimes be only too happy to have me out of the picture, now that Jodie's recovering, because it would simplify everything, wouldn't it?"

"It would, if you're going to start messing with my sister's emotions. I'm not having that, Dev, I'm just not. Are you in love with her?"

"Don't ask me that."

"I'm her sister and I care about her."

"It's not fair. You're right, we shouldn't have kissed. And yes, I'm phrasing it that way because you must have seen that she kissed me back." *And if you could have seen her in the park, gasping when I suckled her breast, arching her back, clinging to me and moaning...*

"She's vulnerable."

"I know. It won't happen again."

It couldn't. It was too big a risk.

That pang he'd felt just now when he thought DJ might be ill... Imagine if Jodie tried to shut him out because he'd slept with her and messed with her emotions and she couldn't forgive. Imagine if he lost his daughter because of one piece of very male loss of control. His whole body ignited in Jodie's arms, but his head and his heart had to rule right now. His body didn't get a vote.

"So you're not in love with her?"

"I don't even know what that means, Elin."

"Sure you do."

"I care about her." Otherwise why the heck would he be busting his gut to help her bond with her baby, when it could so easily backfire on him? It didn't make sense.

"You'd damn well better!"

"We have DJ. I don't want conflict. I want whatever we decide, long-term, to be the best outcome we can find for DJ."

She snorted, part pacified, part bristling and protective. "If I think you're going to hurt her…"

"I would never hurt my daughter."

"My sister. I know you wouldn't hurt DJ. That's the only thing that's stopping me from hitting you right now." She bracketed her hands on her hips. "But if you hurt my sister…"

She didn't finish, and he didn't dare to make a promise he might not be able to keep. Sometimes it just wasn't in one person's power to stop the other person from getting hurt. The idea of hurting Jodie… Well, it hurt *him*, it made his chest go tight and his breath catch. But that didn't mean he had the power to prevent it.

"I hear you, Elin," he said wearily. "You've said the right things. I won't forget. I'm glad you came."

The weather was perfect, with a breeze from the northwest making a rare break in the summer's humidity and heat. Jodie couldn't have wished for a better day. Mom and Elin had both said they wished they could come to Oakbank with her, but they had errands to run this morning and Jodie wasn't sorry. The idea of being alone with Dev and DJ frightened her the way it always did—two very different reasons, there—but it was still less daunting than the prospect of her mother and sister watching her like a hawk the whole morning.

DJ was awake and happy when Dev arrived to collect them, to Jodie's relief. It meant he focused on the baby, on cooing at her and picking her up. It gave both of them a distraction and a way to keep their distance from each other after everything that had happened last night.

The unsuspected vulnerability he'd shown over his memories of the accident. The bone-deep need she'd felt to soothe his fear away. The explosive power of their lovemaking. On the hood of the car, for crying out loud, with both of them climaxing within seconds of each other, not caring that they were right in the open air, not caring about the previous agreement they'd made.

He regretted it.

Every word he spoke and every movement he made telegraphed the fact.

Minimal eye contact.

No touching at all.

When his body softened and his voice went tender, it was because of DJ. When he smiled, he smiled at his daughter, and she smiled back. It was the right thing, Jodie knew, the only thing. She should be grateful for it. Instead, she had to fight not to feel shut out. Still, DJ hadn't yet once smiled for her.

Mom and Dev had a little back-and-forth over whether he'd packed enough diapers, and whether she'd be sheltered enough from the sun. "She's too young for sunscreen," Mom said.

"I have a hat for her," Dev promised, "and the stroller's canopy shades her when she's in that."

"Wipes?"

"Right here."

"Pacifier."

"She doesn't like it."

"You mean you don't like it. You don't believe in them. But I raised all four of mine and they were never too attached—"

"I have a pacifier, Barb," he said patiently, "but she just spits it out again whenever I try it."

"It's not important, is it?" Jodie said, and they both looked at her, their frustration with each other spilling in her direction.

"Ready?" Dev asked.

"More than."

DJ was getting on for four months old now, and growing every day, her periods of alert wakefulness getting longer and her body strengthening as fast as Jodie's. You would scarcely know that she'd been born seven weeks premature. Dev strapped her into the car seat and they were away in just a few minutes, after those first awkward moments, heading west out of town to the rolling green hills where Oakbank's twenty horses grazed.

Their route covered part of the same road they'd taken on the way back from the restaurant last night, but it seemed so different in the daylight, none of the menace and memory, and they turned onto a different road before reaching the sign and turnoff leading to Deer Pond Park.

Oh, Oakbank was so familiar and so well-loved and she'd forgotten so much of it, but it all came flooding back, every fresh sight and sound. The gravel of the long driveway entrance popping beneath the tires, the lush shade of the summer-clothed trees, the white-painted fences, the loom of the big red barn as they turned into the parking area.

Behind the barn, beyond a screen of greenery, was the manager's cottage she'd been living in at the time of the accident. Katrina and her boyfriend had it now, although they hoped to buy their own place soon, apparently. Jodie's family had moved all her things back to Mom and Dad's after the accident because no one had known if she'd ever be able to return to her little home. She'd recovered so much better than they'd all feared, but still it might be a while before she could live independently.

Independently…

On her own?

Her and DJ?

She couldn't picture it, tried to imagine herself and a baby in the manager's cottage, but it was such a scary idea. Her fine motor control would have to improve a heck of a lot before she could even think about it. The thought came with a flood of both relief and guilt.

*So don't think about it, Jodie, think about just being here right now instead.*

She saw a string of kids on horseback heading out on a trail ride with members of the summer staff at the head and tail of the group, and realized they must be a batch of vacation day-campers. There was another group doing a beginner lesson in the outdoor arena, where morning shadow still stretched across the sand from a line of cool oaks.

Anna and Katrina, the two full-time riding instructors, knew she was coming. Dev had phoned this morning from his place. They came hurrying out as soon as they saw her climb from the car, and she had to blink back tears as she hugged them both.

"Oh, it's so good to see you!"

"We wanted to visit more...."

"We're so glad you're here."

They'd each come to visit her once in the hospital, but hadn't seemed to know what to say. She'd been a little hurt at the time. They couldn't have come more often? They couldn't have stayed longer, and talked more?

Now, of course, she understood how hard it must have been. They'd known about the baby, but couldn't talk about it because of the medical decision that Jodie herself wasn't yet recovered enough to know. She felt their apology about all those unsaid things in the warmth of their greeting, and something inside her eased a little.

"And I'm so glad I've come," she said. "It's the best thing. Do—do you want to see DJ?"

Dev was unstrapping her carrier from the back of the car. She'd gone to sleep, lulled by the journey. "Can we bring her inside first?" he said. "The sun's so bright." He draped a soft flannel blanket over the top of the carrier handle to shade her.

Anna and Katrina led the way, and Jodie almost kept up with them, she felt so strong and energized just by being here.

The barn was cool and quiet, its wide end doors flung open to catch the fresh breeze. Clean sawdust covered the arena, horses poked their heads over the half doors of their stalls and there was Bess, saddled and working, walking patiently down one long side with a child holding the reins and a therapist by her side.

Dev put DJ's car carrier on one of the bleachers that overlooked the arena and took off the flannel blanket. Anna and Katrina both bent over the carrier, clucking and cooing at the sight of the sleeping baby. "It's incredible, Jodie," Anna said.

"I guess it seems so right and natural to you now," Katrina said. "But we're still in shock. She is beautiful."

"And you are amazing."

That word again. Dev had said it last night.

"I don't feel amazing." And if they knew that it didn't feel right and natural at all with DJ, if they knew she still hadn't smiled at her...

"No, you never do," Katrina said, "but trust me, you are."

"Tell me that once I'm in the saddle!"

"You really want to ride?"

"Katrina, have you ever known me to *not* want to ride?"

"Holly's about to finish her session," Anna said. "You're next."

"Oh, that's Holly?" Jodie looked at the girl in the saddle. "Wow, she's grown since I last saw her!"

Holly had cerebral palsy, and had been coming to Oakbank for hippotherapy since she was six years old. She adored her riding lessons, and had shown significant improvement in muscle tone and coordination over the past four years. As always, she slid down from Bess's back wearing a huge smile, put her arms around the horse's neck and kissed her. "I love you, Bess."

Jodie hung back a little, not knowing if Holly would recognize her after ten months of absence and so much change. Her hair was shorter. Her body moved so differently. She was thinner and so much of her athlete's muscle tone had disappeared. Jodie didn't think that she looked actively *scary,* or anything, but still...

"Say hi, Jodie," Dev prompted. "I don't think she's seen you."

"I— Yes, okay. Of course I'm going to say hi. She's a great kid."

But the moment had gone. With the therapist at her side, Holly had started toward the arena's opposite exit where her mother was waiting, already full of news about her ride. "Did you see me trot, Mommy? I was on the correct diagonal the whole time."

Oh, well, there'd be another time. Jodie walked up to the patiently standing horse. "Hi, Bess," she said softly.

Bess turned a big brown eye toward her, and gave a satiny little prod with her nose. Recognition? Probably. Horses had good memories. Jodie rubbed the horsey face gently, fighting to keep her coordination so that it felt good on Bess's shaggy cheek. "There? Is that okay? Is that how you like it, Bessie-girl?"

Katrina brought a mounting block, something Jodie had never needed before. Then, remembering, she proclaimed, "My helmet!"

"Here," said Anna. She'd crossed the soft sawdust with barely a sound. "It's been hanging on the hook behind the office door this whole time."

"Need help?" Dev offered.

"I'm fine." But it was tricky, and in the end she couldn't manage the helmet's plastic catch and had to accept his offer. His fingers brushed her jawline and the tender skin beneath her chin as he fastened the clasp and she closed her eyes, thinking of last night. Was Katrina watching? Could she see…?

*See that I'm thinking about kissing him, about feeling him inside me.*

It had kept her awake for far too long. The need and wanting. The powerful body memories. The regret. Why had she let it happen? Why had his vulnerability caught so strongly at her heart? Why hadn't she found a different way to respond? How could her awareness of him surge so fast when she had so much else to deal with? It didn't make sense. She didn't want it.

And she didn't want one simple brush of his fingers to take her back to last night with such immediacy and power. The clasp snapped into place and she stepped back, unsteady but very relieved.

"Ready?" Katrina asked.

"Not sure how we do this."

"You've helped other riders a thousand times, Jodie." Kat's voice was an odd mix of deference and encouragement. She was five years younger than Jodie, and had begun working here part-time at seventeen, when Jodie was twenty-two and already a well-qualified riding instructor. Their relationship of mentor and student had changed, too, because of the accident. "You were the one who taught me how to assist a rider with special needs, remember?"

"Different when it's me. Different when my legs don't work right. Can we talk it through?"

"Of course." Katrina talked her through each movement, where each hand and foot went, when she would give a boost.

It felt wrong, and then as soon as she arrived in the saddle, she was at home. "Oh, Bessie, you good girl!"

The horse's broad back was alive and warm beneath the saddle, her mane shaggy in front. Jodie reached forward and ran her fingers awkwardly through it, while the familiar horsey smell rose to her nostrils. "Are you going to lead me, Kat?"

"Yep, if you want."

"I haven't been led on a horse since I was seven years old!"

"Well, I could set up a show-jumping course for you,

with twelve fences and five-foot-high rails, but you'll have to give me a few minutes for that."

"Okay, just for you, we'll save that for the next ride," Jodie said.

It was so weird and at the same time so good. Katrina led Bess at a walk, and the horse's rocking rhythm was more even and steady than Jodie could yet manage on her own legs. This was one of the benefits of therapeutic riding. It gave people a sense of the natural rhythm of movement that they might never have experienced on their own.

Soon she was smiling broadly. Her family had never understood her passion for horses. Where had it come from? No one knew. No one else shared it. No cowboys or rodeo riders in the family history, that they knew of. But somehow it was just there, growing in her bones from when she was seven years old and had taken her first pony ride on the woolly back of a chubby Shetland pony.

Sitting on Bess now, she felt like *herself* for the first time since the slow slide out of her coma, and it was so wonderful to discover that the old Jodie still existed somewhere inside her, even if her body couldn't show it yet.

*I'm me. I'm still me.*

*And I'm a mother. I have a baby girl.*

"Could DJ come up here with me?" She didn't even think about it, just said it.

The baby was awake now, Jodie knew, because she could hear the start of some little fussing sounds coming from the car carrier. Dev had turned a couple of times to check on her. She was getting bored, all the way over there on the bleachers. Maybe she couldn't see her mommy riding, from so far away, and wanted to take a closer look.

Katrina asked Bess to halt. "Could she? I think it's up to you, Jodie. You know better than me that Bess is the safest horse in the world, and she's not depending on your cues with the reins. You want to sit DJ up there and hold her?"

"Is it okay with you, Dev?" It felt strange to be looking down on him. He stood there, watching her intently, head a little tilted to one side, eyes narrowed. She must have shocked him with the idea of having DJ up on a horse at less than four months old, but not a bad shock, apparently. He was thinking about it, not rejecting it.

Jodie held her breath. *Please agree. Please. Just say yes. Don't question it.*

If he wanted to know why it was so important, she knew couldn't explain in words.

"She does seem to be getting a little bored over there." He'd echoed her own thought. "You think she's going to be a pony gal, like her mom?"

"Hope so!"

He gave a brief nod, didn't say anything out loud, then began walking in DJ's direction. A minute later he'd unstrapped her and brought her over. She was wriggling, sitting up in his arms. She was reaching the same kinds of milestones as Jodie herself. Growing stronger. Becoming more alert.

"How is this going to work?" Dev asked.

"Could you hand her up to me? And then keep ahold of her, just in case? I'll sit her here at the front of the saddle so she's leaning against my stomach. If you just put a hand on her front…"

"Should work," he agreed.

DJ seemed to like the idea. She was waving her arms,

taking happy little breaths and making sounds. Katrina stood beside Bess's head, stroking her nose and cheek and telling her, "You're getting another passenger, but she doesn't weigh a whole lot. Is this a first for you? I think so."

Dev lifted DJ up and settled her against Jodie's front. Jodie wrapped a hand around her middle and found Dev's hand there already, as she'd asked. Their fingers touched and laced together because there was no room for them to do anything else, and the downy back of DJ's little head bumped gently against Jodie's stomach.

With Dev's other arm behind her on the saddle, she felt so close to him. Closer, in some ways, than she'd felt last night with his hands and mouth on her breasts. He could have pillowed his head against her thigh by moving just an inch or two. She remembered what he'd said that first evening at his place, when she'd learned the truth about DJ's birth. *We're a family.* For the first time, with Bess's warm, living strength beneath her, and DJ and Dev both so close, she actually believed it might be true.

"She seems real excited about this," Katrina commented.

"Is she smiling, Kat?"

"No, not smiling, but so alert. Are we standing still, or walking?"

"Walking," Jodie answered. "Ready when you are, Kat. Dev, are you? Will you be able to keep pace in that position?"

"I'm fine. She is really happy, look at her, she's bouncing."

"Still not smiling? I can't see."

"Serious, still, but so eager. You're not missing anything by not seeing her face. It's her body doing the talking."

"Oh, it is, I can feel it. Oh, DJ, you're so happy, aren't you?"

Not smiling, but maybe just as good.

Katrina clicked her tongue and told Bess to walk, and the wonderful rocking motion of the horse began again. Her hooves barely made a sound on the soft sawdust, and when they passed the big open doors where the sun came streaming in, her brown coat gleamed. DJ bounced and made her cooing and gurgling sounds. Dev muttered, "Just managing to keep up, here" beneath his breath, and then, a little louder, said, "She's loving it. Isn't she?"

All Jodie could say was, "Oh! Oh!" Her face hurt from smiling, and her vision blurred with tears.

*I'm holding her and it feels right. We're on a horse together and she loves it. She feels like my daughter. My very own daughter. For the first time. I can feel it. I can feel what Dev feels about her. If only I could see her face! That's the only way this could be any better. I never understood. I never knew this was how it could feel.*

Oh. Oh.

There were just no words.

*I must not let her see how scared I am,* Dev thought.

It was perfectly safe. He knew it with his head. His heart couldn't feel it. DJ? His precious baby girl? Fifteen weeks old and on a horse, five long feet from the ground?

But he could see what it was doing for Jodie and that made the fear unimportant. It was such a beautiful sight. Jodie's smile. DJ's excited bouncing, her little mouth open but serious, her hands batting in the air. The horse so slow and steady and patient.

He had to walk almost leaning against the warm equine body in order to keep one hand in place against DJ's stomach. The other hand he rested on the back of the saddle, an inch from Jodie's rounded backside. She'd worn stretchy jodhpurs, sand-colored, because that was what she always wore for riding, and man those things looked good on a woman's body!

His half-side-on position gave him a perfect view of the rhythmic rock of her hips in the saddle, and the only thing that stopped him looking too long and hard and thinking all sorts of forbidden thoughts about last night and those rocking hips on the warm hood of the car was the better view he got from looking higher up, where the big, teary-eyed, dazzling grin on her face just wouldn't go away, and the slight crookedness and lack of control in her arms and shoulders didn't seem to matter at all.

"Oh!" she kept saying. *"Ohh!"* And kind of laughing and crying at the same time, while DJ sat pressed up against her and all that Jodie body language of reluctance about holding and touching her baby had miraculously gone.

He wanted to wrap his arms around her and plant exuberant smooches of congratulation all over her face. *You're amazing!* He wanted to soften those same arms and give her kisses that were tender and wondering and soft on her mouth. *You're amazing.*

This was what he'd been drawn to at eighteen, even though he'd never acknowledged or acted on it back then. This was what still drew him—the combination of fragility and strength, the petite body that had a warrior's fight in it, the determination and perseverance along with a huge, dazzling, sexy smile.

If this was his old life, in New York, he knew what his next move would be. Whisk her away somewhere so that this fizzing need inside him could find a happy release. Ten days in Paris, a three-day weekend in the Bahamas. It had worked for him, in the past.

He always picked the right kind of woman, sophisticated and high maintenance and impossibly well-groomed. Always had a great time, while in the back of his mind—and the woman's—the clock ticked and the objections mounted up.

He couldn't have spent his life with a woman whose grooming rituals took up two hours of every single day. She—a series of them, over the years—couldn't have spent hers with someone who read the international section of the newspaper every day like he was prepping for an exam and then actually wanted to *talk* about it. He couldn't have seriously fallen for someone who paid that much attention to shoes and whose voice went whiny and childlike the moment she didn't get her own way. A few weeks together, though…great.

He'd been smug about it, he now realized. He'd been far too certain and confident about his choices. The right kind of relationship, with the right kind of woman. He'd had it all sewn up, all his bases covered.

Jodie wasn't the right kind of woman.

But she was the mother of his child.

And he'd be stepping back from the whole situation as soon as she was able to take care of DJ herself, as soon as he trusted that they had the right arrangement in place. It was the only thing that made sense. It was— even though they never said it straight out—what her family wanted.

But hell, she looked fabulous up there, grinning from ear to ear, with DJ nestled against her front. He didn't want it to end.

His first inkling of the new arrivals was the sound of Barbara Palmer's voice. "Oh, sweet jeepers, and she has the baby up there, too!"

Before Katrina, Jodie or Dev himself could react, Barb and Lisa came hurrying across the arena. He couldn't see them fully, as Bess's body masked his view, but there could be no doubt about their attitude. Katrina told Bess to halt, which she obediently did, while Jodie had stiffened in the saddle and tightened her arm around the baby.

Dev tightened his own fingers, so that their two hands were knotted tightly together. He felt Jodie squeezing, and squeezed her back. *It's okay, they seemed to be saying to each other. We're in this together, and we're not going to apologize for any of it.* He came so close to laying his cheek against her thigh.

*You're amazing....*

"It's fine, Mom," she said. "Katrina has the horse, Dev has DJ, nothing bad is going to happen."

"It's not fine! How can you be so irresponsible with your own daughter? How can you even put this as a priority, coming here, at this point in your rehab? Getting on a *horse?* When walking and showering and brushing your hair are still so much of a challenge? How can you?"

"I thought you had errands this morning."

"Lisa called, and I told her you were coming here, and she wanted to take a look. I decided the errands could wait."

"Honey," Lisa said to her sister, "Mom's right, don't you think?"

She was already reaching up, standing on Bess's other side. Dev would have had to fight her for the baby, snatch the little body from Jodie's front with a rough movement, to keep her under his own control. He didn't do it.

"Never mind yourself," Lisa went on, "although that's bad enough. But to put a fifteen-week-old pree-mie baby on horseback?" She had DJ safely in her arms in a couple of seconds, and began to stroke her silky little head, kiss and hug DJ against her sun-darkened collarbone. She loved her baby niece, no doubt about that. She seemed genuinely shaken by the idea that DJ had been all the way up there on scary Bess's back.

"She liked it," Jodie said.

"Liked it? How could you? Project that onto her? I mean, seriously!"

"We could tell. It was clear."

"You are *projecting,* Jodie. I'm actually pretty angry about this! After we've been so careful, so worried—"

"Lisa, I promise you—"

"Honey, Lisa doesn't mean to sound so—" Barb began, cutting in.

Lisa shook her head back and forth. "Yes. Okay. I'm sorry. Not angry. Just questioning your judgment, okay? And your priorities. Sure, I mean, I guess it sounds great." She mimicked, "'Wow, I was back in the saddle four weeks after I came home from the hospital. My daughter started riding when she was less than four months old.' But it shouldn't be about your ego, should it?"

"It's not about my ego." Jodie's voice had grown strained and tense. The happy grin had gone. And the tears. She was frowning, dry-lipped. "Is that what you think?"

"It's what I thought when you tried to give my Izzy riding lessons when she was three years old. You wanted to turn her into a superstar in a few months, winning ribbons in show-riding competitions and heaven knew what else."

Dev felt his tension level climb as the argument grew more heated. He knew about siblings. He had an older brother in California, a criminal defense attorney, who could still push his buttons when they met up at family gatherings. *Just keep DJ out of it,* he wanted to say, but managed to press his mouth shut.

"That was ten years ago," Jodie was saying, "and I was only just starting out instructing. Izzy didn't like it and so we let it go."

"After she almost fell."

"She didn't *almost*. I had the pony by the bridle and he settled down in about five seconds. I had no idea you were still upset about that, after so long. And it was never about winning ribbons."

"I'm not still upset. I'm not." Lisa shook her head frantically again. "Just seeing you there with DJ reminded me, makes me question what it's really about. Photos for the Oakbank website?" She gestured behind her.

"Photos?" Jodie and Dev both looked where she was pointing, over at the bleachers nearest the office, and discovered Anna there with a camera.

Anna began to walk toward them, her movement a little graceless and awkward as if in apology for the tension she sensed in the air. "I'm sorry, did I do the wrong thing? I didn't want to interrupt and get you to pose, but you looked so great, I just couldn't resist grabbing the camera."

"Great?" Barb exclaimed.

"I didn't know Anna had the camera," Jodie said tightly, then turned to her friend and spoke in a bright tone. "But it's fine. Did you get some? I'd love to see them."

"So they're not for the website?" Lisa persisted.

Dev answered her. "Of course they're not for the damned website! And if they were…"

Had they not seen how Jodie had looked relaxed and happy and *herself* for the first damned time since she'd woken up, how she'd held DJ like a mother for the first damned time since she'd learned the truth about her pregnancy? Had they not even taken a moment to notice any of that before barging in? Would it be such a terrible thing to have a picture of Jodie and her baby girl on the Oakbank website, when she loved the place so much?

"I'm tired," Jodie suddenly announced. "My legs are starting to shake. I think I'd better call it quits for today."

"For today?" Barb wailed.

"Yes, I want to keep doing this. Get better at it. Move on from Bess to Snowy, and see how I go."

"You can't mean you're going to try to ride again the way you used to?"

"You said you hadn't sold Irish."

"Because I knew you'd want to see him. Not *ride* him. You'll never ride him, Jodie."

There was a sharp, painful silence. Dev could have shoved his daughter's grandmother facefirst into the sawdust floor, he was so angry with her. Nobody yet knew whether Jodie's recovery would be complete enough to allow her to ride the way she used to. How could Barb preempt the worst-case scenario like that? How could she shatter Jodie's hopes?

Jodie's jaw set hard and stubborn at her mother's words. "Then DJ will ride him instead. He's only nine years old. She can start on him when she's ten. She'll be a strong rider by then, and he'll be mellow as a lamb at nineteen."

"This is ridiculous," Lisa muttered.

"You got that right," Dev said, his own jaw painfully tight.

It was ridiculous that they'd come. Insane that they were creating conflict out of something that had been so joyful until five minutes ago. Ridiculous and insane and just plain insensitive.

He managed not to say any of this out loud. But he pulled DJ out of Lisa's arms. "I think she needs a diaper change."

"Kat, can you get us back to the mounting block?" Jodie asked in a strained voice.

"Sure, of course. You okay to get that far?"

"I'm fine. As long as Dev has DJ."

"I have her." He turned his back on Lisa and Barb, not certain which of them owned the greater share of his anger. He'd thought of Lisa as an ally, until now. Out of all of the Palmer women, she was the one who was least inclined to underestimate Jodie or overprotect her, the one who might understand that Jodie's bonding with DJ was incomplete and that they might need to try some pretty imaginative strategies to get things on track.

Like putting the two of them up on a horse.

But now he felt betrayed. She was the one who'd gotten Barb's blood up this morning. So Lisa had "wanted to take a look"? Wanted to sabotage the whole event, more like. He didn't doubt that her motives were good. Pristine and pure. She loved her baby sister. Maybe that long-ago episode with Izzy and the riding lessons really did still scare her, even if at heart she knew it wasn't Jodie's fault. The whole family loved her. But boy could love be blind sometimes!

He wanted to tell both women, "You have ruined the best moment Jodie has had since the accident." Even better than last night, because it was right, while last night, in hindsight, probably wasn't. He wanted to say, "You have set her back weeks with DJ. Maybe even months."

And there would be no second chances on those months. They would be the months when DJ would learn to laugh and sit up and look at picture books and maybe even crawl. They would be the months when her sounds would start to mean something to her, and when she would start to distinguish between the faces that looked at her with love and the ones that didn't.

If Jodie lost that little spark of love and rightness that had ignited in her today, when the two of them had sat on Bess together… If it didn't fan into a bright, life-long flame because Barb and frigging Lisa had come along and put it out…

Freaking hell, he would find that hard to forgive.

## Chapter Nine

Maybe a real mother, a good mother, wouldn't have done it. Maybe it was the last thing a normal, good mother would have done, asking to have her tiny baby up there with her in the saddle.

Jodie thought about it all day, through the drive home with DJ and Dev, through the tense lunch of chicken salad rolls that her mother made for the two of them after DJ had had her bottle and Dev had gone.

She and Dev had barely spoken to each other in the car, so different from the mood last night when he'd revealed so much and she'd felt so much care. "Are you angry?" she'd asked him.

"Of course I am. Not with you."

She'd wanted him to say more, but he hadn't and she hadn't felt able to push. Angry with Mom and Lisa for interrupting? Angry with them for being right? Angry with himself? He drove less smoothly than usual, those strong hands sliding around the steering wheel, foot stabbing at the brake, eyes unreadable behind his sunglasses.

The powerful body language made her intensely aware of him, the way she'd been up on Bess, with their fingers twined together and his head so close to her thigh. She had to fight not to steal sideways glances the whole time, and itched to touch him, too, to place her hand on his shoulder or his thigh, in an attempt to connect. It wasn't a very obedient hand, though, Ole Lefty. It tended to crab into a tight claw, or twist its fingers at the wrong time. Even if she had dared to touch him, the touch would have turned out all wrong.

He wasn't just angry, but absent. Somewhere else. His thoughts ticked furiously—she could almost hear them—but she didn't know what they were about. They'd almost reached home when she ventured to say, "I guess we'll wait a bit before we try this again."

"Mmm?" Her words had pulled him back from a faraway place, it seemed.

"Before we go back to Oakbank," she explained.

"Look, I don't want to create a rift between you and your family."

"I know. I hate being at odds. They care about me. And they care about DJ."

"Yeah, Oakbank…" He was still deep in his thoughts. Oakbank apparently fit someplace in there, but she didn't know where.

"Well, here we are.…" she told him. Unnecessarily, as he was already turning into the driveway.

And now lunch with Mom, and DJ's spreadsheet-dictated schedule, and a quiet afternoon, when Jodie had half hoped to be at Oakbank most of the day, watching the day campers and group lessons, visiting her favorite horses in their stalls. The whole morning had left a sour taste, far more so than what had happened between her and Dev last night, and she questioned everything about it.

Lisa called in that evening, saying, "I'm sorry," before she'd even entered the house, and they sat in the kitchen together and drank glasses of iced tea. Mom had DJ out on the porch swing at the front of the house, and Jodie could hear the sound of lullaby singing.

"I think I came on too strong this morning," Lisa said. "I know I did. I was just so scared, that's all, when I saw you there, and with the baby."

"I was perfectly safe, Lise. I had Dev and Katrina right by me. Bess has been a fully trained hippotherapy horse for ten years, and she is incredibly well looked after so she doesn't get tired and sour. She is wise and perceptive and calm as a pond. I would trust her with my life."

"We're just a little worried about your priorities, that's all."

"I want to get as strong as I can. I want to put the accident behind me and start being normal again. And riding has always been so much a part of normal for me."

"I just question—" Lisa stopped, huffed out a breath. "Look, I'll just put it out there. How often are you going to blow off your rehab to go to Oakbank?"

"Don't say it that way. I didn't blow it off. Dev called Trish and she thought it was a great idea, as long as I was careful."

"We're just concerned. We care about you."

"I know. Just don't smother me, okay? I hate it."

"Is she fussing tonight? Is that why she's out on the porch swing with Mom?"

"Um, I think she's fine."

Mom had kept DJ to herself all afternoon, telling Jodie that she needed to rest "after that whole mess this morning." And it was true that she'd felt extra tired, emotional and not as capable as she wanted to be. She'd spent too much time trying to recapture the morning's wonderful, heart-melting sense of certainty about DJ and her own role, but she couldn't. Was it because the mood had been bruised so abruptly? Or was it her own fault?

She didn't want the baby to pick up on all her self-questioning. Horses had such an uncanny instinct about human emotions that they were practically psychic, so why shouldn't babies be the same? It meant something that DJ hadn't yet smiled at her. It hurt her and scared her and she didn't want to make things any worse. So she stayed away, and DJ seemed to have a contented, peaceful afternoon.

Dev hadn't called. The spreadsheet said he was supposed to have DJ overnight today, but the spreadsheet hadn't seen what had happened at Oakbank this morning, so it was even more out of the loop than usual.

"Anyway, I'm sorry," Lisa said again, repeating it and explaining her motives until this, too, felt like a form of smothering.

Mom came into the kitchen with DJ propped on her hip. She rubbed at the small of her back with her free hand as if it were aching, and every pore of her skin looked tired.

"Mom, give her to me," Jodie said, too concerned about that aching back and tired skin to remember her own fears and doubts until after the words were spoken.

Mom shook her head. "It's fine."

"Are you sure?" But, so help her, she felt relieved.

"She'll be ready to go down as soon as she's had her bottle, I think. Dev hasn't called, and he's usually here earlier than this. Is he coming, I wonder? Well, I'm not going to call him. If he wants her, he needs to say so, and if she's down for the night and he shows up, I'm not disturbing her."

"We're all tired," Lisa announced, as if it solved everything.

Dev arrived at the Palmers' twenty minutes too late.

"She's down," Barb told him at the front door. "She went down at seven. Why didn't you call?"

"Because it was already settled that I was having her tonight." He tried to sound patient and pleasant about it, but knew he wasn't succeeding. He gentled his tone further, but still couldn't keep the frustration at bay. "Was she that tired you couldn't have kept her up? It's not like she's asleep at the exact same minute every night."

"You're usually here by six."

"I was…caught up." He'd had a crazy afternoon, getting back to the office to encounter an unexpected crisis with a longtime client of his father's, and then a long call from New York about the international legal case he was supposed to be working on in London in the fall.

The call pulled him back into his work, reminded him how much he enjoyed it. For the first time since DJ was born, he almost forgot her existence, and then he remembered with a flood of conflicting emotion… all that love, all that uncertainty.

He'd spent hours on the phone and at the computer, dealing with the client's problems and the London case while at the same time trying to put a plan in place that he had no intention of sharing with Barbara at this stage.

He just might share it with Jodie's dad, Bill, because occasionally the quiet man gave an inkling that he was more on the ball about Jodie's needs than he let on.

He'd grabbed coffee and a sandwich on the run, had twice been about to send a text to Barb or Jodie to tell them he was running late, but then something else had come up and the text never happened. In the back of his mind, because of Barb's own spreadsheet, he hadn't thought it mattered that much. Now, she'd used a poor excuse yet again to keep DJ under her own roof.

If this was so that Jodie could spend more time with the baby, then he wouldn't have a problem with it, but that wasn't happening. None of the Palmer women seemed to have any thought that Jodie needed help, not with baby-care but with bonding. They were in a state of massive denial, and if he didn't take drastic action soon, then his relationship with the entire family would descend into open conflict.

He couldn't let it happen, because if they or Jodie somehow managed to shut him out of DJ's life... His scalp tightened with dread at the very thought.

"You're not going to wake her?" Barb asked, telegraphing her disapproval very clearly.

"No, I won't wake her. Is Bill around, though?"

"In the basement. Shall I call him?"

"No, I'll go down."

Ignoring Barb's visible curiosity about why he might be seeking out her husband, Dev found him at his workshop bench, planing a curved piece of oak with an old-fashioned handheld plane. Dev couldn't work out what the piece of oak was for, and said so.

"It's the main," answered Bill.

"The main what?"

Bill chuckled. "No, m-a-n-e. I'm making a rocking horse. For DJ."

"Oh. Oh, wow."

They both stood there in a manly silence for several moments, while Dev took in the other pieces of the rocking horse. He began to see how it would all fit together. It was going to be a beautiful piece of workmanship. "I'm not good at the fussy stuff," Bill said eventually.

"This doesn't look fussy at all. It looks…like a piece of art. Incredible."

"I mean the fussy stuff with diapers and bottles."

"Right. You must have done your share."

"When I had to." He chuckled again. "But I like to be involved in my own way. Things like this."

"She'll love it."

"Her first Christmas, I thought. She'll be able to sit on it by then, with help."

"It's going to be really wonderful."

"Going to paint it like Jodie's Irish, dapple gray." He fell silent again, and his laconic manner transmitted itself to Dev, who couldn't find a way to say what he wanted to say. He wasn't even quite sure what he was trying for. In the end it was Bill who helped him out. "I love my wife and my girls," he said, "but it's not going right, is it?"

"No…"

"With DJ, I mean, and Jodie."

"No, I don't think it is."

"Right now, she's everybody's baby, the way Jodie was when she was little, especially after she was ill. She fought it. The horses were the best thing that ever happened to her, although Barb still can't see it. I don't want to watch Jodie hanging back with DJ, not knowing where she fits, not trusting herself with the baby. My wife and my daughters are trying to help, but they're doing it wrong. You can see it, can't you?"

"Yes, I can."

There was another silence. Bill picked up his plane. "Should we get involved?"

"I think we have to."

"Any ideas?"

"That's what I wanted to talk to you about," Dev said.

"And...score!" Trish said.

"Yay, it went in the tub." Jodie clumsily clapped her hands. "That's three times, now."

"Wow, Jodie!" Elin said. She'd dropped in as she occasionally did, to play cheerleader to Jodie's efforts.

Trish moved to retrieve the tennis ball from the big pink plastic bucket, which was about three feet in diameter, six feet away and hard to miss. But the close proximity hadn't stopped Jodie from missing it with the ball about nine times before her first hit. "I'll get it," she said quickly.

"Sure?"

"You and Elin keep scrambling up, and it's good for me to do it, right? Makes the whole exercise more complex and useful." She stood up, walked over, bent down, put in an intense mental effort and got her fingers to close around the ball. Back in her seat, she threw it again—*let go, crazy fingers!*—and there came another rubbery plop as it landed in the bottom of the tub. "Yeah, all right!"

"You're getting much better at this," Trish said.

"Wanna move the tub farther away?" Jodie asked.

"Not today. Practice a little more on your own, if you

want, before we break for lunch. I need to go check on Alice." Trish gestured across to another rehab patient working on a puzzle on the far side of the room.

"Of course I want," Jodie said, and went once again to pick up the ball—before Elin could do it for her.

She threw it, let go at the wrong time and missed by a mile.

She went to retrieve the ball from under the occupational therapy unit craft table—before Elin could do it for her—but someone else had gotten there first.

Dev.

He had a fabric baby pouch strapped over his shoulders, with DJ cradled against his chest.

She went hot and flustered at the sight of them, since Mom's spreadsheet hadn't breathed a word to suggest they were coming. Dev looked somehow formidable today, despite the softening accessory of a baby dressed head-to-toe in pink, right down to a tiny bucket-shaped pink sun hat. His jaw was set, and there was an electricity of intent humming inside him. It flustered her even more, as soon as she picked up on it. "Hi," she said, and asked—before Elin could do it for her—"What are you doing here?"

"It's all okayed with Trish and Lesley."

"It is? What is?" She looked in Trish's direction and received a smile and a thumbs-up in reply.

"Yes, Dev," said Elin, who hadn't been looking at Trish. "What are we talking about?"

"Um, Elin, if you don't mind this is between me and Jodie."

"Well, it isn't, really." She frowned at him. "If you recall our talk the other night."

"Talk?" Jodie came in. "What talk?"

They ignored her. "This has nothing to do with what

we talked about the other night," Dev said to Elin. "I've already agreed you were right about that. So would you mind please—?"

"Butting out? You're telling me to butt out? Mom told me what happened yesterday at Oakbank."

"I told you, too, Elin," Jodie said. "I told you it was great."

Again, they ignored her, glaring at each other, then Dev very deliberately turned in her direction. "I'm a little early, Jodie, because DJ woke up earlier than usual and it seemed best to show up now, before she gets fussy. Ready to go?"

"If you tell me where."

"Can't do that." He picked up her purse.

"Devlin!" Elin said.

"I am not dealing with you right now, Elin. I am not justifying myself to you, or to Lisa, or to your mom. Talk to Trish about it, if you want, but I need to get going before DJ falls apart. Jodie?"

He began to walk toward the door, his stride so long and assured and angry that Jodie had this dizzy, illogical panic that she would never see DJ again if she didn't follow him, so of course she did.

It was as if he had a gun pressed to DJ's head. Or to her own. It was a hostage situation or a kidnapping, he was that cool and controlled and ruthless about it. Elin seemed rooted to the spot. Trish was watching carefully from the far side of the room. When Elin took a pace forward, she called her quickly, and Elin went over to her, chin defiantly raised but ready to listen. A moment later they were in a very female huddle, with Elin nodding and frowning, and Trish persuasively arguing… something.

In a summery skirt and white lacy top, Jodie wasn't

dressed for a kidnapping. In fresh blue jeans and a designer polo shirt, neither was Dev. Where was the no-brand jacket and pulled-down baseball cap? The baggy clothing where he could hide the gun? "Dev, you have to explain."

"When we're in the car."

"Okay. I mean, I'm pretty hungry, so if it's lunch…"

It couldn't be lunch. You didn't kidnap someone to take them to lunch.

"Lunch is included."

"Good." She managed a skipping step to keep up with him, and almost fell.

He stopped. "Sorry, I'm going too fast."

"A little. Some people might say it's me going too slow."

He kind of gathered her against him, running his arm beneath hers and around her back, reaching up to settle her uncooperative left hand on his shoulder. Her whole body began to blur. That was how it felt. Blurry and fuzzy and soft. Happy. Her mind was racing but her body was happy, where it belonged.

His hip pressed into her side and DJ in the front carrier was right there with her little leg flapping against Jodie's stomach. Her hat was about to fall off. Jodie made an ineffective reaching movement with her right hand, and Dev saw what was happening and flipped the darling little pink-flowered bucket back into place.

"Let's not go slow, if we can help it," Dev said, in the corridor, and she could feel the vibration of his voice against her ribs. "Elin's probably sending out an APB, as we speak."

"So I'm right." She'd gone breathless, could he hear? "You are kidnapping me?"

"Yep, me and DJ."

"Oh, she's in on it?"

"Joint criminal masterminds, the two of us."

"That's a relief. I was scared she might be the hostage."

He turned serious suddenly. "Never, Jodie. I promise you that. I'll never try to use her as any kind of weapon or leverage or— But I think we really need to do this."

"I—I think so, too. Whatever it is."

"Thank you." He lost a little of the gun-to-the-hostage's-head feeling, and they walked together, in step, with DJ making sounds against his front and it just went on feeling way too nice, a complication Jodie didn't need when there was so much else to work out.

"Can I ask what it is?" she managed to ask.

"We're not telling you till we're on the road, are we, little pink person?"

"DJ, you'll tell me, won't you?" she said to the baby.

But DJ wouldn't spill.

Dev's car was parked in the visitor spaces out front. The day was bright and sunny and hot, and the effect of the air-conditioning had worn off during the time it had taken him to come into the rehab facility and collect her, so he opened all the doors to vent the hot air before strapping DJ back into her car carrier.

Jodie stood waiting and watching. She couldn't do that yet, the bending with DJ in her arms, the adjustment of the little body in the carrier, the fiddly, fine-motor-control-requiring snap together of the safety straps. He straightened and closed the car door. "Need some help getting in?"

But this she could manage on her own.

He went around to the driver's side, started the engine and the air-conditioning and they swung out of the parking lot and into the street.

"Now explain," she said. "You're not taking me to Oakbank behind my family's back?"

"Would that be terrible?"

"I— They're driving me crazy, if you want the truth, but they're doing so much to help. I hated that Mom and Lisa just showed up like that yesterday. It ruined the moment—"

"You got that right."

"—but it's because they care."

"Starting to wish they cared a little less. Or thought a little more."

"So we're not going to Oakbank?"

"Nope, although we can go visit horses at some point, if you want."

"At some point? What is this, Dev? Trish approves, I could see that. She was arguing with Elin back there and going blue in the face about it. Do Mom and Dad and my sisters know?"

"Your dad does. I talked to him last night. He packed your bag for you."

"Mmm, that might be interesting…"

"I gave him a list. He said he hadn't had any trouble with it."

"That might be even more interesting."

"Your mom and Lisa must know by now, because Elin would have told them the second Trish finished explaining. But your dad agreed it was best to keep quiet till we swung into action. Of course you can tell them, as soon as you want. Call them," he suggested, "once we're fully on the road."

It wouldn't be long. The car swooped between the traffic lights, made a tidy right and a wide left. Another two minutes and they'd be out of town. Jodie felt a surge of exhilaration and freedom that she hadn't had since before the accident. It was such a familiar feeling, yet distant somehow, because she hadn't had it for a long time. It was like urging Irish into a gallop across a wide green field, scary and wild and wonderful. Free, yet not alone. In control of something stronger than you were yourself.

"Yesterday was— I am not having that happen again," Dev said. "And even to find Elin there with you this morning. I appreciate she wants to support your therapy, but yet again, it turned everything into a big deal when it shouldn't be. That's why you need this. We both do. DJ does."

"You mean it really is a kidnapping?" She began to laugh. "You're not giving me back? There's not even a ransom note?"

"Not for at least a week. We need some time on our own, the three of us—I've found a cabin, made a reservation—and this is the only way it's going to happen."

"So you haven't even given them an address?"

"When I talked to Trish about it, she could see how important it was, and she's happy to have you take a break from rehab for a week or so, since you're tiring yourself out trying to make progress. She has the address."

"But she'll only hand it over once there's five million dollars in unmarked bills deposited in a locker at the bus station."

"You're really getting into this kidnapping idea."

"Yep."

He thought for a moment, then laughed. "Me, too."

They hit the highway and he sped up. DJ lay quiet in her seat. Jodie turned to look at her and found her kicking her feet in her tiny pink cotton shoes as if she were getting into the kidnapping idea, too. She smiled at the baby. *Hello, sweetheart.* But the smile was self-conscious and she wasn't surprised when DJ didn't smile back.

*You can't make it happen, Jodie. Just give it time.*

"Can I be the one to fire the gun from the car window to blow out Elin's tires when she comes after us?"

"Sure, since you've decided you're in on this, too."

"What should it be? A rifle? A sawed-off shotgun? I'm not real clued in on weaponry."

"Me, neither. But let's go for total overkill and make it an AK-47. You'll find it on the backseat next to your daughter."

She laughed again, then thought…daughter…mom. "What's my mother going to think? She's not going to let it rest with Dad."

"Your dad sees and knows more than he lets on. And he's strong-minded, when he wants to be."

"Oh, you noticed that, too?"

"He'll handle her."

"He will." Once more, she laughed. "He sure will!"

Dev pulled off the road at a shaded picnic area where there were wooden tables with bench seats and playground equipment and a picturesque pond with a viewing platform for spotting turtles and water birds. He'd brought a simple lunch of sub-style sandwiches and cartons of juice, and DJ watched them eat it from a commanding position in her car carrier, resting on top of the table. Dev cooed at her and she batted her hands for him and broke into the most dazzling smile.

*So I do get to see her smile, even if it's not smiling for me,* Jodie thought. "It's so quiet," she said out loud, because the smiling thought was painful despite how sensible she tried to be. "I love the quiet."

"Yeah, no phone calls, so far."

"They're probably running hot, back in town."

He packed up the picnic things, strapped DJ back in the car and they set off again, zoomed along in their bubble of air-conditioning, changed from highway to county road and the bends beckoned like a movie's happy ending, and DJ, without a care in the world, fell sound asleep.

## Chapter Ten

Dev buzzed with victory and optimism the whole drive. To tweak Jodie's kidnapping comparison a little, he felt as if he were driving the getaway car after a billion-dollar heist. Yes, he had the precious cargo right here with him, and there was no one on his tail and he owned the world.

Almost four weeks ago, he'd told Jodie that the three of them were a family. Now at last they might have a chance at working out what that meant, the way he'd wanted from the beginning. He was a lawyer. He liked to know where he stood. He liked the ground rules in place.

Most importantly, he had a deep-seated need to see Jodie being a mother. Something would have to fall into place then, wouldn't it? She would find out what she wanted. She'd talk about it. They would come up with their own much simpler version of Barb's ridiculous spreadsheets, and if they could present a united front, then the three Palmer women would surely step back and give them some space.

He accepted that he wouldn't get to have DJ under his own roof, long-term, as much as his heart wanted, but he thought—or told himself—that he could deal with this as long as everything was amicable and settled. He'd *have* to deal with it.

It might even be pretty nice, down the track. He pictured a tomboy of an eight-year-old girl arriving at his place for regular visits with a purple backpack full of stuff. He saw himself on the phone with Jodie, negotiating in a friendly, casual way over what each of them would give DJ for her birthday and which of them would get to have her for Thanksgiving and Christmas. He saw himself returning from consultancy work in Asia or Europe with exotic trinkets for his daughter and her mom.

Braking to a halt in front of the cabin, it struck him that this picture was a little too simplified and idyllic to be plausible. DJ would probably acquire a stepfather at some point, for example. Jodie was too amazing to spend her life without a loving partner, if she wanted one.

And would Dev always buy those exotic trinkets himself, or would there be another woman in the picture with him, tolerating his absorption in his growing daughter, for the sake of a short-term sizzling affair?

New York was ten-hour's drive from Leighville. London and Hong Kong were a heck of lot farther. Right now, twenty-four hours without seeing DJ seemed like too long. What made him think it was going to get easier? What would happen if Jodie's bond with DJ became so strong that his own role ceased to matter?

The sense of victory ebbed like water out of a bath, but he pushed the doubts and questions aside. He'd been told the keys to the cabin would be waiting for them, beneath a flowerpot containing a red geranium beside the front door, and he could see the geranium from here.

Jodie stirred herself beside him. She hadn't been sleeping but she'd been very quiet, almost dreamy, and had now been roused by the dying of the engine. "So this is it?"

"Take your time. DJ's asleep. I'll bring in our stuff."

"Okay. Might grab a drink of water." She stretched in the passenger seat and found the water bottle he'd given her earlier.

Dev hit the trunk catch and brought out his bags and the cooler and boxes he'd packed with food. Jodie had opened the car door and pivoted to stretch her legs down to the ground. She was sipping on the water, looking around, apparently liking what she saw. She stood up and pushed all the car doors wide to give DJ plenty of fresh air while she slept. With the car parked right in front of the house in the shade and the whole place quiet and secluded, it would be perfectly safe to keep her there until she woke up on her own. Jodie bent to brush her cheek with one soft finger, then began to walk toward the cabin, a soft smile on her face as she took in the peaceful setting.

*I've done the right thing,* Dev decided. The only thing.

The place was beautiful, more like a log home than a cabin, larger than they really needed, only a few months old and built by the people who farmed this land to rent out for family vacations. It was also adjacent to a state park. He'd found it on the internet, looked at the photos and the map, liked the high ceilings and huge stretches of double-glazed window, the loft bedroom upstairs that he could use, and the master bedroom downstairs for Jodie, so that she wouldn't have to climb up and down.

Behind the cabin was a huge stretch of forested state park, with walking trails and a lake for boating, while the view through those enormous windows took in rolling green farmland and a wide bowl of sky. Outside, there was a garden and a deck, a swing set and a barbecue, while inside he liked the huge open-plan kitchen and living area, with its big squishy tan leather sofas and clean-cut décor. There was even a bookshelf crammed with vacation reading, ranging from crime fiction to teen vampire novels to romance.

The only downside, made apparent before Jodie had even made it through the front door, was the cell phone reception.

It was wa-a-ay too good.

When Dev came out for a second load of gear, Jodie had her phone pressed to her ear and was seated on the wooden steps that led up to the deck. She hadn't even made it inside. "It's beautiful.… No, she's asleep.… Plenty of space, it looks huge… Do? Does it matter what we do…? No, please don't call that often, Mom, you'll only get frustrated.… Why? Because I'm switching it off!"

She slid the phone shut with a click, stuffed it into her bag, looked up at Dev and gave him an upside-down smile, which he read like a book and reflected right back to her.

*Families.*

*It's so great to be here.*

*Oh, you understand? Perfect.*

They should be looking away from each other at this point. It had gone on for too long, and it was dangerous, after the massive flare of heat between them two nights ago. But he couldn't do anything about it, he just kept looking.

She leaned her head against one of the sturdy verticals of the deck railing, while Dev had stopped with his hand holding the door. His breath caught in his chest at the sight of that amazing, contradictory Jodie package. The strong will. The petite body. The forgiveness toward her family. The stubborn, triumphant action with the phone. The failed bond with her baby that his head understood the reasons for, while his heart just couldn't get at all.

Then she raised her arms in the air and deliberately broke the moment with a goofy grin and an exuberant yell, that echoed into the forest. "Woo-hoo!"

How was he going to keep from touching her? He'd promised Elin and himself that he wouldn't, but how? How was he going to make this week work the way it needed to?

He had to tough it out, that was all, pure and simple, keep his focus and his priorities, and he thought that Jodie did, too.

She'd yelled too loud, Jodie soon realized. She'd woken the baby.

Which was probably a good thing.

Because if she and Dev were going to look at each other like that again anytime soon, she might just conclude that way too much interference from her mother and sisters was exactly what they both needed. She had so little willpower where Devlin Browne was concerned.

DJ began with a whimper and a snuffle, progressed to a short riff on her current favorite sound—

"eeaaaah"—and then began to cry, building to full volume in around forty-five seconds.

Dev just stood there.

Jodie looked at him, heart sinking, head a mess. Her sense of peace had vanished so fast.

By now, at home, there would already have been at least two pairs of feet hurrying across the grass, two voices cooing and two pairs of hands reaching out, neither of them hers. She would have seen DJ safe in someone's loving arms being soothed and settled, and possibly changed and fed and made to smile, before she'd even pretended to herself that she was getting up and going over, before she'd begun to wrestle with the frightening, horrible reality that she didn't want to.

But Dev just stood there. Daring her. Waiting her out.

Judging her how much? Seeing how much?

Seeing *everything*.

She could see the muscles bunched at his jaw and his fingers tightening against his palms. He wanted to go to DJ. But he wanted Jodie to go more. And he understood exactly how much she struggled with it. It shocked her that he knew what was in her heart. She felt naked and guilty and defiant and just miserable. Why had she thought going away, just the three of them, would be a good idea?

"Don't make it into a big deal," she blurted out.

"You're the one who's doing that."

"No, I—" She stopped. "Am I?"

"I can't stand to hear her cry, by the way."

"Are you angry?"

"Not at all. Can you stand it? Listen to her."

"Please, please don't make it into a big deal."

"I'm not."

It was true. He wasn't *making* it into a big deal, because it already was one, all on its own. Dev didn't need to do a thing. The problem was her.

"I'm afraid I'll let her fall."

"I won't let that happen." He moved a little closer, treading down the front steps to ground level as if to reassure her that he'd be close behind.

"I'm afraid she'll cry worse if I pick her up, because I'm not the one who's familiar and I want her to love me and I'm scared of what she can see and feel. She's never yet once— Dev, she's never—"

"Come on." He reached out and pulled her up, and she decided not to make the horrible confession. *She's never smiled at me.*

Oh, DJ was a mess already! No question of smiling now. Her face was red and screwed up and even though Dev had parked in the shade and they'd left all the doors open her fuzzy, dark little hairline was slicked down with sweat from the effort of her crying.

Jodie fumbled with the clips of the car carrier, hating the fact that her fingers were still so wrong. They gripped when they should be loosening, they wouldn't obey her at all. Dev had to step in. He had the straps undone and loosened and out of the way in a couple of economical movements, intending to help but only underlining Jodie's inadequacy in the process. How could she take care of a baby safely?

She slid her hands behind DJ's back and managed to lift her. "I'm sorry I'm so bad at this, sweetheart…."

Sweet.

Heart.

*She is, but I'm not feeling it. All I'm feeling is the fear. All I'm hearing is the sound of her cry, and it's so*

*loud and piercing and desperate, and makes me feel
so helpless because I don't know how to make it stop.*

She couldn't even feel Dev, although she knew he
was right beside her. He was a pillar of rock, hard and
blind. She straightened with DJ in her arms, and the
baby was so wriggly and heavy. Jodie's disobedient left
hand made a claw on the little pink-clad back. "Are my
fingers digging in? Am I hurting her?" she asked in a
panic.

"No, you're fine. Your hand's a bit tense, but it's
okay." He covered her hand with his, eased the claw position into softness. "Can you carry her into the house?
Let me know the second you think you're losing it. She's
due for her bottle. She wasn't ready for it when we had
our lunch but now she's probably crying from hunger,
so let's just head right for the couch."

"Can I get that far?"

"If you can't, I'm here. Try."

And she knew he was asking for much more than
simply making it to the couch.

So she tried.

*This is my baby. I love her. She's precious and tiny
and such a massive bundle of potential. Dev and I
made her. She's the two of us in combination, but she's
unique. She's dynamite. She might be president, some-
day. An Olympic champion, a world-famous musician, a
beloved wife. Beautiful and clever and kind and brave.*

*Who are you, DJ? When will you stop crying? When
will you smile at me?*

They climbed the steps. The cabin was cool inside,
shaded by the nearby woods, its screened windows
thrown open so that the breeze came right through. The
place was so new it still smelled like cedar and pine.

Jodie reached the couch and sank into its softness.

Dev slid a pillow beneath her arm for DJ's head. She wasn't so frantic now, but still she was crying. The sound and movement of it consumed her whole body and she didn't even seem to know that she was cradled in someone's arms.

Her mother's arms.

"I have a bottle made up for her," Dev said. "It's in the diaper bag. She'll need it warmed up, but that'll only take a minute or two."

They seemed endless, those minutes. DJ's eyes were screwed tight with crying. Jodie tried smiling down at her. Babies smiled when they saw someone smiling at them. So far it hadn't worked for her and it wasn't going to work today. "I love you, precious girl," she said, wondering what punishment life had in store for a woman who lied to her own baby.

"Here," Dev finally said, handing her the cylinder of plastic, warmed to blood heat.

Jodie shoved it into DJ's mouth. Oh, she didn't mean to do that, but her muscles weren't cooperating and it just happened. The plastic circle that kept the rubber teat in place bumped hard against DJ's gums and the baby shrieked.

"Oh, no… Oh, no…" Jodie said.

"It's okay. Did you slip?"

"Yes."

"It's okay."

"I hurt her."

"She's forgotten about it already."

And she had. Her little pink mouth had closed around the teat and she knew exactly what to do. She sucked it and the bottle began to make a singing sound as it emptied. "Will she get gas?"

"Give her a break. Lift her onto your shoulder and pat her back. Can you do that?"

"I think so." Clumsy, but still. DJ gave a burp and then a big wobble. Jodie half expected her to start crying again but she didn't, and with Dev's help she was soon in that lovely cradle position again, crooked in Jodie's left arm, beneath her breast, ready to finish her liquid meal.

She slowed toward the end of it. She was getting sleepy again. Jodie thought about enlisting Dev's help to put her down in the bassinet he'd brought, but decided there was no hurry. Okay, so DJ hadn't smiled yet, but she wasn't crying. Okay, so there was no overwhelming wave of love like the one Jodie had caught such a short, lovely glimpse of in her own heart at Oakbank, but still, this felt… It felt…

Peaceful.

Unhurried.

Unpressured.

Worthwhile.

*Maybe I'll close my eyes for a little, too…*

She woke up when Dev took DJ gently from her arms. "How long was I—?"

"Half an hour or so."

"And you've been sitting there the whole time in case I let her fall."

"Not the whole time. I took out some insurance." He gestured to a big, soft nest of pillows laid out on the floor in front of the couch. "She wouldn't have gone far. So I did some unpacking, set up the kitchen. It's beautiful outside. Hot, but there's a breeze, and the woods are shady. Want to explore?"

DJ did. She was wide-awake, bouncing in her daddy's arms, a pink frenzy of energy. With a dexterity borne of experience, Dev strapped her into her little front pouch carrier, facing forward so she could see everything that was going on.

"I'd love to explore," Jodie told him. "Let me change out of this skirt, though."

Dev screwed up his face and said slowly, "Yeah, about that…"

She gave him a questioning look.

"Remember in the car when you questioned your dad's capabilities in the packing department?"

"Uh, yes, I do."

"Well, you'll see for yourself."

"You're scaring me now." She stood up and made her way to the bedroom at the back of the cabin that looked out onto the woods. It was a lovely room, spacious and clean-lined, with the greenery outside giving it a cool light.

Dev and DJ followed her into the room and she saw that he'd opened the suitcase Dad had packed for her, but had left it on the bed with the top flipped back and everything still in place inside. "Just so you don't check the contents and decide I sabotaged them," he said. "This is exactly the way he had it."

She looked at the tangle of garments in the crammed piece of luggage. "This is it? This is what he packed?"

"I gave him a list, remember? He told me he'd followed it."

She looked some more, dipped her hands into the tangle and pulled out a pair of scarlet pantyhose she'd once worn as a Moulin Rouge dancer to a fancy dress ball. "Can I ask what was on the list?"

"Underwear and socks, a swimsuit, something warm in case the nights chill down, a couple of outfits for going out, daywear, et cetera."

She rummaged a little more. "Well, okay, I guess it's all there."

She set everything out on the bed, while Dev and DJ watched. DJ seemed to love the color and movement.

Item one—what looked to be the entire contents of her underwear and sock drawer, and she'd had "tidy underwear drawer" on her to-do list for a good six months before the accident. She thought about apologizing for the number of bras, since Dev had been the one to lug the suitcase inside, but didn't want to call attention to it.

For some reason, he seemed to be smiling.

"Did, um, my family toss any of my stuff when they moved it out of the cottage at Oakbank?"

"You tell me. You seem to own forty pairs of socks now. How many did you own before?"

"What can I say? Horse people need a lot of socks." She turned back to the suitcase.

Item two—a chocolate-brown halter-neck bikini she hadn't worn in five years, because on vacation in Florida where she'd bought it, it hadn't seemed too skimpy, but in Ohio it definitely did. Well, at least it didn't weigh much.

No comment from Dev.

But he was still smiling. Or had it progressed to a grin at this point?

Item three—the huge, vibrantly colored and fringed silk-and-wool gypsy shawl was warm, for sure, and finely woven and beautiful, but she kept it hanging in her room more as a decoration than something to wear.

"Where'd that come from?" Dev asked.

"Lisa bought it for me when they went to Europe."

"I think DJ likes it." Facing out at his chest height,

she was kicking her legs and flapping her arms. Not smiling, but close.

Item four—the bridesmaid dresses from Maddy's and Lisa's weddings. Maddy had gone for a sophisticated look, and her bridesmaids had worn strapless gold-and-silver sheaths. Lisa had wanted a Victorian feel with a hint of burlesque, which for some reason added up to sage-green satin overlaid with black lace. DJ liked both of those, too.

Item five—a single summer top, one pair of shorts and some hiking boots. "Those will team great with the shawl once the sun goes down," Dev said.

"Well, as long as I color-coordinate the socks…" She'd reached the bottom of the suitcase. "There's no pajamas or shoes."

"Huh. Sorry. My bad." He spread his hands, but they were grinning at each other, because how could you not? The whole bed was a mess of fabric and balled socks.

"Or toothbrush or makeup."

"Those were meant to be covered by the et cetera."

"Not as far as Dad was concerned, apparently."

"I should have checked."

"Or brush or comb or shampoo." She looked helplessly at the mess and thought of Dad, Dev's coconspirator, his intentions so good and the result so…*not*. "It's too funny, Dev. I love it!"

"You do?" DJ jiggled her little legs some more, against his front.

"It's so Dad. It's— Mom and Elin would have packed perfectly and sensibly and used up three suitcases. Dad just wanted us to make a clean getaway and didn't think it through."

"The clean-getaway part was pretty important."

"Yep."

"So…shop first and then explore the place, or the other way around?"

"The other way around. I didn't come all this way to buy a toothbrush. Even the hospital gift shop had those."

"And dinner out tonight, I'm thinking. Some low-key kind of place where they won't hate us for bringing a baby."

"Is there any other kind of place in Southern Ohio? Not sure I'll be wearing either of those dresses, though."

They took an easy ramble around the cabin, finding the start of the trail through the woods, a bench for sitting and looking at the view over the rolling woods and farmlands, a stone birdbath, and a newly planted stretch of garden that would look fabulous in a few years, especially in spring when the dogwood trees came into their extravagant white and pink colors.

With the baby right in the thick of things against Dev's front, Jodie expected him to push her a little, the way he had earlier when she'd been crying in the car, but he didn't and she was thankful for that. She needed breathing space. She couldn't bear to rush, or push herself.

In case DJ felt her tension and doubt.

In case Dev guessed just how blocked and lost she was, and despised her for it.

"It's so peaceful here," she said, aware of him watching her too closely, as he sometimes did. Did he see as much as DJ? She mustn't let him see. "So beautiful."

*Look at the beauty, Dev, don't look at me.*

Beyond a field of tall corn, they could see the farmhouse belonging to this piece of land. Jodie wondered if they'd meet the owners during their stay. She'd like to thank them for this place. "We'll definitely be back," she would want to tell them, but she didn't know if that would be possible. Who was "we"? Herself and DJ? All three of them?

"Like it, then?" Dev asked.

"Very much."

"DJ seems pretty happy, too." Okay, that was a push from him. The baby dangled against his front, completely at home in that position.

Because Dev expected it—and because she knew he was right—Jodie said to her, as brightly as she could, "Are you happy, DJ? Are you having fun?" And DJ gazed back at her with those big, wise eyes and didn't smile.

## Chapter Eleven

That night, as planned, they went to a family-style place where no one minded that DJ lay in her stroller right beside the table and sat on Dev's lap for her bottle, and where there was a change table in a space of its own adjacent to the bathroom. The place quickly filled up with groups of all sizes, parents and grandparents and kids, couples with toddlers, dads with daughters, moms with sons.

An older couple came past on the way to their table, while Dev and Jodie waited for their entrées, and paused when they saw the baby, back in her stroller and growing sleepy. "Oh, she's beautiful!" the woman said.

"I'm sorry," the woman's husband apologized, standing back a little. "She never can resist a baby."

"It's fine," Dev said. "We think she's pretty hard to resist, too."

Jodie smiled and nodded and felt so exposed.

"How old is she?" The woman turned instinctively to Jodie.

*Because I'm the mom.*

"I— She's—" Her mind went blank and she didn't have the right answer. Did she say four months? DJ looked too small for that. So did she explain right away that the baby was born early?

"Almost four months," Dev answered easily, before Jodie had solved the dilemma in her head. He'd met these kinds of questions before.

"She's tiny!"

He'd met this reaction before, also. His answer was as easy and cheerful as before. "Getting bigger as fast as she knows how."

"What's her name?"

"We call her DJ."

"Oh, but that's short for something, right? My niece is CJ, short for Caroline Jean."

"We haven't decided yet, so for the moment it's just DJ."

"You haven't decided? And she's four months old? Well, if that don't beat all!" The woman laughed, not unkindly but definitely in surprise, as if today's new parents were a mystery to her, in a cute sort of way.

Jodie said quickly, "I like DJ. I can't imagine calling her anything else."

"Well, she is adorable."

"You make a beautiful family," her husband said, and the couple moved on.

"You like DJ?" Dev echoed quietly, once they were out of earshot. He leaned a little closer across the table and she felt their complicated connection like honey melting over her.

"I do. It belongs to her now." She remembered that

shocking day four weeks ago when she'd found Dev at his front door with his crying daughter in his arms. "It's…how we were introduced."

He sat back again. "I'm sorry, it just worked out that way."

"You don't have to apologize."

"We do need to find something, though, or she'll get that woman's reaction about her initials for the rest of her life."

"Dani Jane," Jodie blurted out, because suddenly it seemed important for DJ to have a proper name, one that came from her mom, one that was chosen with joy, even if no one used it very often.

"Yeah?" The intent look came again, coupled with a spark deep in his eyes. "You want it to be Dani Jane?"

"I don't know where it came from. But I just had a feeling. It's kind of sassy and strong, as well as being feminine. It's not too big a step away from DJ. When she's older, it gives her some choices about what she calls herself."

"I like it. What do you think, baby girl?"

But DJ had fallen asleep and couldn't give an opinion. Their meal arrived, in the form of two steaming plates of home-style meat and vegetables—one meat loaf, one sirloin tips. The other adult diners were tucking into similarly hearty fare, while kids mostly had plates of nuggets and fries or spaghetti with meatballs. There were at least four high chairs in use, and lots of messy kid faces streaked in ketchup or sporting milk moustaches.

"We fit right in," Jodie said.

"Weird, huh?" He frowned, suddenly.

"Not so weird."

"Different, then."

"You don't like it?" All Jodie wanted right now was to fit in, to be a normal mom.

"Let's just say, I'm a little suspicious when I fit in too well."

"You're an outlaw at heart?"

"I like a little adventure, for sure."

"This gravy is an adventure, as far as I'm concerned. What is that?" She speared a dark blob.

"Mushroom, I'm pretty sure."

"Okay, not such an adventure. Well, but it is, actually. Just being here. When a few months ago I was… nowhere. Something strange happened at first, Dev, although it's ebbing now. Sometimes when I smelled or tasted or touched something, the sensation was so strong and new. The day of the barbecue, when Dad was cooking those onions. It was as if no one in the world had ever smelled fried onions before, and the ketchup, too. It was like discovering gravity or gold."

"I've had that feeling sometimes with DJ," he answered slowly. "I hadn't thought of it that way, but you're right. As if I'm the first person in the world ever to take care of a baby. Just the smell of her hair…"

"Adventures and experiences don't have to be big and splashy, do they? The tiniest moments can be precious, and so fresh they sparkle."

"That's true…" His eyes had gone smoky and thoughtful.

*I just wish I could find those moments with our baby,* she wanted to tell him. *I wish the smell of her hair would make me feel as if the whole world was new. I wish I could see her smile for me.*

Should she say it?

But she left it too long and the moment passed and she was too scared. It was good being here with Dev.

She couldn't bear to spoil it, couldn't stand the idea of seeing his face change if she said too much about what was and wasn't in her heart.

DJ stayed asleep for the whole of their meal but wakened and grew fussy as they drove back to the cabin. Dev could tell that Jodie was tired, she knew, and he gave her the kind of easy way out she'd come to expect from her mother and sisters, not from him.

"You need a good night's sleep. Find something to read from that shelf of books to lull you off, and I'll take care of DJ. She can sleep in my room upstairs, and that way we won't disturb you if we're up in the night."

She should have argued. A normal mom would. A normal mom would never have reached the point where her baby was four months old and she'd never yet wakened in the night to handle a feed or a diaper change. But she didn't want to argue. What if she did wake for DJ and couldn't get the baby to settle again? What if she ended up calling for Dev because nothing was working, including her left hand as she attempted a solo diaper change?

To hide her feelings, she teased, "I must have worked pretty hard today to get that kind of a break."

But he was very serious when he answered. "You did great today, Jodie. You named her."

"I—I guess I did. Must have really taken it out of me, because I'm wiped." Don't cry, Jodie. Don't let him see. Step back so he doesn't feel how close you are to the edge. "Thank you," she said, falling back on those very useful words, not even knowing what she was thanking him for, right now. "In that case, I'll see you in the morning."

For nearly an hour she lay in bed listening to the

sounds he made as he took care of DJ, settled her in her bassinet, then relaxed in the living area with music playing.

Aching for him.

Aching for herself and what she was missing.

Aching for DJ, who had the best dad in the world.

The baby had a good night, Dev said. They ate breakfast out on the deck, just cereal and fruit and coffee. Since it would be kind of useful to have a toothbrush and more than one pair of pants, they drove half an hour to a major store and picked up a few essentials. Jodie would have bought more, but DJ began to signal that she thought shopping was way overrated, so the one extra pair of shorts and a strappy tank would have to do.

After lunch and naps for both mom and baby, Dev suggested exploring the trail through the woods, and that sounded safe. A family thing to do. A time when the dad carried the baby in that little front pouch.

"Time to break out the new shorts, you mean?" she said, so that he wouldn't guess what she was thinking.

"Sounds like a plan."

He left her alone to change. She was getting faster at it, but Ole Lefty still made some of the movements a challenge at times. In ten minutes or so, she met him back in the living area and they left the cabin, found the start of the marked trail leading into the woods and lost themselves in the cool greenery.

They walked slowly, because that was all she could do, but the pace didn't matter. Side by side, Jodie could hold on to Dev when she needed to, and he seemed to have an instinct about that, turning a little whenever the terrain grew too uneven. There were simple wooden benches at intervals, really just two tree stumps with a plank nailed across the top, but they gave her the chance to sit and regroup, and meant that they could go farther.

There was a stream gurgling just out of sight, tantalizing them with its delicious sounds. There were cardinals and warblers, and they saw a greenish-brown salamander flick itself beneath a rock. The air had a fresh, peaty smell and it was so peaceful and quiet, just the sounds of water and leaves, their footfalls on the mushy earth, and Dev talking to DJ about the things they saw.

"See the cardinal? It's red. Look at it flashing through the trees, baby girl."

Jodie felt shut out of his ease with the baby, even though she was right by his side. How could he talk to her like that, so unselfconscious about it, when DJ couldn't possibly understand? Red? Cardinal? How old would she have to be to learn colors and birds? She looked so happy there against his front in her pink outfit, with his voice so familiar in her ears.

*I'm jealous....*

Jodie felt the painful, complicated twist of it and hated herself. How could she ruin such a perfect afternoon with her own messed-up feelings? She'd thought a walk in the woods would be so safe, but instead she felt as if she'd walked into an ambush.

"She's a little young for the nature talk, isn't she, Dev?" The sour twist of shame and disappointment came out in her tone, despite her best efforts.

"I hate when I hear parents talking to kids as if they're not really people," he answered easily, as if he hadn't heard the tone. He must have.

"But you coo at her." Her throat was tight. She'd cooed at DJ, too, but it felt as if she were acting a role that she'd been cast in by mistake. Faking it. And badly.

Like last night, when she hadn't been able to answer a simple question about DJ's age.

"I coo at her," Dev said. "I talk to her, I sing to her, I even confess things to her, sometimes."

"Confess things?" What did Dev have to confess? He had become the most amazing father in such a short time. He was doing everything right, the way he always did, without making a big deal out of it in any way.

He mimicked himself. "Man, honey, I'm not so keen on this diaper change stuff. I'm hoping you'll potty train real early."

She gave an upside-down laugh, disappointed. "Oh, that kind of confession." She blinked fast, feeling the wash of tears.

"Why, what did you think?" He leaned a little, his shoulder giving a gentle, playful push against hers. He couldn't have seen the tears. She'd blinked them away. He mimicked again. "DJ, don't tell the cops, I wrapped the gun in a rag and buried it in the backyard under the red rose bush."

But she couldn't laugh about it. "Thank you for kidnapping me," she said, her voice even tighter, unsteady now.

"We're back to that?" He put his arm around her.

"I need this. I'm not getting it right yet. You're being…so patient. But I need it so much." She stopped and pressed her lips together. Could she tell him? A part of her wanted to hold it back. Because what would he think if he knew? But then the words just came. "I'm afraid I'll never get it right."

"Get it right?"

"The love. Loving her. Being her mom." She was crying now. "It was a bad start. But that shouldn't matter. Other mothers have bad starts. A difficult birth, or a baby in the NICU so they don't get to hold her right away. I don't know why it matters for me, what's gone wrong, why I can't feel it. Don't tell me I need professional help. I have a ton of that with the rehab, and it's great, Trish and Lesley are both amazing, but I don't need any more of it. I just couldn't bear to have a therapist teach me how to be a mom, no matter how sensitive and skilful and well-meant."

"Hey… Hey…" He half turned her to him and she buried her face against his shoulder so he wouldn't see just how much she was crying.

Oh, who was she kidding? He didn't need to see. He could feel.

Her shoulders were shaking and she couldn't make them stop. For a long time she just let herself cry about everything in the whole world. About the accident and Dev's suffering that night and the birth. About the struggle with her body and brain. About Mom and Dad and Elin and Lisa and Maddy caring so much but understanding so little. About Dev putting his high-flying career in New York on hold, whether temporary or permanent, so he could be DJ's dad.

Oh, and why not just throw in war and the environment and a few natural disasters at the same time, and cry about those, too? She couldn't remember when she'd cried this hard.

Finally she spoke again. "I love her." DJ made the third side of their triangle. She'd gone quiet now, against Dev's chest. "I must. I do." Those little legs had stopped jiggling. "But I can't feel it. That's the most awful thing, Dev, such a terrible thing." Of course Dev talked to DJ like a grown-up, because those big, swimmy eyes of hers seemed to be taking in every horrible word Jodie spoke, every sobbing gasp of breath. "You must hate me right now."

*Both of you.*

He said gently, "What, you think I didn't guess from the beginning that you were having problems?"

"I—I— Mom and Elin and Lisa keep telling me it's because of the rehab, because I get too tired."

He made an impatient sound.

"But you don't buy that idea...."

"Maybe they really think that," he said. "Or maybe they're in denial. Or maybe they want to go easy on you for the best reasons in the world."

"That's pretty pointless, when I can't go easy on myself."

"You have felt it, the love. You felt it on Thursday at Oakbank, when you had her sitting up in front of you."

"I—I did. It was so wonderful. Such a relief. But it didn't survive Mom and Lisa showing up, and yesterday I struggled so hard, and that's crazy, for it to be so fragile."

"So it's fragile, for now. Dressing yourself was fragile a few weeks ago. Before that, talking was fragile. Your brain and body got stronger."

"It's not my brain. It's my heart."

"Don't worry about your heart."

"How can you say that, when for you it's so easy."

He gave a snort of laughter. "Easy?"

"It is easy. You change her and feed her and bathe her and carry her around and all the time you just love her without even trying."

It was true.

So help them both, it was true.

Dev fought to find an answer, a reassurance that wouldn't be glib and wrong, but he couldn't find one.

Jodie was right. Against everything he would have predicted about himself a year ago, he found it so easy to love DJ, and he couldn't just tell her mom how to do it, step-by-step, not when she was crying and crying like this, when the difficult words she spoke were just temporary lulls in the storm of sobbing and tears. He thought that the crying was vital and necessary, and it had been a long time coming, he guessed.

Tell her how to do it?

*First, kiss her darling forehead and blow a raspberry on her tummy....*

No. They were both out of their depth. Everything seemed like a platitude.

*Relax. It will happen.*

The only thing he could think of, the only thing that seemed to make sense at the moment, was to give love and reassurance to Jodie, and hope she'd be able to pass it on. Love worked that way, didn't it? The more you gave, the more there was. DJ had taught him that, just as Jodie had taught him that adventures could happen in the tiniest sparkling moments. He was still thinking about that.

"So maybe you shouldn't try, either," he finally said. "Maybe you should let go, and forgive yourself, and have some trust."

"Mmm." She sniffed and he clapped a hand to the back pocket of his pants in search of the wad of clean tissues he kept in there for DJ's needs. Jodie mopped at her face and he led her back to the last bench they'd passed, about fifty yards along the track, and they sat.

Just sat.

Shoulders pressed together, bodies like magnets, hearts in tune.

She needed this.

"I think you've always worked for what you wanted, haven't you?" he said, after a while. "I remember when you were sixteen when we put on that play and you wanted to do the lighting. You didn't know anything about theater lighting, but you promised you'd learn, and you did. You worked so hard at it. You've worked so hard at your riding, worked to gain the management skills so you could run the whole stable."

"You remember the lighting?"

"I wanted a red spotlight for my big speech and you wouldn't give me one because you thought it was melodramatic. You argued with the director—I've forgotten her name—until she saw your point."

"And you've hated me for it ever since. I'm amazed you remember this."

"Haven't hated you. Got over my ego, discovered you were right and admired you for fighting. But I don't think you can fight and work in that same way to learn love. Love just…happens."

"How did it happen for you?"

"With DJ?"

"Yes. Tell me about it, Dev. You've told me about the birth and how much she weighed and how much oxygen she had to have and all of that. Tell me about you. Because you were there. And I wasn't."

So he told her. Because she was right, she wasn't there, and *of course* he needed to tell her, and he should have realized it weeks ago. Just like her family, he'd protected her too much. While he spoke, DJ sat in her little pouch against his chest and listened to the sound of his voice coming through his shirt until she fell asleep.

"Well, after the first shock of the blood test showing you were pregnant, it was a while before anything happened," he said. "They focused on getting you stable, and I was pretty busy with getting the plates in my leg. Then they did an ultrasound and I saw her. Saw the beating of her heart."

"Oh, wow."

"I'm so stupid, they gave me pictures and I put them away and there was too much else to think about and I haven't shown them to you."

"It's okay. I'm picturing it now. I can see the real pictures later. I want to."

"They did another ultrasound at twenty weeks and I was so scared they'd find something was wrong with her because of the accident, but everything was normal and we could see she was a girl."

"So you knew she was a girl three months before she was born."

"And you weren't there to talk about names with me. And I didn't want to give her a name you turned out to hate. So she has the two initials on her birth certificate. We're allowed to change it officially later. The more I think about Dani Jane, the more I like it."

"Thank you."

"No, thank you. You gave her her name. That's important. Maybe if—"

"You're skipping ahead. Don't. Please."

"I am. Sorry. The next thing that happened was seeing her move, watching your tummy rippling and kicking up. It was…hard…amazing. But hard."

"Hard, why?"

"For your mom and dad and sisters. They laid their hands on your stomach and felt her kick, while you weren't moving at all and we didn't know if you ever would."

"Oh."

"It was… Yeah, the doctors weren't saying much

about your recovery at that point. Some encouraging signs with your scans and tests, but a long way to go."

"And did you, too?"

"Did I, what?"

"Put your hand on my stomach."

"Once. It seemed— I wasn't sure that I had the right to. But your mom wanted me to."

They both sat and thought about this for a moment. Dev remembered it so vividly, but couldn't put it into words. Jodie with her eyes closed, never moving, with those high-tech mechanical guardians around her, the monitors and alarms and tubing. The cool weave of the white hospital sheet. It had grown warm to his touch. He'd thought the baby had stopped moving for the moment and that he was going to miss out. He couldn't feel anything. She was as still as her mom. But then…

A twitch. A flutter. And then an actual kick, two or three of them, hard little bumps against his hand.

And he believed that day, as they all did, that if the baby could move so vigorously then Jodie had to be functioning in there somewhere. She had to be making progress.

"Were Mom and Dad angry that I was pregnant?" she asked.

"Angry? Jodie, it was just about the only thing that got them through it. Something to hope for. A sign that your body was still working enough to grow a healthy new life. None of us ever once thought about the fact that it hadn't been planned. It felt as if it *was* planned, by something greater than ourselves."

"And what happened next?"

"Well, you opened your eyes." Could she hear the scratch in his voice? Could she see him blinking too much? "That was pretty exciting. We'd been talking to you all along. We did tell you about the accident and the baby, but you don't remember."

"Not at all. Not even an inkling."

"We stopped talking about the baby at some point, because the doctors thought it might be too confusing for you, too stressful, if you kind of half understood in the coma but couldn't speak or react."

"I don't remember opening my eyes."

"No, well, it didn't last long, the first few times. That was hard for your mom. She expected too much, too quickly. She kind of nagged you about it and got very frustrated and upset and had to back off."

"I can imagine."

"Then DJ put on a growth spurt and they didn't like the fact that you couldn't move. They were afraid the blood supply would be compromised. They started talking about inducing labor early, but it happened on its own. Your mom was sitting with you and she could see the contractions, the tightening. You grimaced when they happened, and we all got pretty excited about that, too."

"Were you there at the birth?"

"Yes, right there the whole time. It was a quick labor, only a few hours, I think I told you that. Dr. Forbes had me cut the cord. They had to get her stable, but within a few hours I was able to hold her. They had us skin-to-skin."

"Skin—? Both of you? You and DJ? You mean you had your shirt off?"

"Yes, and she was just in a diaper. They do it a lot, now. It helps the baby's breathing and heart rate. They've done studies. Preemie babies gain weight faster if they can have skin-to-skin contact with their mom or dad."

She was quiet for a little while, thinking about this, and then she asked, "Did I have her skin-to-skin with me?"

He had to clear his throat. "Yes, a couple of times, the first few days."

"Oh. Oh, wow. I think— I think— No, for a moment I thought I could remember it. But no. I don't think it's a memory, I think it's just— Why didn't they keep doing it?"

"You got an infection and you were very sick for a while, and it wasn't safe for DJ to be with you. She went home, and that was when you started to wake up, and you were so confused."

"Confused… Maybe I remember that, a little. I didn't like it."

"You moaned a lot and seemed very distressed for several days. They didn't know at that point if you had permanent brain damage, and they decided it would be best to keep the baby away."

"Oh, I wish that hadn't happened."

"We just didn't know at that point, you see, if you'd ever be able to take care of her, or even take in that she was yours. It's been a miracle, really. It's so amazing to see you now, walking in the woods, talking and laughing, when a few months ago… Don't beat yourself up, Jodie. About anything. You're amazing."

*You're amazing….*

*Pull back, Dev. This is too strong. This isn't what she needs, or what you need, either.*

They both knew it. Jodie eased away from the shoulder-to-shoulder contact, pressing her lips together, visibly fighting to steady her breath. "Thank you," she said. "I've said that about five thousand times since I came home. But this is the biggest. Thank you. I needed to hear all of that. It's hard. This dramatic life story that I don't remember. But it helps. It will help, I think."

She stood up and walked to the nearest tree. Her movement was unsteady and lopsided and Dev wanted to jump up and give her his arm but he held himself in place, tried to watch her without it being too obvious that he was concerned. They both needed some space.

She leaned on the tree, her good hand running up and down the smooth trunk, then pressed her forehead against it as if it could infuse her with strength. She was thinking about something, wrestling with it, trying to decide what to say. He could see it, didn't know whether to prompt her.

"Need to head back?" he asked.

"We'd better."

He checked his watch and found it was already five o'clock. DJ would be wanting another bottle soon, or a nap first if she wasn't hungry yet. Later they could give her a bath and put a blanket on the floor so she could have a kick and a play. He outlined the plan to Jodie. Would she leave it all to him? Maybe he shouldn't have responded so much to her fatigue last night.

She stood straight, and there were two bright spots of color in her cheeks. "I want to take care of her tonight," she said. "By myself."

Yes-ss!

But there was more, and it was important, he could see. The color flamed even higher and there was a glitter of courage and determination and stubbornness in her blue eyes, the same glitter he'd seen yesterday when she'd told Barb and Lisa that if she could never ride Irish again, then DJ would.

"Dev, I want to have her skin-to-skin, the way I did in the hospital but don't even remember. Could we do that?

There's a spa bath in the master bedroom. We could go in it together. I'd want you nearby in case I slipped. But when you said I'd had her against my bare stomach in the coma when I don't remember… I want to have that happen. Then maybe she'll— Maybe at last I'll get her to—" She stopped and took another shuddery breath. "I want to know how it feels."

## *Chapter Twelve*

"Of course we can do that." His voice came out on a husky rasp. "Absolutely, we can do that. We'll put you both in the spa bath."

"That would be perfect. I—I'd love it."

Forget giving Jodie space, he couldn't help himself, he had to touch her. Because of the color in her cheeks and the brightness in her eyes. Because of the emotional roller coaster that was still taking her on the ride of both their lives. How could he not touch her?

Hand on her hair, brush of his mouth across her lips to say, *I'm proud of you, I know how hard all of this is, you're amazing.*

She responded briefly to his kiss and the magnetism between them would have kicked in as strongly as ever, if there hadn't been this one thing that was even more important.

"Help me get back to the cabin?" Her left hand had

gone into its crab shape on his arm. He was coming to love Ole Lefty, as she often called it, because it tried so hard and was so brave when it failed, clawing and unable to let go, as if a victim of its own determination. Like Jodie herself. "I've done too much walking, Dev. Too much of everything." She laughed. "Crying. Living."

He put his arm around her waist and she leaned against him and they didn't need to speak anymore. It was a slow journey. He could have kept reassuring her, she could have kept apologizing, but they didn't. They didn't need to. The apologies and reassurances were understood between them without words. If he hadn't had the baby against his front, he would have offered to carry her, even though he knew she would have refused.

"So, did I win? Where's my gold medal?" she said as they came up the steps. "What, last place? Oh, well…"

"Last place? Of course you won," he told her.

DJ had gone to sleep. He laid her in her bassinet in the living area, over near the kitchen area, with the curtains and slatted blinds pulled across to darken the room, and she didn't waken, just sighed and snuffled and went quiet. They both stood and watched her in the new dimness, her parents, tangled together by her very existence, helpless about it.

Suddenly, Jodie was crying again, apologizing for it. "I'm sorry. I don't know why."

"It's okay. It's okay." Dev felt a rush of very male inadequacy, coupled with an equally male need to make things okay.

Right now.

In one move.

But he'd already said everything he knew to say. Did she want words? What else was there?

Well, holding her. They were standing so close it would be very easy.

It *was* very easy. Just his arms and her shoulders, the bump of their hips, stillness as she sighed against him. It happened before he planned it, a familiar phenomenon where she was concerned.

And then it changed.

He couldn't have her in his arms like this without wanting her, no matter what his head told him about Elin's warning a few days ago and his own understanding of the emotional risk.

Risk? Wasn't everything already at risk? Would fighting this heat really help?

He couldn't see it, couldn't remember Elin's arguments, or his own. All he could think of was Jodie's sweet, fierce little body pressed against him, proving her womanhood. All he wanted to do was quiet those shaking shoulders with the touch of his mouth on hers.

He did it and her mouth was right there, seeking his, wanting it just as much. It began as a kiss, but they both knew it wouldn't stop there. He could feel her bare legs against his, sliding their warmth across the muscles of his thighs. Her collarbone was bare, too, and he kissed the little hollows above it, making her gasp.

They sank to the cool brown leather of the couch and she stretched her body out, her spine and shoulders against the couch back, her legs half beneath his. He tried to lift her top and she sat up again and peeled it off, her breasts pert and round in a coral-pink satin bra. "Can't manage the catch," she said. "I always twist it around…."

But he'd already reached behind her and flicked the

hooks. You just needed the right angle, and the right movement with your thumb. The straps dropped from her shoulders, he tossed the bra out of the way, and there were those breasts he loved. He buried his face between them, lifted their tender weight with his hands and heard her breathing change. She'd forgotten about her tears.

*I'll make you forget everything, sweetheart.*

It seemed so simple. He forgot why he'd ever thought it wasn't.

It seemed like an adventure, a sparkling jewel of a moment, and those moments were the best adventures of all.

"Stand up," he whispered.

"Can't. Remember that marathon I just ran?"

So he helped her, popped the fastening on her shorts, shimmied them down and then the scrap of cotton and lace beneath. He loved her hips, loved the way they rocked so neatly. He bracketed his hands at her waist, amazed by the shape of her, the curves and lines, that butt so soft and silky against his palms.

She tried to lift his shirt. "This is where it all comes apart, sadly. Ole Lefty doesn't want to do this."

"Ole Lefty can have plenty of help. Don't even have to ask." He pulled off his shirt and she sank her fingers into his chest, rougher than she'd intended, probably, but he didn't mind. Hell, he totally didn't mind. The roughness heightened the beautiful chaos of everything, the sense that he didn't know quite what would happen next, where she would touch him next, whether it would be light or hard, what her breathing might do.

He ripped at his jeans, took his briefs down with them and stepped out, his hardness blatantly apparent. She reached down and touched him there, cradled his weight and he ached, just ached, and the ache radiated outward, up to his hairline and down to his toes.

"I never understand this," she said. "Why it's so magical."

"Just is."

"For you, too?"

"Yes."

How? Why?

Wanting her at eighteen but letting it go because he thought there must be a million women out there he'd want in the same way. Which had never really happened. There'd always been something missing. He'd put it down to his own naïveté. He didn't believe that anymore.

Discovering her last year, and then the accident cutting it all short, never letting him reach the usual moment with a woman where he began to think about how it should end. A final dinner out? Jewelry? A phone call? It could never have ended like that with Jodie.

Discovering her again three nights ago and finding that nothing had changed. If anything, had only grown stronger because of the complexity of what bound them together and pushed them apart.

He'd never known anything like this.

She pushed him onto the couch and sank on top of him, looking down into his face, those neat breasts grazing his chest and pushing higher, the softness at the apex of her thighs making a warm, perfect nest for his throbbing arousal. "You have to understand that this might not be pretty," she said, echoing what he'd said to her the other night as they stood against the front of the car. She was more serious than he'd been with the words, shy and fierce at the same time. "You might have to—"

"I don't care what I have to do," he interrupted. "Hold you, or guide myself. Start over. Shift. Anything. We managed fine the other night."

"You had protection right there in your wallet, the other night."

"Have it right there in my wallet now."

"On the floor?"

"Let me get it."

"I have it." She stretched down, giving him the perfect opportunity to take in the shape of her butt, the delicious curvy paleness of it in the dim room. A minute—quite a long minute—later she slid higher on his body, wearing a triumphant grin, clutching a square packet.

"You do have it."

"You have no idea. A wallet? Wasn't easy."

"Proud of you."

"Are you?"

"You're amazing."

"You always say that.…"

"Yeah, I do. Because it's true. But let's quit talking now.…"

*Oh, yeah, let's definitely quit talking. There's way too much else to do.*

She was right, there were a couple of times when it wasn't pretty, but hell, as always it was beautiful, more beautiful than ever. She laughed when her body wouldn't cooperate, gasped and shuddered and sighed when it did. He held her, rolled her, eased her thighs apart, caressed the whole length of her as he heard the build and raggedness of her breathing.

Inside her, he almost let go within seconds, had to school himself back, let her catch up, and when she did she took him over the edge so fast he lost all sense of time and space, could only feel and cry out and breathe.

They went into a bit of role reversal after this. She was the one who fell asleep within seconds, while he lay there in her arms wondering how to make the universe stop right here in this moment forever. Wishing she would wake up so they could talk and kiss. Glad that she didn't, because it meant he could watch her sleeping with his hand resting across her breasts. Wondering what would happen next.

He was scared of how important this felt, of what an adventure it might be, scared of this strange, vulnerable feeling that he couldn't really find a name for, didn't know what to do about it.

DJ was waking up. He heard the creak of her bassinet, the sound of a snuffle and the beginning of a cry. If she woke Jodie…

He eased himself away from her and she didn't stir. In the bedroom, some of Bill's chaotic wardrobe decisions littered the bed after Jodie's attempts to find something to wear this morning. He swept them aside, back into the suitcase, folded the sheet and quilt aside, then went and gathered Jodie up from the couch.

She was so warm and relaxed. Would she stay asleep? She wanted to have her bath with DJ, her session of skin-to-skin, but she was too tired for that right now. She needed to stay asleep until her energy rebounded.

He caught this tiny moment in himself of wanting her to change her mind about the skin-to-skin idea. How much would it achieve, really? She'd seemed so hopeful about it, what if it ended up a huge disappointment? What if Jodie couldn't manage to hold the baby? What if DJ cried?

*We can deal with all that,* he thought. *I'm making an issue out of nothing. What's wrong with me?*

She murmured something and he told her, "Just carrying you to the bed."

"Mmm."

He tucked her beneath the sheet like a child, laid the gypsy shawl on top because the quilt would be too warm, then went to get DJ before she began to cry in earnest.

Jodie woke some time later to find Dev treading softly out of the bedroom. He turned when he heard her move. "Damn, I woke you up, coming to check on you."

"You didn't. I was ready. How long did I sleep?" She felt a little self-conscious about it, and about what had led up to it. Her fierceness. His acceptance. The fact that it had happened at all. The fact that it had happened *again.*

*Are we dating, Dev?*

"A good hour," he said. "DJ's had her bottle and she's raring to go." He was silent for a moment, then said, "Shall I run the bath now? Do you still want—?"

"That would be great. Of course I still want." Beneath the sheet she began some stretches and range of motion exercises to shake off the heavy blanket of sleep, while Dev made preparations. She could see him through the open bedroom door, adding a generous squirt of bath foam and a sachet of scented salts.

The spa bath sat in the corner of the master bathroom, directly beside the two huge windows. They were made of clear glass and looked onto a thick screen of greenery with a barely visible lattice screen beyond, so that in complete privacy and warmth you would nevertheless feel as if you were bathing in the open forest.

When the water had been running in for several minutes, she levered herself off the bed, took the gypsy shawl he'd spread over her, wrapped it around her body, and went to the doorway. "How are we going to do this?"

"Can you get in by yourself?" He looked at her in the shawl, his gaze running down and up again, hard to read. "Do you need help?"

"It shouldn't be a problem."

"It could be slippery," he warned.

"There are steps and handholds."

"So once you're in, I'll give her to you. I'll stay right close by."

"That's safest, I think."

He seemed relieved. "It'll only be lukewarm, so she doesn't overheat or burn. Might feel a little cool to you."

"It's a warm day. Cool is good." Funny, for a change she was the one reassuring him.

And yet they were both nervous. Or not so much nervous, but keyed up. Was that it?

It was a bath, she told herself. Just a bath. But it was important. Too important even to talk about, so they talked about the tiny practicalities. Did they have enough towels? Was there a diaper and a clean outfit ready for DJ when she came out? Did Jodie need a robe? *Were* there any robes? Ah, yes, thick luxurious ones made of white towelling, two of them, folded in a small closet tucked behind the bathroom door.

She still felt churned up over what they'd said to each other out in the woods. Her painful confession about the state of her love for DJ. His stories about the pregnancy and birth. Now, on top of their lovemaking, it was like the aftermath of a storm, with a renewed sense of calm and a ton of work to do to deal with the litter of damage.

No, *damage* was wrong.

This wasn't about damage anymore, it was about healing.

Did Dev think so? "I'll give you a minute," he said.

For her to let the gypsy shawl drop, he meant, and climb into the water.

She felt crazily self-conscious when he left the bathroom and closed the door, as self-conscious as if he'd just stood there watching. She'd put on some weight in the weeks since leaving the hospital. Her breasts and hips were a little rounder, which was good, as the enhanced curves masked movements that were clumsier and less gracefully athletic than they used to be.

An hour ago when they'd made love, she'd warned him seriously that it might not be pretty. It couldn't have been, with this body. How much had he taken in? Why did the idea of being naked in front of him now seem so much scarier than it had the other night, or just now? It shouldn't have been any different.

She'd just begun the climb into the tub when he called to her, "How's it going?" She heard a creak and a movement, as if he were about to come through the door.

Naked, she froze in place. She didn't want him to see her. The reaction didn't make sense but existed anyway. "Not breaking any world records on the timing," she called to him. "Just climbing in now."

"Tell me when you're ready."

She sank into the water, wondering if the thick, mounded expanse of white foam was deliberate on his part. If it was, she was grateful for it. Beneath the waterline, you couldn't see a thing. "Okay, I'm good."

He opened the door. "Comfortable?"

"It's perfect." She looked up at him. His expression was serious. Worried, even. Reluctant. Out of his depth. He didn't need to be. Not as far as her safety was concerned, anyhow, or DJ's. "There's this sloping section on the side that I can lean against, and a kind of step to prop my feet so I don't slip too far down in the water. I'll be able to hold her. It's so lovely and deep, I'm almost floating."

He had his hand on the door handle, motionless, and for some reason the whole world seemed to echo his attitude. Everything went still and quiet. Beneath the water, her body tingled. "Uh, nice bathroom," he said, pulling the words out of nowhere. "I mean, it's just right for this."

"I know." She tried not to notice his awkward attitude. "The big tub is perfect. It would have been difficult in a smaller one. Where is she?"

"In her bassinet, to give me a chance to set up."

"What's she doing? She's not asleep? Please say she's not. I—I want this to happen, Dev. I'm not feeling patient, right now."

"It's fine. Composing a sonata for creaking wicker and plastic rattle, I'm pretty sure. I'll go get her."

A minute later he was back with DJ, who was wide-awake and happy, gurgling and cooing. He gave her a big squeeze and a fierce kiss on her tummy, then laid her on the bed and took off her clothing and diaper. "What a kick you got there, baby girl," he crooned. "Daddy's little athlete, aren't you, sweet thing?" He picked her up and came into the bathroom, knelt on the tiled step, cleared his throat. "Ready?"

Jodie lifted her arms. "Ready," she whispered.

Ohh.

DJ wriggled as she touched the water. Dev still held her firmly. She was tiny and soft and slippery, and she half floated as her little arms and chin came to rest on Jodie's front. She had no bottom whatsoever, just a series of creases and folds. "Got her?" he said.

"Yes. But stay."

"Of course I'm staying." Right there, he meant. He didn't move from beside the tub, just rested his forearms on the cold white porcelain and watched.

Watched, and belonged.

Ohh.

There were no words for it. DJ's little body. The warmth. The soft lapping of the water. The slipperiness. The tenderness. The way the water helped with Jodie's imperfect coordination and control.

"Can I…play with her, Dev?"

"Play with her?"

"Bob her around, float her from side to side. I mean, she's never been in a tub this big, has she?"

"Of course play with her." He was still watching closely, his hair getting damp with steam from the tub, his shirt wet from the splash of the baby's legs. "As long as the water doesn't get into her mouth."

So they bobbed around and floated from side to side, her little legs making trails in the foam. The foam began to melt away, which was good because then Jodie didn't worry so much about it getting in the baby's mouth and eyes, as Dev had warned.

"Oh, you're beautiful," she crooned. "You're so beautiful."

And something shifted and changed inside her. She let go of the doubt and fear and questions because the moment was too huge and didn't leave any room for those things. She slid DJ a little higher and those pink starfish hands grabbed at Jodie's skin and suddenly it came.

A smile.

A big, sweet, soft-lipped, toothless, beaming baby smile.

"Ohh," she crooned. "You're smiling. Oh, you darling girl! Why are you smiling? Mom says you never smile in the bath."

"Because you're right in there with her," Dev said, "and you're smiling right at her."

"But I've tried that before and it's never worked. She's never ever smiled at me till now. Oh, baby girl!" She just couldn't take her eyes away.

"Tried it." He slid closer, along the side of the tub. "That was the difference. Now you're not trying, you're not thinking about it, you're just smiling."

"Oh. Oh."

No words. Just kisses. On DJ's tender shoulders, her forehead, her wet baby hair, her chubby cheeks. Jodie cradled her against her shoulder and almost swam with her, floating around the generous-size spa tub, bobbing and bouncing DJ through the water.

The sense of rightness coursed through her with as much warmth and vitality as the blood in her veins. *Oh, my baby girl, oh, my sweet precious angel.* It was a part of her, this new feeling. It wasn't like the short-lived flicker of feeling that had come two days ago at Oakbank. That had only been a glimpse. This was real and powerful and bone-deep, an utter, beloved certainty.

The water was getting too cool. Dev turned on the faucet and a blast of warmth jetted in, bringing the temperature back up. They stayed in there until Jodie and DJ were both wrinkle-skinned and even then, as she lifted the baby to pass her to Dev, she didn't want to let her go.

"You can have her for now," she warned him, making it a tease so that she didn't cry instead. "But watch out, because I want her back as soon as I'm out of here." It had been so precious and wonderful. She felt as if she'd recaptured something she hadn't known until today had been lost.

And it would last, this time. She believed it. Knew it. Knew that the overwhelming sensation of love had been real and true and deep enough not to ebb or fade. It was what Dev had. It changed everything.

"Careful, she's so slippery," she told Dev, and there was a wet, drippy tangle of arms and movements as he bent down to take her.

"I've got her," he said gruffly. "I know she's slippery. It's fine." He captured her in the big, fluffy towel and dressed her in a fresh outfit—lilac, this time—right there on the glass vanity while Jodie lolled in the water and watched him with their daughter. When she was dressed, he stepped into the next room and laid her on the bed. Jodie heard the sound of pillows being plumped and settled to keep her safely in place. "That's the way," he sang to her. "Not going anywhere like that, are you, sweetheart angel?"

DJ cooed at him.

"Now let me pass you a towel," he said, back in the bathroom. "Do you need help getting up?"

"No, there's enough to hold on to." But she slipped at her first try and slid back into the tub, her feet squeaking across the porcelain. The water churned. She gritted her teeth. Why was it so hard? How did such a clumsy episode follow so quickly from some of the most precious moments of her life?

*I won't let the clumsiness spoil what I feel,* she vowed, and made another effort, pulling herself from the water and into the towel Dev had waiting for her. *I couldn't let it spoil that, because it was too strong.*

"Everything okay?" he said.

"Like a miracle. Oh, Dev, I can't tell you…I can't describe it. I can't even think about the difference it's already made."

"Good. Good. I'm so glad."

She thought he was going to kiss her. She was sure of it, after the way they'd made love so recently, after the emotion unleashed by her holding DJ in the bath. His eyes had pooled with glinting darkness, half-shielded by a sweep of lashes, his mouth was so soft, his lips had parted and he was looking at her. She swayed closer, and her hands loosened on the towel. It would drop to the floor in another moment, and she didn't care.

As long as Dev kissed her.

But it didn't happen.

He took a long, harsh breath and stepped back, pressing his lips together, turning his head. "Better not leave DJ on the bed for long," he said. "I'll put her on the floor, with her baby gym. Time to think about dinner, too. It's been a big day."

"A great day."

"Yes." He left, picking up the baby on his way out.

Wrapped in the towel in the steaming bathroom, Jodie felt abandoned and hated the ebbing of that glorious feeling of love and relief that had made her so complete and so happy just moments ago.

The change in his mood was as stark and apparent as the sun vanishing behind a dark cloud. The air felt colder. The light seemed different. It no longer streamed like gold through the thick greenery as it had when she'd first climbed into the bath. The sun had almost set, and the bath water had taken on a greenish tinge from the sachet of bath salts Dev had poured in.

There was no more foam, Jodie realized. She and DJ had stayed in the bath for so long that it had gradually disappeared, and she'd been so absorbed in the baby that she hadn't noticed.

Dev would have seen everything. Not just the shape of her body lying there, but the awkwardness of it in movement, and somehow this left her more naked and vulnerable than she'd been the other night when they'd made love, or just now on the couch, because both those times it had been dark, or at least dim, and their need for each other had wrapped both of them in a kind of protective blanket. She'd felt a lot of things, but she hadn't felt exposed.

Now, she did, because Dev's mood had changed so suddenly, it seemed, and this had to be the reason why.

Jodie took a long time to reappear. DJ had grown bored on her blanket, even with the baby gym positioned above her. There was only so much rattle-whacking a four-month-old could tolerate, apparently. Dev picked her up and propped her on his hip while he attempted to put oven fries on a baking tray, toss a salad and grill steaks with one hand.

He'd cooked that way before.

"Wouldn't put you in your bassinet even if I thought you'd stay happy there, would I, baby girl?" he murmured to her, heart lurching in his chest at the stark thought of losing her.

Not losing her.

He couldn't lose her.

Jodie wasn't like that. No matter how strongly her bond with the baby kicked in, today and in the future, she wouldn't punish him with it, would she?

Not deliberately. She surely wasn't like that.

But the punishment could happen anyway, because he wanted too much. He'd been kidding himself so stupidly right up until tonight, thinking through all these plans about shared custody and generous access, about making it work even when he was in New York or Europe, not understanding that the bond he had with DJ was so much stronger because the baby hadn't had the chance to build a bond with her mom.

Just now, in the bath, when they'd smiled at each other, gotten lost in each other for minutes on end, forgotten about him so completely, both of them, and then Jodie had seemed so glowing and different after she stepped out of the tub, so much freer and more full of life, he'd seen it in the look on her face, felt it in the way her body moved.

The shutting out.

Like the slamming of a prison door, with himself on one side and Jodie and DJ on the other.

He felt sick at himself, a miserable wreck of selfishness and blindness and jealousy. Did he *want* to see Jodie go on floundering the way she had been, purely so that she would leave the best of the parenting to him? That was horrible. He was appalled about it.

But he felt it anyway, this sense that he was shut out and that it was a conspiracy coming from both of them.

He didn't understand why it had such a grip on him or what it meant.

Couldn't do a damned thing about it.

Here she was, at last. She was wearing a pair of

stretchy cream long johns and a flowery camisole top—amongst the more useful contents of her underwear drawer, he guessed—and she was wrapped in the gypsy shawl her sister had given her, that he'd laid on the bed. Strangely enough, the outfit almost worked. "Cold?" he asked, pushing his dark, unwanted feelings aside.

"From the bath."

"Right. DJ felt cool, too. You'll both warm up soon."

"Mmm."

"Dinner's nearly on the table."

"Thank you."

"DJ won't last much longer. We can eat, then I'll put her in her sleep suit and give her her last bottle and she'll go down. Can usually count on a good eight hours after that. With luck it'll be getting light before she wakes up. That's mostly how it works with her now." He sounded as if he were giving a lecture, and knew it came from his need to assert his own role.

*I'm the one who took her home from the hospital. I'm the one who saw the sonogram and felt her move in your belly, when you knew nothing about it.*

He'd told Jodie all that stuff himself, just a few hours ago, and it had changed everything, along with DJ's smile and Jodie's tearful smile back, and now he wanted Jodie's glow to fade? He was despicable.

Despicable, and lost.

The steaks were almost done. She helped him serve up and they ate without saying a lot. He talked about what they might do tomorrow—go visit the nearby lake, go back to the store to fill more of those gaps in her dad's packing—but it was all on the surface and they both knew something was wrong.

"May I feed her and put her to bed?" Jodie asked, after she'd finished eating. "Would you mind?"

"Mind? You're the mom," he said stiffly. "And you've missed out on a lot. You don't have to ask."

"No. Right. I guess I don't. Thank you."

"Don't say that."

"Sorry, I didn't mean—"

"We can't go on thanking each other for the most mundane childcare tasks. How's that going to work?"

"It's not, I guess, but— Yeah, okay, I won't keep thanking you."

"Let me know if you need any help."

"I will."

He was worse than Elin and Barb. He left the rest of the dinner mess in the kitchen and hovered around in the open-plan living area, ears almost aching from the effort of listening. He could hear her talking to DJ as she changed the baby's diaper, not the same way that he talked to her, but *right,* all the same, not forced or self-conscious, and the thick knot of incomprehensible jealousy tightened inside him.

## Chapter Thirteen

"Yes, I'm fine," Jodie said into her cell phone. "I keep telling you, Mom… No, I'm not going to keep it switched on, from now on. I'll call you once a day to tell you I'm fine, and that's it."

She stood out on the deck, with her left hand pressed awkwardly against her ear to block out distracting sounds, and she had her back to Dev, even though he could hear her quite clearly. Was she trying to block him out, also?

She listened some more, then said to her mother, "Well, we've been out to dinner, we've explored the woods, we've been shopping to replace all the things Dad forgot to pack for me, we've been to the lake and had a picnic, soaked up the sun, cooked a barbecue here on the deck…" She listened again. "Coming home? Dev told them a week when he made the reservation." She turned and looked at him. "We've only been here three nights."

Was that a question in her face? Did she want to leave sooner?

His gut twisted. Maybe for her, the purpose had been achieved, there was no more point to this, and she wanted to go home. He wouldn't blame her. He hadn't been the best company since that magical session between Jodie and DJ in the bath. Hell, he was trying!

But he was trying to protect himself at the same time. He was floundering and she had to know something was wrong. "It's up to you," he murmured. "If you want to leave sooner…"

"Only if you do," she answered quietly, with her hand over the phone. Her eyes had narrowed, intent on his response.

"I don't."

"Good." She turned her attention once more to her mother. "I'll call again tomorrow." She listened. "Mom, you don't need to know the exact details on how many exercises I'm doing, okay?" Another pause. "Listen, I'm ending the call now. I'm not hanging up on you or anything, but there's nothing more we need to say." She thumbed the phone off and put it down on the outdoor table.

"Only if you do," she repeated deliberately, fixing Dev with those blue eyes.

"I don't," he repeated back.

"So what's wrong?" She crossed the space between them and tried to touch him, but he eased away, as he'd been doing since Saturday night. He didn't trust himself, close to her, and there was this massive sense of risk and vulnerability crashing through him that he didn't understand.

"Nothing," he said. "Just giving us both some space."

Her expression turned fierce and she stuck out her jaw. "Was that a one-off, on the couch, then? A two-off, I guess I should say, counting the other night in Deer Pond Park coming home from the restaurant. Be honest. Tell me up front."

"Up front…"

"It's not so hard, is it? You were pretty good at it, last year, the up-front stuff. You said straight out that you weren't in the market for anything long-term and I appreciated your honesty."

*Maybe if I knew the answer, it wouldn't be hard.* Out loud, he told her, "Just…not a good idea."

"Yeah, you keep saying that."

"Twice. I've said it twice."

"Once for each time. If we go for a third, I'll let you say it again." She put a hand on her hip, jutted her chin in a defiant grin and struck a sassy pose that he knew ran only skin-deep.

"Stop…" he almost begged.

*Stop being so brave. Stop asking for answers I don't have.*

"Oh, me? *I* should stop?" She glared at him.

"No, okay, you're right. That's not fair. It's just… This—coming here—is about you and DJ, isn't it, not about you and me? I don't want anything to get in the way of that. What you're finding together. It's so great. It's beautiful to see."

"Yes, it is." A smile lit up her face, a new kind of smile. "Thank you for making it happen."

"That's her now, waking up."

"Oh, it is? Yes, I can hear her. Yes."

Three days ago, he would have had to urge her, *blackmail* her, almost, into going to her baby. Now she was already on the way, eager and awkward, calling out as she went. "I hear you, baby girl. I'm coming."

It was exactly what he wanted, better than he could have hoped, and she wasn't using it to hurt him, she was still giving him all the time he could want with his baby girl, so why was it killing him like this? What was he so afraid of?

He needed action and answers, not this pointless self-questioning.

Jodie had left her cell phone on the table. His was in his pocket, switched off just as hers had been. He took it out. It felt cool and compact in his hand, a familiar symbol of certainty and control.

Touching the screen, he had his office in New York on the line within seconds, knowing he was kidding himself about what this would achieve, even while he heard his assistant's voice. "Catch me up, Angie," he told her. "Has there been any news from London on the consultancy?"

"Can you believe I changed your diaper and your outfit all by myself?" Jodie cooed to DJ. "Your daddy will be so proud."

*I'm lying to her. Again.*

He wouldn't be proud, he would be uncomfortable and reluctant, and if she told him, "I changed her all by myself," he would say all the right things, but underneath there would be this distance. "Space" he'd called it, just now.

It wasn't space.

It was withdrawal, shutting down.

And she got it.

Yeah, don't worry, she got it completely, even though he hadn't spelled it out.

Mission accomplished, as far as he was concerned. He'd taken her and DJ away from Mom and Lisa and Elin in order to strengthen their bond and deepen her love, and it had worked better than either of them could have hoped. She loved her baby girl, her Dani Jane, in a way she hadn't imagined possible just a few days ago, with none of that thick, ugly layer of self-doubt and fear and unfamiliarity that had held her back.

Which meant that now Dev was free.

He loved his daughter, and he never would have abandoned her to the distance of her mother and the overinvolvement of her Palmer grandmother and aunts, but now that Jodie had her bonding in place, he was free. He could put this "family" thing he talked about onto the same footing as so many other kids had—live with the mom, see the dad occasionally for visits and weekends, while the parents maintained a cordial relationship if the kid was lucky.

Visits, where? Would he go back to New York? Jodie's family always seemed to assume so. Her heart lurched and sank at the idea. It felt so wrong to think of them at such a distance from each other, all the complicated arrangements they would have to make to keep DJ in his life.

She didn't want arrangements. She wanted him.

It was pretty simple, really.

She loved him.

She'd known last fall that he would break her heart when he left, whether they slept together or didn't. He would break her heart when he left now, and little DJ, who knew nothing about any of this, was powerless to help, because there was no way in the world that Jodie would ever use her as leverage or a weapon.

"Look at you, sweetheart," Jodie whispered to her.

"How can I keep you happy and safe? How can I keep you from guessing how much I'm hurting? I can't let him guess, either."

She picked the baby up, put her in her stroller because that was the safest way to move a baby when you weren't sure of the strength of your own arms, and wheeled her back out to the deck, hearing Dev on the phone as she approached.

"Yeah, very glad I called," he was saying. "Sorry I had it switched off. I was trying for some space, but I'll keep it on now in case anything else comes up. It's going to be a mess if we don't straighten it out.… Yes, please, make the reservation.…" He was so absorbed in the conversation, he hadn't seen her. He was staring out at the woods, not seeing them, either. "Yes, for Wednesday, if you can, so I'm there for meetings Thursday and Friday… I can fly out of Columbus to Chicago and then over the Pole, or through New York if that connects better. Just let me know the schedule when you have it.… Okay, talk soon."

He flipped the phone into his pocket, turned and saw her with the stroller wheels resting against the threshold between the living area and the deck. "Something's come up," she said, so that he didn't have to say it. "And you need to get to London before the end of the week."

"Yes. If my assistant can get the right flights, I'll have to leave here tomorrow and I won't be back before Tuesday."

"Tuesday," she echoed.

"I can't leave you here on your own."

She took a deep breath, let go of the instant, aching sense of loss, tried to hold on to what she had, the wonderful new sense of motherhood and love. She didn't have Dev's love, but she had DJ's. "I don't have to be on my own. We have the cabin till Friday. Mom could come out, I expect, or Lisa and the kids. Keep me company. Help pack."

"That's a good idea," he said slowly. "It would be great if you and DJ could stay for the full week. The timing on this is—"

Tough.

And yet he seemed relieved, too, which she understood. He didn't want to be here anymore, and this gave him the perfect excuse.

"What time tomorrow?" she asked, as if everything was fine.

"Depends on the flights."

"She'll get back to you today?"

"Within an hour, I hope. I hate not knowing what's happening."

He didn't have to hate it for long. His assistant got back to him as promised, with details on confirmed flights. By eleven o'clock tomorrow morning, he would be gone.

Jodie called home and spoke to Mom, fighting her way through the usual overanxious questions about her well-being and the baby's until she could get to the point. "Something's come up, Mom, and Dev has to go to London."

"London?"

"For work."

"Well, I gathered that. For how long? When?"

"He's leaving tomorrow."

"So you're coming back?" Mom sounded relieved.

"Well, I'm hoping I don't have to. It's been wonderful here. That's really why I'm calling."

"You can't possibly stay there on your own. You're

not driving yet. There's so much you can't manage. You're not saying that Dev's taking the baby?"

"Mom, if you'd let me get a word in edgewise, I'm not saying I'd stay here on my own, I'm wondering if someone can come out and keep me company. You or Dad or—"

"Of course we can." She sounded eager, now that she'd grasped the situation. "Yes, we absolutely can, one of us at least. You don't have to say another word. We'll work it out. What time do we need to be there?"

"He has to leave by eleven."

"I'll get right on it. We'll work something out. Just leave your cell phone switched on."

"Nope, not doing that."

"Jodie…"

"Because you'll call me every five minutes to up-date. Send a text, if there's anything important."

"Jodie, honey…"

But she stayed stubborn, gave Mom the directions to the cabin, ended the call and switched off her phone.

Again, Dev seemed relieved. "Last dinner out?" he suggested.

"Sounds great."

Sounded so final.

## Chapter Fourteen

Jodie was in the bathroom when she heard the sound of a car arriving at the cabin at ten-thirty the next morning. Dev had almost finished packing. DJ was asleep in her bassinet. She hurried out and almost tripped on one of the rugs in the living area. There was a flash of red, parked out front.

Elin.

Her heart sank. Elin was the bossy sister, the one most likely to lecture, the one bluntest when she disapproved. And Jodie was quite sure she'd find something to disapprove of today.

But they had a big hug anyhow, because they were sisters, and in the end bossiness and lectures and bluntness took second place.

"I was sure Mom would be the one to come," Jodie said, while Elin took her overnight bag from the trunk of the car.

"She would have, if I'd let her. We had a great fight about it, her and Lisa and me. I won."

"So I gather."

Elin put her hands on her hips in a pose that said she wanted answers. "What's gone wrong, honey?"

"Nothing." *Make it bright, Jodie, make it casual.* "It's just business. Dev has to be in London. Only for a week. Less, really. Six days."

"Right." If there was one thing Elin was good at, it was communicating that she had a lot more to say, by means of saying nothing at all.

They went inside and met Dev with his luggage, ready to go.

"So fill me in," Elin ordered both of them.

"Well, she has a proper name," Dev said.

"Oh, she does?"

"Dani Jane."

"Your idea?"

"Jodie's."

"Really, honey?" Elin turned to her, face suddenly lit up. "I like it. I love it."

"It feels good," Jodie said. "Although I can't imagine calling her anything but DJ most of the time."

Nobody spoke. The brief moment of harmony and happiness had gone.

Dev studied his watch as if the hands and numbers had all turned back to front. "I should get going." He snapped his mouth shut, then opened it again and growled, "I wish she wasn't asleep."

"She won't wake up if you kiss her," Jodie told him. For some reason, she needed his goodbye to DJ to be a good one.

Only a week, she kept telling herself. Only a week. Less.

But it felt so much more final than that.

Dev was treating it that way. He'd been silent and distant this morning, as if in spirit he was already on the flight, sitting in his business-class seat and opening his laptop, eager to get to work.

He'd said to her from the beginning that the three of them were a family—himself, her and DJ—but it didn't feel that way, right now. This felt like the breakup she'd dreaded last year, the no-strings, no-regrets goodbye she would have said to him—pretended to really mean—when he went back to New York, if the accident and the baby had never happened.

"Please keep your phone switched on," he said to her, as they stood together beside DJ's bassinet.

"Oh, you want Mom to bug me every five minutes?"

"No. So I can call. To see how things are going."

"You can trust me with her, Dev."

"Of course I can."

It was horrible. There was nothing she could safely say. He tossed his laptop in its carrier case onto the front seat and she realized she hadn't seen it when he unpacked on arriving here. Then, he'd had it in his suitcase, out of sight and out of mind. Now, it occupied Jodie's passenger seat, the prime position.

Replacing her.

Making his priorities clear.

He didn't even hug her in farewell, just let his arm trail briefly across her shoulders. "Take care." Gruff, not looking in her direction.

He drove off, she couldn't help watching him with helpless, miserable longing until the car disappeared behind a patch of thick green summer foliage, and then she had Elin to contend with.

"What was that about?" She was still watching down

the road, where every now and then a flash of color or light from his car would reappear.

"I— What?"

"Did you have a fight? Help me, here, Jodie!" She wheeled around, stepped closer, put her hands back on her hips in what was a classic Elin-wants-answers pose. "I can't work out if it's killing him to leave, or if he can't wait. Whichever, I should be mad as hell at him, right? Shoot, I am mad! I could kill him!"

"We didn't have a fight."

"Then what the heck is his problem? What is yours?"

"Elin, I can't take this right now." She closed her eyes, knowing the tears would squeeze through her lashes anyway, and Elin would see them. She waited for the onslaught of critical big-sister words, but they didn't come.

Until finally, quietly, "You're in love with him, aren't you?"

"Only took you a year to work it out, sis."

"A year?"

"Okay, twelve years. Since high school. Not that I've been pining that long, I only thought about him if I happened to see his parents, or in the holidays wondering if he was back for a visit and I might see him. I saw his brother once, and thought for a second, from the back, that it was him."

"Yeah, you haven't been pining at all."

Jodie ignored this. "But last year, when he came back to town, I knew then, and it went bone-deep in a heartbeat, and—"

"And because of the accident, last year seems like yesterday," Elin said, understanding. "And now you have a baby together, and you don't know if that's the best or the worst thing that could have happened. Ah, honey…"

Elin *understood!*

"Real clever strategy on my part, wasn't it?" Jodie said wearily. "Get pregnant, spend eight months in a coma. Ten points for imaginative variation on the shotgun wedding."

"You didn't get pregnant on purpose."

"No. Which is a plus, really. Since it clearly hasn't worked."

"Hasn't worked?"

"He left. Did you notice?"

"For a week. Less."

"Not just a week. His whole heart left. He left, in spirit, a good thirty-six hours ago. The trick with the departing car just now was only an illusion."

"What happened, honey? What changed?"

"Dani Jane smiled at me. For the first time." Even thinking about it, in the midst of her turmoil about Dev, brought a smile to her face. "And I suddenly discovered how to love her. Which I hadn't known before. Did you—? You must have seen. Or suspected."

"We were worried. We thought maybe you just needed more time with your therapy."

"It was more than that."

"We thought a whole lot of things. Jodie, I realize we've behaved like interfering witches, the whole family, but we didn't know. If you would ever wake up. If Dev would want DJ all to himself and we'd never have that part of you, that legacy. And then when you found out about her and it seemed you weren't bonding with her the way you should, we didn't want to make a big deal of it, in case that made things worse."

"Well, it turns out that was what he was waiting for.

The love. The bonding. So he could pull back, get on with his real life, and know DJ was safe and happy."

"Bull. *Bull!*" Elin challenged.

"What?"

"That's *not* what I saw in his face!" she almost shouted. "That's not what that weird, distant goodbye meant, just now, Jodie. He wouldn't do it like that, if you're right about his reasons and his feelings."

"How do you know, Elin?"

"Because I've seen him, remember?" Her voice softened. "I've seen the way he sat by your bed while you were in the coma. I've seen how he bonded with DJ from the moment she was born, how he did everything he needed to do for her without question or complaint, how he fought with Mom—and, yes, with me—over who should be her primary carer and when you should be told about what had happened."

"So…"

"I can't tell you exactly why he went off like that. I really can't. But I can tell you it's not because he's just been waiting all this time to dump the baby on you and get out. I've accused him of that. Lisa has. We…we had a talk after you came here, Jodie, and we both realized we've let our emotions and our fears dictate the pace too much. But we were wrong to say that to him, or to think it, that he wanted to dump her. He loves her. And whatever else is going on—there's something, there's more—I think you need to find out."

"Find out…"

"Call him." It wasn't a request, it was an order. She pulled out her cell phone, made one press and his number was right there. She pushed it into Jodie's hand and pushed the hand to the ear in time for Jodie to hear a recorded message. Switched off, or out of range.

"So we'll go after him," said the bossiest sister in the Palmer family.

"DJ is—"

"Asleep. So we'll wake her up. It's only the first baby whose sleep schedule is the most sacred thing in the family timetable, honey. Once you get to number two and three… She'll live."

"Wh-what exactly are we doing? Saying to him?"

The hands went back on the hips. "Well, have you *told* him? That you love him?"

"No."

"So we're telling him that."

Easy-peasy, Elin.

Elin had a baby carrier strapped in her backseat. Jodie realized just how much the whole family had stepped in to help with DJ, because Elin's own kids hadn't needed special car seats for years. It was frustrating as hell to have so much family interference, and she loved Elin for it this morning with her whole heart.

Elin flirted with the speed limit out as far as the county road and for several miles beyond. There was no sign of the back of Dev's car. He'd had too much of a head start.

Too much of a head start, but what was this dark blue vehicle coming toward them? Elin screamed to a halt on the shoulder, and the blue car halted also, on the other side.

Dev.

Elin's window slid smoothly down. "What did you forget, Dev?" Her hands weren't on her hips this time, but only because they were on the window and the wheel.

"Couple of things." He opened the car door.

Elin climbed out, also. "One big thing, I hope." She

met him in the middle of the road, both of them ignoring the possibility of traffic.

"Yeah, you could say that." He cleared his throat.

Jodie sank into the passenger seat. She wasn't a fearful sort of person, but she was scared right now.

Scared?

Okay, a person was allowed to be scared.

Giving in to it?

No, she *hated* when she let herself do that.

She began the awkward process of going to join them. Maybe the white line in the middle of a county road was the right place for family treaty negotiations, after all.

Elin seemed to have a pretty clear idea of what was going on. She reached out, pulled Jodie closer, sent her in Dev's direction with a commanding nudge. "She's in love with you, Dev," she announced. "And I damn well hope you feel the same. Talk to her. Work it out. I'll be back at the cabin with Dani Jane."

And then she left, screeching through a turn that curved across both sides of the shoulder and made Jodie glad about the regulations on safety for infants in cars.

"Sometimes I'm glad your family is so keen on baby-sitting," Dev said. He moved to the side of the road, where a line of young sycamore trees gave shade against the summer heat.

She followed him, found a tree trunk to put her hand against, because she wasn't convinced she could stand without support for much longer. "Helps when there are things to work out," she agreed carefully.

He had his gaze fixed on her face, as the sound of Elin's car receded. "What your sister said…" He broke off, swore beneath his breath. He looked like a soldier ready for hand-to-hand combat and she couldn't look away. "Shoot, it almost doesn't matter."

"Doesn't matter?"

"Doesn't make a difference," he explained, frustrated and impatient and bristling with things she couldn't read. "To me."

"Oh."

"Because even if she's wrong about what you feel, I'm stuck with this. I love you, Jodie. Love you. I'm sick at myself, it's killing me."

"Loving me is so…h-horrible?"

"Loving you is horrible when it makes me so scared there isn't any room for me in the mix. When I see you and DJ together and I think my role disappeared, evaporated, the second your bond with her kicked in. I have this horrible jealousy…"

"Of me?"

"No. Of her. I'm jealous of *her.*" He stepped closer, close enough to touch, but then he didn't touch her. "Of my own baby. For earning your smile, for earning that soft look on your face that says you have all the answers and everything that matters. For having your arms around her and owning your whole heart." Finally, he touched her, ran his hands around her back, looked into her eyes with his mouth just a few inches from hers. "Jodie, I need you to look like that at me," he whispered. "I need you to feel like that about me. That I'm your world. Not instead of DJ, but as well as her. Both of us. Your world. If Elin's right… Is she right? Can you look like that at me?"

"Aren't I looking at you like that already?" she whispered. "Right now?" She brushed her mouth against his. "You are my world, Dev, you and DJ, and when you left just now and I thought you didn't want that… You always said it and I always believed you. You weren't looking for anything long-term. How could I trust that any of that had suddenly changed? I was so scared. I hate being scared. I always fight it."

"You don't need to be scared about this. You're the bravest person I know. You've showed me that love can be the best adventure in the world, if two people want it to be. It doesn't have to be safe and boring and a massive compromise. And if you'll marry me, we'll make a family for DJ and she'll be part of the adventure, too, and neither of us will be scared of losing her or fighting over her or any of that." He dropped his voice still lower. "Will you, Jodie?"

"Yes, oh, yes." Her body decided to have a say in things at this point, and her legs suddenly wouldn't hold her up. She fell against him and he laughed and it was the best thing that could have happened, because what choice did he have now but to kiss her?

A car went past.

And then another one.

And then two more.

"I guess you could call it brave and adventurous to say yes to a marriage proposal on the shoulder of a well-used road," Jodie teased him.

"Brave and adventurous to *make* a marriage proposal in that situation. Some might say foolish. You deserve roses and candles and champagne and a whole heap of romantic planning, and here I am doing it in the exact opposite way, with no planning at all, and maybe I deserve, 'Do it better and you might get a yes,' but it… just didn't pan out like that."

"What was it John Lennon said? You told me, Dev. 'Life is what happens to you when you're busy making other plans.' I love that it happened like this. Of course

I said yes. We seem to have a history of doing things in the wrong way."

"In our own way. The adventurous way. A family."

"Let's go back. I'm missing her already. And I want to tell Elin."

"Wish the cell phone reception wasn't so good. The whole family will know in about five minutes and it won't be our sweet secret."

"Cell phone…" The outside world intruded, as she thought about it. "You'll miss your flight."

"They can wait a day, in London. I'll be away five days instead of six. It'll still seem like five times too long."

"Oh, it will…"

"But for now, I'm spending the day with family. And the night with my future bride."

## Chapter Fifteen

The day Jodie and Dev got married was one of the best days of her life. "Let's not wait," they'd said to each other, and so it happened on a sunny fall day when DJ was still only just learning to sit up, and when Jodie's progress down the aisle of the Palmer and Browne family church was still a little uneven and slow.

The day, Christmas Day, when she and Dev sat DJ on the rocking horse Dad had made for her, was heart-warming and amazing and wonderful.

The day the following spring when she rode Irish for the first time since the accident was pretty good, too. Her friend Bec had kept him in training and given him an hour's workout before the ride, so by the time Jodie climbed into the saddle in the indoor arena at Oakbank, he wasn't in the mood to mistake any of her awkward leg aids as the instruction to go into a full gallop. He nuzzled her after the ride as if to say, "I'm glad to have you back," and if a good part of his appreciation was because of the carrots she gave him, well, that was okay.

The day DJ said her first word—"hot"—the day she took her first steps, the day Dev and Jodie finally tore themselves away from their baby and flew off for a delayed honeymoon in Aruba, were mighty fine days, all of them.

But if you backed her against a brick wall and pointed a water pistol at her head and made her choose the number-one day, the very top, most memorable, wonderful, important day, after eighteen months of wedded bliss, would have to be the one where Jodie discovered that she couldn't stand the smell of ketchup anymore, when it had smelled so good during her rehab.

It was in spring, and DJ had celebrated her second birthday the previous week. She was energetic, happy and talking a mile a minute, even though only her mom and dad could work out what she was saying half the time.

She loved children's music DVDs and playing in the sandbox and petting the ponies at Oakbank. She loved story time and bath time and Daddy coming home. She loved spaghetti and ice cream and strawberries, but her favorite food of all—this month, anyhow—was hot dogs.

Which was where the ketchup came in.

Dani Jane liked ketchup on her hot dogs.

A lot.

"Mo-ore, Momm-eee."

"There's already a big squeeze on it, DJ, honey."

"More, plee-eease?"

"Okay, one more squirt."

They were in the kitchen of their brand-new, log-cabin–style house on their brand-new twenty acres of land adjacent to Oakbank Stables, and Dev was due back from an overnight trip to New York that afternoon.

*I can't wait,* Jodie was thinking as she squeezed the ketchup bottle, and then she caught the smell of it full in her nostrils and almost threw up and she just knew.

It was a Palmer thing. Mom remembered it. Elin and Lisa had both complained of it. Maddy swore it was nonsense, and then had called Mom from Cincinnati in tears one day to say, "I put ketchup on my fries and then I couldn't even look at them let alone eat them, and I didn't dare hope after we'd been trying so long, but John went to the drugstore and bought a test and *I'm pregnant!*"

*I'm pregnant.*

DJ ate her hot dog with her mommy being somewhat less patient than usual about how long it took and how much mess there was to clean up. Her nap time should have followed her lunch and she seemed a little surprised when Mommy bundled her into the car and zoomed off down the road to the nearest drugstore.

Dev arrived home at four, when DJ was still sleeping thanks to the late start to her nap, and when Jodie hadn't been expecting him for another two hours. She heard his car and met him at the door. He pulled her into his arms before she could speak and kissed her, hungry and happy and so familiar. "Finished early," he said. "Raced to the airport and took an earlier flight. Glad I've put the international stuff on hold for another year or two. Couldn't wait to see you."

"Me, too. I've been trying to call you. You had your cell phone switched off, I thought you must still be in meetings... Dev, guess what?"

She told him.

He kissed her again, and she found that his face was

wet with tears. She pulled back a little, looked at his wet lashes and narrowed eyes and mouth pressed tight to contain what he felt, and melted at the sight of such a strong man in such a tender state. She took some of the moisture onto her fingertip and showed him. "Wh-why, Dev?"

"Do you have to ask?" he whispered. "Because you're *here,* this time."

"Here?"

"With DJ, you weren't. You weren't present at all, and we both missed out on so much because of it. To have you here, and healthy, and my beautiful wife… Don't you want to cry?"

"I cried the whole afternoon." And she was crying again, laughing and sniffing and feeling crazy happy and emotional at the same time. "I went back and smelled that ketchup bottle three more times just because I could."

He laughed. "There you go."

"Because you're right, and it's just how I felt, too. I wasn't here, for DJ. This time, I'm having two pregnancies in one, and no one is going to stop me."

It was truer than either of them knew. Better than either of them knew. Three weeks later, a routine scan in the dark and quiet of the obstetrician's office showed that in roughly seven months, she and Dev would become the proud and happy parents of twins.

\* \* \* \* \*

# THE DADDY DANCE

BY
MINDY KLASKY

**Mindy Klasky** learned to read when her parents shoved a book in her hands and told her that she could travel anywhere in the world through stories. She never forgot that advice. These days, Mindy works and plays in a suburb of Washington, DC, where she lives with her family. In her spare time, Mindy knits, quilts and tries to tame the endless to-be-read shelf in her home library. You can visit Mindy at her website—www.mindyklasky. com.

To my writers' retreat girlfriends, who gave Rye
his name—Nancy Hunter, Jeri Smith-Ready,
Maria V. Snyder, and Kristina Watson

## Chapter One

Kat Morehouse pushed her sunglasses higher on her nose as the train chugged away from Eden Falls, leaving her behind on the platform. Heat rose in waves off the tiny station's cracked parking lot. Plucking at her silk T-shirt, Kat realized for the first time since she'd left New York that solid black might not be the most comfortable wardrobe for her trip home to Virginia. Not this year. Not during this unseasonably hot spring.

But that was ridiculous. She was a dancer from New York—black was what she wore every day of her life. She wasn't about to buy new clothes just because she was visiting Eden Falls.

Her foot already itched inside her walking boot cast. She resisted the urge to flex her toes, knowing that would only make her injury ache more. Dancer's Fracture, the doctors had grimly diagnosed, brought on by overuse. The only cure was a walking boot and complete rest from ballet for several weeks.

Looking down at her small roller suitcase, Kat grimaced and reminded herself that she wasn't going to be in Eden Falls for very long. Just time enough to help her family a bit—give her mother a little assistance as Susan nursed Kat's father, Mike, who was recovering from a nasty bout of pneumonia. Take care of her niece for a few days while Kat's irresponsible twin sister roamed somewhere off the beaten track. Look in on her mother's dance studio, the Morehouse Dance Academy, where Kat had gotten her start so many years ago. She'd be in Eden Falls for five days. Maybe six. A week at most.

Kat glanced at her watch. She might not live in Eden Falls anymore, but she knew the train schedule by heart, had known it ever since she'd first dreamed of making a life for herself in the big city. The southbound Crescent stopped at one-thirty in the afternoon. The northbound Clipper would churn through at two-fifteen.

Now, it was one forty-five, and Susan Morehouse was nowhere in sight. In fact, there was only one other person standing on the edge of the parking lot, a passenger who had disembarked with Kat. That woman was tall, with broad shoulders that looked like they were made for milking cows or kneading bread dough. Her oval face and regular features looked vaguely familiar, and Kat realized she must be one of the Harmons, the oldest family in Eden Falls.

Shrugging, Kat dug her cell phone out of her purse, resigned to calling home. She tapped the screen and waited for the phone to wake from its electronic slumber. A round icon spun for a few seconds. A minute.

More. The phone finally emitted a faint chirp, dutifully informing her that she was out of range of a recognized cell tower. Out of range of civilization.

Kat rolled her eyes. It was one thing to leave New York City for a week of playing Florence Nightingale in Eden Falls, Virginia. It was another to be cut off without the backbone of modern communications technology. Even *if* Kat was looking forward to helping her mother, a week was really going to stretch out if she didn't have a working smart phone.

Squinting in the bright sunlight, Kat read a message sent by Haley, her roommate back in New York. The text must have come in during the train ride, before Kat had slipped out of range. OMG, said the text. A + S r here. "A," Adam. The boyfriend of three years whom Kat had sent packing one week before, after discovering his side relationship with Selene Johnson. That would be "S," the corp's newest phenom dancer.

Haley had sent another message, five minutes later. 2 gross.

And a third one, five minutes after that. Hands all over.

All over. Right. Kat and Adam were all over. Adam hadn't had the decency to admit what was going on with Selene. Not even when Kat showed him the silk panties she'd found beneath his pillow—panties that *she* had definitely not left behind. Panties that Selene must have intended Kat to find.

Even now, Kat swallowed hard, trying to force her feelings past the raw, empty space in the middle of her chest. She had honestly believed she and Adam were meant for each other. She had thought that he alone *understood* her, believed in all the crazy sacrifices she had to make as a dancer. He was the first guy—the *only* guy—she had ever gotten involved with, the only one who had seemed worth sacrificing some of her carefully allocated time and energy.

How could Kat have been so wrong? In reality, Adam had just been waiting for the next younger, more fit, more flexible dancer to come along. Kat hated herself for every minute she had invested in their broken relationship, every second she had stolen from her true focus: her dancing career. She closed her eyes, and once again she could see that slinky thong in Adam's bed.

"2 gross" was right.

Kat dropped her useless cell phone into her purse and wiped her palms against her jet-black jeans, feeling the afternoon sun shimmer off the denim. At least her hair was up, off her neck in this heat. Small mercy. She started to rummage deep in her bag, digging for her wallet. A place like Eden Falls had to have pay phones somewhere. She could call her mother, figure out where their wires had crossed. Reach out to her cousin Amanda, if she needed to. Amanda was always good for a ride, whenever Kat made one of her rare weekend appearances.

Before she could find a couple of quarters, though, a huge silver pickup truck rolled to a stop in the parking lot. The Harmon woman smiled as she held out her thumb, pretending to hitch a ride. The driver—another Harmon, by the broad set of his shoulders, by his shock of chestnut hair—laughed as he walked around the front of his truck. He gave his sister a bear hug, swinging her around in a circle that swept her feet off the dusty asphalt. The woman whooped and punched at his shoulder, demanding to be set down. The guy obliged, opening the truck's passenger door before he hefted her huge suitcase into the vehicle's gleaming bed.

He was heading back to the driver's side when he noticed Kat. "Hey!" he called across the small lot, shielding his eyes from the sun. "Kat, right? Kat Morehouse?"

Startled by the easy note of recognition in the man's voice, Kat darted a glance to his face, really studying him for the first time. No. It couldn't be. There was no possible way Rye Harmon was the first guy she was seeing, here in Eden Falls. He started to walk toward her, and Kat started to forget the English language.

But those were definitely Rye Harmon's eyes, coal black and warm as a panther's flank. And that was Rye Harmon's smile, generous and kind amid a few days' worth of unshaved stubble. And that was Rye Harmon's hand, strong and sinewy, extended toward her in a common gesture of civil greeting.

Kat's belly completed a fouetté, flipping so rapidly that she could barely catch her breath.

Rye Harmon had played Curly in the high school production of *Oklahoma* the year Kat had left for New York. Kat had still been in middle school, too young to audition for the musical. Nevertheless, the high school drama teacher had actually recruited her to dance the part of Laurey in the show's famous dream sequence. The role had been ideal for a budding young ballerina, and Kat had loved her first true chance to perform. There had been costumes and makeup and lights—and there had been Rye Harmon.

Rye had been the star pitcher on the high school baseball team, with a reasonable baritone voice and an easy manner that translated well to the high school auditorium stage. Sure, he didn't know the first thing about dancing, but with careful choreography, the audience never discovered the truth. Week after week, Kat had nurtured a silly crush on her partner, even though she *knew* it could never amount to anything. Not when she was a precocious middle-school brat, and he was a high school hero. Not when she had her entire New York career ahead of herself, and he was Eden Falls incarnate—born, bred and content to stay in town forever.

In the intervening years, Kat had danced on stages around the world. She had kissed and been kissed a thousand times—in ballets and in real life, too. She was a grown, competent, mature woman, come back to town to help her family when they needed her most.

But she was also the child who had lived in Eden Falls, the shy girl who had craved attention from the unattainable senior.

And so she reacted the way a classically trained New York ballerina would act. She raised her chin. She narrowed her eyes. She tilted her head slightly to the right. And she said, "I'm sorry. Have we met?"

Rye stopped short as Kat Morehouse pinned him with her silver-gray eyes. He had no doubt that he was looking at Kat and not her twin, Rachel. Kat had always been the sister with the cool reserve, with the poised pride, even before she'd left Eden Falls. When was that? Ten years ago? Rye had just graduated from high school, but he'd still been impressed with all the gossip about one of Eden Falls's own heading up to New York City to make her fortune at some fancy ballet school.

Of course, Rye had seen plenty of Kat's sister, Rachel, around town over the past decade. Done more than see her, six years ago. He'd actually dated her for three of the most tempestuous weeks of his life. She'd been six months out of high school then, and she had flirted with him mercilessly, showing up at job sites, throwing pebbles at his window until he came down to see her in the middle of the night. It had taken him a while to figure out that she was just bent on getting revenge against one of Rye's fraternity brothers, Josh Barton. Barton had dumped her, saying she was nuts.

It had taken Rye just a few weeks to reach the same conclusion, then a few more to extricate himself from Rachel's crazy, melodramatic life. Just as well—a couple of months later, Rachel had turned up pregnant. Rye could still remember the frozen wave of disbelief that had washed over him when she told him the news, the shattering sound of all his dreams crashing to earth. And he could still remember stammering out a promise to be there for Rachel, to support his child. Most of all, though, he recalled the searing rush of relief when Rachel laughed, told him the baby was Josh's, entitled to its own share of the legendary Barton fortune.

Rye had dodged a bullet there.

If he had fathered Rachel's daughter—what was her name? Jessica? Jennifer?—he never could have left town. Never could have moved up to Richmond, set up his own contracting business. As it was, it had taken him six years after that wake-up call, and he still felt the constant demands of his family, had felt it with half a dozen girlfriends over the years. With a kid in the picture, he never could have fulfilled his vow to be a fully independent contractor by his thirtieth birthday.

He'd been well shed of Rachel, six years ago.

And he had no doubt he was looking at Kat now. Rachel and Kat were about as opposite as any two human beings could be—even if they were sisters. Even if they were twins. Kat's sharp eyes were the same as they'd been in middle school—but that was the only resemblance she bore to the freakishly good dancer he had once known.

That Kat Morehouse had been a kid.

This Kat Morehouse was a woman.

She was a full head taller than when he'd seen her last. Skinnier, too, all long legs and bare arms and a neck that looked like it was carved out of rare marble. Her jet-black hair was piled on top of her head in some sort of spiky ponytail, but he could see that it would be long and straight and thick, if she ever let it down. She was wearing a trim black T-shirt and matching jeans that looked like they'd been specially sewn in Paris or Italy or one of those fashion places.

And she had a bright blue walking boot on her left leg—the sort of boot that he'd worn through a few injuries over the years. The sort of boot that itched like hell in the heat. The sort of boot that made it a pain to stand on the edge of a ragged blacktop parking lot in front of the Eden Falls train station, waiting for a ride that was obviously late or, more likely, not coming at all.

Rye realized he was still standing there, his hand extended toward Kat like he was some idiot farm boy gawking at the state fair Dairy Princess. He squared his shoulders and wiped his palms across the worn denim thighs of his jeans. From the ice in Kat's platinum gaze, she clearly had no recollection of who he was. Well, at least he could fix that.

He stepped forward, finally closing the distance between them. "Rye," he said by way of introduction. "Rye Harmon. We met in high school. I mean, when I was in high school. You were in middle school. I was Curly, in *Oklahoma*. I mean, the play."

*Yeah, genius*, Rye thought to himself. *Like she really thought you meant Oklahoma, the state.*

Kat hadn't graduated from the National Ballet School without plenty of acting classes. She put those skills to good use, flashing a bright smile of supposedly sudden recognition. "Rye!" she said. "Of course!"

She sounded fake to herself, but she suspected no one else could tell. Well, maybe her mother. Her father. Rachel, if she bothered to pay attention. But certainly not a practical stranger like Rye Harmon. A practical stranger who said, "Going to your folks' house? I can drop you there." He reached for her overnight bag, as if his assistance was a forgone conclusion.

"Oh, no," she protested. "I couldn't ask you to do that!" She grabbed for the handle of the roller bag as well, flinching when her fingers settled on top of his. What was *wrong* with her? She wasn't usually this jumpy.

She wasn't usually in Eden Falls, Virginia.

"It's no problem," Rye said, and she remembered that easy smile from a decade before. "Your parents live three blocks from mine—from where I'm taking Lisa."

Kat wanted to say no. She had been solving her own problems for ten long years.

Not that she had such a great track record lately. Her walking boot was testament to that. And the box of things piled in the corner of her bedroom, waiting for cheating Adam to pick up while she was out of town.

But what was she going to do? Watch Rye drive out of the parking lot, and then discover she had no change at the bottom of her purse? Or that the pay phone—if there even *was* a pay phone—was out of order? Or that no one was at the Morehouse home, that Mike had some doctor's appointment Susan had forgotten when they made their plans?

"Okay," Kat said, only then realizing that her hand was still on Rye's, that they both still held her suitcase. "Um, thanks."

She let him take the bag, hobbling after him to the gleaming truck. Lisa shifted over on the bench seat, saying, "Hey," in a friendly voice.

"Hi," Kat answered, aware of the Northern inflection in her voice, of the clipped vowel sound that made her seem like she was in a hurry. She *was* in a hurry, though. She'd come all the way from New York City— almost five hundred miles.

It wasn't just the distance, though. It was the lifetime. It was the return to her awkward, unhappy childhood, where she'd always been the odd one out, the dancer, the kid who was destined to move away.

She'd left Eden Falls for a reason—to build her dream career. Now that she was back in the South, she felt like her life was seizing up in quicksand. She was being forced to move slower, trapped by convention and expectation and the life she had not led.

Determined to regain a bit of control, she turned back to the truck door, ready to tug it closed behind her. She was startled to find Rye standing there. "Oh!" she said, leaping away. The motion tumbled her purse from her lap to her feet. Silently cursing her uncharacteristic lack of grace, she leaned forward to scoop everything back inside her bag. Rye reached out to help, but she angled her shoulder, finishing the embarrassing task before he could join in.

"I didn't mean to startle you," he drawled. He reached inside the truck and passed her the seat belt, pulling it forward from its awkward position over her right shoulder.

"You didn't!" But, of course, he had. And if she made any more protest, he might take more time to apologize, time she did not want to waste. It was all well and good for him to take all day on a run to the train station. What else could he have to do in slow-paced Eden Falls? But she was there to help her family, and she might as well get started. She pulled the seat belt across her chest, settling it in its slot with the precision of a brain surgeon. "I'm fine. And if you don't mind, I'm sort of in a hurry."

She almost winced when she realized how brusque she sounded.

Recognizing dismissal when he heard it, Rye shut the door carefully. He shook his head as he walked around the front of his truck. Ten years had passed, but he still remembered Kat's precise attention to detail. Kat Morehouse had been a determined girl. And she had clearly grown into a formidable woman.

Formidable. Not exactly the type he was used to dating. Certainly not like Rachel had been, with her constant breaking of rules, pushing of boundaries. And not like the sweet, small-town girls he had dated here in Eden Falls.

His brothers teased him, saying he'd moved to Richmond because he needed a deeper dating pool. Needed to find a real woman—all the girls in Eden Falls knew him too well.

He hadn't actually had time for a date in the past year—not since he'd been burned by Marissa. Marissa Turner. He swallowed the bitter taste in his mouth as he thought of the woman who had been his girlfriend for two long years. Two long years, when he had torn apart his own life plans, forfeited his fledgling business, all to support her beauty salon.

Every time Rye mentioned making it big in Richmond, Marissa had thrown a fit. He had wanted her to be happy, and so he had circumscribed all of his dreams. It was easier, after all. Easier to stay in Eden Falls. Easier to keep doing the same handyman work he'd been doing all of his adult life. At least Marissa was happy.

Until she got some crazy-ass chance to work on a movie out in Hollywood, doing the hair for some leading-man hunk. Marissa had flown cross-country without a single look back, not even bothering to break up with Rye by phone. And he had been left utterly alone, feeling like a fool.

A fool who was two years behind on his business plan.

But not anymore. With Marissa gone, Rye had finally made the leap, moving up to Richmond, finding the perfect office, hunting down a tolerable apartment. He was finally moving on with his life, and it felt damn good to make choices for himself. Not for his family. Not for his girlfriend. For him.

At least, most of the time.

Lisa was chatting with Kat by the time he settled into the driver's seat. "It's no problem, really," his sister was saying. "Rye already came down from Richmond to get me. Things are crazy at home—Mama's out West visiting her sister, and Daddy's busy with the spring planting. Half my brothers and sisters sent up a distress call to get Rye home for the weekend. He's walking dogs for our sister Jordana—she's out of town for a wedding, so she can't take care of her usual clients. At least he could fit taxi service in before coaching T-ball practice this afternoon, filling in for Noah."

Listening to Lisa's friendly banter, Rye had to shake his head. It was no wonder he had moved all the way to Richmond to make his business work. Of course, he loved his family, loved the fact that they all looked to him to fix whatever was wrong. But here in Eden Falls, there was *always* a brother who needed a hand, a sister with one more errand, cousins, aunts, uncles, friends— *people* who pulled him away from his business.

He'd only been living in Richmond for a month, and he'd already come back to Eden Falls a half-dozen times. He promised himself he'd get more control over his calendar in the weeks to come.

Lisa nudged his ribs with a sharp elbow. "Right? Tell Kat that it's no big deal, or she's going to get out at the traffic light and walk home from there!"

Rye couldn't help but smile. He could grouse all he wanted about being called home, but he loved his family, loved the fact that they needed him. "It's no big deal," he said dutifully, and then he nodded to Kat. "And you shouldn't be walking anywhere on that boot. Broken foot?"

Kat fought against her automatic frown. "Stress fracture."

"Ow. Our brother Logan had one of those, a couple of years back. He plays baseball for the Eagles. It took about a month for his foot to heal. A month until he could get back to playing, anyway."

Kat started to ask if Logan pitched, like Rye had done, but then she remembered she wasn't supposed to have recognized Rye. She settled for shrugging instead and saying, "The doctors say I've got about a month to wait, myself. I figured it was a good time to come down here. Help out my parents."

Rye gave her a sympathetic glance. "I was at their house a few months ago, to install a handheld shower for your father. How's he doing?"

"Fine." Kat curved her lips into the smile she had mastered in her long-ago acting classes. Her father was fine. Susan was fine. Jenny was fine. Everyone was fine, and Kat would be on a northbound train in less than a week.

"Colon cancer can be rough." Rye's voice was filled with sympathy.

"They say they caught it in time." Kat was afraid to voice her fears—Mike's recovery had taken longer than anyone had expected. He'd been in and out of the hospital for six months, and now, with pneumonia…

At least Rye seemed to believe her. He didn't ask any more questions. Instead, he assured her, "Everyone's been real worried about them. Just last week, my mother had me bring by some of her chicken almond casserole. It'll get your father back on his feet in no time."

Kat couldn't remember the last time she'd cooked for a sick friend. Oh, well. Things were different down here. People had different ways to show they cared. She tried to recall the lessons in politeness that her mother had drilled into her, years before. "I'm sure it was delicious. It was kind of you to bring it by."

Rye wondered if he'd somehow made Kat angry—she sounded so stiff. Her hands were folded in her lap, her fingers wrapped around each other in perfect precision, like coils of rope, fresh from the factory. She sat upright like a soldier, keeping her spine from touching the back of her seat. Her eyes flashed as they drove past familiar streets, and each intersection tightened the cords in her throat.

And then it came to him: Kat wasn't angry. She was frightened.

One thing Rye had learned in almost thirty years of dealing with siblings and cousins was how to ease the mind of someone who was afraid. Just talk to them. It was easy enough to spin out a story or two about Eden Falls. He might have moved away, but he could always dredge up something entertaining about the only real home he'd ever known.

He nodded to the row of little shops they were passing. "Miss Emily just closed up her pet store."

Kat barely glanced at the brightly painted storefront, and for a second he thought she might not take the bait. Finally, though, she asked, "What happened?"

"She couldn't stand to see any of the animals in cages. She sold off all the mice and gerbils and fish, and then she took in a couple of litters of kittens. She gave them free rein over the whole shop. Problem was, she fell in love with the kittens too much to sell them. If she took money, she couldn't be sure the animals were going to a good home. So instead of selling them, she gave them away to the best owners she could find. In the end, she decided it didn't make much sense to pay rent. Anyone who wants a kitten now just goes up to her house and knocks on the front door."

There. That was better. He actually caught a hint of a smile on Kat's lips. Lisa, of course, was rolling her eyes, but at least his sister didn't call him a liar. As long as he was on a roll, he nodded toward the elementary school they were passing. "Remember classes there? They had to skip the Christmas pageant last December because the boa constrictor in the fourth-grade classroom got out. None of the parents would come see the show until the snake was found. The kids are going to sing 'Jingle Bells' for the Easter parade."

Kat couldn't help herself. She had to ask. "Did they ever find the snake?"

"He finally came out about a week ago. The janitor found him sunning himself on the parking lot, none the worse for wear. He was hungry, though. They used to feed him mice from Miss Emily's."

Kat wrinkled her nose, but she had to laugh. She had to admit—she couldn't imagine the National Ballet School having similar problems. And they would *never* have postponed a performance, snake or no snake, especially a holiday showcase like a Christmas pageant.

Rye eased up to the curb in front of her parents' house, shoving the gearshift into Park. He hopped out of the truck as Kat said goodbye to Lisa. She joined him by the deep bed. "Thank you," she said. And somehow, she meant to thank him for more than the ride. She meant to tell him that she appreciated the effort he had made, the way that he had tried to distract her from her worry.

"My pleasure," he said, tipping an imaginary hat. "Harmon Contracting is a full-service provider." He hefted her suitcase out of the truck, shrugging it into a more comfortable position as he nodded for Kat to precede him up the driveway.

"Oh, I can get that," she said, reaching for the bag.

"It's no problem."

"Please," she said, carving an edge onto the word. She'd learned long ago how to get her way in the bustling streets of New York. She knew the precise angle to hold her shoulders, the exact line to set her chin. No one would dare argue with her when she'd strapped on her big city armor.

Rye recognized that stance; he'd seen it often enough in his own sisters, in his mother. Kat Morehouse was not going to give in easily.

And there really wasn't any reason to push the matter. It wasn't as if he didn't have a thousand other things to do that afternoon—the dog walking Lisa had mentioned, and the T-ball practice, but also phone calls back to Richmond, trying to keep his fledgling business alive while he was on the road.

And yet, he really didn't want to leave Kat here, alone. If he turned his head just a little, he could still see the girl she'd been, the stubborn, studious child who had defied convention, who had done what *she* wanted to do, had carved out the life *she* wanted, never letting little Eden Falls stop her in her tracks.

But there would be time enough to see Kat again. She wasn't going to disappear overnight, and he was in town for the whole weekend. He could stop by the next day. Think of some excuse between now and then. He extended the handle on the roller bag, turning it around to make it easier for Kat to grasp. "Have it your way," he said, adding a smile.

"Thanks," Kat said, and she hustled up the driveway, relying on the roller bag to disguise the lurch of her booted foot. Only when she reached the door did she wonder if she should go back to Rye's truck, thank him properly for the ride. After all, he'd done her a real favor, bringing her home. And she wouldn't mind taking one last look at those slate-black eyes, at the smooth planes of his face, at his rugged jaw....

She shook her head, though, reminding herself to concentrate. She was through with men. Through with distractions that just consumed her time, that took her away from the things that were truly important, from the things that mattered. She might have been an idiot to get involved with Adam, but at least she could translate her disappointing experience into something useful.

Waving a calculatedly jaunty farewell toward Rye and Lisa, Kat threw back her shoulders, took a deep breath and turned the doorknob. Of course the front door was unlocked; it always was. In New York, Kat had to work three different locks on the door of the apartment she shared with Haley, every single time she went in or out. Things were simpler here in Eden Falls. Easier. Safer.

Boring.

Pushing down her automatic derogatory thoughts about the town that had kept her parents happy for their entire lives, Kat stepped over the threshold. And then she caught her breath at the scene inside the old brick rambler.

Chaos. Utter, complete chaos.

A radio blasted from the kitchen, some mournful weatherman announcing that the temperature was going to top ninety, a new record high for the last day in March. A teakettle shrieked on the stovetop, piercing the entire house with its urgent demand. In the living room, a television roared the jingle from a video game, the same four bars of music, over and over and over again. From the master bedroom, a man shouted, "Fine! Let me do it, then!" and a shrill child's voice repeated, "I'm helping! I'm helping!"

All of a sudden, it seemed pretty clear how Susan had forgotten to meet Kat at the train station.

Resisting the urge to hobble back to the curb and

beg Rye to take her to a motel out on the highway—or better yet, back to the train station so she could catch the two-fifteen northbound Clipper—Kat closed the front door behind her. She pushed her little suitcase into the corner of the foyer and dropped her purse beside it. She headed to the kitchen first, grabbing a pot holder from the side of the refrigerator where her mother had kept them forever. The kettle stopped screaming as soon as she lifted it from the heat. The blue flame died immediately when Kat turned the knob on the stove. She palmed off the radio before the local news break could end.

Next stop was the living room, where Kat cast the television into silence, resorting to pushing buttons on the actual set, rather than seeking out the missing remote control. A scramble of half-clothed Barbie dolls lay on the floor, pink dresses tangled with a rose-colored sports car that had plunged into a dry fuchsia swimming pool. A handful of board games was splattered across the entire mess—tiny cones from Sorry mixing with Jenga rods and piles of Monopoly money. Kat shook her head—there would be plenty of time to sort that mess later.

And that left the voices coming from the master bedroom, down the hallway. Kat could make out her father's gruff tones as he insisted someone hand him something immediately. The whining child—it had to be Jenny—was still saying "I'm helping," as if she had to prove her worthiness to someone. And Kat surprised herself by finding tears in her eyes when she heard a low murmur—her calm, unflappable mother, trying to soothe both her husband and her granddaughter.

Kat clumped down the hall, resenting the awkward

walking boot more than ever. When she reached the doorway, she was surprised by the tableau before her.

A hospital bed loomed between her parents' ancient double mattress and the far wall. Mike lay prone between the raised bars, but he craned his neck at a sharp angle. He held out a calloused hand, demanding that a tiny raven-haired child hand over the controls to the bed. The girl kept pressing buttons without any effect; she obviously did not understand how to make the bed work. Susan was framed in the doorway to the bathroom, her gray face cut deep with worry lines as she balanced a small tray, complete with a glass of water and a cup of pills.

"Kat!" Susan exclaimed. "What time—?"

"I caught a ride home with Rye Harmon," Kat said, wrestling to keep her gait as close to normal as possible. The last thing she wanted was for her mother to fuss over a stupid stress fracture. Not when Susan obviously had so much else to worry about.

Kat plucked the bed controls from her niece's hand and passed the bulky plastic block to her father. She settled firm fingers on the child's shoulder, turning her toward the doorway and the living room. "Thank you, Jenny," she said, pushing pretend warmth into the words. "You were a big help. Now there are some toys out there, just waiting for you to straighten up."

Jenny sighed, but she shuffled down the hallway. Kat leaned down to brush a kiss against her father's forehead, easing an arm beneath his shoulders as he started to manipulate the mechanical bed, fighting to raise himself into a seated position. When she was certain he was more comfortable, Kat said, "Come sit down, Mama." She heard the hard New York edge on her words, and she smiled to soften her voice. "Why don't you rest, and let me take care of that for a while?"

Even as Susan settled on the edge of the double bed, Kat heard the distant whistle of the Clipper, the New York-bound train, leaving town for the day. The wild, lonesome sound immediately made her think about Rye Harmon, about how he had offered to come inside, to help. He'd scooped her up from the train station like a knight in shining armor—a friendly, easygoing knight whom she'd known all her life. Kat blinked and she could see his kind smile, his warm black eyes. She could picture the steady, sturdy way he had settled her into his truck.

She shook her head. She didn't have time to think about Rye. Instead, she handed her father his medicine, taking care to balance her weight, keeping her spine in alignment despite her cursed walking boot. She had come to Eden Falls to help out her family, to be there for Susan and Mike. And as soon as humanly possible, she was heading back to New York, and the National Ballet Company and the life she had worked so hard to attain. She didn't have time for Rye Harmon. Rye Harmon, or anything else that might delay her escape from Eden Falls.

## *Chapter Two*

Three hours later, Kat wondered if she had made the greatest mistake of her life. She leaned against the headrest in her cousin Amanda's ancient sedan, resisting the urge to strangle her five-year-old niece.

"But *why* isn't Aunt Kat driving?" Jenny asked for the fourth time.

"I'm happy to drive you both home, Jenny," Amanda deflected, applying one of the tricks she'd learned as a schoolteacher.

"But *why*—"

Kat interrupted the whining question, spitting out an answer through gritted teeth. "Because I don't know how!"

Amanda laughed at Kat's frustration. The cousins had been quite close when they were children—certainly closer than Kat had been to her own sister. Nevertheless, Amanda always thought it was hysterical that

Kat had never gotten her driver's license. More than once, she had teased Kat about moving away to the magical kingdom of Oz, where she was carried around by flying monkeys.

Jenny, though, wasn't teasing Kat. The five-year-old child was simply astonished, her mouth stretched into an amazed O before she stammered, "B-but *all* grown-ups know how to drive!"

"Maybe your Aunt Kat isn't a grown-up," Amanda suggested helpfully.

Kat gave her a dirty look before saying, "I am a grown-up, Jenny, but I don't drive. The two things are totally separate."

"But how do you go to the grocery store?"

"I walk there," Kat said, exasperated. How could one little girl make her feel like such a sideshow freak?

"But what do you do with the bags of groceries?"

"I carry them!"

Kat's voice was rough enough that even the head-strong Jenny declined to ask another follow-up question. It wasn't so ridiculous, that Kat couldn't drive. She'd left Eden Falls when she was fourteen, long before she'd even thought of getting behind the wheel of a car. She'd spent the next ten years living in Manhattan, where subways, buses and the occasional taxi met her transportation needs. Anything heavy or bulky could be delivered.

But try explaining that to someone who had never even heard of the Mason-Dixon line, much less traveled above it.

Amanda's laugh smoothed over the awkward moment as she pulled into the driveway of a run-down brick Colonial. Weeds poked through the crumbling asphalt, and the lawn was long dead from lack of water—

just as well, since it had not been cut for months. One shutter hung at a defeated angle, and the screen on the front door was slashed and rusted. A collapsing carport signaled imminent danger to any vehicle unfortunate enough to be parked beneath it.

"I don't believe it!" Kat said. The last time she had seen this house, it had been neat and trim, kept in perfect shape. Years ago, it had belonged to her grandmother, to Susan's mother. The Morehouses had kept it in the family after Granny died; it was easy enough to keep up the little Colonial.

Easy enough, that was, until Rachel got her hands on the place. Susan and Mike had let Rachel move in after she'd graduated from high school, when the constant fights had become too difficult under their own roof. The arrangement had been intended to be temporary, but once Rachel gave birth to Jenny, it had somehow slipped into something permanent.

Now, though, looking at the wreck of Granny's neat little home, Kat could not help but begrudge that decision. Did Rachel destroy *everything* she touched?

Amanda's voice shone with forced brightness. "It always looks bad after winter. Once everything's freshened up for spring, it'll be better."

Sure it would. Because Rachel had such a green thumb, she had surely taken care of basic gardening over the past several years. Rachel always worked so hard to bring good things into her life. Not.

Kat swallowed hard and undid her seat belt. *One week,* she reminded herself. She only had to stay here one week. Then Jenny could return to Susan and Mike. Or, who knew? Rachel might even be back from wherever she had gone. "Well…" Kat tried to think of something positive to say about the house. Failing miserably, she fell back on something she *could* be grateful for. "Thanks for the ride."

Amanda's soft features settled into a frown. "Do you need any help with your bag? Are you sure—"

"We'll be fine."

"We could all go out to dinner—"

That was the last thing Kat wanted—drawing out the day, eating in some Eden Falls greasy spoon, where the food would send any thinking dancer to the workout room for at least ten straight hours, just to break even. Besides, she really didn't want to impose on her cousin's good nature—and driver's license—any more than was strictly necessary. "We'll be *fine,* Amanda. I'm sure Aunt Sarah and Uncle Bill are already wondering what took you so long, just running Jenny and me across town. You don't want them to start worrying."

At least Kat's case was bolstered by her niece's behavior. Jenny had already hopped out of her seat and scuffed her way to the faded front door. Amanda sighed. "I don't know what sort of food you'll find in there, Kat."

"We can always—" What? She was going to say, they could always have D'Agostino deliver groceries. But there wasn't a D'Agostino in Eden Falls. There wasn't *any* grocery store that delivered. She swallowed hard and pushed her way through to the end of the sentence. "We can always order a pizza."

That was the right thing to say. Amanda relaxed, obviously eased by the sheer normalcy of Kat's suggestion.

As *if* Kat would eat a pizza. She'd given up mozzarella the year she'd first gone on pointe. "Thanks so much for the ride," Kat said. "Give my love to Aunt Sarah and Uncle Bill."

By the time Kat dragged her roller bag through the
front door, Jenny was in the kitchen, kneeling on a
chair in front of the open pantry. Her hand was shoved
deep in a bag of cookies, and telltale chocolate crumbs
ringed her lips. Kat's reproach was automatic. "Are you
eating cookies for dinner?"

"No." Jenny eyed her defiantly.

"Don't lie to me, young lady." *Ach*, Kat thought. *Did
I really just say that? I sound like everyone's stereo-
type of the strict maiden aunt.* Annoyed, Kat looked
around the kitchen. Used paper plates cascaded out of
an open trash can. A jar of peanut butter lay on its side,
its lid teetering at a crazy angle. A dozen plastic cups
were strewn across the counter, with varying amounts
of sticky residue pooling inside.

On top of the toaster oven curled three bananas. Kat
broke one off from the bunch and passed it to her niece.
"Here", she said. "Eat this."

"I don't like them when they're brown."

"That's dinner."

"You said we were ordering a pizza."

"Pizza isn't good for you."

"Mommy likes pizza."

"Mommy would." Kat closed her eyes and took a
deep breath. This wasn't the time or the place to get
into a discussion about Rachel. Kat dug in the pantry,
managing to excavate a sealed packet of lemon-pepper
tuna. "Here. You can have tuna and a banana. I'll go to
the grocery store tomorrow."

"How are you going to do that, when you don't
drive? It's too far to walk."

Good question. "I'll manage."

Kat took a quick tour of the rest of the house while
Jenny ate her dinner. Alas, the kitchen wasn't some

terrible aberration. The living room was ankle-deep in pizza boxes and gossip magazines. The disgusting bathroom hadn't been cleaned in centuries. Jenny's bedroom was a sea of musty, tangled sheets and stuffed animals.

Back in the kitchen, Jenny's sullen silence was nearly enough to make Kat put cookies back on the menu. Almost. But Jenny didn't need cookies. She needed some rules. Some structure. A pattern or two in her life. Starting now.

"Okay, kiddo. We're going to get some cleaning done."

"Cleaning?" Jenny's whine stretched the word into four or five syllables at least.

Kat turned to the stove—ironically, the cleanest thing in the house, because Rachel had never cooked a meal in her life. Kat twisted the old-fashioned timer to give them fifteen minutes to work. "Let's go. Fifteen minutes, to make this kitchen look new."

Jenny stared at her as if she'd lost her mind. Squaring her shoulders, though, and ignoring the blooming ache in her foot, Kat started to tame the pile of paper plates. "Let's go," she said. "March! You're in charge of throwing away those paper cups!"

With the use of three supersize trash bags, they made surprising progress. When those fifteen minutes were done, Kat set the alarm again, targeting the mess in the living room. The bathroom was next, and finally Jenny's room. The little girl was yawning and rubbing her eyes by the time they finished.

"Mommy never makes me clean up."

"I'm not Mommy," Kat said. She was *so* not Mommy—not in a million different ways. But she knew what was good for Jenny. She knew what had been good for her, even when she was Jenny's age. Setting goals. Developing strategies. Following rules. When Kat had lived in her parents' home, Susan had built the foundation for orderly management of life's problems. Unlike her sister, Kat had absorbed those lessons with a vengeance. Her *rules* were the only thing that had gotten her through those first homesick months when she moved to New York. As Jenny started to collapse on the living-room couch, Kat said, "It's time for you to go to bed."

"I haven't watched TV yet!"

"No TV. It's a school night."

"Mommy lets me watch TV every night."

"I'm not Mommy," Kat repeated, wondering if she should record the sentence, so that she could play it back every time she needed it.

Over the next half hour, Kat found out that she was cruel and heartless and evil and mean, just like the worst villains of Jenny's favorite animated movies. But the child eventually got to bed wearing her pajamas, with her teeth brushed, her hair braided and her prayers said.

Exhausted, and unwilling to admit just how much her foot was aching, Kat collapsed onto the sagging living-room couch. Six more days. She could take six more days of anything. They couldn't all be this difficult. She glanced at her watch and was shocked to see it was only eight-thirty.

That left her plenty of time to call Haley. Plenty of time to catch up on the exploits of Adam and Selene, to remember why Kat was so much better off without that miserable excuse for a man in her life.

Kat summoned her willpower and stumped over to her purse, where she'd left it on the kitchen table.

She rooted for her cell phone. Nothing. She scrambled around, digging past her wallet. Still nothing. She dumped the contents out on the kitchen table, where it immediately became clear that she had no cell phone.

And then she remembered spilling everything in the cab of Rye's truck in her rush of surprise to see him standing beside her. She had been shocked by the elemental response to his body near hers. She'd acted like a silly schoolgirl, like a brainless child, jumping the way she had, dropping her purse.

But even as she berated herself, she remembered Rye's easy smile. He'd been truly gallant, rescuing her at the train station. It had been mean of her to pretend not to remember him. Uncomfortably, she thought of the confused flash in his eyes, the tiny flicker of hurt that was almost immediately smothered beneath the blanket of his good nature.

And then, her belly did that funny thing again, that flutter that was part nervous anticipation, part unreasoning dread. The closest thing she could compare it to was the thrill of opening night, the excitement of standing in the wings while a new audience hummed in the theater's red-velvet seats.

But she wasn't in the theater. She was in Eden Falls.

And whether she wanted to or not, Kat was going to have to track down Rye Harmon the following day. Track him down, and retrieve her phone, and hope she had a better signal at Rachel's house than she'd had at the station.

All things considered, though, she couldn't get too upset about the lack of signal that she'd encountered. If she'd been able to call Susan or Amanda, then Rye would never have given her a ride. And those few minutes of talking with Rye Harmon had been the high point of her very long, very stressful, very exhausting first afternoon and evening in Eden Falls.

By noon the next day, Kat had decided that retrieving her cell phone was the least of her concerns.

Susan had swung by that morning, just after Kat had hustled a reluctant Jenny onto her school bus. Looking around the straightened house, Susan said, "It looks like you and Jenny were busy last night."

"The place was a pigsty."

"I'm sorry, dear. I just wasn't able to get over here before you arrived, to clean things up."

Kat immediately felt terrible for her judgmental tone. "I wasn't criticizing *you,* Mama. I just can't believe Rachel lives like that."

Susan shook her head. Kat knew from long experience that her mother would never say anything directly critical about her other daughter. But sometimes Susan's silences echoed with a thousand shades of meaning.

Pushing aside a lifetime of criticism about her sister, Kat said, "Thank you so much for bringing by that casserole. Jenny and I will really enjoy it tonight."

Susan apologized again. "I can't believe I didn't think of giving you anything last night. The church ladies have been so helpful—they've kept our freezer stocked for months."

"I'm glad you've had that type of support," Kat said. And she was. She still couldn't imagine any of her friends in New York cooking for a colleague in need. Certainly no one would organize food week after week. "How was Daddy last night? Did either of you get any sleep?"

Susan's smile was brilliant, warming Kat from

across the room. "Oh, yes, sweetheart. I had to wake him up once for his meds, but he fell back to sleep right away. It was the best night he's had in months."

Glancing around the living room, Kat swallowed a proud grin. She had been right to come down here. If one night could help Susan so much, what would an entire week accomplish?

Susan went on. "And it was a godsend, not fixing breakfast for Jenny before the sun was up. That elementary school bus comes so early, it's a crime."

Kat was accustomed to being awake well before the sun rose. She usually fit in ninety minutes on the treadmill in the company gym before she even thought about attending her first dance rehearsal of the day. Of course, with the walking boot, she hadn't been able to indulge in the tension tamer of her typical exercise routine. She'd had to make due with a punishing regimen of crunches instead, alternating sets with modified planks and a series of leg lifts meant to keep her hamstrings as close to dancing strength as possible.

As for Jenny's breakfast? It had been some hideous purple-and-green cereal, eaten dry, because there wasn't any milk in the house. Kat had been willing to concede the point on cold cereal first thing in the morning, but she had silently vowed that the artificially dyed stuff would be out of the house by the time Jenny got home that afternoon. Whole-grain oats would be better for the little girl—and they wouldn't stain the milk in Jenny's bowl.

There'd be time enough to pick up some groceries that afternoon. For now, Kat knew her mother had another task in mind. "So, are you going to drop me off at the studio now?"

Susan looked worried. "It's really too much for me

to ask. I shouldn't even have mentioned it when I called you, dear. I'm sure I can take care of everything in the next couple of weeks."

"Don't be silly," Kat said. "I know Rachel was running things for you. She's been gone for a while, though, and someone has to pick up the slack. I came to Eden Falls to help."

Susan fussed some more, but she was already leading the way out to her car. It may have been ten years since Kat had lived in Eden Falls, but she knew the way to the Morehouse Dance Academy by heart. As a child, she had practically lived in her mother's dance studio, from the moment she could pull on her first leotard.

The building was smaller than she remembered, though. It seemed lost in the sea of its huge parking lot. A broken window was covered over with a cardboard box, and a handful of yellowed newspapers rested against the door, like kindling.

Kat glanced at her mother's pinched face, and she consciously coated her next words with a smile. "Don't worry, Mama. It'll just take a couple of hours to make sure everything is running smoothly. Go home and take care of Daddy. I'll call Amanda to bring me back to Rachel's."

"Let me just come in with you…."

Kat shook her head. Once her mother started in on straightening the studio, she'd stay all morning. Susan wasn't the sort of woman to walk away from a project half-done. Even *if* she had a recuperating husband who needed her back at the house.

"I'll be fine, Mama. I know this place like the back of my hand. And I'm sure Rachel left everything in good shape."

Good shape. Right.

The roof was leaking in the main classroom, a slow drip that had curled up the ceiling tiles and stained one wall. Kat shuddered to think about the state of the warped hardwood floor. Both toilets were running in the public restroom, and the sinks were stained from dripping faucets. Kat ran the hot water for five minutes before she gave up on getting more than an icy trickle.

The damage wasn't limited to the building. When Kat turned on the main computer, she heard a grinding sound, and the screen flashed blue before it died altogether. The telephone handset was sticky; a quick sniff confirmed that someone had handled it with maple syrup on their fingers.

In short, the dance studio was an absolute and complete mess.

Kat seethed. How could students be taking classes here? How could her parents' hard-earned investment be ruined so quickly? What had Rachel done?

Muttering to herself, Kat started to sift through the papers on the desk in the small, paneled office. She found a printout of an electronic spreadsheet—at least the computer had been functional back in January.

The news on the spreadsheet, though, told a depressing story. Class sizes for the winter term had dwindled from their robust fall enrollment. Many of those payments had never been collected. Digging deeper, Kat found worse news—a dozen checks, dating back to September—had never been cashed. Search as she might, she could find no checks at all for the spring term; she couldn't even find an enrollment list for the classes.

Susan had been absolutely clear, every time Kat talked to her: Rachel had shaped up. Rachel had run the dance studio for the past six months, ever since

Mike's diagnosis had thrown Susan's life into utter disarray. Rachel had lined up teachers, had taken care of the books, had kept everything functioning like clockwork.

Rachel had lied through her teeth.

Kat's fingers trembled with rage as she looked around the studio. Her heart pounded, and her breath came in short gasps. Tears pricked at the corners of her eyes, angry tears that made her chew on her lower lip.

And so Kat did the only thing she knew how to do. She tried to relieve her stress the only way she could. She walked across the floor of the classroom, her feet automatically turning out in a ballerina's stance, even though she wore her hated blue boot. Resenting that handicap, she planted her good foot, setting one hand on the barre with a lifetime of familiarity.

She closed her eyes and ran through the simplest of exercises. First position, second position, third position, fourth. She swept her free arm in a graceful arc, automatically tilting her head to an angle that maximized the long line of her neck. She repeated the motions again, three times, four. Each pass through, she felt a little of her tension drain, a little of her rage fade.

She was almost able to take a lung-filling breath when heavy footsteps dragged her back to messy, disorganized reality. "*There* you are!"

Rye stopped in the doorway, frozen into place by the vision of Kat at the barre. All of a sudden, he was catapulted back ten years in time, to the high school auditorium, to the rough stage where he had plodded through the role of Curly.

He had caught Kat stretching out for dancing there, too, backstage one spring afternoon. She'd had her heel firmly anchored on a table, bending her willowy limbs with a grace that had made his own hulking, teenage body awaken to desire. He could see her now, only a few feet away, close enough for him to touch.

But his interest had been instantly quenched when he'd glimpsed Kat's face, that day so long ago. Tears had tracked down her smooth cheeks, silvering the rosy skin that was completely bare of the blush and concealer and all the other makeup crap that high school girls used. Even as he took one step closer, he had seen her flinch, caught her eyes darting toward the dressing room. He'd heard the brassy laugh of one of the senior girls, one of the cheerleaders, and he'd immediately understood that the popular kids had been teasing the young middle-school dancer. Again.

Rye had done the only thing that made sense at the time, the one thing that he thought would make Kat forget that she was an outsider. He'd leaned forward to brush a quick fraternal kiss against her cheek.

But somehow—even now, he couldn't say how—he'd ended up touching his lips to hers. They'd been joined for just a heartbeat, a single, chaste connection that had jolted through him with the power of a thousand sunsets.

Rye could still remember the awkward blush that had flamed his face. He really had meant to kiss her on the cheek. He'd swear it—on his letter jacket and his game baseball, and everything else that had mattered to him back in high school. He had no idea if he had moved wrong, or if she had, but after the kiss she had leaped away as if he'd scorched her with a blowtorch.

Thinking back, Rye still wanted to wince. How had he screwed *that* up? He had three sisters. He had a lifetime of experience kissing cheeks, offering old-fashioned, brotherly support. He'd certainly never kissed one of his sisters on the lips by mistake.

Kat's embarrassment had only been heightened when a voice spoke up from the curtains that led to the stage. "What would Mom think, Kat? Should I go get her, so she can see what you're really like?" They'd both looked up to see Rachel watching them. Her eyes had been narrowed, those eyes that were so like Kat's but so very, very different. Even then, ten years ago, there hadn't been any confusing the sisters. Only an eighth grader, Rachel hadn't yet resorted to the dyed hair and tattoos that she sported as an adult. But she'd painted heavy black outlines around her eyes, and she wore clunky earrings and half a dozen rings on either hand. Rachel had laughed at her sister then, obviously relishing Kat's embarrassment over that awful mistake of a kiss.

Rachel must not have told, though. There hadn't been any repercussions. And Rye's fumbling obviously hadn't made any lasting impression—Kat hadn't even remembered his name, yesterday at the train station.

Kat stiffened as she heard Rye's voice. A jumble of emotions flashed through her head—guilt, because she shouldn't be caught at the barre, not when she was supposed to be resting her injured foot. Shame, because no one should see the studio in its current state of disarray. Anger, because Rachel should never have let things get so out of hand, should never have left so much mess for Kat to clean up. And a sudden swooping sense of something else, something that she couldn't name precisely. Something that she vaguely thought of as pleasure.

Shoving down that last thought—one that she didn't have time for, that she didn't deserve—she lowered her arm and turned to face Rye. "How did you get in here?"

"The front door was open. Maybe the latch didn't catch when you came in?"

Kat barked a harsh laugh. "That makes one more thing that's broken."

Rye glanced around the studio, his eyes immediately taking in the ceiling leak. "That looks bad," he said. "And the water damage isn't new."

Kat grimaced. "It's probably about six months old."

"Why do you say that?"

"It's been six months since my father got sick. My sister, Rachel, has been running this place and…she's not the best at keeping things together."

Rye fought the urge to scowl when he heard Rachel's name. Sure, the woman had her problems. But it was practically criminal to have let so much water get into a hardwood floor like this one. He barely managed not to shake his head. He'd dodged a bullet with Rachel, seeing through to her irresponsible self before he could be dragged down with her.

But it wasn't Rachel standing in front of him, looking so discouraged. It was Kat. Kat, who had come home to help out her family, giving up her own fame and success because her people needed her.

Rye couldn't claim to have found fame or success in Richmond. Not yet. But he certainly understood being called back home because of family. Before he was fully aware of the fact that he was speaking, he heard himself say, "I can help clean things up. Patch the roof, replace the drywall. The floor will take a bit more work, but I can probably get it all done in ten days or so."

Kat saw the earnestness in Rye's black eyes, and she found herself melting just a little. Rye Harmon was coming to her rescue. Again. Just as he had at the train station the day before.

That was silly, though. It wasn't like she was still the starry-eyed eighth grader who had been enchanted by the baseball star in the lead role of the musical. She hardened her voice, so that she could remind herself she had no use for Eden Falls. "That sounds like a huge job! You'll need help, and I'm obviously in no shape to get up on a ladder." She waved a frustrated hand toward her booted foot.

Rye scarcely acknowledged her injury. "There's no need for you to get involved. I have plenty of debts that I can call in."

"Debts?"

"Brothers. Sisters. Cousins. Half of Eden Falls calls me in from Richmond, day or night, to help them out of a bind. What's a little leak repair, in repayment?"

"Do any of those relatives know anything about plumbing?"

Rye looked concerned. "What's wrong with the plumbing?"

For answer, Kat turned on her heel and walked toward the small restroom. The running toilets sounded louder now that she was staring at them with an eye toward repair. She nodded toward the sink. "There isn't any hot water, either."

Rye whistled, long and low. "This place looks like it's been through a war."

"In a manner of speaking." Kat shrugged. "As I said, my sister's been in charge. She's not really a, um, detail person."

"How have they been holding classes here?" Rye asked. "Haven't the students complained?"

And that's when the penny dropped. Students would

have complained the first time they tried to wash their hands. Their parents would have been furious about the warped floor, the chance of injury.

Kat limped to the office and picked up the maple-coated telephone handset. She punched in the studio's number, relying on memories that had been set early in her childhood. The answering machine picked up immediately.

"We're sorry to inform you that, due to a family emergency, Morehouse Dance Academy will not be offering classes for the spring term. If you need help with any other matter, please leave a message, and one of our staff will contact you promptly."

Rachel's voice. The vowels cut short, as if she were trying to sound mature. Official. Kat's attention zeroed in on the nearby answering machine. "57" flashed in angry red numerals. So much for "our staff" returning messages—promptly or at all.

Kat's rage was like a physical thing, a towering wave that broke over her head and drenched her with an emotion so powerful that she was left shaking. If students hadn't been able to sign up for classes, then no money could possibly come into the studio. Rachel couldn't have made a deposit for months. But the water was still on, and the electricity. Susan must have set up the utilities for automatic payment. Even now, the studio's bank account might be overdrawn.

Susan was probably too stressed, too distracted, to have noticed any correspondence from the bank. Fiscal disaster might be only a pen stroke away. All because of Rachel.

Kat's voice shook with fury as she slammed her hand down on the desk. "I cannot be*lieve* her! How could

Rachel do this? How could she ruin everything that Mama worked so hard to achieve?"

Of course Rye didn't answer. He didn't even know Rachel. He couldn't have any idea how irresponsible she was.

Somehow, though, Rye's silence gave Kat permission to think out loud. "I have to get this all fixed up. I can't let my mother see the studio like this. It would break her heart. I have to get the floor fixed, and the plumbing. Get people enrolled in classes."

"I can do the plumbing myself," Rye said, as calmly as if he had planned on walking into this particular viper's nest when he strolled through the studio door. "I'll round up the troops to take care of the leak. You can get started on the paperwork here in the office, see if you find any more problems."

"You make it sound so simple!"

He laughed, the easy sound filling the little office. "I should. It's my job."

She gave him a confused look. "Job?"

"Believe it or not, I can't make a living picking up stranded passengers at the train station every day. I'm a building contractor—renovations, installations, all of that."

That's right. He'd said something as he handed her the roller bag yesterday, something about Harmon Contracting. Rye was a guy who made the world neater, one job at a time. A guy who made his living with projects like hers. "But didn't Lisa say you were living up in Richmond now?"

A quick frown darted across his face, gone before she was certain she had seen it. "I moved there a month ago. But I've been back in town every weekend. A few more days around here won't hurt me."

What was he saying? Why was he volunteering to spend *more* time in Eden Falls?

Kat wasn't even family. He didn't owe her a thing. What the hell was he thinking, taking on a job like this? More hours going back and forth on I-95. More time behind the wheel of his truck. More time away from the business that he really needed to nurture, from the promise he'd made to himself.

This was Marissa, all over again—a woman, tying him down, making him trade in his own dreams for hers. This was the same rotten truth he'd lived, over and over and over, the same reflexive way that he had set his dreams aside, just because he had the skills to help someone else. Just because he could.

But one look at the relief on Kat's face, and Rye knew he'd said the right thing.

And Harmon Contracting wasn't exactly taking Richmond by storm. He didn't need to be up the road, full-time, every day. And it sure looked like Kat needed him here, now.

She shook her head, and he wasn't sure if the disbelief in her next words was because of the generosity of his offer, or the scale of the disaster she was still taking in, in the studio. "I don't even know how I'll pay you. I can't let my mother find out about this."

"We'll work out something," Rye said. "Maybe some of my cousins can take a ballet class or two."

Kat just stared. Rye sounded like he rescued maidens in distress every day. Well, he had yesterday, hadn't he? "Just like that? Don't we need to write up a contract or something?"

Rye raised a mahogany eyebrow. "If you don't trust me to finish the job, we can definitely put something in writing."

"No!" She surprised herself by the vehemence she forced into the word. "I thought that *you* wouldn't trust *me*."

"That wouldn't be very neighborly of me, would it?" She fumbled for a reply, but he laughed. "Relax. You're back in Eden Falls. We pretty much do things on a handshake around here. If either one of us backs out of the deal, the entire town will know by sunset." He lowered his voice to a growl, putting on a hefty country twang. "If that happens, you'll never do business in this town again."

Kat surprised herself by laughing. "That's the voice you used when you played Curly!"

"Ha!" Rye barked. "You *did* recognize me!"

Rye watched embarrassment paint Kat's cheeks. She was beautiful when she blushed. The color took away all the hard lines of her face, relaxed the tension around her eyes.

"I —" she started to say, fumbling for words. He cocked an eyebrow, determined not to make things easier for her. "You —" she started again. She stared at her hands, at her fingers twisting around each other, as if she were weaving invisible cloth.

"You thought it would be cruel to remind me how clumsy I was on stage, in *Oklahoma*. That was mighty considerate of you."

"No!"

There. Her gaze shot up, as if she had something to prove. Another blush washed over her face. This time, the color spread across her collarbones, the tender pink heating the edges of that crisp black top she wore. He had a sudden image of the way her skin would feel against his lips, the heat that would shimmer off her as he tasted....

"No," she repeated, as if she could read his mind. Now it was his turn to feel the spark of embarrassment. He most definitely did not want Kat Morehouse reading his mind just then. "You weren't clumsy. That dance scene would have been a challenge for anyone."

"Except for you." He said the words softly, purposely pitching his voice so that she had to take a step closer to hear.

Her lips twisted into a frown. "Except for me," she agreed reluctantly. "But I wasn't a normal kid. I mean, I already knew I was going to be a dancer. I'd known since I was five. I was a freak."

Before he could think of how she would react, he raised a hand to her face, brushing back an escaped lock of her coal-black hair. "You weren't a freak. You were never a freak."

Her belly tightened as she felt the wiry hairs on the back of his fingers, rough against her cheek. She caught her breath, freezing like a doe startled on the edge of a clearing. *Stop it,* she told herself. *He doesn't mean anything by it. You're a mess after one morning spent in this disaster zone, and he's just trying to help you out. Like a neighbor should.*

Those were the words she forced herself to think, but that's not what she wanted to believe. Rye Harmon had been the first boy to kiss her. Sure, she had pretended not to know him the day before. And over the years, she'd told herself that it had never actually happened. Even if it had, it had been a total accident, a complete surprise to both of them. But his lips had touched hers when she was only fourteen—his lips, so soft and sweet and kind—and sometimes it had seemed that she'd been spoiled for any other boy after that.

She forced herself to laugh, and to take a step

away. "We all think we're freaks when we're teenagers," she said.

For just an instant, she thought that he was going to follow her. She thought that he was going to take the single step to close the distance between them, to gather up her hair again, to put those hands to even better use.

But then he matched her shaky laugh, tone for tone, and the moment was past. "Thank God no one judges us on the mistakes we make when we're young," he said.

Rye berated himself as Kat sought refuge behind the desk. What the hell was he doing, reacting like that, to a woman he hadn't seen since she was a kid? For a single, horrible second, he thought it was because of Rachel. Because of those few tumultuous weeks, almost six years before.

But that couldn't be. Despite the DNA that Kat and Rachel shared, they were nothing alike. Physically, emotionally—they might as well live on two different planets. He was certain of that—his body was every bit as sure as his mind.

It was Kat who drew him now. Kat who attracted him. Kat whom he did not want to scare away.

He squared his shoulders and shoved his left hand deep into the pocket of his jeans. "Here," he said, producing a small leather case. "You left your cell phone in my car. I found it this morning, and I called your parents' house, but your mother said you were over here."

Kat snatched the phone from his open palm, like a squirrel grabbing a peanut from a friendly hand. She retreated behind the desk, using the cell as an excuse to avoid Rye's eyes, to escape that warm black gaze. Staring at the phone's screen, she bit her lip when she realized she still had no reception. "Stupid carrier," she said.

"Pretty much all of them have lousy reception around here. It's better up on the bluffs."

The bluffs. Kat may have left town when she was fourteen, but she had already heard rumors about the bluffs. About the kids who drove up there, telling their parents they were going to the movies. About the kids who climbed into backseats, who got caught by flashlight-wielding policemen.

But that was stupid. She wasn't a kid. And it only made sense that she'd get better cell phone reception at the highest point in town. "I'll head up there, then, if I need to make a call."

Damn. She hadn't quite managed to keep her voice even. Well, in for an inch, in for a mile. She might as well apologize now, for having pretended not to know him.

She took a deep breath before she forced herself to meet his eyes. He seemed to be laughing at her, gently chiding her for her discomfort. She cleared her throat. "I'm sorry about yesterday. About acting like I didn't know who you were. I guess I just felt strange, coming back here. Coming back to a place that's like home, but isn't."

He could have made a joke. He could have tossed away her apology. He could have scolded her for being foolish. But instead, he said, "'Like home, but isn't.' I'm learning what you mean." At her questioning look, he went on. "Moving up to Richmond. It's what I've always wanted. When I'm here, I can't wait to get back there, can't wait to get back to work. But when I'm there…I worry about everyone here. I think about everything I'm missing."

It didn't help that everyone in Eden Falls thought he was nuts for moving away. Every single member of his family believed that the little town was the perfect place to raise kids, the perfect place to grow up, surrounded by generations. Marissa had said that to him, over and over again, and he'd believed her, because Eden Falls was the only place he'd ever known.

But now, having gotten away to Richmond, he knew that there was a whole wide world out there. He owed it to himself to explore further, to test himself, to see exactly how much he could achieve.

Like Kat had, daring to leave so long ago. If anyone was going to understand him, Kat would.

He met her gaze as if she'd challenged him out loud. "I have to do it. It's like I…I have to prove something. To my family and to myself—I can make this work, and not just because I'm a Harmon. Not just because I know everyone in town, and my daddy knows everyone, and his daddy before him. If I can make Harmon Contracting succeed, it'll be because of who *I* am. What *I* do."

Kat heard the earnestness in Rye's voice, the absolute certainty that he was going to make it. For just a second, she felt a flash of pain somewhere beneath her breastbone, as if her soul was crying out because she had lost something precious.

But that was absurd. Rye had moved to Richmond, the same way that she had moved to New York. They both had found their true paths, found their way out of Eden Falls. And she'd be back in her true home shortly, back with the National Ballet, back on stage, just as soon as she could get out of her stupid walking boot.

And as soon as she got the Morehouse Dance Academy back on its feet. She pasted on her very best smile and extended her hand, offering the handshake that would seal their deal. "I almost feel guilty," she said. "Keeping you away from Richmond. But you're the one who offered."

His fingers folded around hers, and she suddenly had to fight against the sensation that she was falling, tumbling down a slope so steep that she could not begin to see the bottom. "I did," he said. "And I always keep my word."

His promise shivered down her spine, and she had to remind herself that they were talking about a business proposition. Nothing more. Rye Harmon would never be anything more to her. He couldn't be. Their past and their future made anything else impossible.

## Chapter Three

Three days later, Kat was back in the studio office, sorting through a stack of papers. Rye was working in the bathroom, replacing the insides of the running toilets. The occasional clank of metal against porcelain created an offbeat music for Kat's work.

She'd been productive all morning long. That was after seeing Jenny off to school, ignoring the child's demands for sugar on her corn flakes, an extra sparkling ribbon for her hair and a stuffed animal to keep her company throughout the day. Kat had a plan—to bring order to Jenny's life—and she was going to stick with it. If it took Jenny another day or week or month to get on board, it was just going to take that long.

Not that Kat had any intention of still being in Eden Falls in a month.

That morning, Susan had driven her to the studio. When her mother had put the car in Park and taken off her own seat belt, Kat had practically squawked. "You have to get back to Daddy!"

"I can stay away for an hour," Susan had said. "Let me help you here."

"I'm fine! Seriously. There's hardly anything left for me to do." Susan had looked doubtful, until Kat added, "I just want to have a quiet morning. Maybe do a few exercises. You know, I need to keep in shape." Kat was desperate to keep her mother from seeing the devastation inside the studio. "Please, Mama. The whole reason I'm here in Eden Falls is so that you can rest. Take advantage of me while you can. Relax a little. Go back home and make yourself a cup of that peach tea you like so much."

"I *did* want to get your father sitting up for the rest of the morning. He's feeling so much stronger now that he's getting his sleep."

"Perfect!" Kat had said, letting some of her real pleasure color the word. If her father was recovering, then it was worth all the little struggles to get Jenny in line. "Go home. I'll call Amanda to pick me up when I'm done here."

Susan had smiled then. "My little general," she said, patting Kat's hand fondly. "You've got a plan for everything, don't you?"

Planning. That was Kat's strong suit. Over the weekend, she had written up a list of everything that had to be done at the studio, from computer repair to roofing. She had placed her initials beside each item that she was taking charge of, and she'd dashed off Rye's initials next to his responsibilities. A few items—like the computer—needed to be outsourced, but she would take care of them one by one, doing her best to support the Eden Falls economy.

Goals. Strategies. Rules.

Those were the words that had brought her great success over the years. Sure, as a young girl, miles away from home in New York, she had wondered how she would ever succeed at National Ballet. But she had built her own structure, given her life solid bones—and she had succeeded beyond her wildest dreams.

Okay. Not her wildest dreams. Some of her dreams were pretty wild—she saw herself dancing the tortured maiden Giselle, the girl who died when her love was spurned by the handsome Prince Albrecht. Or the playful animation of the wooden-doll-come-to-life in *Coppelia*. Or the soul-wrenching dual roles of the black and white swans in *Swan Lake*.

All in due time, Kat told herself. As soon as she was out of her hated walking boot, she would exercise like a demon. She would get herself back in top dancing form in no time, transform her body into a more efficient tool than it had been before her injury. Goals. Strategies. Rules.

She could do it. She always had before.

Just thinking about her favorite roles made her long for the National Ballet Company. She hadn't spent more than a weekend away from her ballet friends since moving to New York ten years before. Sitting down at the desk in the office, Kat punched in Haley's phone number. Her roommate picked up on the third ring.

"Tell me that they're making you work like dogs, and I'm impossibly lucky to be trapped here in Small Town Hell," Kat said without preamble.

"I don't know what you're talking about," Haley responded with a mocking tone of wide-eyed wonder. "The company has been treating us to champagne and chocolate-covered strawberries. Free mani-pedis, and hot stone massages for all."

"I hate you," Kat said, laughing.

"How are things on the home front?"

"Well, the good news is that my father seems to be doing better."

"I know you well enough to read *that* tone of voice. What's the bad news?"

Where to start? Kat could say that her niece was a brat. That her sister was a lazy, irresponsible waste of an excuse for a grown woman. That the dance studio was falling down around her ears.

Or she could step back and make herself laugh at the mess she'd volunteered to put right. Squaring her shoulders, she chose the latter route. "There's not a single coffee cart on one corner in all of Eden Falls. And they've never heard of an all-night drugstore."

Haley laughed. "I'd send you a care package, but you'll probably be gone by the time it could get there. Any sign of the prodigal daughter?"

"Rachel? Not a hint. As near as I can tell, she actually took off about three months ago."

"Ouch. You guys really *don't* talk to each other, do you? But didn't your mother just tell you last week?"

"Exactly," Kat said grimly, not bothering to recite the hundreds of reasons she didn't keep in touch with her sister. "Mama didn't want to worry me, or so she says." Kat wouldn't have worried about Rachel. Not for one single, solitary second. Getting *enraged* with her, now that was something else entirely....

"Do they have any idea where she is?"

"She sends my niece postcards. The last one arrived two weeks ago, from New Orleans. A picture of a fan dancer on the front, and postage due."

Haley clicked her tongue. "She really is a piece of work, isn't she?"

Kat sighed. "The thing is, I don't even care what she does with her own life. I just hate seeing the effect it has on my parents. And Jenny, too. She's not a bad kid, but she hasn't had any structure in her life for so long that she doesn't even know *how* to be good."

"How much longer are you staying?"

That was the sixty-four-thousand-dollar question, wasn't it? "I'm not sure. At first, I thought that I could only stand a week here, at most."

"But now?"

"Now I'm realizing that there's more work to take care of than I thought there was. Mama's dance studio has been a bit…ignored since Daddy got sick."

"I thought your sister was taking care of all that."

"I'll give you a moment, to think about the logic of that statement." Over the years, Kat had vented to Haley plenty of times about Rachel. "I've got my goals in place, though. Rye should be able to get everything pulled together in another week or so. Ten days at most."

"Rye?" There were a hundred questions pumped into the single syllable and more than one blatantly indecent suggestion. Kat's heart pounded harder, and she glanced toward the hallway where Rye was working.

"Don't I wish," Kat said, doing her best to sound bored. Haley had been intent on making Kat forget about her disastrous relationship with Adam; her roommate had even threatened to set up an online dating profile for her. Haley would be head over heels with the *idea* of Rye Harmon, even though she'd never met the guy. Trying to seem breezy and dismissive, Kat said, "Just one of the locals. A handyman."

But that wasn't the truth. Not exactly. Rye had driven down from Richmond that morning, to take care of the studio's plumbing. And he wasn't just a handyman—he was a contractor. A contractor who was taking her project quite seriously...

"Mmm," Haley said. "Does he have any power tools?"

"Haley!" Kat squawked at the suggestive tone.

"Fine. If you're not going to share any intimate details, then I'm going to head out for Master Class."

A jolt of longing shot through Kat, and she glared at the paneled wall of the studio office. She had really been looking forward to the six-week Master Class session taught by one of Russia's most prominent ballerinas. She pushed down her disappointment, though. It didn't have anything to do with her being trapped here in Virginia. In fact, she would have felt even worse to be out of commission in New York, completely surrounded by an ideal that she couldn't achieve.

"I want to hear all about it!" she said, and she almost sounded enthusiastic for her friend.

"Every word," Haley vowed. They promised to talk later in the week, and Kat cradled the phone.

Her conversation with Haley had left her restless, painfully aware of everything she was missing back home. She wanted to dance. Or at least stretch out at the barre.

But there was other work to complete first. She sighed and sat at the desk, which was still overflowing with coffee-stained papers. Even if Rachel *had* maintained perfect records, they'd be impossible to locate in this blizzard. Tightening her core muscles, Kat got to work.

* * *

Two hours later, she could see clear physical evidence of her hard labor. Raising her chin, Kat clutched the last pile of sorted papers, tapping the edges against the glass surface of the newly cleaned desk. Pens stood at attention in a plastic cylinder. Paper clips were corralled in a circular dish. A stapler and a tape dispenser toed the line, ready to do service. The entire office smelled of lemon and ammonia—sharp, clean smells that spurred Kat toward accomplishing even more of her goals.

Next up: the computer. She had to find out if any of the files could be salvaged, if there was any way to access the hard drive and its list of classes, of students.

She frowned as she glanced at her watch. She could call Amanda and ask for a ride to the tiny computer shop on Main Street. But she was pretty sure Amanda was taking an accounting class over at the community college, taking advantage of her flexible teaching schedule. There was Susan, of course, but Kat wasn't certain that she could deflect her mother again. Susan would almost definitely insist on coming into the studio, and then she'd discover the water damage, the plumbing problems, the utter chaos that Rachel had left behind.

Not to mention the bank account. Kat still dreaded stopping by the bank on Water Street, finding out just how short the studio's account really was.

She sighed. She'd been cleaning up after her sister for twenty-four years. It never got any easier.

Well, there *was* another option for dealing with the computer. There was an able-bodied man working just down the hall. An able-bodied man with a shining silver pickup truck. Firming her resolve, Kat marched down to the bathroom.

She found Rye in the second stall, wedged into an awkward position between the toilet and the wall. He was shaking his head as she entered, and she was pretty sure that the words he was muttering would not be fit for little Jenny's ears—or the ears of any Morehouse Dance Academy students, either. He scowled down at the water cutoff with a ferocity that should have shocked the chrome into immediate obedience.

"Oh!" Kat said in surprise. "I'll come back later."

Rye pushed himself up into a sitting position. "Sorry," he said. "I don't usually sound like a sailor while I work."

"Some jobs require strong language," Kat said, quoting one of the stagehands at the National. "Seriously, I'll let you get back to that. It was nothing important. I'm sorry I interrupted."

"I'll always welcome an interruption from you."

There was that blush again. Rye could honestly say that he hadn't been trying to sweet-talk Kat; he had just spoken the truth, the first thing that came to mind.

That rosy tint on her cheeks, though, made her look like she was a kid. The ice princess ballerina melted away so quickly, leaving behind the girl who had been such an eager dancer, such an enthusiastic artist. He wondered what they had taught her at that fancy high school in New York City. How had they channeled her spirit, cutting off her sense of humor, her spirit of adventure? Because the Kat Morehouse he had known had been quiet, determined, focused. But she had known how to laugh.

This Kat Morehouse looked like she had all the cares of the world balanced on her elegant shoulders. He was pleased that he had made her blush again. Maybe he could even make her smile. A smile would make the whole day worthwhile, balance out the drive down from Richmond, the day spent away from Harmon Contracting business.

"What's up?" he asked, climbing to his feet. The flange was frozen shut. He was going to have to turn the water off at its source, then cut out the difficult piece.

She cleared her throat. It was obviously difficult for her to say whatever she was thinking. "I just wondered if you could drive me down to Main Street. I need to take in the computer, to see if they can salvage anything from the hard drive."

Huh. Why should it be so difficult for her to ask a favor? Didn't people help each other out, up in New York? He fished in his pocket and pulled out his key ring. "Here. Take the truck. That'll give me a chance to talk to this thing the way I really need to."

Kat backed away as if he were handing her a live snake. She knew he didn't mean anything by the casual offer of the keys. He wasn't trying to make her feel uncomfortable, abnormal. But as the fluorescent light glinted off the brass keys, all she could hear was Jenny's querulous voice asking, "But why *can't* Aunt Kat drive?"

She cleared her throat and reminded herself that she had a perfectly good excuse. It would have been a waste of her time to get behind the wheel in New York—time that she had spent perfecting her arabesque, mastering her pirouettes. "I can't drive," she said flatly. She saw a question flash in his eyes, and she immediately added, "It's not like I've lost my license or anything. I never had one."

"Never—" he started to say, but then he seemed to piece together the puzzle. "Okay. Give me a minute to wash up, and we can head there together."

"Thank you," she said, and a flood of gratitude tinted the words. She was grateful for more than his agreeing to run the errand with her. She appreciated the fact that he hadn't pushed the matter, that he hadn't forced her to go into any details.

It felt odd to watch as Rye lifted the computer tower from beneath the desk in the office. It was strange to follow him out to the truck. She was used to being the person who did things, the woman who executed the action plan. But she had to admit she would have had a hard time handling the heavy computer and the studio door, all while keeping her balance with her walking boot.

Rye settled the computer in the back of the truck, nestling it in a bed of convenient blankets. She started to hobble toward the passenger door, but he stopped her with a single word: "Nope."

She turned to face him, squinting a little in the brilliant spring sun. "What?"

"Why don't you get behind the wheel?"

So much for gratitude that he hadn't pressed the issue. She felt iron settle over her tone. "I told you. I don't know how to drive."

"No time like the present. I'm a good teacher. I've taught five siblings."

A stutter of panic rocketed through Kat's gut. She wasn't about to show Rye how incompetent she was, how unsuited to life in Eden Falls. She forced a semblance of calm into her words. "Maybe one of them will drive me, then."

Rye's voice was gentle. Kind. "It's not that difficult. I promise. You don't have to be afraid."

Kat did not get afraid. She leaped from the stage into a partner's arms. She let herself be tossed through the air, all limbs extended. She spun herself in tight, orchestrated circles until any ordinary woman would have collapsed from dizziness. "Fine," she snapped. But her spine was ice by the time she reached the driver's door.

With her long legs, she didn't need to move the seat up. She fastened her seat belt, tugging the cloth band firmly, and she glared at Rye until he did the same. She put her hands on the steering wheel, gripping tightly as she tried to slow her pounding heart. The muscles in her arms were rigid, and her legs felt like boards.

"Relax," Rye said beside her. "You're going to do fine."

"You say that now," she muttered. "But what are you going to say when I crash your truck?"

"I know that's not going to happen."

She wished that she had his confidence. She stared at the dashboard, as if she were going to control the vehicle solely through the power of her mind.

"Relax," he said again. "Seriously. Take a deep breath. And exhale…"

Well, that was one thing she could do. She'd always been able to control her body, to make it do her bidding. She breathed into the bottom of her lungs, holding the air for a full count of five, before letting it go. Alas, the tension failed to flow away.

Rye reached over and touched her right leg. Already on edge, Kat twitched as if he'd used a live electric wire. "Easy," he said, flattening his palm against her black trousers. She could feel the heat of his palm, the weight of each finger. Nervous as she was, she found his touch soothing. Relaxing. Compelling.

Leaving his hand in place, Rye said, "The pedal on the right is gas. The one on the left is the brake. You'll shift your foot between them. You want to be gentle— I told my brothers to pretend that there were eggs beneath the pedals."

He lifted his hand, and her leg was suddenly chilled. She wanted to protest, wanted him to touch her again, but she knew that she was being ridiculous. Any fool could see that she was just trying to delay the inevitable driving lesson.

"Put your foot on the brake," he said. "Go ahead. You can't hurt anything. I promise."

*I promise.* He was so sure of himself. He had so much faith in her. She wanted to tell him that he was wrong, that he was mistaken, that she didn't know the rules for driving a car. She didn't have a system. Tenuously, though, she complied with the instruction. He nodded, then said, "Good. Now, take this."

She watched him select a key, a long silver one with jagged teeth on either side. He dangled it in front of her until she collected it, willing her hand to stop shaking, to stop jangling all the other keys together. He nodded toward the ignition, and she inserted the key, completing the action after only two false starts.

"See?" he said. "I told you this was easy."

"Piece of cake," she muttered, sounding like a prisoner on the way to her own execution.

Rye chuckled and said, "Go ahead. Turn it. Start the truck."

"I—I don't know how."

"Exactly the same way you open the lock on a door.

You do that all the time, up in New York, don't you? It's the exact same motion."

Tightening her elbow against her side to still her trembling, she bit on her lower lip. Millions of people drove every single day. People younger than she was. People without her discipline. She was just being stupid—like the time that she'd been afraid to try the fish dives in *Sleeping Beauty*.

She turned the key.

The truck purred to life, shuddering slightly as the engine kicked in. Her hand flew off the key, but Rye only laughed, catching her fingers before she could plant them in her lap. He guided them to the gear-shift, covering her hand with his own. His palm felt hot against her flesh, like sunshine pooling on black velvet. She thought about pulling her hand away, about blowing on her fingers so that they weren't quite icicles, but she was afraid to call even more attention to herself.

"The truck is in Park. You're going to shift it into Drive." His fingers tightened around hers, almost imperceptibly. The motion made her glance at his face. His black eyes were steady on hers, patient, waiting. "You can do this, Kat," he said, and the words vibrated through her. She didn't know if her sudden breathlessness was because of his touch, or because she was one step closer to driving the truck.

She shifted the gear.

"There you go." He crooned to her as if she were a frightened kitten. "Now, shift your foot to the gas. The truck will roll forward just a little—that's the power of the engine pulling it, without giving it any fuel. When you're ready, push down on the gas pedal to really make it move." He waited a moment, but she could not move. "Come on," he urged. "Let's go."

She looked out the windshield, her heart pounding wildly. "Here?" she managed to squeak.

"We're in a parking lot. There's not another vehicle around. No lights. Nothing for you to hit." He turned the words into a soothing poem.

He was being so patient. So kind. She had to reward his calm expectation, had to show him that his confidence was not misplaced. She tensed the muscles in her calf and eased her foot off the brake. As he had predicted, the truck edged forward, crunching on gravel with enough volume that she slammed back onto the brake.

Rye laughed as he slid his thumb underneath his seat belt, loosening the band where it had seized tight against his shoulder. "That's why they make seat belts," he said. "Try it again."

This time, it was easier to desert the brake. She let the truck roll forward several feet, getting used to the feel of the engine vibrating through the steering wheel, up her arms, into the center of her body. She knew that she had to try the gas pedal next, had to make the silver monster pick up speed. Steeling herself, she plunged her foot down on the gas pedal.

The truck jumped forward like a thoroughbred out of the gate. Panicked, she pounded on the brake, throwing herself forward with enough momentum that her teeth clicked shut.

"Easy, cowboy!" Rye ran a hand through his chestnut curls. "Remember—like an egg beneath the pedal."

She set her jaw with grim determination. She could do this. It was a simple matter of controlling her body, of making her muscles meet her demands. She just needed to tense her foot, tighten her calf. She just needed to lower her toes, that much…that much…a little more….

The truck glided forward, like an ocean liner pulling away from a dock. She traveled about ten yards before she braked to a smooth stop. Again, she told herself, and she repeated the maneuver three times.

"Very good," Rye said, and she realized that she'd been concentrating so hard she had almost forgotten the man beside her. "Now you just have to add in steering."

She saw that they were nearing the end of the parking lot. It was time to turn, or to learn how to drive in Reverse. She rapidly chose the lesser of the two evils. Controlling the steering wheel was just another matter of muscle coordination. Just another matter of using her body, of adapting her dance training. Concentrating with every strand of her awareness, she eased onto the gas and turned the truck in a sweeping circle.

Rye watched Kat gain control over the truck, becoming more comfortable with each pass around the parking lot. He couldn't remember ever seeing a woman who held herself in check so rigidly. Maybe it was her dancer's training, or maybe it was true terror about managing two tons of metal. He longed to reach out, to smooth the tension from her arms, from the thigh that had trembled beneath his palm.

Mentally, he snorted at himself. He hadn't lied when he told her that he'd taught each of his siblings. They'd been easy to guide, though—each had been eager to fly the nest, to gain the freedom of wheels in a small Virginia town.

Suddenly, he flashed on a memory of his own youthful days. He'd been driving his first truck, the one that he had bought with his own money, saved from long summers working as a carpenter's apprentice. He'd just graduated from college, just started dating Rachel Morehouse.

She hadn't been afraid, the way that Kat was. Rachel had tricked him with a demon's kiss, digging into his pockets when he was most distracted. She had taken his keys and run to his truck, barely giving him time to haul himself into the passenger side before she had raced the engine. She had laughed as she sped toward the county road, flooring the old Ford until it shuddered in surrender. Rachel had laughed at Rye's shouted protest, jerking the wheel back and forth, crossing the center line on the deserted nighttime stretch of asphalt. When a truck crested a distant rise, Rachel had taken the headlights as a challenge; she had pulled back into their own lane only at the last possible instant.

He had sworn every curse he knew, hollering until Rachel finally pulled onto the crumbling dirt shoulder. He'd stomped around the truck, glaring as she slid across the bench seat with mock meekness. He'd dropped her back at her house, pointedly ignoring her pursed lips, her expectation of a good-night kiss.

And he'd broken up with her the next morning.

He would never have believed that Rachel and Kat were related, if their faces hadn't betrayed them. Their personalities were opposites—a tornado and an ice storm.

He cleared his throat, certain that his next words would lock another sheet of Kat's iron control into place. "All right. Let's go out on the road." He wasn't disappointed; she clenched her jaw tight like a spring-bound door slamming shut.

"I can't do that," Kat said. It was one thing to drive in an abandoned parking lot. It was another to take the truck out onto the open road. There would be other drivers there. Innocent pedestrians. Maybe even a dog or two, running off leash. She could cause immeasurable damage out on the road.

"The computer store isn't going to come to you." Rye's laugh made it sound as if he didn't have a care in the world. "Come on, Kat," he cajoled when she stopped in the middle of the parking lot. "What's the worst that can happen?"

"A fifteen-car pileup on Main Street," she said immediately, voicing the least bloody of the images that tormented her.

"There aren't even fifteen cars on the road at this time of day. You're making excuses. Let's go."

There. He'd set their goal—she would drive them to the store. She knew the strategies—she needed to put the truck in gear, to turn out onto Elm Street, to navigate the several blocks down to Main. She was familiar with the rules, had observed them all her life: stay on the right side of the road, keep to the speed limit, observe all the stop signs.

At least there weren't any traffic lights, dangerous things that could change from green to red in a heartbeat, with scarcely a stop at yellow.

She took a deep breath and pulled onto Elm.

For the first couple of blocks, she felt like a computer, processing a million different facts, arriving at specific conclusions. She had never realized how many details there were in the world around her, how many things moved. But she completed her first turn without incident. She even followed Rye's instruction when he suggested that she take a roundabout path, that she experiment with more right turns, and a single, terrifying left.

She wasn't thinking when Rye told her to take one

more left turn; she didn't realize that they were on the county road until after the steering wheel had spun back to center. There was oncoming traffic here—a half-dozen cars whooshed by at speeds that made her cringe.

"Give it a bit more gas," Rye said. "You need to get up to forty."

She wanted to yell at him, to complain that he had tricked her onto this dangerous stretch of road, but she knew that she should not divert her attention. She wanted to tell him that forty was impossibly fast, but she knew that he was right. She could see the black-and-white speed limit sign—she presented more of a danger to them, creeping along, than she would if she accelerated. She hunched a little closer to the steering wheel, as if that motion would give her precious seconds to respond to any disasters.

Maybe it was her concentration that kept her from being aware of the eighteen-wheeler that roared by, passing her on the left. One moment, she could dart a glance out at freshly tilled fields, at rich earth awaiting new crops. The next, a wall of metal screamed beside her, looming over her like a mountain. She thought that she was pounding on the brake, but she hadn't shifted her foot enough; the pickup leaped forward as she poured on more fuel, looking for all the world like she was trying to race the semi.

The surge terrified her, and she shifted her foot solidly onto the brake. At the same time, the truck cut back into her lane, close enough that the wind of its passing buffeted her vehicle. Kat overcorrected, and for one terrible moment, the pickup slid sideways across the asphalt road. She turned the wheel again, catching the rough edge of the shoulder, and one more twist sent her careening out of control.

The pickup bucked as it caught on the grass at the roadside, and she could do nothing as the vehicle slid into the ditch at the edge of the road. Finally, the brake did its job, and the truck shuddered to a stop. Kat was frozen, unable to lift her hands from the wheel.

Rye reached across and turned the key, killing the idling motor. "Are you okay?" he asked, his voice thick with concern.

"I'm fine," Kat said automatically. *I'm mortified. I nearly got us killed. I'm a danger to myself and others.* "I'm fine," she repeated. "How about you?"

Rye eased a hand beneath his seat belt once more. "I'm okay."

"I'm so sorry," Kat said, and her voice shook suspiciously. "I don't know how that happened. One minute everything was fine, and then—" She cut herself off. "I could have killed us."

"No blood, no foul," Rye said.

Kat burst into tears.

"Hey," he said. "Come on. You can drive out of this ditch. We don't even need to get the truck towed."

She nodded, as if she agreed with everything he said. At the same time, though, she was thinking that she was never going to drive again. She was never going to put herself in danger—herself or any innocent passenger. What if Susan had been with her? Or Mike, in his weakened state? What if, God forbid, Jenny had been sitting there?

She fumbled for the door handle and flung herself out of the truck. Rye met her by the hood, settling his firm hands on her biceps. "What's wrong?" he asked.

"I can't do this!" Her words came out more a shout than a statement.

"You've just been shaken up. You know the drill—back up on the horse that threw you."

"I'm not a rodeo rider."

"No, but you're a dancer. And I have to believe that you stick with adversity on the stage better than this."

She shook her head. This wasn't dance. This wasn't her career. This was—literally—life or death. She couldn't think of working anymore for the day. "Please, Rye. Will you just drive me back to Rachel's?"

He looked at her for a long time, but she refused to meet his eyes. Instead, she hugged herself, trying to get her breathing back under control, trying to get her body to believe that it wasn't in imminent danger.

At last, Rye shrugged and walked around the cab of the truck, sliding into the driver's seat with a disgruntled sigh. Kat took her place meekly, refusing to look at him as he turned the key in the ignition. The truck started up easily enough, and it only took a little manhandling to get it up the side of the ditch, back onto the road.

Rye knew that he should press the matter. He should make Kat get back behind the wheel. She had to get over her fear. If she walked away from driving now, she'd probably never return.

But who was he to force her to do anything? He was just a guy she'd met ten years before, a guy who lived in Richmond, who kept coming home to a little town in the middle of nowhere, because he couldn't remember how to say no.

*Kat* was the one who'd had the guts to leave for real. She was the one who'd gone all the way to New York, far enough that it had taken a real disaster to bring her back to Eden Falls. Not the piddling demands that his family made on him day after day.

He tightened his grip on the steering wheel. It had been a mistake to agree to renovate the dance studio. He was building his own life away from Eden Falls. He couldn't let the first woman who'd caught his attention in months destroy his determination to make Harmon Contracting a success.

But he'd already done that, hadn't he? He'd already roped himself into finishing that damned plumbing job. And repairing the ceiling leak wasn't going to be easy, either. And he had a really bad feeling about what he'd find when he really looked at the hardwood floor.

He glanced over at Kat. What did Gran always say? "In for a penny, in for a pound." He'd started teaching Kat how to drive, and he'd let her scare herself half to death. She was his responsibility now. It was up to him to convince her to change her mind. To find the nerve to get back in the truck—if not today, then tomorrow. Wednesday at the latest.

He barely realized that he was committing himself to spending half a week away from Richmond.

Kat hopped out as soon as Rye pulled into the driveway. She didn't want to look at the weeds, at the lawn that was impossibly exhausted, even though it was only spring. "Thanks," she said as she slammed her door, and she tried to ignore the hitch in her stride as her boot slipped on the gritty walkway.

Rye didn't take the hint. He followed her to the front door, like a boy walking her home from a date.

Now, why did she think of that image? Rye wasn't her boyfriend. And they most definitely had not been out on a date. Besides, it was broad daylight, the middle of the afternoon.

She opened the unlocked door with an easy twist of her wrist. Not daring to meet his eyes, she pasted a cheery smile on her face. "Thanks for all your help at the studio this morning. Everything's coming along much faster than I thought it would." She stepped back and started to close the door.

Rye caught the swinging oak with the flat of his palm. "Kat," he said, but before he could continue, she saw him wince. He tried to hide the motion, but she was a dancer. She was an expert on all the ways that a body can mask pain.

"You *are* hurt!"

"It's nothing major," he said. "My shoulder's just a little sore from the seat belt."

"Come in here!" She opened the door wide, leaving him no opportunity to demur.

"I'm fine," he said.

She marched him into the kitchen, switching on the overhead light. "Go ahead," she said, nodding. "Take off your shirt. I need to see how bad this is."

Rye shook his head. He was used to his mother clucking over him like a nervous hen. His sisters bossed him around. And now Kat was giving him orders like a drill sergeant. From long experience, he knew he'd be better off to comply now, while he still had some dignity intact. He undid the top two buttons of his work shirt before tugging the garment over his head.

That motion *did* twinge his shoulder, and he was surprised to see the darkening bruise that striped his chest. The seat belt had done its job admirably, keeping him safe from true harm, but he'd have a mark for a few days.

Kat's lips tightened into a frown. "Ice," she said. She turned toward the pantry with military precision, collecting a heavy-duty plastic bag. The freezer yielded enough ice cubes to satisfy her, and then she twisted a cotton dishrag around the makeshift cold pack.

"I don't think—"

"I do." She cut him off. "Believe me, I've had enough bruises that I know how to treat them."

He didn't want to think about that. He didn't want to think about her body being hurt, her creamy skin mottled with evidence of her harsh profession. As if he were accepting some form of punishment, he let her place the ice pack over his chest.

"That's cold," he said ruefully.

"That's the idea." There wasn't any venom in her retort, though. Instead, her hands were gentle as she moved the ice, as she stepped closer, maneuvering the bag until it lay right along his collarbone. The action shifted the midnight curtain of her hair, and he caught a whiff of apricots and honey. Without thinking, he tangled his fingers in the smooth strands, brushing against her nape as he pulled her close. He heard her breath catch in her throat, but she didn't try to edge away. He found her lips and claimed them with his own, a sweet kiss, chaste as schoolkids on a playground.

"There," he whispered against her cheek. "That's a little warmer."

The rasp of his afternoon scruff against her face made Kat catch her breath. Her entire body was suddenly aware of the man before her, aware of him as a *man,* not just a collection of parts that could be manipulated into an entire encyclopedia of ballet poses. Her lips tingled where he had kissed her, ignited as if she had eaten an unexpected jalapeno.

Without making a conscious decision, she shifted her arms, settling into the long lines of his body. She felt his ribs against hers, measured the steady beat of his heart. She matched his legs to her own, shifting her thighs so that she could feel the solid strength of him. He chuckled as he found her lips again, and this time when he kissed her, she yielded to the gentle touch of his tongue.

Velvet against velvet, then, the soft pressure of eager exploration. She heard a sound, an urgent mew, and she realized with surprise that it rose from her own throat. His fingers, tangled in her hair, spread wide and cradled her head. She leaned back against the pressure, glorying in the sensation of strength and power and solid, firm control.

He lowered his lips to the arch of her neck, finding the solid drumbeat of her pulse. One flick of his tongue, another, and her knees grew weak, as if she had danced for an entire Master Class.

Danced. That was what she did. That was what she lived for.

She couldn't get involved with a man in Eden Falls— or Richmond, either, for that matter. She was only visiting; she was heading north as soon as she straightened things out in her parents' home, as soon as Rachel came back to keep an eye on Jenny.

Kat steeled herself and took a step away.

"I think heat might be better than ice for my shoulder," Rye said, a teasing smile on his lips. He laced his fingers between hers.

Those fingers!

Kat remonstrated with herself to focus on what was important. She freed her hand and took another step back. "Ice is better for bruises." She couldn't avoid the confusion that melted into Rye's gaze. "I—I'm sorry," she stammered. "I…" She wasn't sure what to say, didn't know how to explain. "I shouldn't have let myself get carried away."

Carried away. He hadn't begun to carry her away yet.

"I'm sorry," she said again, and this time he heard something that sounded suspiciously like tears, laced beneath her words. "I shouldn't have done that. I'm only here for a few… I can't… I belong in New York."

*You belong here,* he wanted to say. *Right beside me.* And then he wanted to prove that to her, in no uncertain terms.

But he had no doubt that those words would terrify her. She'd be right back to where she'd been in the ditch—rigid with fear. Rye forced himself to take a steadying breath. To let her go.

"Go ahead," she said after her own shaky breath. "Take the ice pack. You can give me back the towel at the studio, tomorrow."

Rye shrugged, resigning himself to her decision. "Yes ma'am," he said. "But aren't you forgetting something?"

She'd forgotten a lot. She'd forgotten that she was here to help out her parents. Her sister. Her niece. She'd forgotten that she lived in New York, that she had a life—a *career*—far away from Virginia. "What?" she croaked.

"You have a broken computer in the back of my pickup truck."

"Oh!" She hesitated, uncertain of what to do.

"Don't worry," he said, and she sensed that he was laughing at her. "I'll take it down to the shop."

She frowned, and her fingers moved involuntarily toward his shoulder. "But get someone else to lift it out of the truck."

"Yes, ma'am," he said again, but the glint in his eyes said that he was anything but a respectful schoolboy. She showed him to the door before she lost her resolve.

As she heard the truck come to life in the driveway, she shook her head in disbelief. Obviously, she'd been traumatized by her disaster of a driving lesson. She'd been terrified by the thought of dying in a ditch, and the adrenaline had overflowed here in the kitchen. She'd been overtaken by the basest of all her animal instincts.

Well, there was nothing to be done but to rein in those physical responses. Goals. Strategies. Rules. She grabbed a notepad from the drawer beneath the phone and started to revise her schedule for finishing up the studio renovation, for getting all the class records in order for the new term. If she pushed herself hard, she could be out of Eden Falls in one more week.

When she'd finished her schedule, though, she leaned against the counter. Her fingers rose to her lips, starting them tingling all over again. Maybe she'd been too optimistic when she wrote up that list. Seven days wasn't a lot, not to complete everything that needed to be done, and to keep an eye on Jenny, too. Maybe she should plan on staying in Eden Falls a little longer. Ten days. Two weeks. There was no telling *what* might happen in two full weeks.

She laughed at herself as she tore up her list. The renovation would take as long as it took.

And she had to admit—that wasn't a terrible thing. No, it most definitely was not a terrible thing to spend some more time with Rye Harmon. She shook her head and thought about how Haley would tease her when Kat explained why she was staying in Eden Falls a little longer than she had planned at first.

## Chapter Four

Kat ushered Susan to the kitchen table, telling her mother to sit down and relax. "You don't need to wait on me like I'm a houseguest," Kat insisted. "I can put the teakettle on to boil."

Still, Susan fussed. "I just want you to rest that foot. You need it to heal, if you're going to get back to New York. Does it still hurt a lot?"

Kat shrugged. She didn't pay a lot of attention to pain. It was all part of her job. She took down two teacups and matching saucers, enjoying the look of the old-fashioned china that had once belonged to her grandmother. "Don't worry about me," she chided Susan. "You have enough on your plate."

"Your father looks so much better. I cannot tell you how much it means, that he's finally able to get a full night's sleep. Jenny is a sweetheart—she's so excited to be reading a book to her Pop-pop right now. But she is a *busy* child."

*Busy* was one word for her. Spoiled rotten was another. Kat was tired of playing policewoman, constantly telling her niece what to do and what not to do. Just the night before, Kat had caught herself complaining to Haley, saying that Jenny had been raised by wolves. Okay, that was an exaggeration. But not much of one.

But then, just when Kat thought that she had exhausted her last dram of patience with her niece, she was forced to realize that Jenny was just a little girl—a very little girl, who was working through one of the greatest challenges of her short life. Only that morning, after finishing her bowl of corn flakes, Jenny had looked up with such transparent sorrow in her eyes that Kat's heart had almost broken. "When is my mommy coming home?" Jenny had asked.

For once, her lower lip wasn't trembling because she wanted sugary cereal for breakfast, or a plate full of syrupy carbs, or some other disaster for her growing body. Instead, she was trying very hard to be stoic.

Kat had pushed down her own emotions, all of her anger and frustration with Rachel. "Soon," she'd said. "I hope she'll be home soon." She'd given Jenny a brisk hug and then sent her toward the toy chest, telling the child that she needed to collect all the scattered crayons at the bottom of the container, returning them to a plastic bucket neatly labeled for the purpose.

Hard work. That was what had carried Kat through the loneliness and confusion of being on her own in New York. That was the only prescription that she could offer Jenny now.

Standing in Susan's kitchen, Kat rescued the teakettle just before it shrieked. She filled the pot and ferried it over to the table before turning to snatch up a plate of gingersnaps. Somehow, though, her booted foot slipped on the worn linoleum. She caught her balance at the last possible second, but the china plate shattered on the floor.

"Oh, no!" she cried. "I am so sorry! I don't know how I could be so clumsy."

Susan rose from her chair.

"No," Kat cried. "You're only wearing your house shoes! I don't want you to cut your feet. Just sit down." She limped over to the laundry room, quickly procuring a dustpan and broom. Berating herself the entire time, she brushed up the debris, consigning shattered china and dirty cookies to the trash. "Mama, I am so sorry. I can't believe I did that. Here I am, trying to help, and I just make everything worse!"

"Nonsense," Susan said. "It was an accident. Nothing to get so flustered about. Now, sit down, dear, and pour yourself a cup of tea."

Kat complied, strangely soothed by her mother's calm. Susan pushed forward the sugar bowl, but Kat merely shook her head. She hadn't added sugar to her tea since she was younger than Jenny was now.

"Mama, I'll go online. I can find a plate to replace that one—there are websites to help people locate old china patterns."

"Don't worry about it."

"But it belonged to your mother!"

"And she'd be very upset to see you so concerned about breaking it. Please, Kat. Not another word."

Still not satisfied that she'd made appropriate amends, Kat fiddled with her teacup. She avoided her mother's eagle eye as she turned the saucer so that the floral pattern matched the cup precisely.

"I worry about you," Susan said, after Kat had finally taken a sip.

"That's the last thing I want, Mama! I'm here so that you don't have to worry. That's the whole idea!"

"And you're doing wonders, keeping an eye on Jenny and getting everything ready for the first summer classes at the studio."

Kat felt guilty about that. She still hadn't told her mother about the condition of the studio, about the utter lack of students for the spring session. Four times in the past week, she'd started to broach the matter of the bank account, of the money that Rachel had not accounted for during the winter term. Each time, though, Kat had chickened out, dreading the moment when she destroyed her mother's fragile peace of mind. Kat's cowardice was certain to catch up with her. There couldn't be much more time before Susan's life got back to normal, before she found the wherewithal to check her financial statements. Who knew? She might even stop by the columned bank building on Water Street, learn about the disaster firsthand. In public.

And that disaster would be made much worse, because Kat was involved. Kat, whom Susan expected to run things smoothly. Kat, who had never been irresponsible like Rachel. Every day that Kat remained silent was a horrible, festering lie.

She steeled herself to make the admission. After all, if she said something today, then she might still be able to help Susan to recover. Kat could stay on another week or so, help sort out the finances with the help of a sympathetic—or, at the very least, a professional—banker.

She took a deep breath, but Susan spoke before Kat could confess. "Sweetheart, it's *you* that I worry about.

I wish that you could learn to relax a little. To sit back and enjoy life." Susan shook her head, running her finger along the edge of her saucer. "You've always been such a grown-up, even when you were a very little girl. I could leave a slice of pie on the kitchen table, right between you and Rachel, and I always knew that *you* would have the self-restraint to eat your vegetables first." Susan smiled fondly, as if she could still see her twins sitting at her dining room table. "Sometimes, I wish that you still played Magic Zoo."

"Magic Zoo?"

"Don't you remember? It was a game that you invented, to entertain Rachel when she was recovering from that broken arm, the summer when you were six years old. The two of you and your cousin Amanda played it every single day!"

"I have no idea what you're talking about."

"Of course you do! You had all sorts of elaborate rules. Each of you girls chose an animal, and then you drew crayons out of a bucket. Each color crayon corresponded to a different magical food. The foods gave you special powers—you could be a flying horse, or a talking elephant, things like that. The three of you played it for hours on end."

Kat blinked. She had absolutely no recollection of such make-believe games. She couldn't imagine spending "hours on end" with Rachel—not without descending into screaming matches. Maybe Amanda had been a full-time referee?

Susan sighed. "I guess I'm just saying that sometimes you need to be more of a kid. Don't worry as much. Take whatever happens and just roll with it. Forget that you're an adult, for just a little while."

"Like Rachel does, every day." Kat said the words before she could stop herself, but even she was surprised by how bitter they sounded.

Susan's face grew even more serious. "Yes. If I were queen of the universe, I would give Rachel some of your maturity. And I would give you a little of her... what's that phrase? The French one? Joie de vivre?"

"I don't think it's joie de vivre to stay away from home when your own parents, your own *daughter,* need you. When was the last time you heard from Rachel? Do you have any idea when she's planning on coming home?"

"A postcard arrived just yesterday. It had a picture of the Eiffel Tower, but not the real one. She was in Las Vegas. At least that's where the postmark was from."

A postcard, sent what? Three or four days ago? Rachel had to know the phone number here at the house, the one that hadn't changed since they were children. She could have managed to call home, at least once. Responded to the text messages that Kat had sent. She obviously didn't want to be found. She wasn't ready to face up to her adult responsibilities.

Kat fought to keep her voice even. "I'm sure she's very happy there."

"Don't judge your sister," Susan said. "She's never had a skill like yours. She's never known what it means to succeed."

Kat bit back an acid response. Rachel had been given every opportunity Kat had; she had enjoyed the exact same chances in life. Even now, she could come back to Eden Falls, raise her daughter, do the right thing. She could help her parents and prove she was a responsible adult. But she'd rather play in Vegas, drawing out her childhood for countless more years.

Susan sighed. "I sometimes think being twins messed everything up for you girls. Each of you was supposed to get a mixture of responsibility and fun. Of adulthood and childhood. Instead, all the grown-up qualities ended up with you and all the rest..." She let her words drift for a moment, and when she continued she softened her words with a smile. "I want you to have fun, Kat. Go stomping in mud puddles for a change. Somersault down a hill. Don't always think about what something means for your future, for your career."

"Mama, I *need* to worry about my career. I'm a dancer. I don't have much longer to prove myself to the company director."

Susan shook her head. "Sometimes I wonder if we did the right thing, sending you to New York."

"How can you say that?" Kat's voice was etched with horror. She couldn't imagine what her life would have been like without New York. Without dancing.

"Don't look so shocked," Susan murmured. "Your father and I are very proud of you. But sometimes I worry that we took too much away from you by pushing you so hard. You had to grow up so young. You never got a chance to play, to make mistakes. You never even went to your senior prom. We just wanted you to be happy."

"I *was* happy," Kat said. As if to convince herself of the truth behind her words, she went on. "I *am* happy, Mama. The day I stop being happy dancing is the day I'll leave the company. I promise." Susan still looked doubtful. As if to finish the conversation, once and for all, Kat leaned over and gave her mother a hug. "I love you, Mama. You and Daddy, too. And I love everything that you've let me become. Now, can I freshen up your cup of tea?"

She pretended not to see the proud tears glinting in Susan's eyes.

A couple of hours later, after a lunch of tomato soup and grilled cheese sandwiches, Kat could see that her father was tiring. "Come on," she said to Jenny. "Let's go down to the park. Run off some of your energy."

Susan smiled gratefully as she saw them out the door. "Are you sure you're all right walking there?"

"It's only two blocks," Kat assured her. "That's why they call this a walking boot." She made a point of keeping her gait even as they made their way down the street.

When they arrived at the park, it seemed as if half of Eden Falls was taking advantage of yet another unseasonably warm April day. Children screamed with delight on the swings, and a pileup of toddlers blocked the bottom of the slide. A group of teenagers sat beneath a cluster of cherry trees, staring up into the cotton candy blossoms, carrying on a passionate discussion about something.

"What's that?" Jenny said, pointing toward a baseball diamond.

Kat narrowed her eyes against the brilliant sunshine. "A T-ball game."

"I love T-ball!" Jenny bounced on her toes, showing more enthusiasm than she had since Kat had come to town. "Can I play? Please? Please?"

"Let's go see." Kat started across the park, watching Jenny as the child raced ahead. Halfway to the playing field, Kat heard the coach call out, "Good job, Jake! Run! Run to first base!"

Kat knew that voice. She'd listened to it at the dance studio, smiled as it interrupted her organizing class records. She'd imagined it, in her dreams, ever since it had teased her in Rachel's kitchen. She met Rye's gaze as Jenny circled back to clutch at her hand.

"Hey," he said, nodding to include both of them. "Kat. Jenny."

"Hello, Mr. Harmon."

Kat smiled at her niece's polite greeting, and she remembered to model her own good behavior. "Mr. Harmon, Jenny was wondering if she could play T-ball with you."

"Absolutely." Rye gestured toward the outfield. "Go out there, between first and second base. You can play right field for us." Jenny trotted out, beaming as if her most secret wish had been granted.

"Thanks," Kat said, less formal now that none of the kids was paying attention. Her heart was skittering in her chest. It had been, what? Two days since she'd seen Rye? Two days since he had completed fixing the plumbing at the studio, and torn out all the rotten ceiling tiles and the damaged flooring. Two days since he had driven off, with the pair of silent cousins he had brought along to help. Or to serve as chaperones.

As if by agreement, Rye and Kat had made sure they did not spend a minute alone together. Not after that searing kiss they'd shared. Not after Kat had reminded herself that she had no time for an Eden Falls relationship.

She had to clear her throat before she could ask, "What are you doing down here? I thought you went back to Richmond Wednesday night!"

Of course he'd gone back to Richmond. He'd gone back to his rented office, to two beige rooms that had somehow shrunk while he'd been in Eden Falls. He'd gone back to his studio apartment, to a bachelor pad that should have been more than adequate for his needs.

He hadn't slept at all that night.

Every time he rolled over, he imagined having another conversation with Kat. Every time he punched his pillow into a more comfortable lump, he remembered another detail of the studio renovation. Every time he threw off his blankets, he thought about how he had let Kat down with the driving lesson, how she had panicked. And how she had warmed to him, afterward.

No.

It had taken him years to fight his way free, to sever enough family ties, enough social obligations, to give himself permission to live and work in Richmond. That whole mess with Marissa—the way he had pinned his hopes on her, on the life he thought they would have together... A white picket fence, two perfect kids and a dog. Until she decided that Hollywood was more glamorous, and she dropped him like a hot potato.

He might have taken too long to come to his senses, but he had finally carved out a life for himself. He could not—*would* not—let a woman drag him back to Eden Falls. Not now. Not when everything was about to break big for him.

Even a woman as intriguing as Kat. *Especially* a woman as intriguing as Kat. Part of her mystique was the fact that she didn't belong in his hometown. After ten years of living on her own, she had become a New Yorker, through and through. She'd be leaving, as soon as her father had recovered.

He'd be an idiot to forfeit his own life plans—again—for a woman who wasn't going to stick around.

But damn, Kat managed to distract him. Over and over again, even when she was a hundred miles away. And now? Standing beside her at the T-ball bleachers? It was all he could do not to cup a hand around her jean-clad hip. All he could do not to twist a strand of her mesmerizing hair around his finger and make a joke or two, draw out a smile on her lips. All he could do not to forget that a couple dozen kids were clamoring on the baseball diamond behind him, waiting for him to step up to the plate as their dedicated coach.

He cleared his throat and answered Kat's question, even though it seemed like a century had passed since she spoke. "I *was* up in Richmond. But something came up, and my brother Noah had to bail on T-ball practice."

"That seems to happen a lot," Kat said, remembering that Rye had filled in for Noah on her first day back in Eden Falls. "Nothing serious, I hope?"

"Her name is Britney."

Kat laughed. "You're a good brother."

"I'm keeping a log. So far he owes me 327 hours of favors. I get gas money and double credit for Saturdays."

"Oh, what else would you be doing today?"

"I'd find something to occupy my time," he said, giving her an appraising glance. There was no mistaking the rumble beneath his words, and her memory flashed back to the feel of him holding her, to the scratch of his jaw as he kissed her. She felt her cheeks grow warm.

"Mr. Harmon!" one of the kids called. "When do we start to play?"

Rye sighed in fake exasperation, careful to keep the

team from hearing him. "Duty calls. And you're going to have to help out, if we let Jenny play."

She gestured to her boot. "I don't think I'm really up to umpire work."

"I've got that covered. Your place is on the bench, behind home plate. Behind me. You get to be head cheerleader."

Kat caught a flicker of Rye's eyebrows, a comic leer as if he were envisioning her in a short skirt, carrying pom-poms. The expression was wiped away before she could even be certain he was teasing her. Laughing, she headed over to her seat, grateful to give her foot a rest.

Enjoying the fresh air outside the studio and—truth be told—the view of Rye's denim-clad backside behind home plate, Kat put her elbows on the bench above her. Stretching out like a long black cat in the heat of the spring sun, she closed her eyes and leaned her head back. She filled her lungs with the aroma of fresh-cut grass, focusing on what Rye was saying to his young players.

He helped one little girl choke up on the bat, instructing her on how to spread her legs for a more balanced stance. The child was not a natural athlete, but he talked her through two wildly missed swings. On the third, she toppled the ball from its plastic stand. "Run, Kaylee!" he shouted. "Run to first! You can make it!"

His enthusiasm for his charges was obvious. Each child improved under his tutelage. Everyone eventually connected the bat to the ball, and some even got a shot past the infield. Soon enough, the teams switched sides, and Kat watched as Jenny came to the plate.

"Okay, Jenny," Rye said. "Oh, you're left-handed? No, don't be embarrassed, I'm left-handed, too. Here, move to the other side of the plate. Now, Jenny—"

"I'm not Jenny."

Kat sat up, wondering what devilment her niece was working now.

"Really?" Rye said. "I was certain that your Aunt Kat told me your name was Jenny."

"I hate that name." Kat started to climb to her feet, ready to tell Jenny to adjust her tone or they'd be heading back home immediately. Before she could speak, though, the little girl whined pitiably, "There are two other Jennys in my class."

Rye nodded. "I guess that would be pretty annoying. I never had anyone else with my name in school. Should I call you Jennifer instead?"

The little girl shook her head. "I'm only Jennifer when I'm in trouble."

Kat started to laugh—her niece was only telling the truth. Rye, though, screwed up his face into a pensive frown. "What should we do, then? How about another nickname?"

"Like what?"

"Jen?"

"There's a Jen at Sunday School."

"Then how about Niffer?"

"Niffer?" She repeated the name like she'd never heard the last two syllables of her own name.

"Do you know anyone else called Niffer?" The child shook her head. "Then what do you say? Should we try it?" Rye was granted a grudging nod. "Okay, then, Niffer. Step up to the plate. Nope, the other side, for lefties. Now focus on the ball. Bring the bat back. And *swing!*"

The bat cracked against the ball, clearly the best shot of the afternoon. The tiny center fielder scrambled to catch the soaring ball, fighting the sunshine in his eyes. Rye shouted, "Go Niffer! Run around the bases!"

Fulfilling her role as head cheerleader, Kat was shouting by the time her niece completed her home run. The kids exploded with excitement, too, both the batting and the fielding teams chanting, "Nif-fer! Nif-fer!"

Obviously recognizing a climactic ending for the game when he saw one, Rye declared the practice over five minutes early, sending the kids off with their appreciative parents. Kat sat up straighter on the bench, watching Rye talk to the other adults. Several ribbed him about filling in for Noah, one telling him that he was taking his best man's duties too far. So, things must be really serious between Noah and…what was her name? Britney.

Rye was absolutely at home with every person he talked to. He shook hands with all the men; he accepted kisses on the cheek from most of the women. Kat supposed that he'd known these people all his life—he had gone to school with them, grown up with them.

She'd gone to school with them, too. Well, four years behind. She should have been every bit as comfortable in Eden Falls as Rye was. After all, how many places were left on earth where someone could leave her front door unlocked to go play T-ball in the park? How many places would band together to fill Susan and Mike's freezer with countless nourishing, home-cooked meals?

Kat was beginning to understand what had kept her parents here all these years. She even caught herself smiling as Rye crossed the diamond, Jenny at his heels.

"Aunt Kat!"

"You looked great out there, Jenny."

"I'm Niffer, now!"

"Niffer," Kat agreed, sternly reminding herself to use the new nickname.

"Can I go climb on the castle?"

"*May* I?" Kat reminded. Grammar rules were just as important as the other rules that Niffer needed to maintain while they lived together.

"*May* I go climb on the castle?"

"Go ahead," Kat said. "But we need to go back to Gram and Pop-pop's house in ten minutes."

Niffer was halfway to the jungle gym before all of the words were out of Kat's mouth. Rye settled on the bench beside her, grunting with mock exhaustion. "They'll wear a man out."

"You're great with them," Kat said. "I never know how to talk to kids."

"Most people think about it too much. It's better to just say what you're thinking."

"Easy for you! I've been living with…Niffer for a week and a half, and that's the first I heard that she didn't like her name. It's like you two share some special bond."

Special bond. Rye tensed at the words and the responsibility that they conjured up. Years ago, he'd worried about just such a "special bond," worried that the then-unborn Niffer was his daughter. Rachel had set him straight in no uncertain terms. If any guy shared a "special bond" with Niffer, with Rachel, it was Josh Barton.

And just as well. Rye could never have taken off for Richmond if he had a daughter here in Eden Falls. The games that Marissa had played, tying him to the town, would have been nothing compared to the bonds of fatherhood.

"She's a good kid," he finally said.

His lingering tension was telling him something, though. His lingering tension, and a couple of sleepless nights. Even if he had no hope for anything long-term with Kat, it was time to man up. Past time, actually. He flashed on the feel of her body pressed close to his in Rachel's kitchen, and he cleared his throat before saying gruffly, "I should tell you. Your sister and I went out a couple of times. It was a long time ago. Five, six years. We were only together for a few weeks."

Kat's face shuttered closed. "Rachel never mentioned anything. We, um, we haven't been close for a very long time."

Rye wanted to kick himself for making Kat pull away like that, for bringing out that guarded look in her eyes. Over the past few days, he'd relived that kitchen kiss so many times. He'd remembered the swift surge of passion that had boiled his blood as Kat settled her body against him, as her lips parted beneath his. Back in Richmond, he'd picked up the phone a half-dozen times, just wanting to hear her voice. Hell, he'd even grabbed his keys once, thinking about making the drive south in record time.

And he had to admit that he'd wondered—more than once—if she would bring that same sudden passion to his bed. He'd imagined her shifting above him, concentrating on their bodies joined together, fulfilling at last the promise that he'd made with a blushing kiss ten years before.

He was being an idiot, of course. He wasn't going to see Kat in his bed. He was going to honor her clearly stated desire, keep his distance, and finish up his work at the studio. Get the hell out of Eden Falls, and back to Richmond, where he belonged. That was the professional thing to do. The gentlemanly thing to do.

Damn. Sometimes, he hated being the good guy.

Still, his family had dragged him down here for the weekend, and he'd be an idiot not to take advantage of the fact that Kat was sitting right beside him. He just had to reassure her. "It was nothing serious, Kat. Rachel and me."

"With Rachel, it never is."

"She was really interested in another guy, a fraternity brother of mine. After about a month, we both realized the truth, and that was it."

"Of course."

Kat heard the stiffness in her tone. She knew that she had pulled away from Rye as soon as he mentioned Rachel. She was holding her back straight, as if she were about to spin away in a flawless pirouette.

She hated talking about her sister. She hated going over the poor choices Rachel had made, the easy ways out that she'd taken, over and over and over again. Just thinking about the old battles made Kat freeze up, clutching at her old formula—goals, strategies, rules. That's what she needed, here in Eden Falls. That's what she needed throughout her life.

But what had Susan told her, just that morning? *Go stomping in mud puddles for a change. Somersault down a hill.*

Impossible. Mud and hills were both in short supply, here in the public park. But Kat *could* let herself go. Just a bit.

"I'm sorry," she said, forcing herself to relax. "I really do appreciate your telling me about Rachel."

He continued to look grave, though. Her natural reaction had driven a wedge between them. But she could change that—even with stomping and somersaults off the menu for the day. Consciously setting aside her anger with Rachel, Kat dug her elbow into Rye's side. "Come on! I'd race you to the far end of the park, but I'm pretty sure you'd win."

He looked at her walking boot. "Yeah. I wouldn't want to take unfair advantage. What do you think, though? Could you manage the swings?"

"That's about my top speed, these days."

She took the hand that he offered, letting him pull her to her feet. They fell into step easily as they crossed to the swing set. She actually laughed as he gestured toward the center leather strap, waving his hand as if he were presenting her with a royal gift. "Mademoiselle," he said, holding the iron chains steady so that she could sit.

She settled herself gracefully, pretending that the playground equipment was some elegant carriage. Her fingers curled around the chains, and he sat next to her. Neither of them pushed off the scraped dirt, though. Instead, they braced their feet against the ground and continued talking.

"I feel terrible," she said, throwing her head back to look up at the clear blue sky. "Keeping you working in the studio when you should be up in Richmond."

"You shouldn't. A job's a job."

"But this job is taking so much of your time. What do you need, up in Richmond? What am I keeping you from doing?"

*Sleeping,* he wanted to say. *Concentrating on my work. Focusing on running a business instead of imagining what would have happened if I hadn't let you chicken out the other night.*

"I need to build a website," he said, somehow keeping his voice absolutely even. "Order business cards.

Envelopes. Stationery for bids. I'm lousy at that sort of stuff."

She nodded, as if she were writing down every word. "What else?"

"I've joined the Chamber of Commerce, but I haven't made it to a meeting yet. I've got to get the ball rolling with a little in-person networking. Start building that all-valuable word of mouth."

"That all sounds manageable."

"I've got some paperwork that I have to file with the state. Copies of my license, that sort of thing."

"I've got to say, Mr. Harmon. It sounds like you've got everything pretty much under control. Even *if* I keep dragging you back to Eden Falls."

"I'm glad one of us thinks so." He smiled, to make sure that she didn't take offense. It was his own damn fault that he couldn't stay away from here. His own damn fault that he put thousands of miles on the truck, wearing the tires thin on constant trips up and down the interstate. Old habits died hard.

Time to change the topic of conversation. Time to get away from the way he had screwed up his business plans, over and over and over again, ever since he'd graduated from college.

"So," he said, purposely tilting his voice into a light-hearted challenge. "What do you think? Who can pump higher, here on the swings?"

For answer, Kat laughed and pushed off, bending her knees and throwing back her head. Before he could match her, though, the bells on the courthouse started to toll, counting out five o'clock.

"Wait!" Kat said, stopping short. "Niffer and I have to get home. Mama will start to worry."

He bit his tongue to keep from cursing the bells.

Kat looked around the park, surprised to see that nearly everyone else had left. Of course, it was a Saturday in Eden Falls. Everyone had an early-bird dinner waiting at home. She glanced toward the castle jungle gym, ready to call Niffer and leave.

Except Niffer was nowhere to be seen.

Kat shook her head, forcing herself to swallow the immediate bile of panic. Of course her niece was on the playground equipment. She'd headed over there just a few minutes before.

Kat scrambled to her feet, taking off at a lopsided jog toward the castle. "Niffer!" she called. And then, "Jenny! Jenny!" The bright pink climbing bars mocked her as she reached the base of the toy. Up close, it looked impossibly tall, far too dangerous to be sitting in a public park. "Jenny!"

She looked around wildly. This couldn't be happening. She couldn't have lost her niece. She couldn't have let anything happen to Niffer, to Jenny, to Rachel's daughter.

"Kat! What's wrong?"

Rye skidded to a stop beside her, his ebony eyes flashing. She tried to pull up words past the horror that closed her throat, over the massive wave of guilt. He put a hand on her back, spread his fingers wide, as if to give her a web of support. She started to pull away—she didn't deserve to be touched. She was too irresponsible for anyone to stand near her. She had been given one single goal—watch Jenny—and she had broken all the rules by letting the child wander off unsupervised. Broken all the rules, just so that she could sit on the swings and flirt with Rye Harmon.

Broken all the rules, like Rachel.

"I can't find her," she sobbed. "I told her that she

could go to the castle, and I only looked away for a couple of minutes, but she's gone!"

Without thinking, Rye moved his hand from Kat's back, twining his fingers around hers. He felt her trembling beside him, understood that she was terrified as she darted her gaze around the park. She wasn't seeing anything, though. She was too frightened. No, beyond frightened. Panicked. Not thinking clearly.

He narrowed his eyes, staring into the deep shadows by the oak trees on the edge of the park. There! In the piles of leaves, left over from last autumn. Niffer was plowing through the dusty debris, obviously pretending that she was a tractor, or a dinosaur, or some imaginary creature.

"Look," he said to Kat, turning her so that she could see the child. "She's fine."

Kat stiffened the instant that she saw her niece. Instinctively, Rye tightened his grip on her hand, letting himself be dragged along as Kat stumbled across the uneven grass to the oak tree border.

"Jennifer Allison Morehouse, just what do you think you're doing?"

The little girl froze in midswoop, guilt painting her face. Instead of answering her aunt, though, she turned to Rye. "See? I told you that Jennifer is a bad name."

Incredibly, Kat felt Rye start to laugh beside her. He managed to wipe his face clear after only a moment, but he was standing close enough that she could feel his scarcely bridled amusement. For some reason, his good humor only stoked her anger. "I asked what you are doing over here, young lady! Didn't I give you permission to play on the castle. Not under the trees?"

The child's lower lip began to tremble. "I *was* playing on the castle. I was a princess. But the unicorn mermaids told me that I had to find their diamond ring over here."

Unicorn mermaids. Like Kat was going to buy that. She filled her lungs, ready to let her niece know exactly what she thought of unicorns and mermaids and diamond rings.

Before she could let loose, though, Rye squeezed her hand. Just a little. Barely enough that she was certain she felt it. Certainly not enough that Niffer could see.

Kat remembered her mother, sitting in the drab kitchen, sipping her cooling tea and saying that Kat should be more playful. She remembered Rye coaching the children, encouraging each of them in whatever they did best. She remembered the relaxed camaraderie of the T-ball parents, picking up their kids.

She took a deep breath and held it for a count of five. She exhaled slowly, just as she had when Rye taught her how to drive. No. Not like that. That had ended in disaster.

This was a new venture. A new effort to achieve a different goal. "You'll have to teach me about the unicorn mermaids," she said. "But that will be another day. Right now, we have to get home to Gram and Pop-pop."

Niffer looked as if she thought a magician might have somehow enchanted her Aunt Kat, turned her into a newt, or something worse—a bewitched, unreliable adult. "Okay," she said uncertainly.

"Come on, then," Kat said. "Let's go."

As Niffer started scuffling through the leaves, Kat caught a harsh reprimand at the back of her throat. Instead, she whispered to Rye under the cover of the rustling, "She scared me."

"I know," he whispered back, and he squeezed her hand again.

"She really, really scared me."

"But she's fine," he said. "And you will be, too."

Kat had to remind herself to breathe as they walked out of the park and down the block to her parents' house. Somehow, she forgot to reclaim her hand from Rye's.

## Chapter Five

Kat raised her voice over the band, practically shouting so that Amanda could hear her. The crowd was raucous at Andy's Bar and Grill that night, and the musicians were making the most of having a full house. "Okay," she shouted. "You win! You said the music was great and I didn't believe you!"

Amanda laughed and clinked her mug of beer against Kat's. "Drink up!"

Kat obliged. After all, a bet was a bet. This mug tasted even better than the first had.

Kat couldn't remember the last time she'd had so much fun on a Friday night. Amanda had called her around noon, reporting that she'd already arranged for Susan and Mike to keep an eye on Niffer for the evening. Her cousin had picked her up at Rachel's house, only to frown when Kat answered the door in her skinny black jeans and a silk T-shirt. They'd made an emergency stop back at Amanda's house—Kat still wore black, but Amanda had rounded out the outfit with a flame-red scarf, lashed around Kat's hips like a belt. That, and a ruby-drop necklace that had belonged to their grandmother made Kat feel like she was someone new. Someone daring. Someone who wasn't afraid of being a little bit sexy, on a Friday night out on the town.

In fact, when Kat was hanging out with Amanda at the crowded bar, listening to her cousin's running commentary about the cute blond bartender, she felt like she was discovering a whole new world of fun. What had Susan said, the week before? That Kat had been cheated out of going to prom? Maybe Kat *had* lost out on a thing or two in New York, if this was what it felt like to hang out with her cousin, to cut loose, without a care in the world.

Kat certainly couldn't remember the last time she had indulged in drinking alcohol, anything more than a sip or two of champagne at an opening-night gala. Her entire body thrummed in time to the crashing music, and the roof of her mouth had started to tingle. Amanda, on the other hand, seemed entirely unaffected by the single glass of beer that she had sipped.

Before Kat could challenge Amanda to keep pace properly, a man shuffled over to the table. "Hey, Amanda," he said, mumbling a little and looking down at his boots.

"Hey," came Amanda's cool reply. "Brandon Harmon, don't be rude. You remember my cousin Kat, don't you?"

"Hey, Kat," the man said, still intent on studying the floor.

Brandon Harmon. Kat blinked hard and looked at

him as closely as she dared. Nope. She didn't remember him. This being Eden Falls, though, they had probably sat next to each other in fourth-grade social studies. From his name, he had to be one of Rye's countless siblings. Or cousins. Or whatever. It seemed like they comprised half the town.

As if he could read Kat's mind, Brandon looked over his shoulder. There was a cluster of men standing at the bar, their broad shoulders, chestnut curls and midnight eyes all proclaiming them part of the same clan.

Rye stood in the center of the bunch. He lifted his mug toward Kat in a wry salute. She was surprised by the sudden rush of warmth she felt at his attention. Unconsciously, she flexed her fingers, thinking about how strong his hand had felt in hers the Saturday before, after she had panicked about losing Niffer in the park. She'd spent the better part of the past week thinking about Rye's touch. His touch, and the patient humor in his voice… And that truly spectacular kiss that they had shared in Rachel's kitchen…

Kat's belly swooped in a way that had absolutely nothing to do with the beer that she had drunk. She'd felt the same sensation a hundred times in the past week. The past week, while Rye had been working up in Richmond. In between taking care of Niffer and running some errands for Susan, Kat had put in a lot of hours at the studio, but Rye had been nowhere in sight. The hardwood for the new floor had been delivered, though. It needed to spend a week acclimating to the temperature and humidity in the studio. A week when Rye had tended to other business. A week that Kat had been left alone with her memories, with her dreams.

But she was being ridiculous, mooning around, missing Rye. She knew perfectly well that he lived in Richmond now, that he was never moving back to Eden Falls.

And what did it matter? *She* had already spent two weeks in Eden Falls—seven days longer than she'd planned. It was time to turn her attention back to New York. Back to her career. She couldn't daydream about the way Rye's lips quirked just so when he smiled....

In front of her, Brandon shifted his weight from one foot to the other. "Amanda," he said, apparently summoning the nerve to bellow over the music. "Do you want to dance?"

Amanda laughed. "I'm sorry, Brandon. I can't leave my cousin here alone."

The poor man looked so crushed that Kat immediately took pity on him. She feared that he might never screw up his courage to ask out another woman again if she didn't free Amanda now. "Go ahead," she shouted to her cousin. "I'll be fine."

"Really?"

"Go! It's not like I can join you!" Kat gestured at her walking boot.

Amanda laughed and cast a quick glance toward Kat's mug, as if questioning her cousin's judgment. Kat shook her head. She wasn't drunk—not exactly. But she was definitely feeling...relaxed. Loose. Free, in a way that she hadn't felt since coming to Eden Falls. That she hadn't felt in *years*.

As Amanda mouthed a quick "Thank you" from the dance floor, Kat realized just how much her cousin had hoped Kat would let her go. Curious, Kat studied the cowboy, surprised to see how quickly he gained the confidence to place his hands on Amanda's trim waist, to guide her into a smooth Texas Two-Step.

There was something about those Harmon men....

Something about a Southern gentleman with the determination to go after something that he wanted… She swallowed hard, thinking once again of a very different Harmon. She wished that she and Amanda had been drinking soda, or sweet tea, or anything that came in a tall glass with ice, so that she could cool the pulse points in her wrists.

"You're a kind woman," Kat heard, close to her ear. She whirled to find herself face-to-face with Rye.

"What do you mean?" He was close enough that she barely needed to raise her voice. Thank heavens the band was playing, though. Otherwise, he would have heard her heart leap into high gear.

"It took Brandon two whiskey shots to get up the courage to ask Amanda to dance. If you hadn't let her go, all that booze would have gone to waste."

Kat laughed and said, "False courage for a silver-tongued devil like that?" As if to emphasize her words, she set the flat of her palm against Rye's broad chest. The action seemed to surprise him almost as much as it did her—he stiffened at the touch for just a moment. She tossed her hair, though, and thought, *What have I got to lose?* She continued in her best imitation of a carefree flirt. "Why, I bet that Brandon could have any woman in this place."

"Really?" Rye lowered his voice and stepped closer to Kat. He practically nuzzled her neck as he said, "*Any* woman?" She shivered, a delicious trembling that made him think truly evil thoughts. "Come on," he said. "Let's get some fresh air."

"I can't leave Amanda!"

He cupped his hands around his mouth and bellowed, "Hey, Amanda!" When the woman looked up from the dance floor, he pointed once to Kat, once to himself, and once to the door. Amanda laughed and nodded, waving goodbye to both of them. Rye settled one hand on the small of Kat's back as he guided her through the crowd.

A cool evening breeze hit them like an Arctic blast. "Come here," he said, pulling her around the corner of the building. They were sheltered from the wind there, and from the prying eyes of new arrivals to the bar. A bench was pushed up against the rough wooden wall. He gestured toward it and waited for Kat to take a seat. Before she had fully settled, he sat beside her, closer than was strictly necessary.

She wore some sort of sleek black top, one that revealed every bit as much of her figure as it covered, even with its long sleeves. The neckline swooped down, way down, reminding him of the sensitive hollow at the base of her throat. That patch of vulnerable flesh was now marked by a sparkling ruby pendant—as if he could forget it. His fingers twitched, and he resisted the urge to pull at the matching crimson scarf around her waist.

Shivering in the twilight air, Kat rubbed her hands against her arms. "I bet this is where you take all your women." She surprised him for the second time that night, squirming closer to his side, as if she wanted to soak up every ounce of his body heat.

"Just the ones I want to hear talk," he said, yawning a little in a useless attempt to clear the dullness from his ears. Andy's joint was always fun on Friday nights, but the band was far too loud.

"Talk," Kat purred, placing a hand on his thigh. "Is that why you asked me outside?"

This was a Kat he hadn't seen before. Sure, she'd let him kiss her in Rachel's kitchen. And it had seemed second nature to take her hand when she was so worried about Niffer. He'd enjoyed that feeling, that closeness, that sense of protecting her, and he hadn't let go as he walked her back to Susan and Mike's house.

He'd spent the week up in Richmond, though. A week of business. Of remembering his priorities. With his contractor's license properly filed and a dozen business meetings completed, he was newly charged with determination to make Harmon Contracting a success.

Except… Now that he was away from the office? Back in Eden Falls? And breathing in Kat's intoxicating scent…?

Her fingers started to move in distracting patterns, tracing the double-stitched seam on his jeans as if she'd glimpsed his dreams all week long. His body leaped to immediate attention, and he barely swallowed a groan. He leaned forward and found her face already tilted toward him, her lips eagerly parted for his kiss. Heat rolled through him as he breathed in the honey apricot of her hair. He tangled one hand in the lush strands, using the other to trace the shape of that incredible, clinging black top.

He outlined her lower lip with the tip of his tongue, grinning as he heard a needy moan gather at the back of her throat. Her hands were working their own magic, one fiddling with the top button of his shirt, the other continuing its exploration of his increasingly tented jeans. "Kat," he breathed, and then he sealed their kiss.

Heat, and slick velvet, and a pounding, urgent need. But behind that, under her sweet cry, he tasted the sharp bite of hops. Beer. He was shocked to realize that she'd been drinking. Sure, she was an adult; she was allowed to drink alcohol. But his mind refused to reconcile the notion of Kat, the ice princess, cutting loose. Kat, the tightly bound queen of control, tossing back a couple.

All of a sudden he understood the boldness in her hands, the brazen teasing in her words.

He shifted his hand from the back of her head, stopped crushing her close. Instead, he brought his palm around to cup the line of her jaw, using the motion to soften the end of his plunging kiss. She pulled back, just enough for him to look into her platinum eyes. He asked, "How much have you had to drink?"

She looked confused. "Just a couple of beers."

A couple of beers. With her frame? And he was willing to bet that she didn't have any tolerance at all— she couldn't possibly make a practice of hanging out at bars, pounding down a few brewskis on a Friday night.

He leaned in for another kiss, this one quick. Chaste.

"What?" she protested. "I'm an adult. I'm allowed to have a couple of beers."

"Of course you are. But I'm not going to take advantage of you like this."

"It's not taking advantage if I want it, too."

Her blustering response made him certain he was making the right decision. The Kat he knew would never throw herself at him like that. What had she told him, one of those days when he was hanging out at the dance studio? She had *goals* and *strategies* and *rules*.

He clenched his jaw and pulled away from her. "Come on," he said, keeping his voice as light as possible. "Let's get something to eat."

Kat shivered, freezing now that Rye had pulled away from her. She plucked at the scarf around her waist, suddenly ashamed. Two lousy beers. How much could that have impaired her judgment?

But the world was just starting to swirl around the

edges—not enough to make her dizzy, but more than enough to tell her she was over her limit. She thought about what she had done, about where her hands had just been, and she was overwhelmed with a scarlet wash of embarrassment.

"Kat?" Rye's voice was gentle. "Let's go get some dinner at the Garden Diner."

"I don't want dinner," she whispered.

"What? You're going to tell me that dinner goes against your dancer rules?"

*More than fooling around on a bench outside a backroads bar*? he meant. Her eyes shot up at the amusement in his voice, and her shame started to morph into anger. "What about you?" she challenged him. "Did it take you a couple of shots to come over and talk to me, just like Brandon? I bet you shouldn't be driving around Eden Falls right now."

"I don't need liquor to help me do what I want to do," Rye said. She heard the passion behind his words, the absolute certainty that he *had* wanted to talk to her, to be with her. Even if he'd been gone for the entire week. Even if he'd been the one to pull back just now. His voice was only marginally less fierce as he said, "I stuck to soda water tonight. I have an early day tomorrow, back up in Richmond. A site visit for a prospective client."

Ashamed of her actions all over again, she shook her head and hugged herself, trying to ignore the incipient spinning of the world around her.

"Come on, Kat. You're the one who said you're an adult. Let's be adults together." She flashed him a mortified glance. "Let's go get something to eat," he clarified.

She sighed and let him pull her to her feet. One

single step, though, on the gravel footpath, and she found that her balance was compromised by the damn walking boot. What had she been thinking, betting Amanda about the band, drinking that second beer?

She let Rye slip an arm around her waist, helping her to his truck. At least there was no question of his demanding that she drive tonight. That was one reason that she could actually thank Amanda. She closed her eyes in mortification as Rye reached across her to work her seat belt.

He made small talk as he drove to the diner. She couldn't be sure what he was saying, something about his father finding a new seed-line of heirloom carrots to plant on the family's organic farm, and Rye's sister Jordana developing a series of recipes based on the vegetables, something for a restaurant she was planning to start.

The more Rye talked, the hungrier Kat realized she was. By the time they got to the diner, she was fantasizing about home-cooked food—turkey dinner with mashed potatoes and gravy, meat loaf with peas and carrots. Rye helped her out of the truck, and he kept a protective hand beneath her elbow as he guided her into the diner, but she was already feeling much steadier on her feet.

She studied the entire menu, front to back, but ultimately, she followed Rye's lead. A bacon cheeseburger, slathered with blue cheese, thick with lettuce and juicy tomato. Fries on the side, with a single sizzling onion ring to top it all off.

Rye watched Kat tackle her meal with the single-minded determination that she devoted to everything. He'd half expected her to chicken out at the last moment, to order a side salad with a slice of lemon or some other girlie excuse for a meal.

But he had to hand it to her—she matched him bite for bite, washing down burger and fries with generous amounts of sweet tea. Maybe it was the beers that Amanda had conned her into drinking, maybe it was simple craving for a single ridiculous splurge of a meal, but Kat dug in with a gusto that astonished him.

Okay. Maybe not "astonished." He'd felt the illicit energy coiled inside her on the bench outside of Andy's. He'd felt a little of the wicked damage she could do when she let herself go unleashed.

But he'd never imagined that she would wreak so much havoc on a Smoky Blue Burger Platter. And he was damned pleased to see that she could.

"So," he said when they both finally came up for air. "The floorboards should be ready for installation next week. It'll take two days to get them down. Another day to set the ceiling tiles, and then a couple of days for painting. We'll be done in a week."

Seven days, Kat thought. Seven days, and then all the damage would be repaired. Rye would be finished at the studio, free to stay up in Richmond forever.

"Wonderful!" she said, forcing every ounce of fake cheerfulness that she could summon into the word. Oops. She must have poured it on a little *too* thick. Rye was looking at her funny. She cleared her throat. "I worked with Niffer's teacher, and I've sent home flyers with all the kids in the elementary school. We've already got two summer sessions of Beginning Ballet filled, and one of Intermediate."

"That's great! But I thought that you didn't have anyone to teach."

"Oh, I didn't tell you. I found an old recital program

in the back room on Tuesday. It was from last summer's performance, so I could still track down most of the teachers listed there. Three of them agreed to come back."

"I knew you could do it." There. That was the way enthusiasm really sounded.

Kat took another long swig of sweet tea. It was impossible to find the stuff in New York—not that she would have indulged at any point in the past ten years. Stirring artificial sweetener into iced tea didn't come anywhere close to savoring the supersaturated syrup of her childhood.

Feeling a little rebellious, she tried to imagine what her dance colleagues would say about her Eden Falls night out on the town—beer, burgers and enough sweet tea to float a luxury yacht. What did it matter, though? She couldn't remember the last time she had laughed as hard as she'd laughed with Amanda. And there were a lot worse ways to spend an evening than sitting across from a man as gorgeous as Rye Harmon.

Even if her fellow dancers would vow to eat nothing but lemon juice on iceberg lettuce for an entire week, if they had indulged like Kat.

"Hey," Rye prompted. "Are you okay?"

"I'm fine." She smiled. And she was. She was more than fine. She was relaxed and happy. "I was just thinking about what everyone is doing in New York. It's Friday night, so there's a lot of scrambling. The company does matinees on Saturday and Sunday, so everyone is probably a bit crazy."

He heard the fondness in her voice, the easy familiarity with routine. Sure, she might call them "crazy", but it was a craziness she knew and loved. "You must really miss it," he said.

"I do," she answered, but he caught the pause before she went on. As if she were looking for words. Searching for a memory. "I miss the feeling of testing myself, of pushing myself to do the most my body can do. I miss the feeling of becoming another person, someone totally different from me." She sighed. "I miss..." She trailed off, swirling an orphaned fry in ketchup.

"What, Kat?"

"Sometimes I'm not sure that I can do it." The admission seemed to unlock something in her, to free her to rush on with more words, more confessions. "The big parts, the principal dancer roles...I need to impress the company director, to prove I have what it takes. That's why I pushed myself so hard before I got hurt—extra rehearsals, extra sessions at the barre. And all I ended up with was this stupid boot and a forced month off."

He knew what she wanted him to say. He knew that she wanted to hear that she would succeed, that she would conquer her injury, that she would come back stronger than ever.

But he couldn't be certain of that. He didn't know enough about her world, about the demands of ballet life in distant New York City. No matter what *he* thought of her, how great he thought she was, he couldn't say that she had the pure strength, the unalloyed physical power to master her chosen profession's greatest challenges.

"You'll do the best that you can," he said. "And if the people who make the decisions are too foolish to take every last drop of devotion that you can give them, then you'll figure out the next step. And you'll master that. Goals, strategies and rules, right? That's what someone told me once."

She rolled her eyes. "Whoever said anything that stupid?"

"Not stupid." He shook his head. "Not stupid at all."

She flinched under the intensity of his gaze. Now that she had finished eating, the last tendrils of her tipsiness had floated away. She was sober, but her body still remembered the way that she had used it. She felt tired, raw. And with Rye staring at her that way, she felt totally exposed.

"I don't know," she said. "That stupid formula helped me when I was fourteen years old. It's probably not good for anything anymore. Not ten years later."

"It's good enough for me," Rye affirmed. "Up in Richmond this week, I applied your 'stupid formula.' I got more done in five days than I had in five weeks before that." Of course, that was the first time that he'd spent five consecutive days in his new office. The first time that he hadn't let a so-called emergency drag him back to Eden Falls.

"I'm glad I was able to help you," Kat said, trying to ignore the fact that her smile was a little wobbly around the edges.

It was funny, really. It was almost like there was a limited amount of "get up and go" to go around. Rye had listened to her, and he was moving forward with his career plan, full steam ahead. Kat, meanwhile, caught herself repeatedly musing on what life would be like if she stayed in Eden Falls.

How would it feel to teach at Morehouse Dance Academy? To stand in the center of the room, clapping out a rhythm for aspiring ballerinas, for good girls who wanted to be graceful and pretty and never, ever dance professionally on any stage, anywhere? How would it feel to stop by Susan and Mike's home every day, to watch her father continue to gain back his strength, to sit at her mother's kitchen table and drink tea using her grandmother's china? How would it feel to greet Niffer every afternoon as she got off her school bus, chattering about art projects, and reading class, and learning the capitals of all the states?

Wonderful, Kat realized, even as she was astonished to recognize that truth. Absolutely, unqualifiedly *wonderful*. In two weeks of living in Eden Falls, Kat had already had more fun than she had in the past two *years* in New York.

And what did that say about her chosen home? Her chosen career?

"Hey," Rye said, interrupting her thoughts. "Ready to get out of here?"

She nodded, sliding out of the fake leather booth. Rye paid at the cash register, waving away her attempt to reach her wallet. He held the door for her, and he ushered her into the truck, but this time she fastened her own seat belt. He smiled and stroked a single finger across her cheek before he closed the door. She shivered at the unspoken promise of that touch.

It took less time than she expected to drive to Rachel's house. Rye put the truck in Park and killed the engine. "Where's Niffer tonight?"

"Sleeping over at Mama and Daddy's. She has them wrapped around her little finger."

"Kids have a way of doing that."

She knew that it was her turn to say something, to make a joke about Niffer, about family, about something light and easy and funny. For the life of her, she couldn't imagine what she could possibly say. "Want to come in for a drink?" she finally settled on. "Of tea," she hastened to add. "Or, er, water. That's all we have inside."

"That'll be enough." Kat watched as he took the keys from the ignition, carelessly tossing them by his feet. That was yet another aspect of life in Eden Falls that she'd never see in New York. If anyone were foolish enough to own a pickup in New York, they'd keep it secured under lock and key—maybe with a mad Doberman in the cab to deter potential thieves. Somehow, it made Kat's heart sing to think of a place that was safe enough to leave car keys on the floor mat.

Inside Rachel's home, Kat headed toward the kitchen. "Let me get you a drink."

Rye caught her before she could cross the foyer, folding his hand across her flame-red scarf. "I have a confession. I'm not really thirsty."

A frisson of excitement raced across her scalp as she registered the rumble of his words. She let him turn her around, felt his other hand settle on her waist.

She was a dancer. She was used to being held by men. She was accustomed to the feeling of strong fingers on her flesh, gripping her tightly, holding her upright.

But all those sensations were her job. They were as routine, as mundane, as utterly bloodless as sitting down at a computer, typing an email, ordering supplies over the telephone.

This was something different. This was something more.

Rye felt the hitch in Kat's breath, and a lazy smile spread across his lips. He'd watched her through the evening; he knew how quickly she had sobered as she ate dinner. He had no qualms about kissing her now. Kissing. Or more.

"You know," he whispered, purposely keeping his voice so low that she had to pull closer to hear him, "we left Andy's too early tonight. We never got a chance to dance."

Her laughter was as soft as her silken hair. "In case you haven't noticed, I'm not exactly in dancing shape." She waved a hand toward her walking boot.

"I wasn't thinking of anything too strenuous. Not your pliés or arabesques or that sort of thing."

"Mmm," she whispered. "You've been doing your homework."

"All part of renovating the studio. I have to know how the space is going to be used, don't I?" That was a lie, though. He had whiled away hours in Richmond, thinking about Kat, thinking about what she did for a living. He had gone online, looking for pictures of her, and he'd picked up a bit about dance along the way.

He should have been working, of course, instead of spending his time online. Should have been focusing on Harmon Contracting. But all work and no play... He'd almost succeeded in convincing himself that his...research was good for business. That there was nothing personal in it. Nothing at all.

"Ready to sign up for a class?" she asked, obviously amused.

"I don't think either of us needs any training." He pulled her close, relishing her surprised gasp even as she yielded to his pressure. She felt marvelous in his arms, pliant but hard, melting into him even as she maintained her dancer's balance. He leaned down and found her mouth, sinking into her sweet silken heat.

Deepening the kiss, teasing her with his tongue, he raised his hand to the marble column of her throat. He could feel her pulse flutter beneath his thumb, a butterfly dancing against his flesh. His fingers wrapped around her nape, urging her closer, then skimming down the length of her spine, molding her fine-boned body to his.

He shifted his weight to match the angle of her hips, signaling his intention by an almost imperceptible tightening of his fingers against her waist. She followed his lead flawlessly, as if this were one of her fancy ballets, as if they'd practiced these moves hour after hour, night after night.

With choreography far more intimate than any Texas Two-Step, he guided her toward the couch. He half expected her to hesitate, to freeze, to refuse to follow his lead. But she sank down before he did, raising her arms above her head like some sort of exotic goddess, summoning him, asking him to join her.

Not that he required much urging.

Kat caught her breath as she lay back on the pillows of the overstuffed couch. Rye looked huge in the dim light from the foyer—sturdy and confident and *present* in a way that made her heart race. Sure, she had kissed other men. She had even fooled around on a couch or two. And practically lived with a jerk. But she had never felt this inner drive, this absolute certainty that she was doing the thing that she was meant to do, that she was with the man she was meant to be with.

For a fleeting moment, she thought of her mantra— goals, strategies, rules. There weren't any rules for the sort of passion she felt now. There wasn't any wrong or right. There was just being. Being in her own physical body. Being with Rye.

She needed to feel him, needed to know the weight of him against her.

She twined her hands around his forearm, tracing

the ropes of hard muscle, the scatter of chestnut hair. She tugged with a decisiveness that left no doubt of her intentions. "Rye," she said. "Please…"

She didn't have to ask a second time. He sank beside her, pulling her onto his lap as he sprawled against the back of the couch. She felt the rigid length of him against her thigh, the absolute confirmation that she wasn't imagining his interest, wasn't fooling herself about his need for her. Knowingly, she traced her fingernail along the denim ridge, barely restraining a grin as he groaned.

But there was more for her to explore, more of his body to know. Even as she yielded to another of his soul-rocking kisses, her fingers found the buttons of his shirt. Summoning all of her concentration, all of her determination, she undid one, and then another, and another. She tugged the tails of his shirt from his waistband and then did away with the garment altogether, tossing it onto the floor with reckless abandon.

All the while, he was doing incredible things to her neck, laving the tender spot beneath her earlobe, tangling his fingers in her hair. A crimson glow ignited in her belly as he stripped away the scarf around her hips. When he trailed the silk across her throat, drifting it over her ruby charm, the throbbing heat that rose inside her nearly made her lose her concentration, almost forced her to yield to his ministrations, to fall back against the soft couch and let him do whatever he wanted to her.

Almost.

Instead, she remembered that groan that she had incited as she traced the outline of his need. She wanted to draw that sound from him again. Relying on her taut dancer's muscles, she pulled herself upright on his lap.

She placed her hands on his shoulders, straddling his waist so that she knelt above him. For one instant, she lost her balance, pulled askew by the unaccustomed weight of her walking boot, but his hands settled beneath her rib cage, holding her, steadying her.

Before she could continue with the exploration she was determined to complete, he stripped his hands up her body, skimming off the clinging black of her top. She gasped at the sensation of cool air bathing her skin, but she was immediately warmed by the satisfaction in his gaze. While one hand spread against the small of her back, giving her the support she needed, the other flirted with the lace edge of her bra, delivering the attention she craved.

His thumb brushed against one nipple, then the other, and the sensitive buds tightened so fast that she cried out. He repeated the motion, adding a caress to the smooth plane of her belly. The red-hot fire inside her turned incandescent. She arched her back, begging him for more attention, and he lost no time complying. One hand sprang the hook on her bra, the other bared her white and willing flesh. His mouth was hot against the underside of her breasts; his tongue traced arcane patterns that left her writhing. When his lips closed over one solid pearl, she thought that she would scream. When his teeth snagged the other, she did.

Panting, eager, she forced herself to concentrate, to return to her original plan. With ragged breath, she pushed against his shoulders, making his head loll back against the couch. She left a trail of kisses along the line of his jaw, featherlight and barely hinting at all that she could do to him, for him. Her lips tingling from his rough stubble, she traced the line that had been bruised the week before, the now-invisible ache that she had given him when she had driven his pickup off the road.

She followed the logical line of that diagonal, adding her tongue to the attention of her lips. She found the dark trail of hair that marched down his tight abs, and she traced its promise, first with her lips, then with all the soft heat of her mouth, ending with the knife-edged promise of a single fingernail.

"Kat," Rye groaned when the pressure became more than he could bear. He had to feel more of her, had to find the liquid heat that spoke to his arousal. He let his palms course over her sides, felt her eager body rise to meet his. He made short work of ripping open the walking boot's straps. She sighed as he eased her foot free of the device, as he tossed the contraption to the floor. His fingers found the hidden side zipper of her crazy New York pants, and he caught his breath at the unexpected gift of lace that he revealed.

She scrambled for his waist, for the familiar bronze button of his jeans, but he caught her wrists, holding them still, bringing the fluttering birds of her fingers to rest beside her hips. There was time enough for his pleasure, time enough to find the complete release that she promised him.

He walked his fingers along the delicate top of her panties, measuring the taut tremble of her belly. She followed his silent command, raising her hips to meet him, to beg him, to invite him to share in the glory that she promised. With the lightest of touches, he traced the hollow behind her right knee, the sensitive cave carved by her tendons. She bucked against the sensation, and he caught a laugh in the back of his throat.

Kat moaned his name, reaching up to pull him down on top of her. She needed to feel his weight against her, needed him to anchor her. Something about the gesture, though, brought full realization crashing down upon her. She'd had no intention of bringing a man back to Rachel's home. She'd had no plan to make love that night.

She had no protection.

"Rye," she whispered, hating every word she had to say. "I don't have…anything. We can't…"

"Hush," he said, and the fingers that he traced along her inner thigh nearly sent her over some crazed edge. "We won't."

Before she could flounder in the sea of disappointment that his words released upon her, his fingers went back to the lace edge of her panties, to the damp panel of silk beneath. "Rye —" she protested.

"Hush," he whispered again, but now he breathed the word against the most secret part of her, turning it into a promise. She closed her eyes as his fingers slipped beneath the lace; she caught her breath as his thumb found the pearl between her legs. One gentle flick, two and she was writhing for release.

He laughed again, ripping away the last of the lacy barrier. She felt his stubble against her thighs, gently raking one leg and then the other. Forgetting her dancer's control, she tilted her hips, longing for the ultimate pleasure that she knew he was prepared to give her.

A single velvet stroke of his tongue. Another. One last, savoring caress, and then she was crashing over a precipice, clutching at his hair, tumbling down an endless slope of clenching, throbbing pleasure.

Rye watched the storm pass over her body, the beautiful twist of her lips as she breathed his name, over and over and over again. When it was past, when he knew that she was drifting on a formless, shapeless sea of comfort, he eased himself up her body. She was utterly relaxed as he pulled her languid form to lie on top of him. Her hair spread across his chest, and the warmth of her flushed cheek soothed his own pounding heart.

"Mmm," she murmured, and her fingers drifted down his torso.

"Rest," he said, smoothing one hand down the plane of her back, while the other cupped the curve of her neck.

"I want…" she whispered, but she drifted into silence before she finished the sentence.

He eased himself to a more comfortable position, telling himself that his body's demands would quiet in a few minutes, that the ache below his belt would ease. He underestimated, though, the force of the woman whom he cradled. He had not considered the power of her honey-apricot scent, teasing him with every breath he drew. He had not taken into account her soft pressure against his chest, his thighs, his entire excruciatingly primed body.

But he managed to take comfort in Kat's utter peacefulness as her breathing slowed. He waited, and he watched, and he held her until she slipped into the deepest of sleeps.

Only then did he look around the living room, seeing the home that Rachel had let fall into disrepair. He could fix things up in short order. Rip out the awful carpet, put down a new floor. Replace the fogged storm windows with something that would insulate the house better. Renovate the entire kitchen, with its creaky old appliances.

It wouldn't take long. A couple of weeks. A month. He could stay in Eden Falls while he worked, keep an eye on every step of the process.

No.

He wasn't going to stay in Eden Falls. He lived in Richmond now. He had a life for himself, a business that he had fought hard for. For the first time in his adult life, he was free to do what he wanted to do, free from family and clinging girlfriends.

Kat shifted in her sleep, spreading her hand across his chest.

What the hell was he doing here? Maybe he had come home with Kat precisely because he knew that *she* wasn't sticking around Eden Falls. She had been absolutely clear—she was heading back to New York, just as soon as he could finish work on the studio. She was safe. She wasn't going to take over his life. She wasn't going to be another Marissa, teasing him, shaping his life to hers, then leaving him in her dust.

Kat had already built a life for herself, a life outside of Eden Falls. She had remained true to herself, true to the promises she'd made when she was just a kid.

Was he really such a wimp that he couldn't do the same? He had *vowed* that he would make a go of things in Richmond. Moving away was what he'd always wanted, what he needed, to prove that he was a real man.

He couldn't give all that away. Not for an impossible future. Not for an unknown, unmeasured relationship with Kat, who had already found her own path to independence.

A chill settled over the room as the final heat of their exertion faded. Rye fought against a shudder, forcing himself to stay perfectly still, lest he ruin Kat's sleep. The night grew long, and he watched and waited and thought about all the futures that might be, and one that he would never, ever have.

## Chapter Six

Rye stood in the dance studio, surveying the stack of hardwood flooring. Brandon was the cousin he'd enlisted for assistance that day. He was pretty sure the guy had only agreed to come over because he hoped Amanda Morehouse would be visiting Kat. Rye had probably implied as much, now that he thought about it. He didn't feel too guilty, though. In the past, Brandon had roped Rye into worse duty on the family's huge organic farm.

"The staple guns are out in the truck," Rye said. "The saw is there, too, along with the rolls of waterproofing to lay out beneath the wood."

"I'm pretty sure that I'm the one who taught *you* how to install a hardwood floor," Brandon retorted.

"Just trying to be helpful," Rye said. He didn't mind his cousin's gruff reply. Instead, he took advantage of

Brandon's expertise to head toward the office, to the private refuge where he knew Kat was hard at work.

Kat. Even now, he could feel her weight on his chest, her body melted and cooling after the pleasure he had given her. The memory, though, made a corner of his heart curl in reflexive avoidance.

He hadn't thought this through. He hadn't realized quite how hard he was falling for Kat, how much she had come to mean to him. There was no way that their lives could ever come together—she was determined to get back to New York the second she was shed of that walking boot, if not before. It had been what? Three weeks already? She'd said that she was only going to wear it for a month. One more week—at most—and then she'd be gone forever.

And he certainly couldn't put all the blame on her for his current discomfort. He hadn't been lying when he'd told her he had an early Saturday meeting in Richmond. Late Friday night, actually early Saturday morning, he had finally carried her to her bed, tucked her in beneath her comforter and stroked her hair until she fell back to sleep. But then he'd left, hitting the road, letting the freeway roll out beneath his headlights as he drove home in the dark of night.

He hadn't called on Saturday. Sunday either. He'd needed to put some distance between them—emotional space to match the physical one.

This whole thing shouldn't be as difficult as it was turning out to be. So what if Kat was heading back to New York soon? Rye could always come down to Eden Falls, stay here until she left. Who knew what would grow between them in the time that they had?

No.

He wasn't going to do that again. Wasn't going to

cash in his dreams. If he walked away from Richmond now, he knew that he would never again find the nerve to build his own business. He would stay here in Eden Falls until he was old and withered and gray, until he couldn't even remember what to do with a woman as intoxicating as Kat.

Damn.

He knocked lightly on the door frame. "Mornin'," he said as Kat looked up from behind the desk.

God, she was beautiful. Her hair was back in one of those twists off her neck, making her look like every schoolboy's fantasy librarian. Her silvery eyes brightened when she saw him, and her smile made his heart ache.

"I missed you," she said. "It was a long weekend without you."

He was supposed to apologize for living in his new hometown. He couldn't. No. He *wouldn't*. Instead, he asked, "What did you do?"

"Niffer had a T-ball game. You didn't tell me that you're a million times better coach than Noah is."

He shrugged, fighting against the pang that told him he should have been there for the game. "Britney was out of town, so Noah didn't have an excuse not to be there."

Kat laughed. "Daddy was feeling so much better that Mama let him walk down to the park with us. We had to take it slow, but he made it. It was great to see him out of the house, soaking up the sunshine."

"That's good news." He felt stiff as he said the words. Awkward. This was terrible—he felt like he was lying to Kat with every word he said. Every word he didn't.

"How was Richmond?" she asked, the faintest hint of worry etching a thin line between her brows.

He forced himself to answer with a hearty smile. "Everything is going great. That Saturday morning meeting was with a new client—a massive kitchen renovation. Yesterday, I met with a computer guy—he's set up all my client files."

Kat wasn't an idiot. She could tell that something was wrong.

Something. There wasn't a lot of mystery about that, was there? What was the one thing that had changed since she and Rye had last talked, had been easy and comfortable and happy in each other's company? Her cheeks grew hot, and she wasn't sure whether the leap in her pulse was because of the memories of what they had done, or her regrets about what they hadn't.

But that wasn't all. She understood the warning behind Rye's stilted conversation. She *knew* that he lived in Richmond now, that he was only here in Eden Falls as a favor to her. He didn't even *want* to be working on the studio. That was just as well. She was going back to New York, after all, leaving all of this behind in just a matter of days.

And that thought left her strangely numb, as it had every time she thought it over the weekend.

But that was ridiculous. New York was her home, had been for ten years. New York was the place where she had her friends, her job, her life.

She thought of the gray concrete canyons, the buildings so tall that sunshine never touched the streets. Before she could be depressed by the memory of such a bleak landscape, though, she forced herself to confront the hard facts of living in Eden Falls. A big night out was stopping by the cinema to watch a first-release film. There wasn't a single twenty-four-hour business in town. The only restaurants that made deliveries were the pizza parlor on Elm Street and the Chinese place on Baker.

But she and Amanda had had a lot of fun at the movies, just last night. She'd left Niffer with her parents, and she and her cousin had shared a huge tub of popcorn, watched some silly chick-flick. After all, who needed to work twenty-four hours a day? And why would she ever need to order in anything other than pizza or Chinese?

No. She could never live in Eden Falls long-term. No matter how much fun she was having on this spring break. Vacation wasn't the real world, even a vacation rooted in caring for her healing father, for her wayward niece.

Bottom line—it was absolutely, positively 100% necessary to drive around a town like Eden Falls. Kat had been imposing on her mother and Amanda for the entire time she'd been here. Sooner or later, her family was going to refuse to ferry her from one place to another. And she had no intention of making another disastrous attempt at getting behind the wheel.

Eden Falls had nothing on New York. She just had to remember that.

In fact, there was one more dangerous thing about Eden Falls: Rye Harmon. She had a sudden vision of his lips on the inside of her thigh. Her cheeks flushed at the memory of the pleasure he had given her. At the thought of the fulfillment he'd denied himself. She had to say something, had to let him know that she had stopped by Doherty's Drugstore the day before. He needed to know that she had purchased a packet of silver-wrapped condoms, to use in the future.

Whatever future they had. She cleared her throat. "Rye, about Friday night," she began, even though she had no earthly idea what she was going to say after that.

He answered her quickly, too quickly. "I shouldn't have… I'm sorry. I live in Richmond now. I —"

"Rye!" She cut him off, touched by how flustered he'd become. "I know that. I understand."

"It's just that in the past… There was someone who…" He ran his fingers through his hair, leaving his chestnut curls in disarray. "I'm making a total mess out of this."

She caught his hands and pulled them close to her chest. "No," she said, meeting his eyes. "You're not. I'm not expecting you to drop everything and move back here to Eden Falls. I'd be crazy to ask that, when I'm only here for a while myself. Friday night was amazing—and I hope we'll spend more time together before I go back to New York. But I'm not expecting you to walk in here with an engagement ring and the keys to your family's Eden Falls house."

Right then, for just that moment, when her smile got a little crooked and she squeezed his fingers between her own, he would have left Richmond. He would have dropped Harmon Contracting, abandoned all his hopes and dreams.

But then he heard Brandon shift equipment out in the studio. It was like his cousin was trying to remind him of his business, of his future, of all the reasons he'd fought to get out of Eden Falls.

Rye was an independent businessman now. And Kat wasn't part of his past. She wasn't Marissa Turner. She was a woman who had found her way clear of Eden Falls years before. That was part of what made her so damned alluring.

He slipped his fingers free from her gentle grip, but he stepped even closer. His palm cupped the back of her neck, and he leaned down to steal a quick kiss. She was more hesitant than he'd expected, though, almost as if she were afraid of the spark that might ignite between them.

Well, spark be damned. His free hand settled on the small of her back, tugging her closer, so that he could feel the whole long line of her body. He traced her closed lips with his tongue, and his blood leaped high when she yielded to him. Before he could follow through, though, before he could think about easing up the rumpled cloth of her blouse, there was another clatter from the outer room.

"That's Brandon," he breathed, settling his forehead on Kat's shoulder and drawing a steadying breath. "He's ready to install the floorboards."

Kat's own breath hitched as she took a step back. What was she thinking, anyway? She wasn't exactly the type of girl to revel in a little afternoon delight—not with countless business details left to take care of.

"Great," she said, trying not to sound too rueful. Then, she repeated the word, broadcasting it for Brandon's hearing. "Great! Let me show you this website that I found. I can use it to design stationery for the studio—letterhead and flyers and business cards."

He edged around the desk, coming to stand behind her as she pulled her chair closer to the computer. She sat like a classical statue, straight and tall. Her hands flew over her computer keyboard, smoothly competent as she called up something on the screen. He didn't care about any stupid website. He was just pleased for the excuse to be standing so close to her.

"Look at this," she enthused. "They have hundreds

of templates—you can choose one that's right for you. Here, I'll show you. Let's make a flyer for Harmon Contracting. Didn't you say that you needed to do that?"

She looked at him expectantly, and he nodded, eager to see her smile. He wasn't disappointed.

"They have themes, like Medicine and Legal." She let the computer mouse hover over those choices for a moment to illustrate the possibilities, and then she swept it toward the top of the screen. "But we probably want Carpentry."

She clicked once, and the screen was filled with the image of a creamy white page. Silvery scrolls curled around the edges, folding into twined hearts in the corners. Ornate writing spelled out the formal words of an invitation: Mr. and Mrs. Robert Smith request the pleasure of your presence at the wedding of their daughter...

"Oops!" Kat slammed her palm down on the mouse, as if it were a living creature that might actually scurry away. "I clicked on Celebrations by mistake."

He couldn't help himself. He grinned at her obvious discomfort. She was acting like that one false click was a much bigger deal than it was. From her level of embarrassment, it was almost like she'd unveiled some deep dark secret, as if he had walked in on her while she was showering.

He felt the first stirring of his body responding to that delightful image, and he shifted his weight from one foot to the other. *Business, Harmon*, he remonstrated with himself. This was a business website that she was showing him.

By the time he had schooled his mind back to professionalism, she had brought up a different page. Hearts had been replaced with tiny images of a hammer and saw in one corner, a toolbox in another. Bold lettering stated John Smith Handyman Services, with a mock address at 123 Main Street.

"See?" Kat said, and she was studying the computer screen just a little too intensely, staring at the page as if it might turn into a bird and take flight. "I can click here, and we can change the name." He watched as her fingers picked out "Harmon Contracting." "We can add your Richmond address. There's room for an email address, a landline, and your cell phone. You can keep the dark brown, or you can make it any other color. Navy, maybe. Or maroon."

"What if I want the silver, from the other screen?"

He couldn't say what made him ask the question. It wasn't fair, really. He just wanted to see emotion skip across her features, flash across her platinum eyes. She darted a glance toward the office door, toward the studio where Brandon served as unwitting chaperone.

Kat cleared her throat, consciously deciding not to take the bait. Instead, she dashed her fingers across the keyboard, pulling up the draft files she had created for her own business, for the dance studio. Toe shoes filled the corners, and the lettering was a professional burgundy. Morehouse Dance Academy. The street address. Eden Falls, Virginia.

She had completed the flyer with information about all of the classes that they offered, from Introductory Ballet to Advanced Showcase. Instructors' names were listed inside parentheses—Miss Sarah, Miss Emma, Miss Virginia. The only blank class was the Advanced Showcase; the former teacher had not responded to the dozen messages Kat had left.

That made sense, actually. Miss Courtney Thomson had been the most accomplished of the studio's instructors. She was likely to take her career the most seriously, to have been the most turned off by Rachel's haphazard management. Kat suspected that she'd already taken on work in a neighboring town, moved on with her life. Kat really couldn't blame her.

"That's great," Rye said, and she realized that he'd been reading the full text on the page.

"It's nothing," she said, but she was pleased by the compliment. She'd spent a lot of time on Saturday writing the brochure. "I need to take it to my mother this afternoon."

"She'll love it. It reads like something from a professional advertising company."

"We can do something similar for you. Specific to plumbing and electricity and stuff."

"Stuff," he teased. "You make it sound so complicated."

"You know what I mean!"

"Yeah, I do," he admitted. Without fully intending to, he placed his hands on the back of her chair, spinning her around to face him. He heard her breath catch in her throat as he edged forward. She looked up at him, an uncertain smile quirking her lips. He leaned down and planted his palms on the arms of her chair, the motion bringing his lips close to hers. "I know exactly what you mean," he growled, and suddenly neither of them was talking about stationery or computers or... stuff.

Before he could follow through on the promise of the suddenly charged air between them, a clatter came from the studio. Something metal hit the floor, followed by a sharp curse.

"Brandon?" Rye called, already turning to the door.

"I'm all right," came the quick reply. "But I could use a hand out here."

Rye set his hand against Kat's cheek. "I—" he said, so softly that Brandon could never hear him. He wasn't sure what he was going to say. *I want to finish what we started Friday night. I don't care about stationery, not when we could be talking about something else. Doing something else. I don't give a damn about Richmond, or New York, or Eden Falls, or anyplace, so long as I'm with you.*

"Go," Kat said, and she watched him swallow hard. "I'll be here. Brandon needs you."

She slumped into her chair as he hurried out the door. She should have Rye check the air-conditioning in the office. It was about twenty degrees too hot in the small room. She pretended not to hear the muffled curses as the men negotiated over some spilled hardware.

Before Kat could pull herself together enough to go back to the stationery website, the computer chimed. She had new email. She clicked on the icon, opening up a message entitled Coppelia. The sender was Haley, writing from New York.

The first paragraph was a breathless apology for failing to write more often. Haley's on-again, off-again boyfriend was back in her life; he'd given her red roses for her birthday—*two dozen!!!* The apartment was fine. Slimeball Adam had finally come and picked up his junk. Skanky Selene had already dumped him and moved on to another dancer in the company. Kat's eyes skimmed over the words, as if she were reading some boring nineteenth-century novel about people she'd never met.

But then she saw the real reason for Haley's message.

Sign up for *Coppelia* auditions closes at midnight, May 1. You have to do it in person; they won't let me add your name to the list. Are you coming back in time?

Kat stared at the screen, at the Xes and Os that closed out Haley's message. *Are you coming back in time?*

*Coppelia*. Kat had always dreamed of dancing the lead role of Swanilda. The ballet had been her absolute favorite, ever since she was a little girl. It told the story of a lonely toymaker in a mountain village, a mad scientist who created a life-size doll who only needed the sacrifice of a human being to come to life. Swanilda was the wise village girl who figured out the madness of the toymaker's work—she saved her betrothed from being sacrificed. Swanilda defeated the mad woodcarver and married her beloved.

The role was physically demanding. In addition to classical ballet moves, the part required executing a number of country dances and one extended section where Swanilda pretended to be the jerky windup doll, Coppelia.

Kat flexed her toes inside her walking boot. Even when she arched them to their full reach, she felt nothing, no twinge of pain. Her foot was almost healed.

She looked around the office. Despite her still-elevated heart rate as she listened for Rye, out in the studio, her work here was nearly done. She could place her order for stationery right now. That would leave one last thing to clean up: the bank accounts. Kat couldn't believe that she'd let the problem linger for nearly three full weeks. But it wasn't really a surprise. The lost money was the one thing she couldn't fix. That was Rachel's one failing that Kat couldn't tidy up, couldn't erase away. Her parents would be devastated, and there was nothing Kat could do—and so she'd let herself shrug off the responsibility, ever since she'd identified the problem.

But for the past week or so, there had been another reason that she'd failed to handle the financial crisis. Once she told her mother about the lost money, there'd be no reason left to stay in Eden Falls. And Kat had to admit that part of her did not want to leave.

That was only natural, she tried to assure herself. Her father had looked so healthy as he walked to the park on Sunday. He was sitting up in his recliner at home, even heading to the kitchen to get his own snacks. Susan would be able to run the studio on her own soon enough; Amanda could probably juggle her own teaching schedule to help out for the first rough weeks of transition.

Even Niffer had calmed down. Sure, the child still whined when she didn't get her way. And she would choose candy over a healthy meal, given half a chance. But she'd taken to the new structure in her life like the duck to water. Just that morning, she had returned her crayons to her toy box without being asked to straighten up the kitchen table.

For all intents and purposes, Kat's work here was done. Except for the accounting ledger.

Out in the studio, Rye laughed at something Brandon said. No. Rye was not a reason to stay in Eden Falls. He lived in Richmond. He was on the threshold of his own successful career.

She flashed again on a memory of how incredible it had felt to lie within the shelter of his arms. His heartbeat had pounded against her own. His warmth had enfolded her as she drifted off to sleep.

She had braved the embarrassment of shopping at the drugstore, of securing the protection they needed, so that they could complete what they'd started Friday night.

No. Rye was a spring fling. A light touch of relief as she juggled all the responsibilities of family. An enjoyable confirmation that her demanding life in New York hadn't ruined her, that she could still be a desirable woman.

She didn't have any right to turn their fun and games into anything more. It wouldn't be fair to Rye. It wouldn't be fair to herself.

Squaring her shoulders, Kat clicked on the button to reply to Haley's email. She typed:

Glad to hear all is well. I'm wrapping things up here and should be home in time to sign up. Thanks a million times over! XOXO. Kat

She read the message four times before she clicked Send. And then she dug out the studio's oversize checkbook, determined to calculate all of Rachel's red ink, down to the last penny. Then, she'd be free to leave Eden Falls. To return to her home. To New York.

Out in the studio, Rye was pleased to find that a drop cloth had caught the spilled staples and oversize staple gun that Brandon had dropped. Nevertheless, he said to his cousin, "Let's take this thing outside. I don't want anything to scratch the new floorboards."

"You're the boss," Brandon said. He hitched up his Levi's before he helped Rye maneuver the heavy cloth out the door.

It was only when they stood in the parking lot that

Rye said, "Wait a second. There's just a handful of staples." He looked over at Brandon. "What the hell made so much noise?"

"You mean this?" Brandon reached into the bed of the truck, fishing out a clean metal tray for painting. He shoved it beneath the tarp and then emptied a box of staples onto it. The clatter was suitably dramatic.

"What the—"

"I had to get you out of that office, buddy."

"What are you talking about?"

"I heard the two of you talking. Don't you realize that girl thinks you're picking out wedding invitations?"

Rye laughed. "You don't know what you're talking about. She accidentally pulled up that screen. She was showing me how to put together flyers for the new business."

Brandon snorted. "You've got it bad, don't you? You'll believe just about anything."

"You couldn't see the computer screen, Bran. I'm telling you, it was filled with ballet shoes."

"*What if I want the silver, from the other screen?*" Brandon quoted.

Rye sighed. "I was just teasing her. There isn't anything serious between us. There can't be. She's heading back to New York in a week or two."

Brandon bent to retrieve the paint tray and staples, taking his time to stow them in the bed of the pickup. He was still facing the truck when he muttered, "That shouldn't be the only reason there isn't anything serious."

Of course, Rye heard him. Rye was pretty sure he was *supposed* to hear him. "What are you talking about?"

"Hey, I've got eyes. And I know you. I knew you a

couple of years ago, when that crazy Marissa chick was jerking you around, and you were practically living on my couch."

"I wasn't living on your couch."

Brandon pinned him with glittering eyes. "No, you just stopped by every other night because I'm such a wonderful cook. Come on, man. That was Johnnie Walker *Gold* that we killed the night your Marissa said she was heading out to California."

"She wasn't 'my' Marissa," Rye said automatically.

"Of course not. She was just the reason you forfeited the lease on your first place up in Richmond. And put off getting your contractor's license, for two years running. And didn't bid on that antebellum mansion gig. Or that showcase house. Or—"

"Okay!" Rye clenched his fists, his stomach churning at the memory of all the opportunities he'd let go because of Marissa.

"No," Brandon said. "It's not okay. Because I see you doing the same thing, all over again. You're throwing away your life, because of a woman. You're staying in Eden Falls, even after you promised to get the hell out of Dodge."

"I have an office up in Richmond, Bran." Rye barely held his temper in check.

"And just look at how much time you're spending up there." Brandon reached into the back of the truck, pulling a soda out of the cooler that was lashed to the bed. He popped the top and passed it to Rye before salvaging another for himself. He downed half the drink in a few noisy swallows before gesturing with the can. "Don't do this, buddy. I'm telling you. She isn't worth it."

*She's worth a lot more than you know*, Rye thought.

*You haven't seen her, the way she can laugh. The way she cares about—really loves—her niece. The way she's set aside her own life, helping out her family when they need her. You haven't seen the way she looks with her hair down, and her lips swollen from a good kiss, and....*

But of course he didn't say anything out loud. Instead, he sipped from his own soft drink can and stared across the parking lot, as if the billboard on the far side held the answer to all the secrets of the universe.

He wasn't going to fight his cousin over this. Especially when he knew that Brandon was right about one thing. Kat was going to leave Eden Falls, and then all the fun and games would be over. Kat was heading back to the National Ballet and New York, to the life that she'd built for herself.

And nothing Rye could say would change that. Marissa Turner had taught him that, for sure. He could never control a woman. Only himself. Only his own decisions.

Brandon finished his soda in another long swig, belching before he crushed the can and tossed it into the back of the truck. "I pity you, buddy. You've sure got it bad."

Rye punched him on the shoulder. "Shut up, Bran, okay? Let's get back in there. It's time to get this job done."

"You're the boss. Just remember, you can hang out on my couch, anytime you need to."

As Brandon headed back into the studio, Rye pretended to remember that he had to make a phone call. He was only standing there, though, with his mobile beside his ear. Standing there and realizing that Brandon was right. Rye did have it bad.

Because no matter how this ended, no matter how broken up he would be when Kat went back to New York, he wasn't ready to stop yet. No, this wasn't the same as it had been with Marissa. He wasn't going to throw his own life away, just because of a woman.

But he was going to enjoy himself while he could. He was going to follow through on the unspoken offer that Kat had made when she invited him in for a drink. He was going to enjoy whatever time they had together—a week, two weeks, whatever.

He just had to make sure things didn't get messy. He just had to make sure that neither of them expected more than the other was offering. He just had to make sure that there were no strings attached.

*Picking out wedding invitations.* Brandon didn't know what the hell he was talking about. Kat wasn't some flighty girl, living her entire life with the single goal of getting a wedding band on her finger. She'd be just as happy as Rye was to enjoy whatever they had, for however long they had it. And when it came time to put her on the Yankee Clipper and send her back north, that was exactly what he would do.

After a few minutes, Rye realized that he must look like an idiot, standing in a parking lot, holding a cell phone to his ear, not saying a word. As he slid his phone back into his pocket, he realized that he felt like an idiot, too. He could bluster and boast all he wanted, but there was a truth he had to admit—at least to himself.

He had fallen for Kat Morehouse. Fallen hard. And no amount of saying otherwise would change the shape of the hole she was going to leave in his heart when she headed back to New York City.

## *Chapter Seven*

Kat watched proudly as Niffer ate the last bite of broccoli on her plate. "Thank you for dinner, Gram," the little girl said. "It was almost as good as dinner last night."

*Well, so much for perfect manners,* Kat thought. At least Susan was smiling at Niffer indulgently. "And what did you girls do for dinner last night?"

Niffer answered before Kat could. "Mr. Harmon took us out for tacos!"

"Oh, really?" Susan arched a smile toward Kat before darting a look at Mike. Kat's father made a show of chewing his meat loaf.

"We just grabbed something quick, Mama. Sort of a celebration for getting the painting done at the studio." Kat heard the way her voice rose in pitch, even though she tried to sound casual. There was just a shadow of a hint of a possibility of a chance that Susan would accept the fact that Rye had treated them to a casual Mexican dinner for no reason whatsoever.

The questions would never stop coming, though, if Kat gave any hint of the midday break she had taken Wednesday afternoon....

It had all started innocently enough. Rye had said that she should leave the office for the rest of the day, that the paint fumes would get too strong. He had driven her home, confirming that Niffer was well-occupied with her after-school program. And then, he had ushered Kat into her bedroom, barely taking time to close the door behind him. They had both laughed as they produced identical silver-wrapped packets from behind the counter at Doherty's.

No. Susan didn't need to know anything at all about that. If Kat had had *her* way, her mother wouldn't have known anything about the taco dinner the night before, either.

Completely innocent, Niffer wiped her mouth with her napkin before folding the cloth and putting it beside her plate. "May I be excused, Gram?"

Susan looked astonished by the polite request, but she nodded at the little girl. "Certainly, Jen—um, Niffer. Thank you for asking so nicely."

Kat helped her niece wriggle down from the dining room chair. When she turned back to the table, Susan was shaking her head in amazement. "You have worked wonders with her, sweetheart."

Kat lifted her chin and smiled. "I really think she wanted some structure in her life. You always said that you and Daddy set your rules so that Rachel and I would know how much you love us."

Mike looked up from his armchair at the head of the

table. "I didn't think you listened to a word your mother and I said while you were growing up."

"Daddy!" Kat laughed. "Of course I did. I can recite all your lessons by heart." She closed her eyes and raised up a finger, as if she were recounting the Ten Commandments. "A fool and his money are soon parted." She added a second finger. "If you don't have anything nice to say, don't say anything at all." One more finger. "Never assume malice, when stupidity is an explanation."

Susan laughed. "She has you there, love. I think the only thing she learned from me is 'stop making that face, or it might freeze that way.'"

Kat shook her head. "No, Mama. You taught us a lot more than that." Before she could elaborate, though, the phone rang.

Susan bustled into the kitchen, only to return with the handset. "What? I can't hear you! There's too much noise in the background!" Susan took the phone away from her ear and squinted at the buttons. She punched the one for volume five times in rapid succession. "Who is this?" she shouted back into the phone.

"Mom!" Now the sound was loud enough that Kat could make out her sister's voice.

"Rachel?" Susan looked as if she might drop the phone. Kat heard a skitter of footsteps, and Niffer was back in the room, hugging her grandmother and reaching for the handset as if it were a lifeline. Susan pulled back a little before she shouted, "Where are you?"

"I'm in D.C., Mom! Staying with friends! We're having a party!"

Mike muttered at the far end of the table, "Tell me something I don't know."

Niffer started whining, "Mommy! Let me talk to Mommy!"

Susan shushed her granddaughter. "Rachel, when are you coming home?"

"That's why I called, Mom!"

Niffer was still whimpering, trying to get her little hands on the phone. "Hush," Kat said. "Come here, Niffer. You can sit on my lap, and we'll talk to Mommy after Gram is done." She measured out the moment when the little girl thought about refusing, but then Niffer let herself be held.

Rachel was still shouting over the line. "I'm catching a ride tomorrow! I'll be there by noon!"

"Wonderful, dear," Susan said. "Niffer has a T-ball game tomorrow afternoon. You can see her play."

"Who?"

"Niffer. Jenny."

There was a commotion on the other end of the line, some sort of shouting match that resolved into a cluster of voices shouting "Ten! Nine! Eight!"

Rachel added her own treble above the countdown. "Gotta go, Mom! See you tomorrow!"

The silence in the room echoed after the connection was broken. Susan stared at the handset as if it might come back to life. Mike scowled, his thoughts about his wayward daughter patently clear on his face. Kat shook her head. Rachel hadn't mentioned her at all, hadn't even asked about their father's health.

Niffer, though, bounced off Kat's lap and ran across the room to hug Susan. "Mommy's coming home! I get to see Mommy tomorrow!"

Susan smoothed her granddaughter's hair. "Yes, dear," she said automatically.

Kat sat back in her chair. Looking at her parents'

faces, she realized that Susan and Mike thought the same thing she did. Rachel was about as likely to show up at Niffer's T-ball game as she was to win a Nobel Prize. The interstate to D.C. might as well have been the Trans-Continental Railroad. And there was no real way to cushion the blow for an excited little girl.

Kat had to do something, though. "Niffer, honey. Go pick up your toys in the other room. Gram is going to drive us home in five minutes."

When Niffer looked up, a spark of her old rebellion glinted deep in her coal-black eyes. "When Mommy's back, Gram won't have to drive us everywhere. Mommy's smart enough to drive a car."

"Niffer!" Susan warned.

Kat, though, waved off the confrontation. "Clean up your toys, Niffer. Now."

The little girl dragged her feet as she harrumphed across the room.

Mike glared after her. "I thought that child was through with all her back-talking."

Kat shrugged. "She's just excited. And I don't have the heart to get angry with her, because I know she's going to end up disappointed tomorrow."

"You don't *know* that," Susan tsked.

Kat sighed. "I hope you're right, Mama."

No one said another word on the topic. But Kat couldn't help but realize her father didn't correct her. He was as mistrustful of Rachel as she was. It was a long ride home, listening to Niffer ramble on about all the presents she hoped her mother would bring.

Rye glanced in the mirror of the hotel lobby, making sure that his tie was straight before he went into the conference room. He could already hear the murmur of conversation inside, the movers and shakers of the Richmond business world conducting their most important deals at the monthly Chamber of Commerce dinner. He was willing to bet that the salads had already been served, that the bone-dry breasts of chicken were on their way.

He'd rather be in Eden Falls. He'd rather be sitting in Susan and Mike Morehouse's dining room, watching Niffer wrinkle up her nose at the broccoli that she had already denounced when he took her out for tacos the night before. He'd made Niffer promise to eat every last bite, saying that her grandmother would be disappointed if she left any vegetables on her plate.

Kat's smile had been blinding. Or maybe he'd just been blinded by memories of Wednesday afternoon. Everything had seemed so simple when he had taken her home from the studio, using the paint fumes as an excuse for playing hooky. So easy. So *right*. Even now, he could hear her laughing as she told him some story about Niffer. He could hardly believe that he had ever thought of Kat as icy. As cold. As utterly, completely controlled in everything she did. He couldn't wait to see her lose that firm control again. As soon as he could get back down to Eden Falls.

"Hey, Rye!"

"Josh!" Rye extended his hand toward his fraternity brother. "I wasn't expecting to see you here."

"This is where the big deals get done, right?" Josh Barton flashed his old winning smile. "I heard a rumor you had set up shop here in Richmond."

"I figured it was finally time to get out of Eden Falls."

"Past time, I'd imagine." Josh had always been restless, even back in college. Rye supposed that was part of his charm with the ladies—the man dreamed big, and he wasn't afraid to have company on his journey. "What sort of work are you doing these days?"

Rye felt himself relax in the face of Josh's easy confidence. "A couple of kitchens, lately. Last winter, I did a complete restore on the old Wilson place. And just this week I finished renovating the Morehouse Dance Studio."

"*That* must have been a pain. Is that crazy Rachel still running the place for her mother?"

"Not for a while. She took off to visit friends out west." Rye shrugged. His explanation sounded better than, *she left town, ditching your daughter with her parents.* "Her sister came down from New York to help out. Kat."

"She's the one who went to that fancy ballet school?"

Rye nodded. He didn't want to talk to Josh about Kat. In fact, now that he thought about it, it was strange that Josh hadn't been around to help with Niffer. Take her for a weekend, at least. Especially since the guy still seemed to be pretty tied in to Eden Falls life. He'd asked about Rachel running the studio. He had to know about Mike Morehouse's illness, about the way the community was rallying to help out the family.

"At least one of those girls turned out sane." Josh gave Rye a knowing wink.

"What do you mean?"

"Come on! You know as well as I do—Rachel is *nuts!*"

No matter how much Rye might have agreed, the blatant criticism raised his chivalrous hackles. "She was always a little wild, yeah, but I wouldn't call her 'nuts.'"

Josh grinned. "Are we talking about the same woman? Played the field after she got out of high school? Spent half her time at the frat house, then tried to frame me for eighteen years of child support?"

A sliver of warning slipped into Josh's tone. "Frame?"

Josh shook his head. "That crazy bitch sued me for paternity. She had to withdraw the case, though, after all the tests came back. I dodged a bullet with that one!"

Rye laughed, because that's what he was supposed to do. Even as he responded on automatic pilot, though, his jaw was tightening into a stony line.

Josh shot his cuffs and nodded toward the conference room. "But enough about Eden Falls. You're in Richmond now. Ready to meet your new business partners?"

"You go ahead," Rye said. "I'm going to make a pit stop."

Rye watched in dismay as Josh disappeared down the hall. His ears were ringing, as if the lobby echoed. A metallic taste coated the back of his throat. *Dodged a bullet.*

Rachel Morehouse had told Rye, in no uncertain terms, that Josh Barton was the father of her baby. Rachel had said that her baby would never have a handyman for a father; no one but a lawyer was good enough for Rachel. Rachel had said that Rye was off the hook. Rachel had said…

Rye clutched at the marble counter in front of the mirror. Closing his eyes, he could see Niffer's jet-black hair, a perfect match for her mother's. But he could see the line of her jaw, as well, a line echoed in a dozen of Rye's nieces and nephews. And he could picture the girl standing at the plate in T-ball, getting ready to swing the bat left-handed. Rye looked down at his own left hand, staring at his palm as if he'd never seen it before.

For whatever twisted reason that passed as logic in

Rachel's rebellious mind, she had lied to him five years ago. Jennifer Morehouse was Rye's daughter.

Kat made sure that her father was comfortably settled on one of the benches behind home plate, and then she nodded toward a vendor who had set up his cart on the edge of the park. "Can I get you a hot dog, Daddy?"

"No, thanks. I'm fine."

"A Coke, then?"

"I don't need anything."

Susan had been worried about the late-afternoon start of the game; she hadn't wanted anyone to go hungry. As a result, she'd spent the afternoon setting out "nibbles"—cheese and crackers and fruit and cookies—three times as much food as any normal meal. Kat didn't think she'd ever be hungry again.

As much as she was inclined to fuss over her father, she had to admit that he *did* look strong. Sure, his shirt hung loose at his throat. And his tight-belted trousers rode a little high on his hips. But the fresh air had brought color to his cheeks. He'd made the walk from the house without getting winded, in his best time yet since his surgery. Kat sat down beside him, but barely a minute passed before she jumped up and looked over her shoulder.

Mike's mouth pursed into a frown. "Don't waste your time looking for her, Kat. You know as well as I do that she's not going to make it."

Kat wanted to berate him. She wanted to say that he was tired, that he was depressed because of his long illness, that he wasn't being fair. But deep in her heart, she knew that she agreed with him. Rachel had said that she'd be home by noon, and it was already almost four. For the hundredth time, Kat wondered what her sister's friends had been counting down. How many more drinks had they downed to celebrate whatever it was? What else had they consumed, substances stronger than alcohol?

Before Kat could figure out an appropriate reply to her father, Susan left a cluster of her friends and came to join them on the bench. "Kat! Lauren says she saw your flyer in every store on Main Street. I can't tell you how many people told me how professional it looks."

Kat smiled automatically, but there was a chill beneath her reaction. Sure, the paperwork looked good. The class rosters were filling up. But she *still* hadn't broached the subject of the bank account with her mother. Every day that passed made Kat more worried, but no matter how many times she promised herself, she just couldn't find the words to deliver the bad news. She felt like she was living a lie, every time she talked about the studio but stayed silent about the money.

Before Kat could respond to Susan's compliment, Niffer came skidding to a stop in front of them. "The game's about to start! Is Mommy here yet?" The child craned her neck, peering around at the benches as if a full-grown woman might somehow be hiding nearby.

Susan answered for all of them. "Not yet, dear. Oh, look! Coach Noah is looking for you."

Niffer, though, directed her eyes over Kat's shoulder. "Mr. Harmon! Guess what! My mommy is coming to see me play today!"

Rye felt like someone had kicked him in his gut as he watched Niffer run back to the T-ball diamond. Rachel? Here?

His hands instinctively flexed into fists, as if he needed to defend himself in some battle. He wasn't ready to see Rachel. Not yet.

After walking out of the Chamber of Commerce dinner the night before, he had spent the entire night thinking about Josh's revelation. He'd tossed and turned on his mattress, tangling himself in his sheets until he swore and got up to splash cold water on his face.

How had he not seen the truth before? Why had he let Rachel's lies derail him? Why hadn't Rachel come after him for child support? And how was he going to tell Kat the truth? How could he tell Niffer?

Over and over, he asked himself what Rachel had possibly hoped to gain, keeping him in the dark.

But it all made sense, in a twisted way. Rachel thrived on drama. In her heart of hearts, she had to know that Rye would have stepped up, faced his responsibility. Rye would have done everything he could to help Rachel, to ease Niffer's strange, unbalanced life.

But Rachel could get far more mileage out of Josh being Niffer's father. She could sulk about being rejected by the guy who'd made it big. She could complain about the vast wealth that should have been hers. She could lash out against a system that had cheated her, denied her rights, cast her loose. And Josh wasn't around Eden Falls often enough to bother setting the record straight.

Rye had to figure out what was right, how he could take responsibility for Niffer now, at this relatively late date. But to do that, he needed to talk to Rachel. Rachel, who Niffer had just sunnily proclaimed was coming to the park.

Shoving down the feeling that his world was rapidly spinning out of control, Rye forced himself to smile at an unsuspecting Kat, to shake hands with Mike. Susan made a big show of coming over to kiss him on his cheek, to tell him how pleased she was about the renovations he'd completed at the dance studio. A quick glance from Kat reminded him of the cover story they'd concocted. According to the lies, Rye had just come in to freshen up the paint, to update the appearance of the Morehouse Dance Academy. Susan was never to know how badly Rachel had managed the business.

He forced himself to smile and make small talk with Kat's mother.

Rachel's mother, too.

What the hell was he going to do when she showed up? For all he knew, she might be in one of her crazy moods. If she saw that Kat and Rye were together, she might announce their past relationship to the entire world, trumpet it to the heavens for all to hear, just to see how everyone reacted.

He could only imagine the look that Kat would turn on him then. He could picture the hurt in her eyes, almost as clearly as if he already saw it. Sure, he had already told Kat that he'd dated her sister for a few weeks. But he'd purposely kept the extent of that "dating" vague. He certainly hadn't given a hint that a child could have resulted from that brief time together.

He needed a break to think this through. "Excuse me," he said. "I'm going to grab a hot dog before the game."

"I'll come with you," Kat chimed in, smiling. His heart sank, but he gave her a hand as she stepped down from the benches. He regretted how easily she twined her fingers between his, how comfortably she fell into step beside him as they made their way to the edge of the park.

Kat deserved better than this. She deserved more from him than being mortally embarrassed when her sister walked into the middle of this supposedly perfect spring afternoon.

"It's going to be okay," Kat said, as soon as they were out of earshot from her parents.

Rye started when she spoke, almost as if he were a child caught stealing cookies from the cooling rack. "What will?" he choked out.

"This whole thing with Rachel. We've tried to let Niffer know that she can't rely on her mother, that just because Rachel *said* she'd be here today, doesn't mean it's going to happen. It's so hard, though. Niffer hears what she wants to hear. I guess all kids do. The whole time we were walking over here, Niffer kept telling us that she's going to hit three home runs, just for Rachel. As if Noah could have coached her on how to do *that*." They walked another few steps in silence before she said, "That was sort of like a joke, Rye."

He shook his head, looking at her as if he were truly seeing her for the first time that day. "I'm sorry. I guess I'm a little preoccupied."

"We all have been. It's one thing for us adults to know we can't depend on Rachel. It's another for Niffer to learn the truth." She squeezed his hand gently. "I'm really touched that you're taking this so hard. It means a lot to me that you care so much about Niffer."

*There*, Rye thought. That was the opening he was looking for. That was the introduction he needed to tell Kat what was really on his mind.

But could he do that to her? Before he'd had a chance to talk to Rachel himself, to confirm the facts one last time? And could he break the news to Kat here, in full view of half the town, with an innocent T-ball game starting up behind them? He could already hear the children's shouts, the good-natured cheering for the kids at bat, for the ones in the field. And Kat was already wound so tight, worried about how Niffer would cope when Rachel didn't show.

*When Rachel didn't show.* Despite Niffer's heart-stopping announcement, Kat didn't think that Rachel was going to make it to the game. In fact, from the look on Mike's face, the man had been pretty certain his other daughter was a no-show. Come to think of it, even Susan had looked unsure.

Well, if Rachel didn't come to the park today, then Rye's secret was safe for a while longer. He could still track her down, get absolute confirmation. Then he could choose his time and his place. He could break things to Kat gently.

Hunching his shoulders, he folded his misery deeper into the nauseating sea of his emotions. He *would* clean this up. He had to. But this was neither the time, nor the place.

"Want a hot dog?" he asked, pulling out his wallet.

"You have got to be kidding." Kat laughed. "Do you know how bad those things are for you?"

"Worse than a burger and fries?" he retorted.

That did the trick. He knew that she was immediately thinking of the booth they had shared at the Garden Diner, of the meal that she had enjoyed with so much primal enthusiasm. Of the passion that had followed, on her couch. And, if her memory worked anything like his, of the follow-through in her bedroom, just a few days before.

"You should be careful," he said, lathering mock concern over his words. "It looks like you're getting a sunburn."

He supposed that he really did deserve the punch that she delivered to his shoulder. It was worth it, to get another look at the blush on her cheeks. He leaned closer, whispered in her ear, "Do you blush all over? Head to toe?"

He loved the little squealing noise she made in protest. He relished the thought that she would make him pay for his impertinence. Later. In private.

As much as Kat enjoyed sitting next to Rye on the bench, basking in the sun and watching the kids play ball, she felt her stomach twist into knots as the innings crept by. She caught herself glancing at her watch for the third time in as many minutes.

It was nearly five o'clock.

Kat caught Niffer looking worriedly at the stands as she came up to bat for the last time. Rye made a point of waving spiritedly to the little girl, starting up a chant. "Niff-er! Niff-er!" The child seemed to perk up at his attention, lifting her chin in a show of athletic determination. Kat almost laughed—her niece seemed to have learned the gesture from her sometime coach.

The bat cracked against the ball, and Niffer took off around the bases. When she stopped at second, she dusted off her hands, looking every bit a pro. Kat's heart almost broke, though, when the child shielded her eyes, gazing plaintively back at the stands.

Another three batters, and the game was over; Niffer's team had won by two runs. Each child trotted out toward the pitcher's mound, shaking hands with the opposition, as if they'd competed in the Olympics. Niffer joined in the group cheer that rounded out the game, and then she raced back to the benches.

"Where's Mommy?" she asked, craning her neck for a better view. "Did Mommy see me bat?"

Mike's face was creased with a mixture of anger and

fatigue. Susan sighed deeply. Kat held out her arms, ready to gather in her disappointed niece. But it was Rye who said, "Sorry, Niffer, your mother didn't come." His tone was matter-of-fact.

"But she said she would be here!"

"She must have made a mistake." Kat was grateful that Rye was being so reasonable, that he was speaking to Niffer as if she were an intelligent person, capable of handling an emotional blow. Anything else, and Kat was afraid that *she* would lose her own firm resolve to stay cheerful.

"Grown-ups don't make mistakes!" Niffer whined.

*Grown-ups make mistakes all the time*, Rye wanted to say. He felt as if his heart was breaking as he faced the result of his own biggest mistake.

Because Niffer's disappointment was yet another consequence of what he'd done with Rachel. If he had insisted on proof, way back when, if he had forced Rachel to share the results of the paternity test, then Niffer would not be so bereft today. She would have known all along that she had one loving parent to watch her accomplishments, to cheer her on.

Unable to say the words that would make everything right, he tried to do the next best thing. Pulling Niffer close to his side, he rubbed her narrow back with a sympathetic hand. "I'm sorry, kiddo. I wish your mommy had made it." He didn't. Not at all. Not yet. But he could fake the words well enough to fool a child. "I can think of one thing that might make everything better."

Niffer dug the toe of her sneaker into the ground, obviously reluctant to accept any comfort. "What?"

"How about an ice-cream cone?" That got her attention. "You can get yours with sprinkles."

"And a cherry on top?"

"Yeah. I think we can manage that." He looked up at the semicircle of adults. "Who's up for ice cream?"

Mike cleared his throat. "I think it's about time for me to head home. It's been a long day."

Susan chimed in immediately. "That makes two of us. That was such an exciting game, Niffer! Thank you for inviting us."

Mike took his time managing the two short steps from the bleachers to the ground. Rye offered him a steady forearm to balance against as he dropped the final few inches. The older man leaned close, clapping Rye on the back. "Thank you, son." The grim look in Mike's watery blue eyes let Rye know that the thanks were for more than a helping hand. "Thank you for taking care of my girls."

Kat's father wouldn't be so grateful if he knew the full story.

For that matter, neither would Kat. Rye's belly tightened as he caught her appreciative smile.

Kat waited until her parents were well on their way across the park before she turned back to her niece. "Okay, Niffer. Go get your glove, and thank Coach Noah." The little girl ran off. Kat looked at Rye. "You don't have to do this, you know."

"I want to."

"I've had a lifetime of being disappointed by my sister. Niffer had better get used to it. And I can assure you, you don't want to get wrapped up in this particular drama. It just repeats itself, over and over and over. Steer as far away as you can get."

"I'm already involved," Rye said, his voice deadly earnest.

Kat half expected him to make a joke as he said the

words. Well, not a joke exactly, but some friendly gesture of comfort, a sly side comment that would make her blush, something that would make her wish that there were a lot more days left in the spring, that New York and Richmond were not so very far apart.

But there was no secret message behind Rye's statement. There was no hidden tweak. He was stating a fact as bare as the red earth of the pitcher's mound behind him—he *was* already involved. He'd become involved the instant that she'd let him drive her home from the train station, the moment that he'd offered to renovate the studio. The second that she had leaned against him in the kitchen, pulling him close for that deeper kiss, for that soul-shocking meld that had echoed through the past couple of weeks, culminating in the afternoon they'd spent in bed—was it already four days before?

He looked like he was thinking of saying something else, but Niffer came bouncing back, glove in hand. "Can I get mint chocolate chip?"

Rye said, "If they have it."

"What flavor are you getting, Aunt Kat?"

Kat smiled and ruffled her niece's hair. "I don't eat ice cream, sweetheart."

"Never?" Niffer's eyes got very big.

"Never."

Niffer scrunched up her nose. "Do you eat ice cream, Mr. Harmon?"

"Every chance I get," he said, making the little girl laugh. "My favorite is coffee mint mango crunch."

"That's not a real flavor!"

"Hmm," Rye said, as if he were considering the matter for the very first time. "Maybe I'll just get butter pecan, then."

As they drew close to the truck, Niffer said, "Mr. Harmon, why don't you let Aunt Kat drive?"

Rye's laugh was short. "That's a great idea. What do you think, Aunt Kat? Want to get behind the wheel?"

Kat shot daggers at him with her eyes. "No, thank you," she said, making her voice as cold as the ice cream the others were about to enjoy. She couldn't resist adding a sarcastic edge. "But I really appreciate your asking."

"My pleasure," Rye said mildly.

He should know better than that, trying to egg her on in front of her niece. There was absolutely no way she was going to get behind the wheel of the silver truck. She was no idiot. She'd learned her lesson, in no uncertain terms. Only after she and Niffer were strapped into their seat belts did she think to ask, "Why do you care so much about whether I know how to drive, Niffer?"

"That's what grown-ups *do,*" the child said, as if the concept were as simple as one plus one. "I'm just a kid, so I need to have a grown-up take care of me. Gram and Pop-pop and Mommy don't love me anymore, but I thought that *you* could be my grown-up. You know. Forever." Niffer had spoken matter-of-factly, but her lower lip started to tremble as she looked out the window. "But you can't do it, Aunt Kat, because you don't know how to drive."

"Oh, sweetheart!" Kat folded her niece into a hug, looking hopelessly at Rye as he pulled out of the parking lot. He seemed to be concerned about the traffic on the road; all of his attention was riveted on the cars that streamed by. She had no idea where to start unpacking all the misunderstandings in what the child had said. "Gram and Pop-pop love you very much, but they need their house to be quiet right now, so that Pop-pop can keep getting better. Your mommy loves you, too, but she just can't be with you now. And grown-ups can take care of you, even if they don't know how to drive. *I* can take care of you."

"Will you be my forever grown-up?"

Kat's throat swelled closed with the sudden threat of tears. "Forever is a very long time, Niffer. I can promise you this. You'll never be left alone. You'll have a grown-up to help you for as long as you need someone. Okay?"

Niffer's dark eyes were very serious, as if she were weighing every syllable of Kat's vow. "Okay," she said at last.

As soon as they arrived at the ice-cream parlor, Niffer saw a friend, and she ran across the room, squealing with delight, their serious conversation completely forgotten. "Yikes," Kat said to Rye as they took their place in line. "I had no idea how to respond to that!"

Yikes, indeed, Rye thought. It had been everything he could do not to stop the truck right there in the parking lot. Not to turn to Kat and Niffer and make his confession. Not to tell them the whole truth, get the horrible weight off his chest, shed it from around his heart.

Of course, he didn't say anything. Niffer would only be confused by what he had to say. The child was fragile enough, without witnessing her aunt's justified, unbridled rage. And Kat would—rightfully—be furious when she learned what had happened. And there was still a chance—a tiny one, but a chance nonetheless—that Rachel would tell him something different when he finally tracked her down, that she would have some other explanation, some proof.

But there was something else. Something he had only just started to work out for himself.

He didn't want to lose Kat, didn't want to miss out on her gorgeous smile, her easy companionship, the unrivaled excitement that she brought to their shared bed. Sure, they seemed great together. But she *was* heading back to New York soon, with or without Rye's big confession. He was going to lose her to the big city, to her life with the ballet—there had never been any other possible ending for their story together. This reckless spring was going to be a memory, probably in a week, maybe less.

Was it really so terrible to let Kat go without knowing the truth about him and Rachel? Was it the end of the world if she went back to her real life thinking fondly of Rye, of the time they had shared in Eden Falls?

Everything would be different, of course, if he had any chance of keeping her with him. But Kat was never going to come live with him in Richmond. She'd never trim her wings and settle for a second-rate city. Not when she could have it all in New York. And he had absolutely no basis for building a business in Manhattan.

It was only fair to Kat that he keep quiet—just for another week or two. Once she was safely in her real life, Rye would face the music. He'd step up and accept his responsibility, treat Niffer like his daughter, make sure that she was safe forever, that all her needs were met. There was just no need to make a formal acknowledgment now. No reason to ruin the short time that Kat had left in Eden Falls. This was a kindness to her. Really.

Rye resolved to ignore the headache that started

pounding behind his eyes as he ran through his justifications one more time.

Niffer came skipping to the counter when they neared the front of the line. Kat was pleased to see that Rye had finally relaxed after the tension of Rachel's no-show. He laughed as he ordered up Niffer's mint chocolate chip, complete with the mandatory sprinkles and cherry. Rye's own butter-pecan cone followed. He passed the ice cream to her so that he could pull his wallet out of his pocket.

Maybe it was the fragrance of the butter-rich ice cream. Maybe it was the freshly made waffle cone. Maybe it was the bright sunshine outside, or the emotional dam she had just built for Niffer. But suddenly Kat found herself saying to the woman behind the counter, "And I'll have a scoop of chocolate, please."

"Cone or cup?"

Cup was safest. No more calories. No greater threat to her dancer fitness.

But this was the first time she'd had ice cream in years. "Waffle cone, please." Rye laughed and paid the total.

"Aunt Kat!" Niffer said as they sat down at a tiny metal table. "You got ice cream!"

"I couldn't let you have all the fun, could I?" She licked her cone, and the ice cream melted across her tongue, cold and rich and satisfying. She laughed in pure enjoyment, marveling at the simple pleasure she had denied herself for so long. Niffer joined in, and Rye wasn't far behind. Before long, Kat couldn't even have said what was so funny. What was so perfect. All she knew was that *this* was living, *this* was embracing the world in a way that she had almost forgotten how to do.

They finished their treats and walked back to the

truck. Before Rye could open the door, a siren began to wail in the distance. Kat automatically looked around for the source, and she spotted a huge fire engine, barreling down the road. The deep horn boomed as the truck approached the intersection, making Niffer huddle against her hip. "It's okay," Kat said automatically. Nevertheless, she held her niece close until the truck had disappeared.

"Hmm," Kat mused, as Rye turned the key in the ignition. "That's the first siren I've heard since I came to Eden Falls. Back in New York, I hear a dozen before breakfast."

"A dozen fire trucks?" Niffer asked.

"Some fire trucks. And police cars and ambulances, too. You can hear the noise all day long. All night, too." Even as Kat thought about it, she realized that her nights had been peaceful in Eden Falls. In fact, she routinely fell asleep as soon as her head hit the pillow, and she slept so soundly that she couldn't remember her dreams in the morning.

Not like New York, at all. Back in the noisy apartment that she shared with Haley, she woke up nearly once an hour. If it wasn't sirens, it was barking dogs, or screeching garbage trucks, or noisy people on the street, six floors below. Even when Kat *did* sleep in New York, she was disturbed by vivid dreams, by nightmares that jolted her awake as she imagined tumbling off a stage, or breaking her leg when her partner failed to catch her after some dramatic leap.

Maybe that was why her foot had healed so fast here in Eden Falls. She was sleeping well for the first time in years.

Speaking of which… "Okay, Niffer. As soon as we

get home, I want you changing into your nightgown and brushing your teeth. Got it?"

"Got it!" The little girl was already yawning as Rye pulled into the driveway.

Kat took extra care tucking Niffer into bed. She smoothed the sheets carefully, folding them so that they weren't too high on the child's chest. She kissed Niffer on her forehead, switched on the night-light, told her to "Sleep tight!" She sat beside Niffer's bed, watching as the little girl's frown smoothed out, as her breathing evened, as she slipped deep into sleep.

*Will you be my forever grown-up?* Kat's heart seized at the earnestness behind Niffer's question.

Rye was waiting in the living room.

"I am going to murder my sister," she said, whispering so that Niffer couldn't hear.

For answer, Rye held out his arms. She let him fold her close to his chest. His shirt smelled of sunlight and spring air and something that was indefinably, unmistakably *Rye*. His arms tightened around her, carving out a refuge, making her feel safe. She felt his lips brush against the crown of her head.

"I'm sorry," he murmured.

She wanted to tell him that it wasn't his fault. She wanted to tell him that Rachel had always been a flake, that Kat truly could not remember a time when she had been able to trust her sister to keep a promise. She wanted to tell him that she was grateful for all that he had done, for coming to the game, for treating them to ice cream. For coming inside now, and for holding her close.

She pulled back enough that she could look up at his face, and all the need for words disappeared. Instead, he touched his lips to hers, sudden urgency overtaking his initial chaste sweetness. Kat laced her fingers between his and led him toward her bed.

## *Chapter Eight*

Kat flexed her left ankle and walked across the dance studio floor. "I can't believe it," she said to her mother. "My foot feels so light!" She glared at the bright blue boot she had just removed.

"Are you sure you should be walking on it?" Susan fussed.

"The X-rays came back fine. Daddy's surgeon said that he could barely see where the original fracture was." That morning, Kat had insisted on visiting her father's doctor. Her foot felt entirely healed; she could not remember the last time she'd felt a twinge of pain. It was time to be shed of the boot.

Still, Susan shook her head. "I worry about you, Kat."

"Mama, I'm fine."

"You push yourself too hard. You always have. At least you've taken a bit of time off while you've been here. It seems like you and that Harmon boy are getting along quite well."

Kat laughed at her mother's not-so-subtle hint, even as she felt her cheeks flush crimson. "No, Mama," she said, meeting Susan's eyes in the mirror. "I *don't* have anything to tell you about Rye and me."

"I wasn't asking!"

"Of course not."

"It's just that I like seeing you happy. I understand that you actually had an ice-cream cone, when he took you and Niffer out after the game?"

"Who told you that?"

"Teresa Rodriguez saw the three of you sitting at a table."

"Does every single detail of everybody's life get broadcast in this town?" Kat tried to sound annoyed, but she was actually quite amused. Susan looked as pleased as a well-fed cat that she had gleaned information about Kat's not-date.

"Not every detail, dear. Teresa couldn't remember if you ordered chocolate or coffee crunch."

Kat's mock frown twisted into a laugh. "You know me. Chocolate was always my favorite. It's Rachel who likes coffee crunch."

"That's right," Susan agreed. "Besides, Teresa wasn't really reporting on ice-cream flavors. She was much more interested in telling me about your boyfriend."

"Rye isn't my boyfriend," Kat said, but she spat out the words a trifle too quickly. She wouldn't have believed herself, if she'd been on the receiving end of that denial. She tried to change the topic. "He *has* done a great job here, hasn't he?"

Susan looked around her studio, her fond smile testifying that she knew exactly what her daughter was doing. "I don't remember the last time the place looked so fine. We should be able to earn back all the lost income by autumn."

Kat's heart stuttered over a few beats. "Lost income?" she asked, as if she'd never heard the words before.

"Those checks from the fall session that Rachel never deposited? The money from spring and all those classes she let fall by the wayside?"

Susan sounded perfectly complacent as she enumerated her other daughter's shortcomings. Kat had rehearsed those words, over and over in her own mind. She'd tried to figure out how to say them simply, without affect, without any hint of the outrage that churned inside her whenever she thought of Rachel's failings. All that time Kat had rehearsed, but Susan had already known the lines. "Mama! When did you find out?"

Susan shrugged. "I've known all along. I kept hoping Rachel would pull herself together, that she'd get the money deposited for autumn term. Every day, I meant to ask her about the checks, to tell her that she wasn't being fair, failing to get the money to the bank. I never got around to it, though, with everything getting so crazy after your father got sick."

"She had an obligation to you, Mama! To the studio!"

Susan's smile reflected a lifetime of quiet hope, decades of constantly readjusting her expectations. "I knew what was going on. Fairness to me wasn't an issue. I never should have counted on Rachel to pull together an entire set of classes for spring. She's never had any interest in dance."

"She didn't have to be interested in dance! She had to be interested in *you!* In you and Daddy! She had to be interested in our family and do whatever she could to help out."

Susan shook her head sadly. "We both know that's not Rachel's strong suit, is it?"

"I don't think Rachel *has* a strong suit," Kat countered. Even as she said the spiteful words, though, she held up a hand. She didn't want to fight with her mother, to force a conversation about difficult things. "Forget I said that," she apologized. "But I still can't believe she just did nothing. That she let the studio fall apart like that."

"It wasn't all her fault, dear. I looked the other way. I knew the classes weren't going forward, and I let that happen. Sure, there were some disappointed little dancers…I know that. But I spoke to as many of the parents as I could, explained what was going on. Most of them already knew, of course. They were stopping by to bring meals, keeping me company at the hospital."

"But it didn't have to come to this! You should have called me back in December, when you first realized that things weren't on track for the spring term. I could have straightened things out before they ever got this bad!"

"And missed *Nutcracker?*"

The question cut like a knife. Of course Kat wouldn't have wanted to miss *The Nutcracker Suite*. She had been featured as the Sugar Plum Fairy. But now that she realized Susan had known what was happening, that Susan had been fully aware of how her lifetime's investment in the studio was fading away to nothing under Rachel's lazy management… "Mama, I would have come here in an instant. You know that."

"I know, dear. And honestly, that's why I didn't call

you. It's not fair that you should always be dragged in
to clean up the messes that your sister leaves behind."

Susan sounded so sad, so utterly bereft, that Kat
didn't know how to respond. She tried: "Mama, I've
been so worried. I couldn't figure out how to tell you
that the account was going to be low. I kept picturing
you writing out a check and only then finding out that
you had nothing left in the bank. The more I imagined
it, the worse it became!"

"I keep a better eye on my checkbook than that,
dear!"

"I know—or, at least, I always thought you did. I just
figured that with Daddy so sick, and you so distracted,
you hadn't even realized what was happening. I think
I started to write you a hundred different letters, out-
lining everything and offering to help in any way that
I could."

Susan shook her head. "I'm sorry this was all so
stressful for you, dear. You should know by now—honesty is the best policy."

"Well I *do* know that, in general. But because Rachel
was involved, I just felt like…" She trailed off, unsure
of how she wanted to finish that statement.

"You just felt like you had to protect your sister."

Hearing those words brought tears to Kat's eyes. She
*did* feel like she had to protect Rachel. Or, rather, she
*had* felt that way. Now she was tired of covering for
her twin, tired of spinning out reassurances and lies. It
had taken twenty-four years, but Kat was finally ready
to accept that she and Rachel were completely separate
people. She wasn't responsible for the bad decisions that
Rachel made. She couldn't change them, couldn't make
them right.

"I'm sorry, Mama," she said, and it was an apology for all the things she'd said, and all the things she hadn't.

"Your father and I will always love both you girls. But we aren't blind. We see what Rachel has done with her life. It's taken us both a number of years, but we accept that we can't do anything to change that. To change her. The most we can do is to make sure that her daughter is taken care of, that an innocent child has the comfort and stability to grow into the person she is meant to be."

Kat thought of Niffer's matter-of-fact statement on the way to get ice cream, the child's certainty that she wasn't loved. "Niffer's a good girl, but she doesn't understand what's going on here. She's afraid she's going to be abandoned."

A shadow ghosted over Susan's face. "Your father and I worried about that when we asked you to come down here. We knew that Niffer would think we were pushing her away. But we hoped that she would find new strength with you, that she would realize there was yet another person who loves her, who wants to see her succeed. And in our wildest dreams, we never imagined that your father would recover so quickly, once the house settled down a little."

"I think I was too tough on Niffer when I first got here. I made her follow too many rules."

"Nonsense," Susan said. "The proof is in the pudding. That child is better than she's been in months."

Kat nodded. She'd seen Niffer's improvement. She'd seen the difference that her presence had made. And that was why Kat had reached a decision.

When she'd arrived in Eden Falls, Kat had planned on staying seven days, maybe ten. Those days, though, had stretched into weeks. And somewhere along the way, Kat had told herself a secret—she had decided to stay for even longer. She was going to stay in Eden Falls forever.

What had she told her mother, way back when she first came to town? She would leave the National Ballet Company the instant that dancing stopped being fun.

Sure, she had planned on dancing in New York for the rest of her life. She *knew* the company, understood the way it worked, knew its system in her very bones. She had set her goals, developed her strategies, lived by her very detailed rules. But somewhere along the way, it had stopped being fun. It had taken its toll on her sleep, on her physical health, on her mental stability.

When was the last time she'd even thought of the company? When had she spoken with Haley? It had been at least a week. No, almost two. Somehow, ballet gossip had become less compelling while she worked on finalizing things here at the studio. The hundred and one backstage dramas that she and Haley usually shared had lost a little—no, a *lot*—of their appeal. Life had come to seem so much richer, here in Eden Falls.

Besides, Kat could never get in shape in time for the *Coppelia* auditions. Of course she had always wanted to dance Swanilda. She was perfect for the role. But she could not deny that she had lost some muscle mass, with her foot confined to a cast. And she'd put on a couple of pounds, indulging in real meals, like a real woman, spending time with a real family.

Before, that weight would have sent her to the workout room, driven her to exercise as if she were harried by a thousand demons. But not anymore. Not now that Kat had made up her mind.

Not now that she was going to be Niffer's forever grown-up.

Amanda and Susan would just have to get used to driving her around town. They wouldn't mind, really. Shared drives would be a chance for all of them to spend time together.

Once Kat made up her mind, she felt as light as air, as certain as she'd been of anything since she'd been fourteen years old, since she'd headed up to New York to seek her fortune. She turned to face her mother. "Mama, I have something to tell you. I think I've known it for a while. Since I realized that we needed someone to teach the Advanced Showcase for the spring term."

"Darling, I can—"

"No, Mama. You can't. But I can. And I want to. I want to stay in Eden Falls." She saw that Susan didn't believe her, didn't truly understand, but she laughed all the same. "This feels right to me, Mama."

"But New York… Everything you've worked for. Everything you've spent your entire life—"

"Not my entire life, Mama. I spent more years here, with you and Daddy, than I've spent in New York. And it's time for me to come home now." Kat surprised herself, realizing how wonderful those words sounded. "It's time. Come on, Mama. Let me show you the calendar I set up on your computer."

She couldn't say whether she laughed because of Susan's expression of pleased surprise, or because her body felt so light and balanced as she crossed the studio floor without the hated walking cast.

By Sunday, Kat's foot felt as strong as it had before her fracture. She had tried hard to limit her time at the

barre, conscientiously keeping from stretching her prac-
tices into hours-long torture sessions. Nevertheless, she
was overjoyed to find that her strength had rebounded
so quickly.

The absence of the boot made it easier to carry
food to the sprawling picnic tables in the park. It was
Sunday—May Day and Eden Falls's traditional Family
Day celebration. In honor of the spring festivities, Kat
had worn a green blouse. She'd actually bought it for
the occasion, dragooning Amanda into driving her to
one of the tiny shops on Main Street. Her cousin had
been only too happy to help her pick out something
more appropriate than New York black. Eventually,
she'd have to choose a whole new wardrobe.

For now, though, Kat wasn't worried about clothes.
Instead, she was worried about balancing the pair of
desserts she had made with Susan. The lemon chess
pie was a family favorite, and Niffer had begged for
blackberry cobbler. Kat suspected that the child really
just wanted to eat spoonfuls of the traditional whipped-
cream topping.

"Go ahead, Niffer," Kat said, as they arrived at the
park. "Go play with the other kids."

"I don't know anyone."

"Of course you do. I can see three different kids on
your T-ball team."

"Will you come with me?"

Kat started to sigh in exasperation, but she thought
better of herself. If Niffer wanted an adult's company,
that was a small enough gift that Kat could provide.
"You go over there, and I'll come see you in a moment.
I just need to set these things down."

Kat added the desserts to a picnic table that looked
like it might break under the combined weight of all

the baked goods. The city of Eden Falls certainly knew how to throw a party. Kat could already smell hot dogs and hamburgers cooking on five or six grills. Another table was laden with salads, and there had to be a half-dozen coolers scattered under the trees, full of soft drinks and sweet tea.

After snagging a diet soda for herself and making sure that Susan and Mike were similarly cared for, Kat went to uphold her promise to her niece. Niffer came running up as Kat approached the gravel-covered playground.

"We're bored!" the child announced.

"How can you be bored?" Kat shaded her eyes, gesturing at all of the playground equipment. "You have a castle, and swings and a slide!"

"We *always* play on those. We need a new game."

A new game. Niffer had no idea just how foolish she was, coming to *Kat* for a new game. Ballet was the only game Kat had known for years. Somehow, she didn't think the kids would be excited about completing a hundred pliés. Then again, they might really get into the grand battements—those were basically an invitation to kick anyone who got within striking distance.

Somewhere between thinking about leg warm-ups and arm stretches, though, Kat remembered something Susan had said, weeks before. She smiled mischievously at Niffer and said, "How about Magic Zoo?"

"What's that?" Niffer sounded suspicious. Nevertheless, a half-dozen kids drew closer. Kat was going to have to make this good.

"First of all, everyone has to choose an animal, something you can find at the zoo. Think of it, but don't tell anyone yet!" She waited while the children selected their guises for the game. Several closed their eyes, as if they were imagining an entire menagerie. What had Susan said? That Kat had played the game by selecting crayons out of a bucket? The colors were supposed to mean something…. Well, there weren't any crayons around, so Kat was just going to have to improvise.

"Okay. Everyone choose a number between one and five. Got it?" Every child nodded, as serious as if they were completing a military exercise. "Now, listen carefully. Each number is a different magical ability. I'm going to tell you the magical abilities, and then you'll have to figure out how your animal uses its special skill. Everyone is going to close their eyes while you do that, and I'm going to hide this…" Kat hadn't thought that far ahead. What was she going to hide? What could the kids hunt for in their imaginary game?

"This bandanna." Rye made the announcement from directly behind her. She spun around to face him, astonished that she hadn't heard him approach. He'd been up in Richmond for the past week, tied up in business meetings, cementing the details on half a dozen new projects that had grown out of his attending that Chamber of Commerce dinner.

She had phoned him a week ago, after talking to her mother.

She had told him about her decision, about her choice to stay in Eden Falls.

He'd been shocked into silence at first, and then he'd started to apologize, started to explain that he had to stay in Richmond, that his business was there. She had laughed and told him that she knew. She understood. It was horrible, rotten luck that she hadn't returned home before he had left, but there were only a couple of hours of freeway between them. Somehow, some way, they would make it work.

She'd even said: "Rye, I know how it's been before.
I know there were women who tied you to Eden Falls.
Who made you feel like you had to stay here. I'm not
those women. It's never going to be that way between
us."

His voice had thickened then, as if he were overwhelmed with some emotion. He'd cleared his throat,
said her name, almost as if he were bracing himself to
make some grand confession. But that was silly. There
wasn't anything for him to confess.

She'd missed him fiercely for the past week—more
than she could have imagined, just a month before. But
now he was back in Eden Falls, for Family Day. He was
standing beside her, lowering his voice as if he were
telling the children ghost stories at a campfire. He brandished his crimson bandanna before the children's fascinated faces. "This bandanna can work magic spells,"
he said. "It belongs to a princess who is being held cap-
tive in a tower, locked in by an evil magician. The princess can only be rescued by someone smart enough and
brave enough to find the bandanna and wear it."

Kat watched the children's eyes grow wide at the
fairy tale that Rye spun. "Okay," she said. "Remember your numbers now. One means you can fly. Two
lets you be invisible. Three lets you walk through
walls. Four gives you the ability to change into another animal. And five…" She trailed off. What was a
fifth magical ability? What else could she factor into
the kids' game?

Rye picked up the instructions, as if he'd known
them all along. "And five lets you read minds."

Perfect. Kat flashed him a smile before she said,
"Okay. Everyone cover your eyes, while the evil magician hides the bandanna!" The kids took the responsi-

bility seriously—they buried their faces in the crooks of their arms. Kat waited until Rye had crossed the playground, planted the bandanna in the shadows at the base of the slide and sidled back to her. "All right, animals!" she shouted. "I'm going to count to five. And when I finish, you'll all be in the Magic Zoo!"

She drew out the count dramatically, stretching out the numbers until she shouted, "Five!" The kids flew off, lumbering like invisible elephants, roaring like flying lions.

Rye laughed as they tumbled across the playground. "That should keep them busy for a while."

"That was the idea," Kat said smugly.

Rye was suddenly nervous, standing alone with Kat. Every night for the past week, he'd tried to reach Rachel, calling her cell phone, sending text messages. While waiting for a response, he'd worked on how to tell Kat the truth about Niffer. He'd started to phone Kat a dozen times, mapping out the words in his mind, figuring out every single thing he had to say, so that it would be proper, so that she would understand.

And every time, he found he just couldn't tell her over the phone. And now, in the park, surrounded by the Eden Falls Family Day celebration, he had to wait yet again.

The breeze carried a whiff of her honey-apricot scent toward him, and he couldn't help but take a step closer. "So," he said, after swallowing hard. "You're wearing green to celebrate your jailbreak?"

"Jailbreak?" She looked confused.

He nodded toward her foot. "The boot?"

"Finally!" She spun in a circle, laughing. "I can move again. I didn't realize how confining that thing was until I had it off. But I'm wearing green for my new life, here in Eden Falls. For spring."

"It looks great on you," he said. "It sets off the color of your eyes." He couldn't resist trailing his hand along the garment's sleeve, touching the fold on the inside of her elbow. The fabric was nearly as soft as the tender flesh it covered. He felt the shiver that rocketed through Kat's body, and he almost laughed out loud.

Before he could lower his voice, though, before he could think of something that would make her move one step closer, a tumble of kids frothed around them, like puppies overturning a basket.

"That was too easy!"

"We found the bandanna!"

"Hide it again!"

Rye laughed and nodded toward Niffer, who brandished the bandanna as if it were a carnival prize. "You go ahead and hide it now. Find a better place. You can use the whole park."

The kids shrieked with excitement, barely managing to cover their eyes. Niffer flew off toward the castle, intent on securing her treasure. Soon enough, the entire herd had thundered away again.

"So," Rye said, stepping closer to Kat. "Where were we?"

"I think I was about to tell you my foot is as good as new." She flexed one of her long legs, extending her toes in a graceful arch that defied the strappy sandals she wore.

Laughing, he closed his hands around her waist. "Wasn't this where we started, ten years ago? With you stretching that leg?" He pulled her close and slanted his lips over hers. He might need to keep this kiss clean enough for a public park, but there was no reason it had to be the fraternal gesture he had tried—and failed—to deliver years before.

"I guess it was," Kat whispered against his throat. "Even though I didn't realize we were starting *anything* that day." She settled her arms around his neck, relishing the feeling that he was claiming her, announcing that she was his, at least for today, for as long as they were both in Eden Falls. She caught her breath against a sudden pang at the thought of being separated from Rye, of losing him forever.

No. She had already told him this. It was best that he continue with his business in Richmond. He had planned so long, worked so hard. He would hate her forever, if she asked him to give up his dreams. That was why she'd been patient for the past week. Why she'd managed not to phone him every single night. She had to be content with everything she had—and do her best to lure him to Eden Falls, early and often. "I have an idea," she whispered against the corner of his mouth. "For how we might *end* this. At least for today."

He chuckled and pulled her closer.

Even as she started to remind him—remind them both—that they were standing in a public park, in broad daylight, there was the sound of one person clapping. The noise was sharp, irregular, and Kat whirled around, barely noticing that Rye's hand on her waist helped her keep her balance on the soft grass.

"What would Mom think, Kat? Should I go get her, so she can see what you're really like?"

Kat recognized the voice, even before her mind processed the old words. "Rachel," Kat said, the two syllables clattering between them like hail.

"Kat," her sister replied evenly. "Rye."

Kat stared into eyes that matched her own silver-gray. But those other eyes were rimmed with heavy eyeliner and multiple coats of mascara. And framed by hair that had been dyed a brilliant, unnatural magenta. Rachel had put on weight since the last time Kat had seen her; the line of her jaw was soft, and there were bags beneath her eyes. But there was no mistaking her twin. And no mistaking the oath that Rye muttered, barely under his breath.

"What are you doing here?" Kat asked, scarcely aware that her fingers were curling into fists.

"You were in the room when I called Mom and Dad. I said I'd visit my baby."

"You were supposed to be here a week ago. Niffer expected you at her T-ball game."

"Niffer?" Rachel's laugh was as harsh as fingernails on a chalkboard. "Who came up with that idiotic name?"

"I did." Rye stepped forward.

Rachel's eyes narrowed. "There was nothing wrong with Jenny."

Rye answered evenly, as if he were measuring out each word with the level in his tool kit. "Except for the fact that she hated it."

Rachel's old look of cunning crept across her face. A block of ice settled in Kat's belly, and she realized that there was another conversation going on in front of her, a whole set of words that she could not understand, dared not predict. "Rye?" she asked, her fingers clutching at his forearm. "What's going on here?"

"Yes," Rachel said. "Why don't you tell her what's going on, Rye?"

There it was again, that complicated flash of meaning between Kat's boyfriend and her twin. Rye's face was ironed into lean planes; she heard him swallow hard. When he spoke, the words were taut, pulled thin as wire. "I don't want to do this here, Rachel. Let's get out of the park, at least. We can talk at your parents' house."

"But Rye! It's Family Day!" Rachel's response was cold, mocking.

Of course Rachel was doing this. Rachel had caught Kat kissing Rye. She was jealous of something she could never, ever have. Rachel had always been that way, whenever she saw Kat succeeding. Kat started to make excuses to Rye, started to explain away her sister's bad behavior. The jagged look in Rye's eyes, though, froze her to the spot. There was more to Rachel's riposte than the sibling rivalry Kat had lived with all her life.

Before Kat could tease out the meaning of what was going on in front of her, a brightly colored bullet shot across the clearing. "Mommy!" Niffer screamed. "Mommy, you're here!"

"Of course, baby. How could your mother be anywhere else?" Rachel put a curious emphasis on the word *mother,* as if she were staking claim to the title for the very first time. Nevertheless, Kat watched Rachel pull away from her daughter's clutching fingers, saw Rachel glare at Rye as if *he* were responsible for Niffer's clinginess.

Rachel's gaze was momentarily obscured by a cloud of Niffer's jet-black hair. Jet-black hair, like Kat's own. Like Rachel's, when it wasn't dyed.

But Niffer had eyes to match that hair. Eyes far darker than Kat's, than Rachel's. Eyes as dark as Rye's.

And as Kat looked more closely, she saw other resemblances, as well. The line of Niffer's jaw. The tilt of her nose. The way that she clutched a red bandanna, tight in her left hand.

Left.

Like Rye.

Suddenly, everything was bright around the four of them, as if they were illuminated from within. There was a buzz in Kat's ears, a humming sound. The roof of her mouth had gone numb, and she realized that her fingertips were tingling. She felt isolated from the world. Cut off. Alone.

"You're her father," Kat said.

Those three words jolted through Rye like a bolt cutter.

His first response was relief. At last, his secret was out. He was through with the lies, done with the stupid disclosure he'd been struggling to make since Josh had told him the truth.

His second response, though, was sickening fear. The color had drained from Kat's cheeks; she looked like she had seen a ghost.

He should have found a way to tell Kat sooner. He should have owned the situation instead of waiting for her to uncover it this way. If he'd stepped up to the plate, he could have broken the news more gently, explained everything more completely. Even over the phone—he could have protected her, guided her, made her see how this had happened.

Well, he hadn't chosen the time or the place, but he could still make Kat understand. Tenderly, he reached out to take her arm, to guide her toward the nearest bench.

She pulled away from him as if his hands were acid. "Don't touch me!" she snapped. Her voice was high.

Broken. She sounded as if she were fracturing into a million jagged pieces.

"Kat, it was a long time ago." He pitched his voice low, unconsciously slipping into the comforting register that he would use for an injured animal, for a sick child.

"Rachel is my *sister.*" Kat's eyes were wide, unfocused. "You slept with my *sister!*"

Of course, what she said was true, the bare words. But there were a dozen things wrong with that sentence, a hundred ways that the facts failed to capture the reality. Starting with: "It was six years ago. We only dated for a few weeks."

"You told me that! But you never said you *slept* with her!"

Rye glared at Rachel, at the pink-haired harpy that was laughing at him over the head of her distraught daughter. "Tell her, Rachel. Tell her that it never meant anything."

Impossibly, Rachel was throwing back her head to laugh. But no. That wasn't *impossible.* Rachel had been manipulating Kat for years. Manipulating him, as well, even when he hadn't realized they were enmeshed in a game.

Now Rachel settled a hand over her daughter's— *their* daughter's—head. "I don't know, Rye," she said. "I wouldn't say that it never meant *anything.*"

A strangled sound caught at the back of Kat's throat. Instinctively, Rye glanced around to see who was watching them. The kids were all playing at the far end of the park, shouting and running around in circles. A couple of the adults had glanced their way, but no one was close enough to hear. Kat whispered, "Were you planning on telling me anytime soon, Rye?"

"I didn't know... I only found out last week."

Rachel laughed—a harsh bark. "Not very observant, then, were you?"

"You stay out of this!" He would have said more, would have lashed out with the anger that flashed through his chest, but he saw Niffer cringe against her mother's side. He forced himself to lower his voice, and he bit out the words, "Rachel, you are not helping here."

"It's not my job to help you, is it?"

"Mommy?" Niffer whispered, but her question was perfectly clear. "Why is Mr. Harmon angry?"

"I don't know, baby," Rachel said, her voice as sweet as molasses dregs. "I think because he was caught lying to Aunt Kat."

"Gram says it's bad to tell a lie."

Rachel's laugh was loud, like the call of a raucous jay. "Yes, baby. Telling a lie is definitely bad."

Rye thought his heart would break as Niffer turned toward him, her jet-black eyes enormous in her pale face. "You shouldn't tell lies, Mr. Harmon."

"It wasn't a lie," he said, before he'd thought out a way to explain all of this to a child. "It was more of a... secret." As Rachel laughed again, Rye turned to Kat. The color had come back to her face with a vengeance; her cheeks were spotted with two hectic patches. He could hear her breath coming in short pants, and she hugged herself like a wounded creature. "Kat," he said. "Let me explain."

Kat heard his plea, and her belly twisted into a pulsing knot. Even so, she felt disconnected from her body, cut loose from the arms and legs and heart that she was so used to working, every minute of every day. Her hurt and fury cut her off from herself, like a shimmering electric curtain. She wasn't certain where her words came from, where she found the strength to ask, "What could you possibly have to say? How could you possibly have forgotten to mention something so important?"

It wasn't fair. It had never been fair. Rachel had always gotten her own way, done whatever she wanted to do, and damn the consequences. Rachel had never bothered with goals, with strategies. Rachel had always broken the rules. Rachel had lied to Susan and Mike all her life, lied to Kat, lied to her own daughter, Niffer.

Why *Rye?* Of all the men that Rachel could have had, why did it have to be Rye?

Kat's thoughts collapsed in on themselves, sending up embers of memories. She was back in the high school auditorium, her cheeks wet with tears of adolescent frustration, with shame at being laughed at by the high school kids. She was staring at Rye, confused by his kiss, even as she was delighted by the tenderness he had shown her.

She'd been mortified to find her sister waiting for her, embarrassed to hear that Susan was waiting outside, ready to drive them both home. Rachel had eyed Kat with a knowing expression. Rachel had bided her time, never telling Susan and Mike what she'd seen backstage in the high school auditorium. Rachel had known even then, even when they were in eighth grade, that she was going to set her hat for Rye Harmon.

But Rachel couldn't have done it alone. She couldn't have broken Kat's heart without an accomplice. She couldn't have turned Kat's life upside down without Rye playing along.

"Rye," Kat said, and her heart was breaking. "How could you?"

He sighed, unsure of the answer, even as he knew he

had to find one. "I swear I didn't know, Kat. Not until last week."

"Last *week?* You admitted that you dated her, but it went a bit beyond that, didn't it? A *lot* beyond that."

"I should have told you everything. I didn't think it mattered." He hadn't wanted it to matter.

Kat shook her head vehemently, clearly rejecting his excuses. "Where?" she demanded. "Where did you sleep with her?"

There wasn't any good answer, nothing that would help Kat to understand. "It doesn't matter."

"Was it in her house? Rye, were you on her couch? In her bedroom?" Kat twisted her mouth around the ugly questions.

Rye knew that she had to be picturing the room where they had embraced, where he had first realized the fragility of the soul inside her steel. Even now, he could picture Kat's mouth open in a perfect O of ecstasy as she shuddered beneath him, as she rode the waves of pleasure that he had given to her—*her*—because she was the woman he wanted to be with. She was the woman he loved.

*The woman he loved.* The realization tore through him, dragging him away from the perfection of memories, pushing him back to the terrible, horrible *now*. He loved Kat, and he had somehow managed to hurt her more than he had ever hurt anyone before. He shrugged helplessly, unable to imagine words that would reassure her.

Tears streamed down her cheeks, and her breath came in short gasps. "I thought we were working together, Rye."

"We were!"

Rachel chortled at his protest, even as Niffer asked her mother what was going on.

Kat could not believe Rye. Not when his secrets involved Rachel. Not when they involved the sister who had let her down—let her entire family down—so many times in the past. Kat laughed herself, but there was no humor behind her words. "I fell for everything, didn't I? Hook, line and sinker. Oh my God, I am so stupid!"

"Kat, you know that isn't true. Listen to me. This doesn't have to change anything between us. This doesn't have to be the end."

"Really? Rye Harmon, why should I believe anything you say, ever again?" Her words chased after each other, tumbling from her lips as if they had a life of their own. She was hurt. She was embarrassed. She was utterly terrified that Rye was telling her the truth now, and she feared that he was not. She didn't know what to believe, not anymore. Not after she'd been so blind.

The only way she could protect herself, the only way she could defend the wounded perimeter of her heart, was to lash out—fast, and furious, and with the sharpest weapon she had in her arsenal. "You don't know how to have a real relationship, do you, Rye? That's why you moved to Richmond in the first place. So that you wouldn't have to deal with *feelings,* with responsibility. Everything was fine between us, as long as we were both just having fun. But when things got serious, you shut down. When you learned the truth about Niffer, you stayed away—avoided me for an entire week! You chose Rachel and Richmond over Niffer, Rye. Over me."

How could she have let this happen?

Her mother had told her to be happy. Her mother had

told her to relax her rigid rules. Her mother had told her to take each day as it came, to enjoy herself.

And this was the result.

Kat had set her rules, years ago, for one simple reason. Rules protected her. Rules kept her safe. Rules preserved her from the jagged pain that was shattering her even now. She never should have relaxed her standards, never should have given in. She never should have let Rye take the fortress of her heart, of her solitude, of all the protective isolation she had built when she was a teenager.

"Kat, I never chose Rachel over you. I stayed in Richmond because I've spent the past week trying to figure out how to tell you the truth. You have to understand. I never meant to hurt you."

"But you did," she sobbed. "You really did, Rye. I thought we had something special. I thought there was a real connection between us. I thought you understood who I am, and what I want, what I *need*."

He had one last chance here. One final opportunity to use words to make it right. "I do, Kat. I promise you, I do."

She shook her head hard enough that her easy chignon fell loose about her face. "No! If you truly understood me, you would know that this is one thing that I can never, ever forgive."

He reached out for her, desperate to change her mind.

"Don't touch me!" That shout was loud enough to get attention. Out of the corner of his eye, Rye could see faces turn. He could measure the moment when everyone recognized Rachel, when they discovered the drama unfolding in their midst.

"Kat," he said again, stepping closer, trying to keep

this horrible, awkward conversation between the two of them.

"Leave me alone!" Kat jerked her arm up, pushing his away. The contact hurt, but not nearly as much as the desolate look in her eyes.

"Hey, buddy." Brandon's voice floated across the playground as his cousin jogged up to his side. "What's going on?"

"Nothing," Rye said tersely. Kat turned away, trying to hide her tear-streaked face. He took a step to close the new distance between them. Before he could say anything, though, Brandon's fingers closed on his biceps.

"Rye," Brandon said. "Buddy—"

"Leave me alone, *buddy.*" He jerked his arm away, letting some of his frustration curl his fingers into fists. "Kat and I are just talking."

"It doesn't look like Kat wants to talk right now." Brandon pitched his voice low.

"Kat—" Rye appealed.

"Please," she said through her tears. "Just leave me alone. I don't want to hear anymore. I can't think about this right now."

"Kat—" he tried one more time.

Brandon shouldered between them. "Come on, buddy—"

Hopeless, helpless anger flashed crimson across Rye's vision. Anger with Brandon, for acting like the town sheriff. Anger with himself, for hurting Kat so deeply. Anger with Rachel, for dragging him into this entire ridiculous mess so long ago, for avoiding his calls until she could inflict maximum damage here, today.

Rye turned on his heel and strode across the park, making his way past the laughing children and their naive game of rescuing the princess. He barely resisted the urge to shout at them, to tell them that the princess was never going to be rescued. The princess was lost forever.

## Chapter Nine

Kat felt everyone's eyes turn toward her as Rye stalked off. Brandon took a step closer, asking, "Are you all right?"

"I'm fine," she said, knowing she was lying. How much did he know? How much had he overheard of her fight with Rye?

Her cousin Amanda appeared out of nowhere. "Kat!" Amanda's eyes slid over to Rachel, to the still-cowering Niffer. "What's going on? Are you okay?"

"I'm fine," she repeated, looking around for an escape, knowing that she had to get away from everyone. Amanda seemed to be the Pied Piper; half of Eden Falls followed behind her. A couple of people called out to Rachel, welcoming her home. A few more hollered for Susan and Mike to join the crowd. Kat looked at the sea of faces, and she felt like she was going to faint.

Susan took one glance at her daughters and set her

lips in a grim line. "Rachel," she said, and then she reached out for Kat. "Come sit down, baby. You look like you've seen a ghost! We're all worried about you."

Baby. That was what Rachel called her daughter. Called *Rye's* daughter. One more time, Kat said, "I'm fine." When it was obvious that no one believed her, she looked her mother right in the eye. "Did you know?"

"Know what?" Susan honestly looked perplexed.

"About Rye and Rachel. About Niffer." Kat watched the crowd jostle closer. She imagined the whispers that were even now skating away to those out of earshot. The scandal would be front-page news in seconds.

Susan said, "Dear, I don't know what you're talking about." Even as her kindly face registered concern, though, Kat read sudden comprehension in her eyes. There. Every single person in Eden Falls would add one and one together. They would all know how Kat had been deceived.

Kat pushed away her mother's fluttering hands. "I have to go, Mama."

"Where?"

"I don't know. I just have to get out of here."

Susan looked around helplessly. "Let me get your father—"

"No, you stay with Daddy. And Niffer, too. And Rachel." She practically spat her sister's name.

Susan sounded panicked as she said, "I don't want you going off on your own, dear. You've had a terrible shock. Amanda can—"

"No!" Kat heard the anguish in her voice, and she knew she shouldn't be shouting at her mother, shouldn't take her anger and pain out on an innocent victim. There had been enough innocent victims this spring—herself and Niffer heading up the list. But Kat couldn't hand herself over to Amanda's solicitous care. She couldn't face her cousin's concerned look, her certain questions. Not when Amanda knew so much already. Not when Amanda had been there, the night that Kat and Rye first… She forbade herself to think about that night, to think about the couch, to think about the white-hot heat that had… Forcing her voice to a quieter register, Kat said, "I'm fine, Mama. I just need to get away from here."

And then, because she knew she could not hold back the fresh tears, because she knew she could not bear the pitying looks of the crowd, because she knew she did not have the first idea of what she could ever say or do to make everything—anything—right again, Kat turned on her heel and strode across the park.

She surprised herself by arriving at the parking lot. Rye's truck hulked in a nearby spot, gleaming silver in the bright afternoon sunlight. And all of a sudden, Kat knew what she had to do.

She glanced at her watch. Half an hour. Plenty of time.

Ignoring the people who must still be staring at her, Kat pulled open the truck's door. His keys were exactly where she expected to find them—on the floor mat, just where he had dropped them the night he took her out to the diner. The night he brought her home. The night he fooled her into thinking she was special to him, that they had shared something beautiful and meaningful and unique.

Her mind was filled with memories of Rye. The weight of him, settling over her. The heat of his mouth on hers. The wild passion that he had stroked to life between her thighs. The crashing release that he had given her, the bonds that had pulled them closer to each other.

Or so she had thought.

Her fingers trembled as she picked up the keys. Even as she wanted to block Rye's voice from her memory forever, she heard him instructing her. Foot on the brake. Key in the ignition. Turn the key. Shift into Drive.

Before, when she had driven the truck, she had been haunted by all the things that could go wrong. She had cringed at every sound, shied away from every fast motion.

This time, she did not care. She did not worry about damaging the vehicle, about embarrassing herself in front of the patient man who had sat in the passenger's seat. She did not think about what it meant to conquer a simple summit, the sort of responsibility that nearly every person she knew had accomplished when they were mere teenagers, when they only *thought* they were burdened by all the cares in the world.

Remembering Rye's instruction, Kat looked left, then right, then left again. She shifted her foot off the brake, fully ready when the truck's massive engine began to pull it forward. She gripped the wheel and drove the pickup out of the parking lot.

Afterward, she could not have said how many stop signs she confronted. She could not have told whether the single traffic light was red or green. She could not recount how many trucks she passed, or how many passed her. She only knew that she drove the pickup to the train station, to the empty asphalt patch where her homecoming had begun, a month before.

Was it only a month? Kat felt as if she'd changed so much. When she had arrived in Eden Falls, she had been bound by her lifelong mantra—goals, strategies, rules. The *rules* especially—she'd had one for every situation. She'd known what to expect of herself, of others.

But in one short month, she'd discovered a new way of living. A way that included Magic Zoo and ice cream and late-night bacon blue cheeseburgers and glasses of beer swilled at an actual roadside bar. What had Susan said? That she wanted to see Kat embrace her impulsive side. Well, here was impulse, all right. Let Susan and Mike and Rye and Rachel settle everything, after Kat was back in New York. They'd work it out between them.

Kat shifted the truck into Park and dropped the keys on the floor mat. Entering the tiny station building, she immediately realized she was alone—no one to sell her a ticket. That was fine. She could buy one on the train.

Kat patted the tiny purse that swung from her shoulder. She had bought it when she splurged on her green blouse—was it only the day before? She'd somehow thought she'd been changing herself, remaking herself so that she could live in Eden Falls for the rest of her life.

Ironic, wasn't it? Kat had finally realized she could stay in Eden Falls, work beside her mother at the Morehouse Dance Academy, teach the Advanced Showcase class, and *be happy,* maybe for the first time in years.

But that was before the *Family* Day picnic. That was before she'd learned the truth about her family. About her sister and the man that Kat had come to love.

No. She couldn't say that. Couldn't believe it. She could not love Rye. Not after what he'd done. Not after the secret he had kept from her. Sure, he might only have known that he was Niffer's father for a week. But he had known that he'd slept with Rachel long before that. Slept with her, and kept the truth from Kat. Slept with her, and minimized the connection, made it sound casual, like nothing more than a meaningless fling.

No. She could not love Rye.

She had only *thought* she loved him. She'd been deceived. Rye had presented himself under false pretenses. Whatever emotions Kat thought she had felt were lies. Lies, like his silence had been.

She couldn't sit still on the station's hard wooden bench. She needed to pace, needed to shed some of the physical energy that still sparked through her. She wrapped her arms around her belly and measured out her steps, planting her heels as firmly as if she'd never been hampered by a walking boot.

She should call Haley. Let her roommate know she was coming back to their apartment. Kat was going to make the midnight deadline for the *Coppelia* sign-up after all. She was returning to her life as a dancer.

Forget about *fun*. Dance was her career.

And all that justifying she had done before, all the ways she had convinced herself that Eden Falls was right for her? That was just Kat's tactic for grappling with fear, just like she'd suffered from homesickness, years before, when she'd first moved to New York. She had been *afraid* to reach out for the role she really wanted. She had abandoned her goals, slashed through her strategies, trampled every one of her rules. All because she was afraid she might not have what it took to dance Swanilda.

What had Rye said to her, the day she ran his truck into the ditch? She had to get back on the horse that had thrown her? She had refused then, but she was never going to back down again. Ballet had thrown her, when she developed her stress fracture. Well, it was high time for her to head back to New York. To get back to her real life.

Of course, she didn't have a way to reach Haley. Her cell phone was useless here. And she didn't have any change with her; she couldn't place a call from the ancient pay phone in the corner.

What did it matter, though? She had a credit card; she could buy her train ticket north. And once she got back to the city, she had an apartment full of belongings.

Kat paced some more. This was what Susan had hoped for, wasn't it? That Kat would cast off all bonds, all limits. Susan just hadn't realized that her daughter would use her hard-won freedom to return to New York, without planning, without luggage, without restraint.

She crossed to the wall of windows and pushed her cheek against the glass to peer down the long line of tracks. No train in sight yet. She glanced at her watch. Five minutes.

A strong breeze gusted through the station as the far door opened and someone stepped inside.

When had she learned to recognize the sound of Rye's footsteps? She knew he was standing behind her. She could hear him breathing. She knew that he swallowed hard. She could imagine him reaching toward her, flexing his hands, letting his empty fists fall to his sides.

"Kat," he said. "Please."

She breathed in deeply, as if the gesture could pour steel down her spine, could give her the strength to withstand the next five minutes, until the Clipper chugged into the station. Setting her jaw so that she couldn't possibly say the wrong thing, she turned to face him.

Rye marveled at the change that had come over Kat in the four weeks since they had last been at the train station. Then, she had been a frigid woman, desperate to control the world around her, iced over with frozen fury at the dancer's body that had failed her. Now, he saw a passionate creature, someone who embraced challenge and battled it on her own ground. He had seen her consumed by passion, not just beneath his fingers, not just in response to his lips, but in the very way she tackled living every day.

He had tested a hundred conversational openings on the way from the park, so intent on finding the words to keep Kat in Eden Falls that he nearly crashed his brother Noah's sports car a dozen times. He thought he had worked out the perfect plea, but now all those eloquent words fled him. He was reduced to repeating the only thing that mattered: "Kat, please. Don't leave me."

She glanced at her watch.

He was afraid to check his own, afraid to discover how little time was left for him to plead his case. Instead, he took advantage of her silence, spinning out all the things he'd meant to tell her, all the confessions he'd longed to make. "I know it seems like I deceived you. Hell, I *did* deceive you. And I can't imagine how I've made you feel. But you have to understand—I didn't know. Not until I saw Josh Barton in Richmond. I've spent the past week trying to find Rachel and ask her if it was true. Trying to figure out the right way to tell you. Trying to figure out all the right words."

"But you didn't tell me. Rachel did."

She spoke so quietly that he almost missed her

words. She directed her speech to the knot of her fingers, white-knuckled across her flat belly.

Nevertheless, he took heart that she had said *something*. If she was willing to spare him any words at all, that meant they were having a conversation. They were still communicating. The door between them was still open, even if he could barely make out a glimmer of light on her side.

Even though he knew he was fighting against time, even though he was certain the hourglass was draining away, he chose his words carefully. "I wish it hadn't happened that way. I wish I had told you the second that Josh walked away, in Richmond. I wish I had taken out my phone, dialed your number and told you everything, all at once."

She did not seem to hear him. Instead, she looked around the train station, like a woman in a trance. "Did you know it was me that first day? Did you think I was Rachel?"

This time, she met his eyes. Her silver gaze was cloudy, shrouded in misery. He heard the tremble behind her words, knew she was questioning the very foundation of everything they'd had together.

He held her gaze and answered slowly, setting every syllable between them like an offering on an altar. "I could never confuse the two of you. Ever. You are so much more than the color of your hair and eyes, the shape of your face. Kat, think back to that day. *I* was the one who called out to you, across the parking lot. I knew who you were, even when you pretended not to recognize me."

She had done that, hadn't she? She had played a child's game, because she was afraid of getting caught in a woman's world. And here she was, more tangled than she'd ever thought she could be.

She thought back to the day she had arrived in town, on that unseasonably warm afternoon, with the heat shimmering off the asphalt parking lot. Then, she had thought she would melt. Now, she feared she would never be warm again. She rubbed at her arms and said, "But after that. When you started seeing me with Niffer. There must have been some part of you that knew. You must have wanted me to be Rachel, to be the woman you'd already slept with. You must have wanted us to be the family that the three of you never were."

The words ate through to the core of her heart. In all her life, she had never been jealous of Rachel. Frustrated, yes. Angry with her poor choices. Disappointed by all the times she had made promises, all the times she had lied.

But this was the first time that Kat had ever truly envied her sister. The first time she had ever wanted to change places, to *be* Rachel. Then she would have known what it was like to be the Morehouse sister Rye first made love to. To be the twin he had first chosen. To be the woman he had been drawn to from the start. If Kat had been Rachel, she never would have let Rye out of her sight.

"No," he said, and it seemed like he was damning every one of her dreams. "Kat, I never wanted you to be anyone but who you are. Don't you understand? I never loved Rachel. I'm ashamed to admit this, but I barely *knew* her. She came to me when I had just graduated from college. She'd been dating one of my fraternity brothers. She wanted to make him jealous. I was flattered and stupid and a little naive. I only knew her for a few weeks, but I think I believed that I could…save her. That I could…I don't know…make her be happy and healthy and whole."

Kat *did* know. She knew how many times she had hoped that she could reach out to her twin. How many times Rachel had manipulated Kat's own emotions, making her believe that *this* time things were different, that *this* time Rachel had changed, that *this* time she would be able to hold it all together.

Still, there was more to Rye's story than that.

"Even if I accept that," she said. "Even if I believe every word you've said about what happened six years ago, that doesn't explain now. It doesn't justify your keeping things secret for the past week. You could have called me, any night. You could have told me everything."

Rye heard the sob that cut short her anguish. And yet, that anguish gave him another faint glimmer of hope. If Kat truly hated him, if she were willing to walk away forever, she'd be speaking with more rage. With less conflict. With more of her famed commitment, holding true to the single path she had chosen.

But even as he told himself that all was not absolutely, irrevocably lost, he heard another sound—one that made his pulse quicken with fear. The train whistle keened as the Clipper neared the station. He was almost out of time.

"Kat," he said, certain she heard it, too. "You have to believe me. I never thought of Rachel when I was with you. I kissed your lips, not hers. I touched your body, not hers. In my mind, you are completely separate people. Two women so different that I can only wonder at the coincidence that you're sisters."

She shook her head, using the motion to pull her

around, to face the windows, the train tracks. The door that would carry her out of his life forever.

He knew that he could not touch her, that he could not rely on the incredible physical spark that had joined them, ever since she first returned to Eden Falls. But he could not let her walk away, either, not without making his last argument. Not without saying the words that had pounded through his head as he completed his breakneck drive from the park.

"Kat, I love you. Please. Don't get on that train."

Kat felt the change in air pressure as the locomotive blew past the station door. The train was braking; metal wheels squealed against the track as it came to a stop.

But those sounds meant nothing to her. Instead, she was trapped by the words Rye had spoken. "What did you say?" she asked, her own question almost lost in the station's dead air.

He took a step closer to her. "Kat, I love you." He glanced at the door, at the train that was almost completely stopped. "I love you, and I don't want you to go. I can't get enough of you. I want you to stay here. I *need* you to stay here. But if you can't, if you won't, then I'll get on that train with you. I'll travel to New York, or to anywhere else you go, until I know that you heard me, that you understand me, that you believe me. I love you, Kat Morehouse, and I don't want to live another day without you."

The train was ticking, temporarily settling its weight on the tracks. A conductor walked by on the short platform outside the station, calling out his bored afternoon chant: "Yankee Clipper, all aboard!"

"Kat," Rye whispered, and now he took a step closer. He held out his hand to her, as if she were a forest animal, some shy creature that he had to charm to safety.

He had hurt her. He had kept a terrible secret for days, long past the time when he should speak.

But hadn't she done the very same thing? Hadn't she kept a secret from her mother, hiding the bad news about the studio's bank account because she could not find the right words? Because it was never the right time to tell the truth?

Susan had forgiven her. Susan had told her that she understood—good motives sometimes led to bad actions. All unwitting, Susan had shown Kat the path to understanding. The way to move forward from a bad situation to one that was so much better.

The train seemed to sigh, grumbling as its engine shifted forward. The cars dragged on the track as if they were reluctant to leave Eden Falls. Kat could still run for the Clipper. With her dancer's grace, she could grab hold of the steel grip beside the stairs. She could pull herself into the vestibule, make her way down the swaying, accelerating car to an overpadded seat that would carry her all the way to New York.

But Rye's eyes were pleading with her. Those ebony eyes, darker than any she had ever seen before. No, that was a lie. Niffer's eyes were just as dark.

The train picked up speed. Its whistle blew as the engine rounded the long curve that would bring it north, to Richmond, to Washington, to New York.

The Clipper was gone.

"Thank you," Rye breathed. He was frozen, though, terrified of upsetting the balance he had somehow found, the miracle that had kept Kat in Eden Falls. His hand remained outstretched, his fingers crooked, as if they could remember the cashmere touch of her hair.

"Oh, Rye," she sighed. "I love you, too."

And then, impossibly, she was placing her hand in his. She was letting him pull her close, letting him fold his arms around her. She turned up her face, and he found the perfect offering of her lips.

He wanted to drink all that she had to give him, wanted to sweep her up in his arms and carry her over the threshold of the station, out to Noah's car, and away, far away, into a perfect sunset. He wanted to stay absolutely still, to turn to stone with this incredible woman in his arms, to spin out this moment forever. He wanted to drag her to the hard wooden bench in the center of the waiting room, to pull her down on top of him, to rip open the buttons on her spring-green blouse and lave her perfect breasts with his ever-worshipful tongue.

He wanted to lead Kat, to follow her, to be with her forever.

"Rye." She said his name again, when he finally pulled back from his chaste kiss of promise. There was so much she needed to say to him. So much she needed to hear him say. She twined her fingers in his and led him out of the waiting room, to the glinting form of his silver truck. He barely left her for long enough to walk around the cab to the driver's seat.

As he closed the door behind himself, she felt an eagerness shoot through his body, the need to confirm that she was still beside him, that she had not left him, that she never would. His fingers splayed wide across the back of her head as he pulled her close; urgency sparked from his palm like an actual electric fire. Now his lips were harsh on hers, demanding, and she might have thought that he was angry, if not for the sob that she heard at the back of his throat.

She answered his desperation with need of her own.

Her hands needed to feel the hard muscle of his back. Her arms needed to arch around his chest, to pull him close, closer than she had ever been in any pas de deux.

His clever lips found the fire banked at the base of her throat; his tongue flicked against that delicate hollow until she moaned. By then, his fingers had made their way beneath her blouse; he was doing devastating things to the single clasp of her bra.

Her own hands weren't to be outdone. She flashed through the simple mechanics of releasing his belt, loosening the leather to reach the line of worn buttons beneath. She slid the fingers of her left hand inside the waistband of his jeans as she worked, and she laughed at the feel of his flesh leaping beneath her touch.

But then, three buttons away from freedom, she paused. She flattened her palm against the taut muscles of his belly, pushing away enough that she could see his eyes.

His heartbeat pounded beneath her touch like a wild animal's, and she felt the whisper of his breath, panting as he restrained himself, as he held back for her. "What are we doing, Rye?"

"If you don't know, then I haven't been doing it right," he growled.

She smiled, but she pulled even farther away. She took advantage of his frustrated whimper to tug her blouse back into place. She ran a hand through her hair, forcing it out of her eyes. "I'm serious," she said, and she was pleased to see his hunger take a backseat to concern. "You're living in Richmond now. You've started your own business and you don't have time to do anything new. You don't need the stress of a new relationship, just as you're finally achieving all your dreams."

He caught her hand and planted a kiss in her palm before lacing his fingers between hers. "You *are* all my dreams."

She laughed softly, but she shook her head. "You can say that now, and you probably even believe it. But what are you going to say next week? Next month? Next year? What are you going to say when I keep you from landing the biggest contract you've ever tried for?"

"That's not going to happen," he vowed.

"It will. Rye, I can see a life for myself in Eden Falls. I think a part of me has seen it from the moment I walked into my parents' home. That's why I delayed getting back to New York, why I delayed signing up for the *Coppelia* audition. My body was telling me something when I broke my foot. It knew the truth before my mind did. Before my heart did. Here in Eden Falls, I can help Daddy with his physical therapy, his rehab. I can help Mama at the studio, take over more of the business side of things, teach a few of the classes. I can keep Niffer with me, help her through the pain when she realizes that Rachel is heading out again. We both know my sister will never stick around."

Rye started to tense when Kat said her sister's name. There was no rancor, though, when she spoke of her twin. Only a matter-of-fact acceptance, with just a twinge of sadness for the woman that Rachel might have been.

He used his free hand to brush back Kat's midnight hair. He wanted to make sure she could read his expression when he spoke to her. He wanted to be certain she knew he spoke the truth. "I don't need Richmond."

"But you—"

He cut her off by shaking his head. "Richmond is

just a place. It's not the magical answer to my problems. It's not the secret to the life I wanted to lead."

"Wanted? I don't understand. What was that life?"

"I wanted to be free. I wanted to be independent. I was tired of being everyone's brother, everyone's cousin, everyone's son. I wanted to make my own decisions, to grow my own business, without constantly turning aside to meet someone else's expectation."

"A-and now?" He heard the hesitation in her voice, the tendril of fear behind her question.

"And now, I *want* to be tied to someone else. To *one* someone else. To you. I want to go to work every morning, knowing I'm the best damned contractor I can be. And I want to come home every night, knowing I'm the best husband I can be." He saw her register his words, saw her amazing silver eyes widen in disbelief. "Marry me, Kat. Make me the happiest man in Eden Falls."

Marry him? Marry Rye Harmon?

Kat started to laugh, a shaky sound that mixed suspiciously with a sob in the back of her throat. "I—" she started to say, but then she gave up on that answer. "You—" She trailed off, as if she could not remember how to shape any words.

He chuckled. "I take it that means yes?"

She stared at him—at the good humor that twitched his lips into a smile. At the confidence that squared his shoulders. At the power that rippled down his arms, in the strength of his cunning fingers. At the man who had seen her heart and understood her soul, who knew who she was, and what she needed to be.

"Yes," she said. "Yes, Rye Harmon, I'll marry you."

His kiss was long and deep and satisfying. He was laughing, though, as he pulled away. "You do realize that we have to get back to the park. Everyone is going to be waiting there, worried."

She quirked a grin. There'd be time enough to follow up on the promise of that last kiss. "We can't have that, now, can we?"

She started to reach for her seat belt, but he shook his head. "Not so fast!" he taunted.

"What?"

"I drove Noah's car over here. You're going to have to drive this thing back to the park." He scooped up the keys from the floor mat and pressed them into her yielding palm. "Go ahead," he said, darting in for a quick kiss. "You lead. I'll follow."

Confident that Rye was with her—would be with her forever—she barely glanced in the rearview mirror as she pulled out of the parking lot.

## *Epilogue*

Kat stood at the stove, flexing her ankles and testing her balance as she dropped biscuit dough into a pot of stewed chicken. The motion reminded her of the exercises she had led for the Advanced Showcase students, just that afternoon. The girls had outdone themselves at the barre. In fact, little Taylor Sutton might be ready to audition for the National come spring, if she continued to work hard under Kat's watchful eyes. And, of course, if she wanted to travel so far away from home.

A gust of wind rattled the windows, and Kat peered out at the gathering winter storm. She was glad Rye had installed the new storm windows. For that matter, it was a good thing he'd anchored all the shutters, as well.

"Niffer," Rye said in the living room. "If you don't bring your dolls in from the front yard, they'll have snow on them in the morning."

"I'll get them after dinner," the headstrong child said.

"Now." Rye's calm order made it clear he would brook no disobedience.

"Mommy wouldn't make me bring in my dolls."

"Mommy isn't here, though, is she?" Rye's voice stayed even. He was merely stating a fact. Rachel wasn't there, hadn't been for months. She hadn't even sent a postcard since…when was it? Halloween? "Niffer," Rye said, making it clear that he was through with petulant games. "Let's go. You don't want dinner to be late—Aunt Kat is making your favorite."

The child trotted over to the door, suddenly content to have lost the round. "Okay, Daddy."

Kat shivered and dropped in another dumpling. She couldn't say if her sudden shudder was a reaction to cold air wafting in the house's front door or the sudden proximity of her husband. Rye's hands closed over her belly, and he pulled her back against his chest, nuzzling her neck until she squirmed even closer.

"Good job, Mr. Harmon," she said, after she had caught her breath. "The way to a child's heart is through her stomach."

"Is *that* the secret, Mrs. Harmon?" His teasing fingers strayed to the neckline of her cobalt-blue sweater. "What do you think it would take to convince Niffer to spend the rest of the evening playing in the basement?"

She laughed and arched against him. "We don't have a basement."

"Damn." He switched his attention to the waistline of her pants, dancing around her hips with enough intensity that she had to suck in a steadying breath. "Do you think she could build herself one? Just for tonight? Even for an hour or two?"

Kat set down the wooden spoon she was using to

form the dumplings, and then she twisted in the circle of his arms. She started to fiddle with the top button of his shirt, amazed as always that he didn't need a sweater in the winter cold. "I've been meaning to talk to you about that."

"About Niffer building a basement?" He started to laugh.

"About you building onto the house," she clarified. "I've been thinking we can close in the carport. Convert it into a third bedroom."

She watched as he considered her suggestion. She saw him contemplate the work, solve the engineering problems, determine the most efficient way to add walls, to move doors. And then she saw him register the true meaning behind her suggestion. His fingers tightened deliciously on her waist.

"Really?" he asked, and there was so much love in the word, so much joy, that she found herself laughing out loud.

"Really," she said. His lips on hers were trembling, as if he were suddenly afraid of hurting her. She wasn't about to put up with that—not for eight more months. She cupped her hand on the back of his neck and tugged him closer, making sure she emphasized the demand with a sudden, quick thrust of her tongue.

"When?" he asked as he came up for air.

"Late August, I think. I haven't been to see the doctor yet."

"See the doctor for what?" Niffer's question came from the doorway, tiny and scared.

Kat whirled toward her niece, automatically kneeling to put herself at the child's eye level. "It's okay, sweetheart. No one's sick. I was just telling Daddy that we're going to have a baby join us next summer."

Niffer's eyes grew as big as pie plates. "Will it be a boy baby or a girl baby?"

"I don't know yet," Kat answered gravely. "Which do you want?"

Niffer thought for a long time, and then she said, "One of each."

Kat and Rye laughed at the same time. "Maybe we'll just take things one step at a time," Rye said, ruffling his daughter's hair. "Come on, now. Help me set the dinner table."

Kat was still grinning as Niffer hurried to grab the silverware out of its drawer. Girl or boy, it didn't matter to her—so long as everyone was healthy and happy and safe in Eden Falls.

\* \* \* \* \*

# MILLS & BOON®

## The Rising Stars Collection!

**1 BOOK FREE!**

This fabulous four-book collection features 3-in-1 stories from some of our talented writers who are the stars of the future! Feel the temperature rise this summer with our ultra-sexy and powerful heroes. Don't miss this great offer—buy the collection today to get one book free!

**Order yours at
www.millsandboon.co.uk/risingstars**

**Don't miss Sarah Morgan's
next Puffin Island story**

# *Some Kind
of Wonderful*

Brittany Forrest has stayed away from Puffin Island
since her relationship with Zach Flynn went bad.
They were married for ten days and only just
managed not to kill each other by the
end of the honeymoon.

But, when a broken arm means she must return,
Brittany moves back to her Puffin Island home.
Only to discover that Zac is there as well.

Will a summer together help two lovers reunite or
will their stormy relationship crash on to the
rocks of Puffin Island?

*Some Kind of Wonderful*
**COMING JULY 2015**
**Pre-order your copy today**

0315/MB507

# MILLS & BOON®
# By Request

**RELIVE THE ROMANCE WITH THE BEST OF THE BEST**

0715/05